THE EMPEROR OF GLADNESS

The

EMPEROR

of

GLADNESS

A NOVEL

Ocean Vuong

PENGUIN PRESS

NEW YORK

2025

PENGUIN PRESS
An imprint of Penguin Random House LLC
1745 Broadway, New York, NY 10019
penguinrandomhouse.com

Designed by Amanda Dewey

LIBRARY OF CONGRESS CATALOGING-IN-PUBLICATION DATA

Names: Vuong, Ocean, 1988– author.
Title: The emperor of gladness : a novel / Ocean Vuong.
Description: New York : Penguin Press, 2025.
Identifiers: LCCN 2024022675 (print) | LCCN 2024022676 (ebook) |
ISBN 9780593831878 (hardcover) | ISBN 9780593831885 (ebook)
Subjects: LCGFT: Novels.
Classification: LCC PS3622.U96 E47 2025 (print) | LCC PS3622.U96 (ebook) |
DDC 813/.6—dc23/eng/20240517
LC record available at https://lccn.loc.gov/2024022675
LC ebook record available at https://lccn.loc.gov/2024022676

ISBN 9798217059225 (international edition)

Printed in the United States of America
2 4 6 8 10 9 7 5 3 1

The authorized representative in the EU for product safety and compliance is
Penguin Random House Ireland, Morrison Chambers, 32 Nassau Street,
Dublin D02 YH68, Ireland, https://eu-contact.penguin.ie.

For Frances,
who found me.

Your worm is your only emperor . . .
We fat all creatures else to fat us
and we fat ourselves for maggots.

—*Hamlet*

Let be be finale of seem.

—*Wallace Stevens*

THE EMPEROR OF GLADNESS

1

The hardest thing in the world is to live only once.

But it's beautiful here, even the ghosts agree. Mornings, when the light rinses this place the shade of oatmeal, they rise as mist over the rye across the tracks and stumble toward the black-spired pines searching for their names, names that no longer live in any living thing's mouth. Our town is raised up from a scab of land along a river in New England. When the prehistoric glaciers melted, the valley became a world-sized lake, and when that dried up it left a silvery trickle along the basin called the Connecticut: Algonquin for "long tidal river." The sediment here is rich with every particle welcoming to life. As you approach, you'll be flanked by wide stretches of thumb-sized buds shooting lucent through April mud. Within months these saplings will stand as packed rows of broadleaf tobacco and silver queen corn. Beyond the graveyard whose stones have lost their names to years, there's a covered bridge laid over a dried-up brook whose memory of water never reached this century. Cross that and you'll find us. Turn right at Conway's Sugar Shack, gutted and shuttered, with windows blown out and the wooden sign that reads WE SWEETEN SOON AS THE CROCUS BLOOM, rubbed to braille by wind. In spring the cherry blossoms foam across the county from every patch of green unclaimed by farms or strip malls. They came to us from centuries of shit, dropped over this place by geese whenever summer beckons their hollow bones north.

Our lawns are overrun with ragweed and quack grass, one of them offering a row of red and pink tulips each spring, heads snared through the chain-link they lean on. The nearby porch overflows with rideable plastic toys, a wagon, tricycles, a fire truck, their primary colors now faded to Easter hues. A milk crate with a flap of old tire nailed across its opening is a mailbox set on a rotted sideboard, *Ramirez 47* written on the rubber in Wite-Out. Beside this is a tin bird feeder the shape of Bill Clinton's head. Seeds spill from his laughing mouth and fall like applause each time the wind comes off the freighter that blows through this place in the night's unseen hours. Though the train never stops in our town, its whistle can be heard in every living room three miles out. *Nothing* stops here but us, really. Hartford, the capital built on insurance firms, firearms, and hospital equipment, bureaucracies of death and catastrophe, is only twelve minutes by car down the interstate, and everyone rushes past us, either on their way in or to get the hell out. We are the blur in the windows of your trains and minivans, your Greyhounds, our faces mangled by wind and speed like castaway Munch paintings. The only things we share with the city are the ambulances, being close enough to Hartford for them to come fetch us when we're near dead or rattling away on steel gurneys without next of kin. We live on the edges but die in the heart of the state. We pay taxes on every check to stand on the sinking banks of a river that becomes the morgue of our dreams.

Down our back roads, the potholes are so wide and deep that, days after a summer downpour, minnows dart freely in the green-clear pools. And out of the dark of an unlit porch, someone's laugh cuts the air so quick you could mistake it for a gasped-back sob. That beige shack flanked by goldenrods is the WWII Club, a bar with three stools and a wood-paneled vending machine stocked only with Marlboros and honey buns. Across from that are brick row houses. First built for men who worked the paper mill on Jennings Road, they now house veterans who come home from every battlefield you can think of to sit on plastic lawn chairs staring at the mountain ridge before shuffling back into smoky rooms where mini-TVs, the size of human torsos, lull them to sleep.

Look how the birches, blackened all night by starlings, shatter when dawn's first sparks touch their beaks. How the last crickets sing through fog hung over pastures pungent now with just-laid manure. In August, the train tracks blaze so hot the rubber on your soles would melt if you walked on them for more than a minute. Despite this heat everything green grows as if in retribution for the barren, cauterized winter, moss so lush between the wooden rail ties that, at a certain angle of thick, verdant light, it looks like algae, like the glacial flood returned overnight and made us into what we were becoming all along: biblical.

Follow the tracks till they fork off and sink into a path of trampled weeds leading to a junkyard packed with school buses in various stages of amnesia, some so old they're no longer yellow but sit grey as shipwrecks. Furred with ivy, their dented hoods pooled with crisp leaves, they are relics of our mislearning. Walk through this yard—as some have done on their way home from the night shift at the Myers sock factory or just out wandering on Sunday afternoons alone with their minds—and you walk through generations of wanderlust burned between faux-leather seats. At the lot's far edge lies the week-old roadkill, its eye socket filled with warm Coca-Cola, the act of a girl who, bored on her way from school, poured her drink into that finite dark of sightless visions.

If you aim for Gladness and miss, you'll find us. For we are called East Gladness. Gladness itself being no more, renamed to Millsap nearly a century ago after Tony Millsap, the boy who returned from the Great War with no limbs and became a hero—proof you could lose almost all of yourself in this country and still gain a whole town. A handful of us wanted to be East Millsap to soak the shine and fill the stores, but the rest were too proud to name ourselves after a kid whose wheelchair never glided over our sidewalks.

Lasting seven months, winter begins by late September, when the frost glitters on the courthouse lawn and over the hoods of cars banked along the roads. As maples, poplars, and sassafras sway, the light filters amber through their leaving leaves. Even the steeple of the boarded-up Lutheran church grows from dove-white to day-old butter by noon.

Though skeptical, we are not ambivalent to hope. Under all this our main drag glows with its two Irish bars, a diner, a florist, the God First beauty salon, the Panda Gate China Wok, a hole-in-the-wall taco joint with no name, a funeral home painted sky blue to comfort the ravages that lie in its calling, a laundromat whose back entrance leads to a basement housing exactly three coin-operated porn booths. Two doors down is the American Legion, where they sell Saran-wrapped slices of pumpkin bread and black coffee every Friday under a windblown tarp. There's the migrant farm laborer's law office behind the YMCA, which last year finally had one of its wings converted to a needle exchange. There's the huge Victorian on Lilac and Main. Home to our first mayor, it's now a halfway house for recovering addicts, the walkway lined with polyester roses that poke out blue and violet from snowbanks after blizzards.

There's the two-story Cape on the corner painted only high as the eldest son could reach, then abandoned the winter he joined the Marines, leaving it half olive green for the past seven years. In late July, a black mini-fridge sits by the road, an extension cord running to the house. Inside, rows of blueberries sweat in green paper pints beside a coffee can with a Post-it that reads *Blueberries $5 Pay What You Can.*

It's a town where high school kids, having nowhere to go on Friday nights, park their stepfathers' trucks in the unlit edges of the Walmart parking lot, drinking Smirnoff out of Poland Spring bottles and blasting Weezer and Lil Wayne until they look down one night to find a baby in their arms and realize they're thirtysomething and the Walmart hasn't changed except for its logo, brighter now, lending a bluish glow to their time-gaunt faces. It's where fathers in blue jeans flecked with wood stain stand at the edges of football fields, watching their sons steam in the reddened dawn, one hand in their pocket, the other gripping a cup of Dunkin' Donuts. They could be statues for what it means to wait for a boy to crush himself into manhood. And each morning you'd sit on the frost-dusted bleachers, a worn copy of *To the Lighthouse* on your lap, and watch the players on the field, blue tomahawks shivering on their jerseys, their plastic pads crackling in the mist. And when you'd turn the page it would slip right off the binding, flutter through the field, gathering inky blotches through the wet grass until it tangles between the boys' legs and disintegrates under a pair of black cleats. The words gone to ground. That town.

Against all odds, we have a library. It used to be an armory that once housed a group of runaway slaves en route to Nova Scotia, cause for the bronze statue of Sojourner Truth at the center fountain, three years now without water. Across from that statue stands the four-foot-eight Lego model of a red T-Rex, the pieces glued into permanence. It is the height of a boy named Adam Munsey, who, a few feet away, was crushed by the very school bus that was to pick him up, the driver shit-faced on a handle of Southern Comfort after staying up all night to watch the Patriots win the 2002 Super Bowl. Further up, where the street widens into Route 4 and the sidewalk crumbles to dust and patches of northern poppy and blue asters spray over the green to your right, you'll find the Colt factory where the founder, Samuel Colt, became one of the wealthiest men in America, selling revolvers to both sides during the Civil War. Now it's a Coca-Cola plant where polished red trucks line the old brick loading bays as the sun slips behind the mountains in the west.

There's Cumberland Road, which takes you to York County Women's Corrections, lined this time of year with pumpkins that flush the drab fields with stretches of ochre—bounties for jackrabbits and starved possums hoarding for winter. Hugging the river beyond are slabs of sandstone pocked with Podokesaurus footprints, made over 195 million years ago, running right up to the Wendy's parking lot. Then the other franchises: Burger King, AutoZone, Mattress Firm, Family Dollar, Dollar General. Then the Nite-E-Nite Motel with its five babyshit yellow doors facing the Kahoots nightclub across the street, which promises NEW GIRLS EVERY SEVEN MONTHS! Beyond that are the hand-painted signs: BRYON'S INSTA-BAIL, FIREWOOD $25 OFF YOUR FIRST CORD, NO FRACKING IN THE NAME OF JESUS, a faded MARTHA BEAN FOR 2006 CITY COMPTROLLER. And one in elegant red script that reads, as if in prophecy, GUNS AHEAD.

What do you really know about what you know of New England?

Past the concrete slab where the Citgo once stood, a deer steps cautious into a grove of milkweed, as if the last of its kind, then leaps into the brush where the creek spills into the river flowing under King Philip's Bridge. A freighter bridge named for the Wampanoag chief who led a rebellion here to take back his land from Puritans, its cement abutment loops with colorful graffiti that reads *SpyKids 2*, *Guerra a los ricos*, *Free Mumia Abu-Jamal!!!*, *Laura & Jonny '92*, *niños malos*, and *9/11 was an inside job.*

It is also the last way out of town.

And it's the very bridge the boy crossed one afternoon on September 15 in 2009. Rain pelted the oversize UPS jacket draped over his shoulders as he walked cradled in the heart of the valley, the land sweeping away from him toward boulderous clouds sinking into the horizon. He was nineteen, in the midnight of his childhood and a lifetime from first light. He had not been forgiven and neither are you. The sky a benevolent grey as the afternoon drained to evening and the cold turned his breath to fog. Under his boots the tracks hummed from steady gales slamming the steel straps. Yes, it *is* beautiful here, which is why the ghosts never leave. I need you to know this as the town rinsed to a blur behind him. I need you to understand, as black water churned like chemically softened granite below, the lights coming on one by one along the cobalt banks, that the boy belonged to a cherished portion of this world as he glanced over his shoulder and saw the phone lines sagging with crows resigned to dusk and the red water tower in the distance announcing us—EAST GLADNESS—in faded white paint, before he turned from this place, swung one leg over the rail and decided, like a good son, to jump.

2

Though it was true the boy had run out of paths to take, out of ways to salvage his failures, he never planned on jumping off King Philip's Bridge that evening. It was only when he glimpsed, between the rail ties, the river swirling so massive below, a place you could slip cleanly into, that something in him both jolted and withered at once. They would say he drowned, of course, like that sophomore from Hebron they fetched from the shallows last summer, who got wasted at a house party and waded out past midnight singing to himself, only to wash ashore the next morning dressed in everything but his shoes. There was no shame, the boy thought, in losing yourself to something as natural as gravity—where one doesn't *jump* but is pulled, blameless, toward the sea. If nothing else, this would hurt his mother least.

But once he raised his leg and lifted himself over the railing, he spotted the second platform below, jutting far enough to make the leap impossible. He paused, stared across the swirling valley charred by the gloam, and glimpsed the spot where the river turned toward Chester County, where the towns are so small you could light a cigarette as you drive in and be someplace else before you blow your first drag out the window. He sucked in a breath, let it mist over him, then toed his way to the lower platform, where he thumbed off his pack until a mute white splash winked below and it was gone. Grasping the steel cables, he inched himself toward the bridge's center, where the fall would be highest, the current below churning through the metal beams.

A few yards in, he paused. The bridge was over a hundred feet tall, he knew, from a field trip back in middle school. It was once the town's most prized achievement, meant to bring passenger trains and money into the heart of Main Street. But the trains never stopped, passing the town on their way to Boston, Providence, Buffalo, Portland, even Montreal. Now only the freighters cut through, carrying strapped lumber or barrels of grain from Ontario. The bridge was painted bright yellow to signal this errant optimism, the color gone now save for a few bolts buried deep enough in the beams to be spared from weather.

Streetlights had come on over the mud shelves hugging the bank, giving the water the brushstroked glow of sunlight touching wet pavement on summer mornings—the kind of light you'd see nowhere else. "Sorry," he whispered to no one over the rush as the wires slickened under his palms. The rain, pouring steady for three days, drenched his hair and ran cold down his neck. The girl back at New Hope had mentioned, without him asking, that if you dive after breaking the surface and rush to touch the river bottom, it'll be enough, that the rapids will drag you forward and all you have to do is close your eyes until the icy water grows warm and quiet in your lungs and your pineal gland floods your brain with DMT and before you know it you're flying in a clear, windless sky, free from the human cage of your body.

What she didn't mention was that when you come up to the edge, there'll be another edge, inside you, one that's both passable and insurmountable at once. He swallowed hard and looked down at his boot wobbling over the beam. That's when he saw the corpse floating toward him, its limbs stretched and opaque beneath the river's surface. The face staring skyward with shut eyes and its clothes billowing from the thin frame. He gasped and wiped the rain from his eyes with both hands and looked again, blinking. But it was still there, clearer even. He hid his face in his sleeve and clung fast to the wire when a voice called out from somewhere across the water. He thought it came from his own head until he heard it again. "Come back. Come back now! Jesus Mother Mary, not now, not today."

He searched the bluffs and saw, set on the riverbank, a two-story clapboard house leaning toward the river. Attached to it was a wrought iron fire escape where a woman was waving her arms about, fighting with some sort of laundry line. He glanced back at the water and realized it wasn't a corpse at all but a bedsheet twisting through the current. A blast of wind ripped another sheet out of her arms and carried it a ways before it wilted around a nearby maple.

"Hey, your blankets!" he shouted from instinct, and quickly regretted it. He stepped back under the beam's shadow, making himself small. But too late.

The woman stopped, leaned over, and squinted at the bridge. Her glasses, reflecting the nearby streetlamp, flickered gold. From her shoulder-length white hair and stooped gait, she seemed elderly.

"Who's there?" She shielded her eyes and called through the rain suturing around her. The boy pressed himself against the struts, a steel bolt digging between his shoulders, and kept still.

"My goodness!" she gasped, eyes wide. "What are you doing? You crazy or what? Father in heaven help us. Get the hell out of there!"

Shivering, he leaned into the cone of light, somehow more troubled that a stranger had caught him on the edge of his life than by his own impulse to end it. "It's not what you think," he yelled back. "I was—I was just studying the water." He pulled back his hood and offered her, like a caught criminal, his boned face, pale as a newt's and framed by a black bowl cut, a girlish but useless tenderness softening his eyes. It was pitiful, being found like this. What kind of idiot puts himself, on a whim, under a bridge and must now convince an old woman that it was all—what, exactly?

"Don't be stupid." She glanced around and pushed her glasses up with her middle finger. "You can't die in front of my house, okay? I don't need any more spirits around here." She made the sign of the cross and gripped the railing as a slew of foreign words droned out of her. Her sheets had all blown away save for one blue towel whipping beside her face.

"Okay, okay! Listen." He held out his hand as if they were steps from each other and not halfway across a river. "I'm not gonna do it. I promise. I . . . I'm just inspecting the bridge. I'm a student—and wanna be an engineer one day." By now his lies came so easily, they rolled off his tongue like train cars heading off a cliff.

"Just get the hell down. I'm serious. Or I call the police."

"Okay, alright. Relax." Gently, he scooted across the beam toward her side of the bank. The woman disappeared into the house, then stuck her head out the next window closer to him, tracking him as he went. At one point his boot juddered over a rivet and she yelped, cursing in her native tongue.

"Put your foot over there. No, there." She was halfway out the window, pointing to a spot he couldn't see. "Now move to the left. Yes, wait—that other left. Good. There's a ladder over there. Go to it and climb. Climb, boy. Hurry." She jabbed her thumb at the sky. "Up, up! That's it."

He footed toward a metal ladder soldered to the bridge and pulled himself, arms jumping from cold, back to track level, then leaned over the rail and gathered his breath. "Thank you, okay?" He waved the woman off. "It's all good. I just wanted to see the girders up close. I'm heading home now, don't worry."

"Bullshit! You wanna die. Come over here." She pointed with her chin toward the shore. "Get over here or you can explain it to the cops. You think I'm kidding?" Her hair was matted from the downpour and a ring of water had darkened the collar of her gown.

The boy rose and scuffed across the bridge as she followed him from window to window, muttering to herself. When the dirt embankment appeared under the platform, he hopped over the rail and hurried toward the house. The street was flanked on both sides by shambled row houses that resembled a set from a war movie. Through the exposed walls, where pink insulation had spilled out, he glimpsed into moldy, moss-lined living rooms. One house was half burnt, its interior filled with grimy clumps of furniture where a young tree had taken root through the floorboards, its top branches clawing a gash in the second floor.

The woman's house was on the river's side, her back door just yards from the water. Through the decades, it had acquired the hues of the riverbank itself, slate grey and beige-speckled, the paint on the clapboard long stripped. As he reached the front steps, the main door opened and a shock of white hair poked above the screen door's frame. She was struggling with the lock, so he gave the handle a yank and the door flew open, revealing a woman who must've been at least eighty. She was tall as his eyes, had a square jaw and a bulbous nose under wire-rimmed glasses that covered her entire face save for a chin that resembled the end of a dinner roll.

His own tortoise frames were beaded with rain, and he saw her as only a smear of beige colors. They watched each other a moment, the dark settling around them as he swayed on his feet.

"I'm sorry," the boy said again, dripping. "I'm not gonna jump off that bridge no more, okay? I promise. Can I go now?"

"COME IN. But take off your shoes. My husband put down these floors." The woman disappeared into the house. The boy hesitated, looking down the empty street. The rain was picking up again. He stepped onto the porch, water running off him in rivulets, took off his boots, and followed her inside.

A creaky rail house built by freight workers over a century ago, the home was one large hallway divided into three rooms: a parlor, a dining room, and a kitchen, whose dim light now glowed at the far end like the hearth of an ancient cave. Furnished in a style the boy had seen only in the black-and-white TV series *Lassie*, whose reruns he watched on a three-channel Panasonic as a kid, the house had the stuffy odor of rooms whose windows rarely opened undercut with the mildewy rank of crawl spaces. As his eyes adjusted, amorphous furniture upholstered in sprawling pale florals came to view. The walls were wood-paneled and adorned with cheap landscape paintings in gilded frames. As he passed the transom that divided the parlor from the dining room, he looked up and saw what was once a white cross, now phantom-grey from decades of dust. On one wall, lit by streetlights, a cluster of grim-faced portraits stared out from an era he couldn't locate. He paused at the kitchen's threshold, water falling from his chin and hair on the laminate floor.

The woman sat down at a small table and nodded toward an empty chair. "Go on, sit. You look like a dunked cookie."

He sat carefully, his eyes taking in the room. Not knowing what to do with his hands, the boy placed them, palms up, on the table but withdrew them to his lap when he realized this looked psychotic.

"Here, dry yourself." She handed him a dish towel. It smelled of raw onions but he wiped his face anyway, his eyes quickly stinging.

"Poor kid," she mumbled to herself. "Hey, it's all over now, okay? Whatever happened is over. But don't you cry, boy. Tears deplete your iron, you know." She grabbed the rag, leaned over and dabbed his eyes some more, deepening the burn. He winced and turned away. "Okay, you're not a boy. You're a man and don't need nobody to wipe your tears."

The kitchen was the size of a large shed and contained a stovetop browned with grime-stuck grease, a sink, and a portion of countertop the size of a cutting board. They sat at a round table covered in plaid plastic meant to look like picnic cloth. From its center, a fabric-shaded lamp trimmed with tulle emitted a sickly amber glow.

She grabbed a nearby pack of cigarettes, a brand he didn't recognize, slipped one between her lips, and put a lighter to it. "I normally don't smoke." She took a drag and stared at him, not unkindly, then leaned over and pushed aside a large stack of magazines. They were decades old and printed in a language he couldn't make out.

"Lithuanian," she said, clocking his curiosity. "Know what that is?"

He shook his head, wiping the onion tears from his cheeks.

"An old country, far away, where I was born." She waved the cigarette about and took a drag. "But all countries are old, if you think about it."

But he had never thought about it. He had rarely thought about any country, least of all the one *he* was born in—only that it, too, was far away.

"Want one?" She handed him a cigarette.

Before he could answer she placed it in his mouth and lit it.

"You like my owls?" She pointed over her shoulder where an armoire loomed behind her. Behind its glass doors was a fleet of owl figurines of many shapes and sizes, some porcelain and shining, others the matte of wood or clay. "Every owl was made in a free country. None of my owls," she leaned back, "came from Communists. Understand?"

He lied by nodding.

Above the armoire were three paintings of owl portraits, their faces bloated as old mobsters, each one depicting, like a Rembrandt study, a new angle to the bird's face. In fact, owl knickknacks, tchotchkes, and icons stared at him from nearly every surface. "I collect them. Don't know why really," she shrugged. "People started giving them to me long ago. Now it's my calling card." She smiled weakly through the smoke. "What's your name anyway?"

"Thanks for this." The boy took a long drag from the bogie. "But I should go."

"Easy, little lamb. I invite you in my home, give you cigarette. And look," she tilted the pack to show him, "I only have two left. I even let you cry in my kitchen. You know it's bad luck to cry in the kitchen, right? You can at least tell me your name."

He stared at the plastic coverlet on the table pocked with holes and considered the name his mother gave him, the thought of it sinking him. It wasn't that he didn't like his name—only that he had been willing to toss it in the river. He had never wanted to throw his name out, just the breath attached to it. The name, after all, was the only thing his mother gave him that he was able to keep without destroying.

"Hai," he mumbled.

"And *hello* to you too. But—"

"No, Hai. It's—"

"Okay," she breathed, "but *who* am I saying hello to?"

"My name is Hai."

"Your name is Hello?"

He decided to nod. "Sure."

"Ah." She brightened and pointed a crooked finger at him. "So your name is Labas!"

"What?"

"Labas means 'hello' in my country." She extended her hand across the table for him to shake. "Hello, Labas. I'm Grazina. Means 'beautiful.'" She grinned, the cigarette smoldering through her yellow teeth.

He shook her hand, cracked dry and warm. "Hello."

"Now we know who's who. So, you were delivering packages and decided that today's the day you had enough, huh? That what they mean when they say you guys *go postal?*"

Hai looked down at his UPS jacket. "Oh," he said. "No, a friend gave me this. I don't deliver anything. But I'm sorry about your sheets."

"Ack." She waved him off. "You live long as I do and everything's a rag."

He stared out the window at the bridge where he'd stood only a half hour ago. Now dark, its row of lights stretched to the other side. "I'm sorry again for all the trouble. But I'm okay now, really."

"Don't be sorry. Living all these years next to a bridge, you see crazy things on it. One time, on Christmas morning, a whole container of chickens tipped over as the train crossed, the top rows falling over the sides. Poor things. They drowned in their cages. But some got loose and swam. Can you believe chickens can swim? Beats being eaten, no?" She let herself laugh. "But I'm glad that you, Mr. Hello, you didn't become another chicken, huh?"

Just then something flickered in her expression and she stopped, her eyes drifting to a spot just over his shoulder. He turned around but found only an old Frigidaire plastered with coupon cutouts, their edges browned and curled. Something about Grazina was off, he realized now. There was a twinkle in her eye that held without pause as they spoke, as if lit by an artificial source. "Labas," she leaned forward and said in a hushed tone, "you want to know the secret to getting rid of every sorrow known to man? Do you?"

He blinked at her.

"I'm serious. Here—grab those dinner rolls hanging behind you and follow me. Go on, they don't bite."

She crossed the kitchen and opened a back door he hadn't noticed before. Rain flew in and broke as mist across the room. Beyond it the river roared up from the banks. "Come, boy," she called from outside. "I'll show you what I mean."

He took the bag of rolls and stepped out, the sound of water filling his empty head. He considered making a beeline across the yard and running for it, but his feet wouldn't budge. The backyard was a plot of dirt flecked with tufts of grass drenched in mud. Twenty feet away, over a concrete embankment crumbling at the lip, ran the river. It was nightfall but the yard was lit weakly by sodium lamps from the street. Grazina hobbled toward the center of the plot, swaying as the wind tugged at her gown, and waved him over.

"What you gonna do with these out here?"

"Just come and put the rolls down. No, open them first. Good, now just dump them."

"What?"

"Just dump them out," she shouted over the river.

He flipped the bag over and about a dozen rolls fell onto the mud.

"You ready?" she said.

Before he could answer she stomped on one of the rolls, flattening it. Then she did the same with another, this time twisting the toe of her slipper, grinding the roll in the ground so the crumbs broke off and disintegrated. "Isn't that wonderful? Now you try, Labas." Her face flushed with delight, she grabbed his hand and pulled him toward her. "Go on, step on one. Trust me."

He pressed a socked foot on a roll, nudging it with his toe.

"For Chrissakes, it's not roadkill. Go ahead and step on it. Good. Now go stronger." Her hands were on her knees, urging him like a deranged coach. "That's it! Yes, with all your weight. Crush those bastards." She grabbed his ankle with both hands and pressed his foot onto the roll. When he lifted his foot, the bread was sunken in the mud, the sock fabric waffling the wet dough. "Don't think about it, just do another. Isn't this fun?"

He crushed another roll, then another as Grazina cheered, her voice cut with childish glee. Before long they were stepping from roll to roll, going in circles. "Anytime I feel my soul going dim," she panted, "I just step on some rolls and it's like a magic spell."

He pushed his heel into one of the last rolls, then dragged it in a wide arc through the dirt, the crumbs sloughing off, leaving a powdery comet shooting across the mud as Grazina clapped and shouted in Lithuanian.

All around them the bread browned and sopped into pale lumps as they went on stepping. From far away, across the river passing in your car, you would've seen two people dancing in a rainstorm in a cone of light on a Connecticut night at the end of the first decade of the century, and forgotten that the country was at war. Hai's laughter, which sounded far away and foreign to him, faded as he caught his breath. There was something to this after all, he conceded.

Grazina patted his back, her spectacles white with rain. "You did it, Labas. You're a natural bread crusher. Before, in Lithuania, bread was precious. We had to eat even hard, moldy bread, green bread that tasted like gasoline. Now we can crush them anytime we like," she made a fist at the word *crush*, "and no one can punish us. But come, come here. We must pray now, boy . . ." She leaned in and gripped his shoulder. "May the Lord forgive us this sin of wastefulness," she began, her voice wobbling with her balance, "may He also watch over the strangers and uphold the orphan and the widow, but the way of the wicked He brings to ruin. For the Lord is not slow to fulfill His promise as some count slowness, but is patient toward you, not wishing that any should perish, but that all should reach repentance."

He watched her as she prayed, this bent stub of a woman, hair matted at her temples, whose voice had earlier coaxed him back to solid ground.

"How do you feel, Labas?" Around them was a circle of decimated bread.

"I feel beautiful," he nodded, refreshed by this bewildering new realm he had entered. "I feel Grazina."

HE WOKE TO the train whistle blowing across the river and knew it was morning. When he spotted his UPS jacket hanging on the wall, a puddle collecting beneath it, last night's events resurfaced. After they'd crushed the bread rolls in the rain, Grazina had offered him, over tea, a spare room to wait out the storm for the night, and he gratefully accepted. But after sinking into a deep, dreamless sleep, he woke in the wee hours to the sound of someone singing. Clear, pristine, lilted singing, like a voice coming up from a cavernous well. Groggy, he glanced around the room and saw, in the half dark, the wooden owl figurine on the desk and realized where he was. He pulled the covers back, left the room, and tiptoed down the carpeted hall before stopping at Grazina's door. It was only when he lowered his ear to the door that he recognized the melody to "Silent Night." He held his breath. Her voice was hollowed out and girlishly high, not the grate of an Eastern European sailor he'd heard earlier. He gave the door a push until, through the widening crack, he saw Grazina lying stock-still and staring at the ceiling, her wide-open eyes catching the wet light from the window as her mouth worked the lyrics through the chorus. He stood staring a moment, feeling both terrified and like a creep at once. "Grazina," he managed, but she kept singing, not that he'd know what to do if she woke. He shuddered, eased the door closed, then hurried to his room and pulled the covers over his head. He didn't know how long it took before her voice dimmed, but eventually it did and he drifted off.

He was lying now in the dusty morning light, collecting himself, when a frying pan started hissing downstairs, followed by the clang of pots. He went over to where his jacket hung and ran a finger down its arm, his attention lingering on the stitching. The jacket once belonged to his friend Noah, a boy he met working tobacco when he was four-teen, the crop blooming verdant along the river that carved East Glad-ness in half. His real name wasn't Noah, but that's what Hai started calling him a week after he died. Because why shouldn't the dead receive new names? Weren't they transformed, after all, into a kind of otherhood? Like many boys throughout the county, the wide green valley swallowed Noah up and spat out a tombstone the height of a shoebox at Cedar Hill, high enough to hold his name and nothing else. It was one of those friendships that came on quick, like the heat on a July day, and long after midnight you could still feel its sticky film on your skin as you lie awake in your room, the fan blowing in what remained of the scorched hours, and realize for the first time in your peep of a life that no one is ever truly alone. It'd been two years since Noah's pine box was hammered shut, and nearly every day since, the UPS jacket draped over Hai's bony shoulders, sometimes even in bed on especially cold nights, the leather torn in places and the *U* nearly peeled off. But skin is skin, he told himself, even when it's not yours.

He dressed and laced his boots, then reached into the jacket's inner pocket. Under the crushed pack of Marlboros, gum wrappers, a few coins, he found the contact lens case, held it to his ear and shook, listen-ing for the pills, then slipped it in his pocket before heading downstairs.

A SINGLE PERFECTLY browned latke slid onto his plate, leaving a trail of oil over the stoneware dish painted with faceless angels circling the rim. Grazina placed one on her own plate, then dropped the pan in the sink with a hush of steam.

"That's my great-aunt." She pointed with her chin to a daguerreo-type on the wall of a scowling woman in a headscarf.

"She looks nice," Hai said.

"She had a humpback and a heart of gold. But her husband was the devil himself, poor Agne. Where are your people?" She closed the fridge with her hip. They had been filling the space with small talk since he came down, but he now sensed a change in her voice.

"I don't got any people. Just my mom across the river. But I can't see her now."

"A son and a mother. That's people enough, no? Why can't you see her?" She placed a bowl of baby carrots before him and sat down fiddling with the table cover. "Probably none of my business."

"I messed up some things, that's all."

"Like your glasses?" She chuckled at the broken corner of his tortoise glasses, wrapped with duct tape.

"One of many casualties, yeah." It had broken back at New Hope during a scuffle he wasn't even a part of.

She looked him up and down, eyes cautious, then lifted an owl-painted teapot and filled their mugs. He drank and wiped his mouth with the back of his hand. He'd never used a saucer before and found the clack that punctuated each sip oddly satisfying. "I heard you singing that Christmas song last night," he said, trying to sound casual. "Think it was 'Silent Night.' You have a great voice."

She shot him a puzzled look. "Don't be silly, Labas. I'm no singer. When I was little I was in the church choir, but then they snipped my tonsils and that was that—kaput. If anyone was singing, I'd hear it. I have good ears." She tugged on one ear. "Like rubber, from my father. Must be those coyotes across the marshes." She nodded across the street. "They go crazy when it rains."

Surely he hadn't dreamt it all up—though the man at New Hope did warn him about having nightmares once he got back to the real world.

She gestured at the bowl of raw carrots. "Those are for you. Eat up."

Hai took a bite from a carrot, then picked up his fork, eager to try the latke.

"No, eat the carrot first. Please." She leaned forward, knife and fork on each side of the plate, a paper towel tucked in her collar. "It's important."

He finished the carrot, then picked another from the bowl and put the whole thing in his mouth.

"They're good for you, believe me." She cut into her latke like it was a steak and ate.

"For the eyes, right?"

"That's a lie the army told in World War Two to hide the fact that they used top-notch radar. Carrots," she paused for effect, "give you the will to live."

He took a bite of the latke, which was perfectly made, crispy at the edges and delicately salted with a touch of herbs he couldn't name. "What do you mean?" he said, chewing.

"It's a root. And roots prevent you from getting the blues." She picked one from the bowl; it gleamed under the kitchen light. "You see, carrots become bright orange because it's so dark in the ground. They make their own light because the sun never reaches that far—like those fish in the ocean who glow from nothing? So when you eat it, you take in the carrot's will to go upward. To heaven." She tucked the carrot back in the bowl, gently, as if it were a tiny person. "Ever heard of a rabbit jumping off a bridge?" she winked. "Of course not. That's because they have the light in them."

He had never heard this before, but somehow it made sense.

"When *I* get the blues, mostly in February, I boil a pot of these and dip them in honey. When my husband died, I ate nothing but carrots for six months straight, and you know what?" She pointed the butter knife at her eye. "Not a single tear. They're stronger raw, but I lost my molars in '91. Bush Senior, what can you do?"

"When did he die, your husband?"

"When does anybody die?" she shrugged. "When God says *Well done*."

By the time the tea was down to its dregs, Grazina grew quiet. Something in the kitchen was ticking. Their eyes met and she looked away, then back at him, on the verge of saying something—but mumbled to herself in Lithuanian, shaking her head. He poured more tea to fill the silence. The kitchen, he realized, was only bright when the back door was opened. Closed now, the place was dim and hourless as a bunker.

"Now," she cleaned her teeth with her tongue, "the place is old and falling apart but there's plenty of heat from the oil boiler, which gets filled every second Friday. There's a leak in the bathroom ceiling but it goes right into the tub, so who cares, right?" She shrugged. "There's no washer or dryer, but you can do it in the tub and hang it on the clothesline. And you'll need to help with fetching the groceries, set the mouse trap, and toss the occasional poor bastard in the river."

"Hold up." He set his cup down. "What are you talking about?"

"You don't gotta pay no rent and you can have my daughter Lina's old room. Where you slept last night. I'm not difficult. I just need help taking my vitamins. And just . . ." She fingered the magazines on the table. "It would be nice to have someone around. I'm eighty-two this year, you know, and . . ." She trailed off, looking down and away.

"You want me to stay here?" He scanned her face, then the owls behind her.

She held up her hand. "Just listen first, okay?" She went on to tell him about this live-in nurse named Janet who was covered by Medicare. Janet was assigned to Grazina after she'd fallen halfway down the stairs and ended up in the ER at Hartford Hospital. But then Janet got married to some biker, hopped on a Harley, and floored it to New Mexico, never to be seen again. Grazina was put on a waiting list for another live-in nurse, which, in these parts, could take months, sometimes years.

Hubbard Street, Grazina went on, was known locally as the Devil's Armpit due to a massive metam sodium spill from a shipping barge coming down from Buffalo back in '88. The toxic sludge had leached into the soil, and then the pipes, so badly the city paid the residents to relocate. Within a year only squatters burning bonfires in ravaged living rooms remained. The Army Corps of Engineers started demolishing houses but left after an electrical fire broke out, exposing asbestos in the walls. They never came back. Homeless camps popped up along the banks through the years, but the land was too cold and blighted for them to last. Grazina and her husband refused to leave, opting to keep their two-story biohazard teetering toward the river. "Our lives are here. I was married in that living room for Chrissakes. How could we leave?" She threw up her hands. "Anyway, a new nurse came—this was right after Janet—I see her car come up the road there, then it stops. She makes a call on her little phone before turning around and zooming right out of here. I never saw her again. No one wants to live in this dump with an old lady. Now I'm back on the list, this time who knows how long." She rested her arms on the table and leaned forward, her tone softening. "Look, if you really have no place to go, like you said, then you can stay long as you need. To get yourself together. But I'm not asking to be a charity case, capisce? I've made it by myself long enough. And you still have your mother, yes? Maybe you need to go to her and make things right." She took a sip of tea, watching him over the mug's lip. "A son should make peace with his mother before anything else."

He listened, his head tilted with the weight of her offer. But even before she finished, he knew he'd say yes. After all, he had never refused anything given him without a price, which was how he ended up where he was in the first place.

"You wouldn't want to live with a kooky owl lady, would you?" She chuckled nervously.

The chair creaked as he leaned back, blinking. "You sure about this?"

She nodded over her glasses.

He reached out and held her hand, surprised by his own relief. "But just to get back on my feet, yeah? Then I'll be out of your hair."

How he would pull this off, there was no telling—but it was a narrow passage worth taking, a feeble tributary that should at least end up somewhere.

Grazina lowered her head, her hair falling across his arms and onto the greasy plate. When she lifted her face, her glasses were askew and her eyes full. "We'll make a good team, right? We'll make do with what the Lord gives us." She exhaled and lit her last two cigarettes, handing him one. "You believe in God, boy?"

He took a long drag and considered this. "He's probably around sometimes."

"Clearly not as much as the devil," she cackled, her missing front tooth winking behind the smoke.

3

Before long, the days grew to weeks and the two strangers found a steady rhythm at 16 Hubbard Street. Hai's main task was to make sure Grazina took her vitamins, like she said, except these "vitamins" turned out to be in a plastic trough filled with prescription bottles. "For my brains," she said, pointing to her head.

The trough was a mess, pharmacy bags with faded print, crumpled paper stuck together by half-melted cough drops, brown-edged receipts, and empty bottles tossed among filled ones. Hai sorted the scripts and allocated the pills into a pink organizer tray labeled with the days of the week. This meant knowing the shapes and sizes of each of the thirteen pills by heart. Every day she had to take three gabapentin for nerve pain in her back, one Lipitor for cholesterol, a Zoloft, two Aricept and two Namenda for cognition, one paroxetine, an antidepressant that also curbed hallucinations, two lisinopril for blood pressure, and a calcium tablet with breakfast.

From patient reports pulled from a manila folder in the armoire drawer, he learned Grazina was diagnosed with mid-stage frontal lobe dementia in the summer of 2004—nearly five years ago. He also learned that missing one dose of Aricept risked the possibility of a "classic attack": confused timelines, aggravation, paranoia, delusions of grandeur, and even unfounded, sudden rage.

Still, they went through those first weeks, soaked in the listless hours, stitching together a kind of life. Like most people, they spent their days watching cable TV in the parlor. Grazina especially loved *The Office*, even if she often mistook it for the news, the close-up interview sessions with suit-and-tie characters resembling special reports. She'd turn to Hai after a while and say, "When they gonna show us the weather, Labas?" Another time, during *The Price Is Right*, while they were guessing the price of a bookcase, she went on listing the names of home furnishing items that he, having grown up in public housing with furniture donated by the Salvation Army, never heard of. "Plush down settee, $90; oak-white credenza, $145; hand-carved wood divan, $340." She went on and on as if reciting prayers on a rosary, even through the commercial break.

Sometimes, to be sure her mind was working the way it should, he'd check on her by asking who the president was. It was the question he asked his own grandmother, his bà ngoại, dead years now, whenever she had one of her schizophrenic fits. He'd be running the bathtub for their laundry and, realizing Grazina had been quiet a little too long, would stop the water, walk to the staircase, and shout, "Grazina! Who's the president?"

"Jesus Christ!" she'd shout up, annoyed. "Obama!"

"Okay, good. Thank you."

Other tasks included a couple runs a week to the packy across the bridge for groceries. The first time he went she watched him from the window as he crossed the rail bridge in case he was tempted to do anything stupid again. Her preferred meal was the Salisbury steak frozen dinner made by Stouffer's, the one that came with a tiny puddle of a brownie that congealed during the third minute in the microwave. Her

EBT card had enough for them to have Stouffer's about three times a week. He wondered what he looked like running across the bridge with a black garbage bag of frozen dinners over his shoulder while some old lady yelled from her window every few minutes that the coast was clear of oncoming trains. His own vice was Pop-Tarts, which he bought in a forty-eight-count box and stored in his room to be eaten untoasted and dipped in instant coffee.

By the second week, he got better at reading her body language, even shifts in her voice. If she started to talk to the painting of the Virgin Mary hung in the dining room, for example, or if she suddenly decided to wander around the house, putting owl figurines in her pockets, they would take the next dose early. He also showed her how to use the microwave and fix the antennae on the old RCA when it went out, teaching her the buttons on the remote, all of which she'd forget by the time the evening news came on. The mind in dementia, Hai learned, can be like one of those Etch A Sketch things he had as a kid: a little shake and it vanishes to a grey and otherworldly blankness. Or worse, when it draws things on its own to fill the gaps, like the time, a few days in, when he woke to the sound of animated talking downstairs. It was 4:53 a.m. according to his Nokia flip phone. He came down in his boxers, the house blued and chilled by the early hour, and found Grazina sitting in the kitchen having a conversation with a pushed-in chair. Seeing him, she pointed to the seat and said, "Labas, why don't you be a good host and make some tea for this nice little girl. She came all the way from Schenectady, can you believe it?"

Quietly freaking out, he ushered Grazina back to bed. "Come back when your father feels better, Anna," she called over her shoulder as he flicked off the light.

Another time he came downstairs after a shower and saw six trays of freshly baked stuffed cabbages cooling on every surface in the tiny kitchen, Grazina slumped in the chair facing the window, sweating and breathing heavily. "Labas, what's happening?" she said without looking up, scared of herself. "What did I do?"

"You hungry or something?" he asked stupidly.

"It's Lina, my daughter. She called," she wrung her hands, "said she'll be over for dinner. Said she finally put down the bottle and now has her appetite again. Did I make enough? She's smart girl." She peered sheepishly at Hai. "An ESL teacher, you know. Out in Pleasanton, Texas."

"And she came all this way just to have your cabbages? She must miss you so much."

Grazina nodded. "That's her over there." She pointed at the armoire where, in the crowd of owl figurines, sat a sepia photo of a grinning ponytailed girl. "She won the fifth-grade spelling bee that day."

Hai put his hand on her shoulder and let it stay until her breath steadied. He helped her clean up, putting the cabbages in whatever Tupperware he could find and shoving them all in the fridge and freezer. Then he took her hand in his, a trick he did with his bà ngoại. Whenever she would see a snake slither from the ceiling or rise from a crack in the tiles between her feet, he'd take her hand and scratch the inside of her palm with his fingernails until the snake crawled back into the fissure in her mind, the ground sealing up like a sutured gash. With Hai scratching her palm, Grazina eventually settled, and they both climbed the stairs, one step at a time. "Lina will come by noon," he said at last.

She faced him, her face halved by the bridge lights, and said flatly, "No she won't. She never comes, that drunk."

HE WAS READING *Slaughterhouse-Five* one morning during breakfast, a copy of which he found wedged in the desk drawer in his bedroom. It turned out Grazina's husband left it there while working on translating the book into Lithuanian, a project he spent over a decade on and ulti-mately left unfinished.

Grazina put down her spring '92 issue of *Town & Country*. "Labas, read me the opening, please."

She stared out the window as he read the first few paragraphs from the story of a man wandering the warscape of his mind after the wars of his body. When he finished, she looked at him from beneath her glasses and said only, "Very well, then. Very well." He was about to say something about the book when the cuckoo clock on the wall behind him went off, the wooden owl shooting out to nod along to a jagged tune spinning in its broken gears. Her eyes lit up. "Ah, 6:43, the hour Vilnius fell to Stalin." She crossed herself, shut her eyes, and said a prayer under her breath.

It was in these moments that he thought this new life, if you could call it that, wasn't so bad. That he could bide his time until something ahead of him lifted, like the mist rising each morning above the river outside his window, revealing what was always there. But he was wrong.

One day Hai came upon a bottle, from a different pharmacy, lying dusty at the bottom of a kitchen drawer among old batteries and ex-pired coupons. He held it up until the light revealed the label and his hopes—hopes he had all along, though hidden even from himself—were realized. No, they weren't codeine or oxys, not even a slow-release Percocet, which could have been crushed and snorted, but a sixty-tablet supply of Dilaudid, half full and made out to her husband, Jonas. It had expired on March 16, 2006, but beggars can't be choosers. Gra-zina came up to him and peered over her glasses at the bottle. "Oh yes. That was for his hernia surgery," she sighed. "He was so happy to ride his bike again after. He loved riding his bike, Jonas."

As soon as she turned away, he pocketed the bottle. If there was one, there would be others.

THAT NIGHT IT RAINED IN TORRENTS, pummeling the second-story windows of the house and casting warped shadows into the room where Hai lay blinking on the floor mattress. Lightning flashed the oak outside, its twisted branches rinsed white as bands of water rolled over the roof and into the gutters, dumping onto the gravel drive below. It was after the second thunderclap, which slammed so hard he felt it ricochet through the mattress springs, that Grazina began to scream.

A sound like someone falling through air without ever touching ground, her voice pierced the thin walls with the hellish mix of a yodel and a howl. Hai hugged his knees to his chest, hoping she'd fall back to sleep. He had known this was coming, the night when all the medicines, the many pills designed in pharmaceutical labs in Indiana and produced in China, would fail them. And yet he was not prepared for this vast, untenable stretch of the mind's vacuous caverns.

After a lull in the thunder, she wailed again, this time louder. The glass knob on her door started jostling, and soon she was shuffling down the hall toward his room, her soles dragging heavy on the hardwood. Outside his door she paused, her breaths hoarse against the hollowed wood. As he put his fist to his teeth to steady himself, the door opened and her stout shadow collapsed beside the mattress. He smelled cooked onions mixed with the peppermint oil she used on her hair before bed. Grazina grunted from the impact and struggled against the floor. He threw off his covers and crouched beside her. Another flash threw the oak's shadow into the room and he made out a tuft of hair on the back of her head. He called to her and grabbed her forearm, slick as a branch pulled from a summer pond. Across the road, the coyotes, spooked by the storm, shrieked against the night.

"Hey, hey. You with me? What's going on?" He shook her shoulders and thought he saw her nod. "Alright, easy now. Who's the president? Who's the president?"

She muttered a few gnarled words, eyes wild in her sockets. He spoke into her opened mouth as if into a well, each syllable a knot on a rope sent down for her to grab. But her brain, like his grandmother's, had ejected her far away from where they were sitting.

"I don't understand," he said. "You gotta try in English, okay?"

She pulled on his neck and planted her mouth to his ear—but only slurred in more Lithuanian.

"No, English," he coaxed. "America, you got it?"

Finally she blinked and shook her head, dislodging one language to make room for another. "My brother," she cried in English. "Get him out, please." She pulled on his shirt collar, tearing it. "Please, sir. My baby brother. He's still inside." She pointed at something a few feet away, the darkness immediately swallowing her arm. A faint glow from the streets illuminated her face, green eyes clear and wide, fixed on a spot ahead of them.

"That's just a desk," he pleaded. "Come on."

"No. It's Kristof." She lunged forward. "I can see his legs."

"I promise you we're the only ones here." He wrapped his arms around her waist and positioned himself to block whatever horror she was seeing. "Your body's right here, in 2009. You just have to step into it, alright? Can you step into it?" He shook her, hoping to loosen her brother from her vision, but she pressed on, tears and snot dripping down her chin. He wiped her face with his shirt only to smear it more, leaving a gash of mucus reflecting the dim light across her cheek.

In the commotion, her flowered nightgown had slipped off her collarbones, revealing her breast. With her neck heavy under his right arm, it was impossible to reach the hem of her gown. Using his free hand, he pulled the nightgown over her, cinching each end together with thumb and forefinger before sliding the button through the eyelet, which caught on the third try. "Sorry," he whispered. Another thunderclap rocked the house and they both ducked, Grazina covering her head with both hands. Shaking, rachitic, she clung to his shirt and kept begging him to rescue her brother. His charred arm, she explained, was poking out from a pile of rubble beside the upturned bread van, her wet eyelids blinking rapidly as the memory flickered behind them.

"It's just a bad dream," he offered. "I promise." He tried rubbing her arms, but she clawed his hands away. As a last resort, he closed his eyes and rocked back and forth, slowly, his brow pinched in concentration as he cradled her. His voice was wobbly at first, but soon he found the notes to the folk song his grandmother would sing him when he'd wake from a nightmare on hot summer nights, asthmatic and delirious. "Chiều đi lên đồi cao, hát trên những xác người," he tried. "Tôi đã thấy, tôi đã thấy bên khu vườn / Một người mẹ ôm xác đứa con." Soon his voice grew stronger, enough to feel its vibration through Grazina's shoulders as he ushered into the room the feeble melody from a country he could barely point to on a map.

Before long, to his surprise, her bones unbuckled from their stiff joints, and he could feel her returning to herself. Her clutch softened around his neck as he sang on, his mouth barely open, as though a single false note would cripple its power.

After a while only the rain peppering the windowsill could be heard. Outside, a truck was turning the corner and splashed through a deep puddle. He studied Grazina's face and posed, once more, the perennial question: "Hey," he whispered, willing her milky eyes to stay on him, "who is the president?"

She blinked, her face exhausted yet vacated by a calm, empty look. "I am," she said. "I'm the president of the United States. And I have made the stuffed cabbages for the secretary of defense. Please send him my best." She spoke without feeling, her eyes staring blankly past him. Then she pushed herself up and leaned against the wall, her hair matted and strewn down her cheek. He reached over, across the half century between them, and cleared the stray hairs from her damp face.

"And who are *you*, boy?" she asked, pointing at him with her chin. "And what's that song? Some sort of magic spell?"

Lightning flicked across their upturned, empty hands as they stared at each other.

"Yeah, for raising the dead," he said.

Grazina's mouth eased into a weak, tired smile, her missing front tooth the darkest thing he'd seen in months. "Good. Then we can live forever."

"I SAID 'what do you *want* to do,' not 'what you need to do.'" Grazina was sitting in the claw-foot tub, her mind clear, the evening dose of paroxetine dissolving an hour now in her bloodstream. Though it was only his third time giving her a bath, they had worked out a system. While she undressed, he wiped the rim of the tub down of grime and loose hair, set her medical booster chair at the bottom, then helped her into it. Once the water came just above her chest, he shut off the tap and started soaping her back with the loofah. The fall she suffered years back had fractured her collarbone. Shortly after returning from the hospital, she had tried scrubbing her back and her arm got stuck, pinning her hand to her lower spine. This was before Janet, so Grazina was alone. She had to pull herself out the tub and dial 911 with her one free hand just to have firefighters, young enough to be grandsons, free her arm as she stood naked and shivering in her own living room.

Once Hai finished scrubbing her back, she did the rest while he sat on the floor outside the bathroom reading *Slaughterhouse-Five*.

"What do you want to do in the future, I mean. Looks like you're some kind of bookworm." She took a long drag from her cigarette, the smoke blowing out the hallway past his face.

He put the book down and stared at a dusty landscape painting hanging across the hall. "You'll think it's stupid."

"Maybe," she said. "No promises." Her amber bracelet clacked against the iron as she flicked ashes in the water.

"I used to want to be a writer. My dream was to write a novel that held everything I loved, including unlovable things. Like a little cabinet." He shut his eyes—it sounded even more ridiculous aloud. "But that was back in high school. Before I realized it wasn't real."

"You wanna be a writer *and* you want to jump off a bridge? That's pretty much the same thing, no? A writer just takes longer to hit the water." She tried to laugh but started coughing. "My husband tried to be a poet, you know, and all that gave him was Alzheimer's."

Hai peeked around the door. "Really?"

"Eh, he never wrote a single word, that bum. Not that I know of, at least. Too lazy. Just talked about it. About writing his life story, Lithuania, the war, this and that, yada yada. Then one day his brain starts to look like Swiss cheese, like mine now probably." Shampoo suds ran down her temples as she looked at him, her lips a taut line.

He turned back to the wall. "I just have to read a whole bunch first. Three or four years of reading, then maybe I'll be ready to write. It's like a pregnancy."

"Sounds more like constipation. In my country, most writers got silent pills."

"Silent pills?"

"Bullets."

A soft rain started pebbling the window.

"Okay then, Mr. Pushkin. How will you do this?"

"I dunno," the boy said, tucking his knees to his chest.

"You need money to do anything, you know. My husband's dead five years now and I still owe for his two-hour funeral. Even dying costs money. Hell, it can cost more than living."

There was a silence. The night was coming down from the mountains and settling thick around the house.

She was right. He had heard stories, which seemed more like myths, of writers who had to enter a lottery just to live in a shack full of mice somewhere deep in the woods for two or three weeks, scribbling away and avoiding their families. They even call it a fellowship. The emo girl with eye bags at New Hope had told him about a school up in Vermont where her sister went for a year, a place where promising young artists, mostly from wealthy families, got to "learn by doing." Where students dressed like the author photos of books they'd yet to write, that some will never write. How come anytime he heard of such unimaginable places, such utopias, he always heard of them too late, the path invisible until he's long past their junction? But what has *he* done anyway—other than dodge the slow-moving "silent pill" of his life only to fall face down in the ditch he was now in?

"Another thing. We're down to thirty-four dollars on the EBT," she sighed. "And it's only the eighth. I know we're saving on the delivery charges since you pick 'em up now. But—"

"Okay." He had a hunch, despite what she had said weeks ago about being good with money, that this was coming.

"For now we'll just eat the rolls instead of stepping on 'em," she said.

Hai searched his mind, then remembered his estranged cousin Sony. Last he heard Sony was working at the HomeMarket on the outskirts of East Gladness, just down Route 4. Maybe he's still there. It would be a long shot, but if Hai apologized, for everything, maybe Sony could get him a job. "I can head to town first thing tomorrow and ask around for work. I'll help out, for sure. Don't worry."

"What's your skill anyway? You have any skills or what?"

He bit his lip, thinking. "Well, I'm good at looking at things. And, I guess, considering them, like ideas and stuff."

"Considering!" she said with a wheezing laugh. "That's a first. I'm afraid being considerate is not a skill. Not in America. Maybe the Vatican, if you're lucky."

"It's called observing. Introspection," he said, miffed.

"You're kidding. That's it?" The cigarette hissed as she chucked it in the water. "Okay, then give me an example."

"Of what?"

"Of you considering. What do you consider?"

"I dunno." Even though she couldn't see him behind the wall, he hid his face between his knees.

The rain was droning steady over the roof shingles. "The rain. Maybe raindrops are like people . . . Well, that's not what I mean—" His voice cracked and he suddenly felt unmoored, incredulous. A child.

"Ha! The rain? Every writer who ever lived talked about rain. You know what writing really is?" She paused for effect. "Complaining. About weather. Beautiful complaining. No wonder why Stalin shipped them to Siberia."

"Please don't laugh at me," he mumbled to the floor, surprised at how much this stung.

Grazina grew quiet. A trickle of water. "You know what? Good for you, boy. You're good at observing. And tomorrow you'll go to town. You'll go to town and get a job where you can be the most considerate observer this county has ever known. You hear me?"

He turned around and their eyes met. "Yeah."

"Good. Now get me out of here. My balls are freezing."

He skipped breakfast the next morning, made a buttered English muffin for Grazina, cutting off the moldy edges, then watched her take her gabapentin and Aricept before heading toward town. He was halfway down the block when she yelled from the door, waving a ziplock bag of baby carrots. "For your heart, for your heart," she shouted. As he crossed the bridge, carrots in hand, she kept calling from the fire escape, but he couldn't hear her over the river's rush—only that she sounded hopeful, which made him hopeful.

It was the end of September now and the steel beams along the bridge gleamed with the season's first frost. A daylit moon was pinned against a taut blue sky as the morning filtered through aspens coppering along the shores. A whiff of woodsmoke floated up from the trailer park as he approached Route 4, and before long the farmhouses came to view, their fields gone to dirt for autumn. Two eagles were soaring over the shanty houses, their mildewed roofs like the backs of century-old whales. Soon the sidewalk crumbled into the highway shoulder, and the gas stations, fast-food chains, and the one packy marked the outskirts of East Gladness. Before long the HomeMarket off Cumberland Lane appeared. It sat in the center of the parking lot of a strip mall called Rushing Oaks Business Park, which also had a Family Dollar, a laundromat, a long-defunct CD store, the windows still plastered with decade-old NSYNC tour posters, and a knitting boutique called Knit Pickers, miraculously still in business. On the edge of the strip was another row of trailer homes. Hai had the sudden thought of being a kid in there, going to bed with the glow of the Family Dollar sign falling through your window, which ached in him a strange and inscrutable tenderness.

As far as franchises go, the HomeMarket was a coveted place to work compared to the McDonald's on Harris, the Taco Bell off Silas Deane, the Wendy's or—worst of all—the Dunkin' Donuts on Griswold, owned by a guy infamous for roofying college girls when he was a high school senior in the nineties. Founded in New England, Home-Market was a fast-casual chain, which meant it was supposed to *seem* fancier, though the pay was still minimum wage. Hai had even heard people bragging about working at HomeMarket. Like Becky Miller, a girl from high school who gave up going to Welles Park, where she'd sit on the bleachers smoking blunts and blasting Mary J. Blige on her boom box with her girlfriends, to scoop mac and cheese and carve up roasted chickens. When someone asked Becky why she stopped coming to the park, she said, "The hell I'm going into that busted-ass park with those busted-ass girls for? I work at HomeMarket now," and walked away smirking, her new cubic zirconia earrings flashing.

As Hai approached, black smoke issued from the restaurant's chimney, the scent of burnt flesh acrid in the air. The building was small and squat, painted white all over save for the red tiled roof. Positioned behind the logo was a neon-lit pioneer girl in a bonnet with maniacal-eager eyes hoisting a basket of bread from her hip.

Inside, the walls were lined to the ceiling with white tiles. Formica tables, bolted to the floor, stretched across the modest dining area. This clinical interior drew Hai's attention to the far wall, where Home-Market's poster-sized menu hung, showcasing, in rich, zoomed-in detail, the steaming dishes served in white bowls and laid across reclaimed wood tables, the cloth ruffled just so to exude a rustic, country-house atmosphere, all of it under the sinister orange lighting common in Thomas Kinkade cottages. Below the image, printed in looping holiday script, was the phrase, *Fill your Home with HomeMarket!* Even as he turned away, heading toward the counter, the poster blazed in the corner of his eye like the residue of a blast.

It was a little after eleven and the store had just opened. A woman in her fifties with dyed red hair tucked into her cap was lifting the metal covers from the heated countertops, revealing smoking vats of vibrant, primary-colored side dishes.

Behind her was a guy loading raw chickens into a seven-row industrial rotisserie oven, the pink meat turning above a row of blistered torsos as fat sizzled mutely behind the glass.

"Deliveries are out back," the woman said without looking up.

"Oh," Hai glanced down at his jacket, "I'm not UPS. I'm——"

"Oh okay—what can I get ya, hun?" She flashed a smile that lasted just long enough for her lips to twitch twice before dropping to a pout.

"Does anyone named Sony work here?"

"He's in the kitchen." The customer service shtick evaporated and her eyes narrowed. "What for? You not gonna beat him up, are you?"

"No—what? He's my cousin."

She examined his hands, as if for weapons. "Hold on." She turned around and shouted through a cupped palm. "Yo, Sony! Some Chinese guy says he's your cousin. Get out here and deal with it."

Squeaky footsteps, then a lanky kid appeared from the back, a head taller than Hai with a long neck and brownish, doe-like eyes. He stood blankly, rubber-gloved hands hovering at his sides.

The woman nodded Sony over. "Don't just stand there like a dead dick." She glanced at Hai, chuckling.

With quick, staccato movements, Sony peeled off his rubber gloves and made a beeline to one of the dining tables.

"Hey. Don't mess with that boy, you hear me?" the oven man called out, loading another rack of chickens and squaring himself at Hai. "His mama's in jail. So if you got any questions, big or small, you can ask me."

Hai smiled weakly, gave the man a thumbs-up, and sat down. It had been over two years since he'd last seen Sony, and he didn't know how to begin. He stared at his hands folded in his lap.

Sony was named after the Sony Trinitron, the first TV his father bought once he arrived in America after being released from a reeducation camp back in Vietnam. Though the TV was made in 1968, his old man didn't get one till '91, the year Sony was born. Naming your child after electronic devices was not uncommon among people in refugee camps back then. Hai knew a kid in Windsor named Toshiba (which got him mistaken for Japanese). Aspirational monikers didn't stop at electronics either, but extended to any cultural relic possessing social or monetary value. One of his mother's coworkers named her daughter Simba because she had watched *The Lion King* on repeat while she was pregnant, sobbing each time Mufasa fell off the cliff. Another was named BMW. One kid from the same refugee camp as Hai's family was called MJKarlMalone Truong; rivals in life, Jordan and Malone would be united in the body of an asthmatic Vietnamese boy with a lazy eye who landed, of all places, in North Carolina, home of Jordan's Tar Heels. Their elders named them after whatever they hoped would manifest in life. Why toil away in factories to save for a Lexus when you could make her yourself?

Hai himself was almost named Honda, on account of a red birthmark on his forehead that had an uncanny resemblance to the car dealer's *H* logo. *He's destined for greatness!* his grandmother, the ultimate hype man to her grandchildren, exclaimed in the hospital room in Saigon. *He's born in Vietnam but made in Japan. And by the best car manufacturer known to man!* Though his mother agreed that such a sign could only come from divine messaging, she had a more sober and austere disposition, and settled for Hai, still heeding the letter on his forehead, which faded by the time he could speak.

"It's good to see you, Sony," Hai said. "What are you up to now?"

"I'm sitting in a chair talking to my cousin. But we're not supposed to be talking. Our moms are fighting."

"That's not how it works. We're adults. And I meant, *how* are you doing? Like, how are things?"

After Bà ngoại died, Aunt Kim and Sony moved up from Florida. But instead of working with Ma, Aunt Kim decided to rekindle something with an old boyfriend who owned a salon in Coventry, causing the sisters to fall out. Aunt Kim wanted to start fresh with a man who actually *owned* his business, and Ma wanted her sister close now that Bà ngoại was gone. *You can't just pop up like a ghost after people die*, Ma had told her days after the funeral. *We're sisters. We got no one else but us.* It sounded simple enough, but when you throw in decades of festering tensions, betrayals, refutations and backstabs, a country still smoldering somewhere in the caverns of memory, the argument became a symbol for everything rotting underneath, both sisters too proud to concede.

"A good soldier can't turn against his ranks." Sony straightened. "General McClellan, the first commanding officer of the Army of the Potomac, had untrustworthy lieutenants and ultimately failed in capturing Virginia. Though he wasn't as incapable as some historians assume. Burnside, on the other hand—"

"Okay, okay." Hai waved him off. "But we're not traitors. Or soldiers. We're related. We're *blood*."

"So were the North and the South during what some still call the War of Northern Aggression."

"Sony. Please. Look, I'm just trying to get a job, okay? You think I can get a job here?" The glow from the giant HomeMarket poster hung over Sony's head, giving him a lopsided halo.

Sony lowered his eyes and fiddled his fingers, which told Hai he was thinking. Their grandmother always believed Sony was chosen by spirits, that he was tuned into a special channel emitted from beyond the human realm. He remembered Sony rocking side to side in the backyard one summer night when they were little, surrounded by fireflies and humming the theme song to the movie *Gettysburg*. "See that boy?" Bà ngoại said, looking out the window. "The elders are using him. He's blessed with that third eye, just like my sister, Chi Sáu."

"What's he talking about with your mom in jail?" Hai nodded toward the rotisserie man.

"Because she is." Sony grabbed at a passing fly, then slowly unfurled his fist for Hai to see, revealing nothing. "And his name's Wayne."

Sony went on to explain, in a barrage of sentences, his eyes never once looking above Hai's chest, how Kim and her boyfriend ended up getting caught for arson after they tried to burn down the boyfriend's nail salon for insurance money when the business was about to go belly-up last winter. "I have her court documents. She can't read English, so I read everything to her. I was supposed to be her lawyer too, but I don't have the jurisdiction to practice as an attorney in the state of Connecticut."

"You also don't have a law degree."

Sony ran a finger down the scar in his head, now bright with sweat under the halogens. A nervous tic.

"Hold on, though," Hai said, looking around. "How did we not know Aunt Kim's in jail? We would've helped you guys. Or something."

"Cause our moms are *fighting*."

"What's the bail?"

"Ten thousand. But if we pay five and half thousand, she gets out. I don't know how that works."

"Where are you living now? Your dad's still in Vermont, right?"

"I'm at the Meyer's Center."

"The one off Lilac? That's a *halfway* house. And you're barely an adult."

"I turned eighteen on July twenty-first at 3:46 p.m." He finally met Hai's gaze, hurt. "And it's not a sober-living home anymore. They changed it in 2006. They're nice to me there. I'm developing life skills. I have no skills and no personality. And I need to develop them. Fast."

"The hell you talking about?"

"That's what Dr. Philbern said."

"Who said you're crazy?"

"Nobody. You're saying that."

"Sony, you doing okay, hun?" called the lady from behind the counter. She raised her cap to peer over at them.

"I gotta get back. We need forty corn breads before the lunch rush and I'm behind."

"You think I can get a job here? I wanna help with Aunt Kim's bail."

"I'm not in charge of team acquisition. You'll have to talk to BJ. She's the best manager HomeMarket has ever employed. Well, at least this one. I can't speak for the others. Only she can judge if you have what it takes. She's in tomorrow at ten." Sony got up, wiped invisible crumbs off the table, and pushed in his chair.

"What's this thing?" Hai picked up an origami bird by the saltshakers, realizing now there was one on each table.

"Those are origami penguins."

"I know, but . . . why?"

"I made them for the tables. They're made just like the traditional swans except I cut off their wings after."

Hai held the paper bird up. It didn't look like a penguin, but it did look like a swan with no wings.

"You can have that one. I'll make another."

"Here," Hai said, remembering the carrots, "take these."

"Baby carrots." Sony examined the bag in his hand.

"They give you courage."

"Hmm. I didn't know that. I'll have them on my break. They'll be great dipped in our gravy. But this will be for nutrition *only*. I have enough courage for at least a hundred twenty men." He walked a few paces and stopped. "Oh, and you should check out *Heroes*."

"What?"

"You loved *Power Rangers* when we were little. So I recommend the series *Heroes*. No offense," he held up his hand, "but I prefer reality-based entertainment. Still, you'll like it. It's *Power Rangers* but with more science."

Hai watched him walk away and realized how much he had missed his cousin.

⌒

SONY WAS BORN with hydrocephalus and had to have emergency brain surgery an hour out the womb at Hartford Hospital. It left a long, pencil-width scar that ran down the middle of his head and ended just above the nape of his neck. The kids at school called him "crackhead," claiming he got it because his mother was a crack addict while pregnant. Sony's father left him and his mother right after he was born. "My sperm can't make a retard," his father said to Aunt Kim while Sony sat peering up at them. "Look at my family line; there is not a *single* retard in the family tree. Not one." He then packed his bags and vanished to the woods in Vermont, marrying a woman who owned three successful local taquerias and never looking back.

One time, when Hai was nine and Sony was seven, the family was milling about on the floor after dinner when Sony ran into the house, excited after sitting out in the grass all evening. He said, "Mama, Bà ngoại, look! I'm normal now. They gonna let me join the Marines. See?" His Vietnamese wasn't too good, so he spoke to them mostly in English. He lowered his head and showed them his scar. "I'm not a crackhead anymore. Look!" To their surprise, his scar was black and uniform like the rest of his hair.

"Oh heavens!" Bà ngoại gasped. "It's a miracle! It finally happened. I knew he was chosen."

"They didn't fix nothing," Aunt Kim snapped in Vietnamese. "Give me that!" She grabbed something from Sony's fist. She held the black Magic Marker before them all, then before her son, who had sunk to his knees. But then something flickered across Aunt Kim's face, something both sad and lonesome and pitiful. And she softened, her eyes glassy. Aunt Kim put the marker in her pocket and pulled her boy close, pressing her lips to the smooth, inky skin of his scar. "I know, I know," she said softly, her lips black with ink. "Now you can join the Marines. But my boy's too smart to get shot, right? He's too bright to die, isn't he?" She stroked his cheek. Ma looked away, her hand over her mouth, as Bà ngoại reached out and squeezed Sony's tiny foot. Sony, normal at last, smiled into his mother's chest.

HAI WAS LEAVING the HomeMarket parking lot when something caught his eye. There, at the far end of the strip mall, in the last store-front, just before the tan brick wall dropped into a dirt lot full of broken glass and a tipped-over dumpster, was a vinyl banner in red letters: GRAND OPENING!!!! SGT. PEPPER'S PIZZA: A FAMILY PLACE.

He was surprised to feel a surge of warmth toward those exclama-tion marks, as if typed into Microsoft Paint in a jolt of ecstatic aspira-tion and quickly printed out and hoisted over the entrance. Outside, a middle-aged man in an orange Sikh turban was wiping down the front windows while a young woman—his daughter?—was inside loading soda cans into an industrial fridge. Taped to the door, above the hours, was a *Yes We Can!* Obama '08 poster. Looking closer, Hai remembered that this spot had once belonged to a debt collection office. Maybe pizza replacing loan sharks meant East Gladness was finally turning a new leaf. He had the urge to shout, *Thank you for believing in our shitty town! I will eat your pizza forever!* but he was already down the road and the words never came.

"IT'S AN INTERVIEW," he said, filling Grazina in over dinner, "so there's no promises. But it's the fanciest restaurant in town. And I found out my cousin's still there."

"Good. So tomorrow you find out for sure." She put down her fork and dabbed her mouth with a napkin, the plastic tray of Salisbury steak empty save for the liquefied brownie. A hand radio, turned low to the news, crackled on the counter behind her.

"You'll get it. I can tell."

"How so?" He lit a cigarette and leaned back.

"I woke from my nap and just had a feeling, that's all. It popped in my head. And I thought, *He's gonna get it.*"

And now rumors from the White House, the man on the radio said, *claim that the president is hoping to broker another round of troop withdrawals—this time from Afghanistan—sometime by Christmas. Let's go over to Lisa, who's in Washington . . .*

The two stopped and listened, their heads angled in attention, truly believing that the worst, both here and elsewhere, was over. It was the kind of day where anything felt possible. As if the charity of the world had tipped, finally, to one side of the rusted scale. The kind of day where you can fill in your scars with Magic Marker and tell yourself you're normal—and it might be true.

4

Hai headed back to HomeMarket the next morning. He cupped his hands over the store window and saw Sony wiping down tables in the dining room. It was ten a.m., an hour till opening.

"Go out back," Sony said through the cracked door.

"There's a back?"

"Yes, to load supplies. Go back and wait. BJ will get you when she's ready."

"Why can't I just sit there at the tables? It's an interview."

Sony rolled his eyes with exaggerated annoyance. "You gotta start at the asshole of things before you can get to the heart. That's what BJ always says. And it's true." He shut the door and locked it with a click.

The back of HomeMarket was a strip of unmarked pavement that stretched toward an abandoned apartment complex whose windows were mostly boarded up, the brick along the edges black with soot from a fire that must have swept through years ago. Hai sat on a cinder block outside the back door and waited. He was there about ten minutes before this skinny white kid with a nose ring came out. The kid nodded vaguely in Hai's direction and leaned on the wall fishing for a cigarette. He had a once-white apron on that was so filthy it looked dragged in mud then washed out in a river.

"You BJ?" Hai said.

"Hell nah, dude," he said with a stoner's chuckle. "I look like a boss to you? Hey, you got a light though?"

Hai threw him his BIC and the boy lit up, his fingertips black with grime. He leaned on the wall smoking for a bit, both of them staring at the dead buildings across the lot. Vines and chokegrass had already pulled some of the nailed plywood off the windows.

"Dude," the kid smirked, his braces catching the sun. "Ever heard of a strawberry shortcake?"

"I think so."

He started to explain it, but Hai wasn't really listening. He was trying to time how long Grazina's last dose would last and whether he had to rush back to the house after the interview.

". . . so that when you're banging the chick, right? Then, just when you're about to pop, you turn her around and knob her right there, in the fucking nose. Then you just"—he made the gesture of an explosion with his hand—"pssssssh."

Hai turned back to the ruined buildings, the iron bars on the ground-level windows, trying to think of the people who had lived there. Did they smell roast chicken each night before they went off to bed? Did it leak into their sleep? How many of them worked at this very HomeMarket? How many of them had to leave in ambulances that must've parked in this lot so that EMTs could bring them out on stretchers past the drive-thru menu board and its crackling voices, the cars snaking around it?

"It's fucked up though, for real," the stoner mumbled. He looked like a character in a haunted house. Hai had grown up with people like him, guys and girls alike, and learned that if you just *uh-huh* your way through whatever they were saying, they'll like you enough to leave you alone or give you a nickname they'll call out in various stages of intoxication.

"This guy I knew said he did it to his ex, but he bullshits all the time. He told me about this other one, though—you know about the Irish plower?"

The kid blew a shaft of smoke that engulfed the side of Hai's head.

"How much this job pay anyway?" Hai turned to him, coughing.

"Shit is what it pays." He dropped the half-burnt bogie and stepped on it. "Why? You trying to get a job?"

"Trying."

The kid's phone buzzed. He flipped it open and laughed. "Yo, check this out! My cousin Danil just sent me this." He shoved a cell phone in Hai's face. Hai pulled back and squinted at what looked like a heavily pixelated video of a squirrel being shot off the roof of a shed by paint-ball rounds, followed by multiple people shouting, one of whom was a woman who kept saying, "Get off my lawn, you cunts! Get off my fucking lawn!"

Before Hai could respond, the metal door swung open. The white boy was already slipping the phone back in his pocket and retying his apron.

Sony stepped out and stood by the door, sentry-like, chin high and staring straight ahead. From the shadows of HomeMarket, a heavyset figure filled the doorframe, then stepped into the light.

"Drive-thru," the figure said and nodded toward the door. To which the white boy bolted inside.

This was clearly BJ. Six foot three with a buzz cut fade and shape-up over a forehead beaded with sweat.

Hai stood, pulled his jacket tight around him, and gave her his hand to shake.

"Hold your horses," BJ said, gently pushing down his hand. "This the cousin you talked about?" she said to Sony, her gaze fixed on Hai.

Sony nodded. "Affirmative, he's looking to join the ranks."

BJ shifted her weight, sand grating under her Skechers. "Open your eyes, man. No, wider." She hunched to examine each of Hai's eyeballs. "Hmm. Pupils still big. Least he's not on heroin," she said to Sony, cleaning her teeth with her tongue. "And if you're on meth, at least you won't nod out on us, right?" She chuckled. "Alright, follow me."

When the fog on Hai's glasses faded, the place came into view, so small you could take three steps in any direction and touch a wall. What followed was a "tour of the facilities," as BJ called it, though the entire back area was no larger than an RV. There was the three-paneled industrial oven, where trays of corn bread were spinning as they rose into golden, palm-sized mounds crusted with sugar, and the long stainless-steel sink where a teenage girl with black eyeliner was now scrubbing away, sweat glistening on the nape of her neck. Then the broom closet, and next to that a door with a Sharpied Post-it note that read *Office*. It looked like any other fast-food place: rubber mats on tiled floors, blocky steel appliances, fluorescent lights, all of it smelling vaguely of ketchup and used dishwater. The whole tour took all of five minutes.

"Now let's show you the front. Where the magic happens," BJ said, rubbing her hands together as Sony hurried behind her. "This right here, *this* is the main protein we serve." She pointed to the back wall behind the counter where, spotlit by overhead gallery lights, was the seven-rack rotisserie oven where the man he saw yesterday was now carving an entire chicken on a polyplastic butcher's counter stained brown and slick from thousands of carcasses.

"This here's Maureen," BJ said, pointing to a redheaded woman. Maureen nodded, not so much smiling but rather moving her lips to another position. "Show him how to make a meat loaf sandwich, no mayo," BJ commanded. Hai was ready to put on a pair of gloves but realized BJ was talking about the computer system when he saw Maureen's fingers fly across the screen, pressing various colored blocks for

ingredients and dressings. In about thirty-five seconds, which to Hai
didn't seem very fast, a receipt shot out from the ticket machine down
the counter.

"She's good, huh?" BJ said. Maureen beamed for the first time. "And
that over there is our chicken man, Wayne." She leaned in close. "He
tells everybody he looks like Al Green, but it's more like the current
Reverend Al Green, you know what I'm saying?"

"Definitely not from the 'Love and Happiness' days." Maureen nodded toward Wayne, a rotund, profusely sweating man whose squat
neck barely rose an inch above his collar.

BJ turned to the sneeze-guard counter that held the rectangular
vats of food. They were heated from above by Nemco commercial hal-
ogen lamps and from below via pools of hot water circulated through
copper wire. The sterile and cold furnishings served to amplify the
hues of the products, giving the food a brilliant luminosity, which was
engineered, he later learned, by a corporate subcommittee backed by
decades of behavioral research conducted at an institute in Ohio funded
by the wife of a Raytheon board member.

"So here's what we're doing, buddy," BJ said. "This counter here,
this is the heart of HomeMarket. This is where America is fed." BJ, Hai
realized, was one of those people whose entire existence hinged on being perceived as an expert. And though experts often made him nervous, he was intrigued by her pristine zeal for this place, which seemed
no more than a tiny cafeteria.

"HomeMarket," she went on, "is not like other fast-casuals—and it
sure as hell's not like those bums down the road like Wendy's, Taco
Bell, and Burger King, run-of-the-mill-type shit. Understand?" She
looked around, gathering momentum, but no one was really paying attention. The white kid with the nose ring was leaning against the
counter by the drive-thru window, his arms folded, bored.

"Affirmative, ma'am!" Sony chirped from behind Hai.

"Good," BJ said. "Because when folks walk into this place, and I do mean this *specific* store," a spray of spit shot out as she said this, one Hai was too timid to duck from, "they're walking into Thanksgiving. Except in here there's no fucked-up relatives, no nasty dried-ass turkey, no cooking or basting or cutting. Hell, not even the shitty decor and moldy pumpkins, none of those stupid cone baskets with squash in them for no reason. This is all about home cooking. And you know what? Even Denny's, which some people got the nerve to call a *sit-down* restaurant, has a goddamn microwave. Have you ever seen a microwave in this establishment?" She waited for Hai to look around, then pulled up her pants and inhaled dramatically. "Russia," she called to the white boy with the nose ring, "you ever see a microwave in here? I didn't think so. What we give to America is the *taste* of the holidays without the pain of holidays. When people come in here, we give them the sensation of home. And they don't even know they're getting that until they bite into this, for example." She scooped a spoonful of the mac and cheese and let it plop back into the vat, then did the same with the sweet potato pie. "See this? See how our pie has the slightly burnt marshmallows on top, just like how their grandma used to make it? Except she didn't!" A vein pulsed wildly along BJ's temple. "Hell, they might not even *have* a grandma, but you bet they're gonna see her face when they got this pie in their mouth."

Maureen pointed at a greenish gruel cooling in one vat. "The creamed spinach is my favorite. Know why?" She raised her brows at Hai. "Cause it don't taste like vegetables. It tastes like dinner."

BJ, slightly annoyed at the interruption, nonetheless nodded in agreement. "That's right. HomeMarket is what's for dinner. Except all the time." She took a step back, stared intensely at the passing trucks on Route 4 outside, and shouted, "We are magicians!" Wayne turned around, startled, and gave her a confused look. She slammed her hand on the counter, knocking a packet of cookies off the register, which

Sony quickly put back in place. "We turn food into *feeling*, folks. You get me? We transform it."

Hai glanced around to gather the other employees' expressions; all remained unmoved save for Sony, whose lips trembled with a mix of awe, reverence, and fear. It seemed this wasn't the first time the crew had heard this.

"You think this is all about being full?" She turned to Hai, who hastily shook his head. "It's about taking care of people, giving them happiness that their shitty jobs suck out of them. Our customers aren't rich pricks in mansions, okay? They come in here tired, broken down by the world. Some of them, like Miss Mabel, haven't seen their family in over twenty years. She knows everybody here by name and even calls Maureen over there her daughter." BJ pointed at Maureen's face. "Isn't that right, Maur? And didn't she give you a ten-dollar tip once?"

Maureen bit her lip and nodded.

"But not all this happens cause of the company. It happens because of our team members. And good teams are *nothing* without good leaders." BJ took from her back pocket an American flag bandana and mopped her dripping forehead. "Now, I'm not out here to be anybody's hero, or even to toot my own horn, but we, lest we forget, folks, are the third," she shoved three fingers in front of Maureen's face, who didn't even blink, "the *third*-best-grossing HomeMarket in all twelve locations in the Northeast."

"Is the one in Reading, Pennsylvania, still number one?" asked Wayne.

BJ sighed and nodded solemnly. "You know very well that one doesn't count. The one in Reading is in the middle of nowhere, *Wayne*. A food desert. If our store was in the sticks like them, we'd make ten grand a night, easy. Out there, where it's just cow pasture for miles, HomeMarket might as well be Times Square!"

"Exactly," said Sony.

The second-best-grossing location was inside Boston's South Station, which was only that high, BJ explained, because people are naturally hungrier when they're waiting. "It's just nature. The more you wait, the more you eat. So, in a way, we're *actually* number one. Now, you might be asking yourself why that is, and I'll tell you why." She leaned back on the counter and folded her arms. "Amanda, bring that corn bread out here!"

The dishwasher girl scuffed out from the back carrying a tray of corn bread and dumped it into a metal cradle on the heat counter. BJ picked one up, held it to the light, then gingerly broke it in half. A puff of steam exhaled from the bread as yellow crumbs flaked onto her palm. She held one half to Hai's lips and said, "Go ahead and taste this truth, friend."

Hai took the piece in his mouth and chewed. The bread, crispy at the edges, quickly dissolved on his tongue, a salty sweetness spreading to a uniform consensus of *corn*, as if, incredibly, the bread inherited the essence of corn—sweet, nutty, mildly buttery—while preserving, perhaps even enhancing, that very corn-ness, despite being transformed into a baked good. It was corn bread more corn-like than any corn he'd ever tasted. The way peach rings are peachier than peaches.

BJ swallowed her half, smiling. Russia's face finally wore an expression: vague agreement. "You gotta admit, that shit's bomb," he said.

"And it's all because of me, BJ, aka Big Jean. And that's pronounced *Jaaang*, the proper French way, we clear?"

"Big Jean," Hai nodded.

"Sure, I might've invented the perfect corn bread—whose recipe only I know, by the way—but I also happen to be one of the top-performing managers in the Northeast."

"Oh God," said Maureen, whose accent Hai now clocked to be from the Midwest. "Here we go again." She turned around and started opening a box of napkins.

"Follow me." BJ headed to the other end of the dining room, where a narrow hallway led to the bathrooms. On the wall was the "Employee of the Month" section with twelve picture frames. All except two displayed BJ's grinning face, with varying lengths of buzz cuts and fades. Sony, who had followed behind, stepped forward and pointed to Maureen's mug-shot-looking photo for the month of June. "This was, of course, when BJ was in Martinique to take care of her grandmother, who was hospitalized for kidney failure."

"Maur was a trooper," BJ said, shaking her head. Then, in a lower voice: "Even though I know she eats the cookies without paying, I let it slide." She patted Hai on the back. "You see. It's a give-and-take world, my friend."

"Who's that?" Hai asked, nodding to what appeared to be a man in a basketball jersey whose portrait took up the latest month of August.

"*That* is none other than Samuel Dalembert." BJ lifted her head and brightened. "A center for the 76ers."

"How come your name is under his photo?" Hai asked.

Apparently corporate had a retirement party last month for one of the founders, so the usual photographer wasn't able to come. Dalembert was BJ's placeholder. "Besides," BJ went on, "as a fellow Caribbean, he and I share a lot of attributes: hardworking, big in the paint, tenacious under pressure, and, let's be honest, one of the finest performers in our respective fields."

"Oh hell no," shouted Wayne from behind the counter. Everyone turned to him. "You can't make nonsense claims just because the guy comes from the same *hemisphere* as you. He's, like, alright—but your guy blocks one or two shots a game, does a layup here and there, and maybe catches an alley-oop once a week. That's what we call a *role player* in the real world. He's no Shaq or Duncan or even Mutombo."

BJ, her trembling hand finally removed from her mouth, said with suppressed calm, "Dalembert is the pride of the French Caribbean. And my grandmother watches basketball *because* of him."

"That's all good," Wayne went on, "but you can't say he's 'the best in his field' just cause you have *whatever* in common. Kevin Ollie's Black too, but I must say that my man objectively . . . sucks."

"I like Vin Baker," Maureen said, looking bored. "He's from Hartford and became an alcoholic. When my son was alive, we'd watch Vinny every week. He was so handsome in that Sonics uniform."

"Hey Russia," Wayne said. "You like that NBA player, AK-47?"

"The Sonics' green was better than the Celtics' green," Maureen went on. "Kinder looking, more class. My father loved the Celtics, that asshole."

Russia pulled off one side of his headset. "What AK-47?"

"Yeah, Andrei Karo-something, that Russian player on the Jazz. You think he's the best in the world just cause he's Russian?"

"I don't like basketball," Russia said, "too much dribbling," and snapped his headset back on.

"Whatever. You all get my point." Wayne turned around and resumed carving up a meat loaf, shaking his head.

BJ faced Hai and Sony. "Don't listen to him. He's been battling diabetes for over a decade and says some wild things, that Wayne." She sighed and looked away. "But he has a good heart. Look, what I'm trying to say to you, kid, is this: I don't call the shots around here." She tapped Dalembert's grinning face. "I just make 'em."

WHEN THE TOUR WAS OVER, Hai followed BJ into the office, which was the size of a large porta-potty. A desktop Dell computer was showing a screen saver of the HomeMarket girl dancing across the screen and tossing corn bread from her basket. BJ dug into a cardboard box under the desk and handed Hai a black polo shirt and an official HomeMarket visor cap. "It's a large but you can tuck it in."

"Wait, I'm hired? What about the interview?"

"Look at me, man. What's the key word in *interview*?"

Hai blinked at her. Sony, somehow still behind him, was breathing heavily on his ear.

"It's *view*. Inter-view. And you got a good view of the place, didn't you?"

Hai nodded.

"Put on that shirt and cap—oh, and this apron too." She handed him a few papers from a drawer. "You start at $7.15, just like any rookie. If you're not a bum you'll be up to $7.25 in no time."

"What's 'no time'?"

"Two years, give or take." She gave him a pen and directed Sony to turn around so he could sign on his back. "There's a ceiling here, though, I gotta warn you. Don't think you're gonna work your way up to owning one of these bad boys. HomeMarket isn't a franchise. We're like Starbucks." She paused to let this sink in. "They don't just hand off Thanksgiving to anybody, you know—not even to me. Corporate keeps that shit in the family."

"HomeMarket controls its teams from the headquarters in Atlanta, Georgia," added Sony, "like an army command center."

"That's right." BJ folded her arms. "This *is* like an army and I'm . . . like its Jesus, I guess."

"Don't you mean *general*?" Hai said.

"BJ's as sharp and steadfast a leader as General McClellan," said Sony.

"You stupid?" BJ said to Sony. "Didn't you say he was opposed to freeing the slaves? Pick another one."

Hai hit Sony on the shoulder. "Would you quit with that Civil War stuff already?"

"He can't help it. It's his thing. He's acoustic." BJ pointed at her own head and gave Hai a knowing look.

"It's not a *thing*," said Sony, buttoning his polo collar. "It's scholarship. I'm a historian." Sony stepped forward, one hand on his heart like the Pledge of Allegiance, and spoke in a rush: "And while there's no denying McClellan's initial moral corruptions, he was the most seasoned and capable field marshal at the time, having graduated top of his class at West Point. I *could* compare you to Sherman, but that would be categorically false as he was far less superior on the field and relied on cruel slash-and-burn tactics, especially in the Southern theater."

BJ glanced at Hai, then at Sony, considering this. "I'm gonna stick with Jesus."

With his shirt and cap on, his papers signed, Hai followed BJ to the front of the house. "Excuse me, team members!" BJ shouted louder than necessary, causing Maureen to cover her left ear. "Please join me in welcoming our newest member to the third-best-grossing Home-Market in history!" There was a smattering of applause; even the dishwasher girl clapped from somewhere in the back.

Sony shook Hai's hand and said, seriously, "I'm proud of you, private."

Something like warmth seemed to flow from Hai's fingers, which startled him. The room spun, then gleamed with colors. He didn't expect this current of relief to flow through him so cleanly. He had a job, which meant he had regained a real, quantifiable foothold in the world. He had a uniform, a cool-looking visor with the logo stitched neatly in cardinal red. His name tag was on the way from the command center in Georgia. He also had coworkers—no, a *team*, one that was the third best at their job. Never in his life had he been so included in something as to be swallowed by it, invisible among a visible human mass.

As the applause died, Russia came over and handed him a chicken drumstick. Hai bit into it and froze, the flavor mounting the feeling already on his chest.

"The hell?" said Wayne, wincing. "Why the fuck is he crying? Come on, dude, it's not even noon yet. I can't work with tears around me. I'm allergic."

Russia said, "Yo, hey, you good, man? You need a break or something?"

Hai shook his head and wiped his mouth of chicken grease. "The chicken's amazing, that's all." Which was partly true. He took another bite as the faces around him warped into watery colors and felt granted into a realm much greater than his sad, little life, which made his troubles seem suddenly ethereal and elsewhere. He not only had a position in the company—but the company had no idea what his past looked like because none of that mattered. He had become an *employee* and thus had obtained an eternal present, manifested only by his functional existence on the time card. He had no history because one was not required of him, and having no history also meant having no sadness. Instead, he was part of a workforce that fed people. He was America's fuel. And he was burning to be used, to be useful.

"See, Wayne," Maureen laughed. "Your chicken's so good it's making the kid cry!"

Wayne swayed on his feet, taking this in. "Really that good, huh?"

BJ placed her hands on her hips with a practiced smile. "Alright, kids, let's open up this damn place already!"

Sony was already at the front door and clicked the lock open.

HAI SPENT THE rest of the day being trained by Sony. First, he had to go inside the broom closet, where they had a twelve-inch TV set and VHS player hooked up on a shelf of paper towel rolls. Hai stood in the dark watching a half-hour customer service instruction video where he was shown how to hold the paper bag of food: arms cradling the bottom of the bag, "like it was a precious baby," said the lady with plastic-looking hair. All of this was demonstrated by a strategically multiracial cast of actors wearing the same uniform he wore, except their teeth weren't jacked up and they looked like they all belonged on Hanes underwear packages. When it was over, Sony opened the door and checked his watch. "You should be done."

"Yeah, I know everything now," Hai said.

"Impossible. Now come with me."

Sony then showed him how to clean the toilets, change the urinal cakes, how to load the roll of toilet paper, which was the size of a car tire, onto the commercial dispenser (by using your knees as a loading bench). Finally Hai was shown how to clock in and out on the keypad outside of BJ's office, by entering his own company code. Sony requested his to be 1865, the year the Union won the war, to which Hai said, "Makes sense."

Hai's number was 2163. He didn't care what that meant but secretly wished it would be the year the sun finally drank up all its gas and blew up the solar system.

"There, you've worked ten seconds so far today," Sony said, pressing Enter.

"Wait, why didn't you clock me in before? I've been here, like, four hours already."

"Human error." He scratched the mole under his left eye and walked away.

That's when BJ's head appeared from the office doorway. "Hey, rook, you got a sec?" Her face was weirdly serious.

Hai stepped inside and she shut the door behind him.

"Sit down and listen here," she said in a throaty voice.

Hai sat down. "BJ, I really . . . I don't mind not getting paid for the four hours—it was just a joke."

She gave him a pinched look, then reached over to type something on the computer, her massive shoulders blocking the screen. When she backed up, a QuickTime player bar appeared, accompanied by ripping heavy bass, followed by someone screaming unintelligible lyrics over the track. Only when BJ gave Hai a playful shove did he realize it was her voice he was hearing, her fingers jabbing at his chest as she lip-synched through the track.

When she finished, his face—only a foot away in the tiny office—was soaked with spit.

"That's, like, kinda good. Right?" he asked.

"You think so?" BJ wiped her neck with her American flag bandana, then, clocking his wet face, gave his cheeks a cursory pat. "You're not just saying that cause I hired you?"

"Not at all. I mean, you have, like, a really good tone. Like System of a Down but, slower kinda?"

"Really? Cause that's what I'm going for. A mix between System and Metallica. Man," she clasped her hands together, "I'm so relieved. This is gonna be the best entrance song ever."

"Entrance song?"

"For wrestling," she said, like this was obvious. "I'm an amateur wrestler on the local circuit. Well, amateur for now, that is. Look, HomeMarket is alright and all, but it's not where I'm about to die, you know what I'm saying? I'm blessed with talent. And my mom said I can't waste that." She spread her arms wide, her fingers touching the frayed schedule sheets pinned up on the corkboard, the chair groaning under her weight. "If God calls on you and gives you a figure of gold, you can't settle with being just a manager. I'm gonna be the next Riki-shi someday."

"Use your skills to get the gold. Right, that makes sense."

"No, no. These arms," she flexed both biceps, "*are* gold. That's the difference between the true ones and posers. Posers want gold but legends *are* gold. It just has to be shined. Never forget that, rook." She leaned back, cocked her head, and looked at him carefully. "How old are you anyway?"

"Nineteen."

"Hmm, I could be your father," she nodded to herself. "I'll be thirty-seven in March."

"Okay," he said.

IT WAS DUSK by the time he left HomeMarket, his uniform smelling of grease and bleach. The evening's red embers flaked off the ridges and settled as soot on the valley floor where he now crossed the strip mall toward the bridge, his uniform inky as the night around him. He spotted, glowing in the far corner of the lot, Sgt. Pepper's Pizza, the grand opening sign still up, but the wind had yanked off one of the corners, folding it over, the sign now reading GRAND OP. The owner, who must've been Sgt. Pepper himself, was sitting on a counter lit by a row of cold fluorescents, sipping a bottle of Coca-Cola, the place utterly empty. Meanwhile the HomeMarket, according to the register he counted out before leaving, must've raked in two grand during his shift alone.

Hai stood a minute in the cold, bituminous air. Someone down the river was chopping wood, probably lit at this hour by the headlight of a car, the axe bites sounding ancient and otherworldly as they pinged up the slopes. He watched the empty pizza shop, his thoughts drifting, for some reason, to his mother. How one night, years ago, she had come home from work after a thirteen-hour shift saying she was craving pizza. Being the sole wielder of English, he got on the phone and ordered one. He must've been eight or nine. After the pizza came and they were all eating, he looked up and saw that Ma had fallen asleep. But not only that—she had face-planted onto a half-eaten slice on her paper plate, making a greasy stain on her white shirt the shape of a warped heart. It was one of those images he could never shake loose from his mind, even though it held no meaning.

Hai had turned to his grandmother, hoping she knew what to do.

"Don't bother her," Bà ngoại said as she placed another slice on his plate. "Let her sleep, son. She's been working since the rooster woke." It turned out his mother had taken NyQuil for back pain when she left work that night and was now deep in a painless dreamland.

Bà ngoại picked up the white plastic divider thing they put in the center of the pizza and set it on the floor. "You see this thing? This is why we always buy from Pizza Hut. They have respect for ancestors."

"How so?" Hai asked, his mother snoring now behind him.

"No other restaurant ever thought to give you a little table to serve the spirits with. Only Pizza Hut." She tapped the crust with her fingernail and smiled. "Give me your other slice." She placed the pizza on top of the three-legged table, making it look like the slice was floating off the floor. Bà ngoại clasped her hands together and, in a low voice, started inviting their dead to come feast on this one piece of mushroom supreme pizza, her body swaying as she chanted. Then she placed the slice back on his plate. "There, we've fed the spirits on their own little table. Now the food is filled with their desire to live, making it more powerful."

He discovered later that the plastic thingy, shaped like a dollhouse lawn table, was there to prevent the top of the pizza box from crushing the pie during delivery.

"The owners of Pizza Hut," Bà ngoại said, glancing at her daughter, "they actually thought about people like us. Can you believe it? Americans making pizza thought of Vietnamese customs." She sighed and wiped her mouth with the back of her hand. "That's why we support them. Good folks," she said, reaching for another slice.

The axe pings were long gone now, along with his grandmother's voice. He turned home, shaking the memory from his head. The sky was raked by an arrow of brant geese calling to each other as they searched for a tree to shelter for the night, and before long the darkness engulfed them. By the time he got to the bridge, the smell of woodsmoke blew off the bluffs, and he saw Grazina's window at 16 Hubbard Street glowing like a scrap of morning among the pitch.

Inside, Grazina was so happy she could barely speak, and kept putting her hand over her mouth and asking, "Do they pay you good? Huh? They pay you fair over there?"

"It's okay, $7.15," he said. "The minimum."

"That's not bad at all. That's two TV dinners when they're on sale at Webster's."

"Oh, here." He put the paper bag he was carrying on the kitchen table and opened it, revealing one of the last corn breads of the day. He held it under the kitchen bulb, like BJ did earlier, and broke it open. It was cold but still moist inside. "Go ahead and try it. It's corn bread."

"I know what this is. I didn't come here yesterday." She took the piece, weighing it in her hand, and gave him a skeptical look. "But is it soft enough for my teeth?"

"Trust me."

She bit into it. He thought he saw her eyelids flutter.

"Oh Jesus Mary," she whispered, yellow crumbs dotting her upper lip. "But how? How do they make it like this?" She shook her head, incredulous, the girl inside peeping through her green eyes.

"Right? I don't know. It's crazy."

"This will be perfect dipped in Salisbury steak gravy. Labas," she gripped his shoulder. "You're working for geniuses. You should be proud of yourself." She brushed invisible dust off his uniform, then grabbed the second piece and swallowed it as she stepped back and regarded him, beaming.

"Ah! Before I forget, Labas..." Her brows arched. "I have something for you too. Come." Grazina walked to a brown door right outside the kitchen, and opened it. This whole time he'd assumed it was a closet. "Go in." She stepped aside and made like an usher.

Through the door was a stairwell leading to a basement full, nearly to the ceiling, with junk. He reached the bottom of the stairs and was immediately confronted by a life's worth of salvaged goods: pots and pans, black garbage bags lumpy with linens and clothes and who knows what, a half dozen filing cabinets partly obscured by old and broken furniture, two sewing machines, a wooden rocking horse with one of its eyes gouged out, a box full of vitamins from the seventies nestled between rolls of film and cassettes, broken vinyl 45s. It turned out Grazina's husband, Jonas, who died in 2004 from a stroke, was some sort of hoarder.

Grazina came down behind him. She leaned on the horse, its hideous head lolling over her shoulder, and told him how Jonas would go on these long walks and come home with armfuls of odd items. As his Alzheimer's got worse, he came home one time carrying an entire front door from an unidentified house, having no recollection of how or where he got it. Baffled, Grazina suggested he toss it out, but he replied, as he always did, by valiantly raising his right hand to the sky, as reenacted by Grazina, saying, "Don't you remember the war? You never know, you never know, woman!" before dragging the door down to the basement. Now it lay across an iron sewing machine velvet with dust.

"Look, I made a path today. I spent all day making a path for you. Go." She ushered him down a single winding path, slightly wider than his waist, that led to a back room. Walking single file, they went deeper, careful to avoid knocking over the towering piles of junk.

Near the far side was a pull string for a single brownish lightbulb. He yanked it and the bulb swayed above them. There, set in an alcove in the wall, were shelves of books, some stacked three volumes deep, running from floor to ceiling. Mostly mass-market pulp fiction from the fifties to the eighties. At the back wall was a white sheet that Grazina now pointed to. "Open her," she said. "That's where you wanna go."

Hai worked through the dust, one arm over his mouth, and peeled back the sheet. As spores swirled through the cone of light, he saw the books, all of them paper gold. Rows and rows of the perennial classics: Homer, Shakespeare, Tolstoy, Austen, Montaigne, Flaubert, Turgenev, Faulkner. But there were also Nabokov, Toomer, Salinger, Atwood, Baldwin, Morrison. Most of them paperbacks, like the ones from Bantam, the pages thin as newspaper, cheaply bound and printed for vast distribution. But that didn't change what was inside. There was also the entire leather-bound collected library of Steinbeck and Hemingway. His mouth agape, heart tapping, dust in his lungs, he ran his fingers along the spines. "Holy shit," he said, breathless. "How did you do this?"

"I didn't do squat," she said. "I told you. My husband was one of those nerds. He read everything. He read so much his eyes dried up in his head. It made him blind, these damn books." A film of dust had covered her glasses. "He used to read me from that Vonnegut book you've been reading," she added in a fallen voice. "We were in Dresden at the same time, that little Billy Pilgrim and me. What a sham, all of it."

This must be why her husband was obsessed with translating the book into their native tongue, he thought. It was an American novel that told their story, if only in brief, apocalyptic glimpses.

Grazina surveyed the shelves and sighed. "My daughter, Lina, is just like her father. Also a nerd. She loved Isaac Asimov. But Jonas never liked her much. She was too close to him, his clone. Strange how that is." She leaned on a felt mannequin and wrapped its arms around her shoulders, making it hug her from behind. "He hated it when he saw her read on the couch. He'd yell, 'All you read about are aliens and goblins. You're stuck in la-la land for Chrissakes. Get yourself back in the real world, girl!' And I'd say, 'Ha! The real world? Where there's poverty, war, babies chucked off the Brooklyn Bridge? What a lovely place, the *real* world.'"

"He sounds like a dick," Hai said. "Why'd you marry a dick?"

Her face softened and she waved her hand dismissively. "He wasn't so bad. Just a coward, really. A wet biscuit of a man, but he hated her for some reason. Maybe he saw in her too much of his own mother, who knows. Parents make babies, God gives them personalities. But one time, you know, I ran away from him, from this very house." Her eyes narrowed and she looked across the room into the past. "They denied him promotion at train yard, so he was a real pain in the ass that week. Just screaming vile things at the poor girl trying to read her little make-believe books. And I said, 'That's enough,' and I grabbed my baby, she was maybe nine or ten, packed a bag, and walked downtown and booked a room at the motor inn—you know the one with just five rooms and an ice machine? I ordered us a pizza, all the toppings. I had two hundred dollars saved up from working at Woolworth's, and those days you can be a king for a day with that much. I sat on the bed, eating pizza and watching my daughter read to me, a smile on her face. It was the sixties and mothers don't just make themselves disappear like that, you know. I felt like the most powerful woman in the world." She pushed her glasses up her nose, causing Hai to do the same with his. "With money I earned by myself, I gave my daughter a room just so she can read in peace for a day. Just one day. And I sat there and watched her read, sipping a scotch from the bar. And I cried like a baby. And Lina, my little Lina, she said, 'Mama, why you crying?' And I said, 'I know how God feels now.' A stupid thing, really, to say to a little girl, but who cares. She must've thought I was finally crazy." Grazina let out a broken laugh. "And hey," she pointed her pinkie at him, "she wrote poems too, you know, my little Lina. Better than Robert Frost, if you can believe it. What did he do anyway, look at trees and feel bad? That's no way to live."

"You're probably right." There was a long silence. Hai searched his pockets for a cigarette he didn't have.

"Maybe you can make use of this mess, huh?"

"It's a good mess," he said, scanning the spines.

The years had glued the covers together, and as he attempted to dislodge them from the shelves, some books came out attached in twos, even threes. Others were eaten, almost entirely, by rats. He lifted a trio of Camus's books and peered into a golf-ball-sized hole burrowing right through *The Stranger*, *The Plague*, and *The Rebel*.

But there was one book whose spine caught his eye. *The Brothers Karamazov.* It was the book he and Noah were going to read together the summer before he died. *This will take us, what, five years to finish?* Noah had said. He wasn't much of a reader but picked up a copy when they were thrifting at Goodwill, saying he liked the title. *Brothers.* Later, while eating Wendy's french fries in Noah's truck bed, Hai read the first chapter aloud as Noah stared at the stars, the engine ticking beneath them as their heads buzzed from oxy and strawberry milkshakes. A week after Noah's funeral, Hai found the book at the bottom of his laundry basket and tossed it in the trash, the bookmark just two chapters in.

He took it off the shelf, a cheaper, smaller edition, the edges fraying, and turned it in his hand.

"You like that one, huh?"

"Think I'll give it a shot." He pressed it to his chest.

"Good, take it. Take it all. It's just kindling at this point. Well, we did it, Labas," Grazina said as the bulb swayed, throwing their shadows about. "Just make sure to bring more of that corn bread tomorrow, yeah?"

Throughout the following week, since he had no laptop and no internet, he would stay up deep into the night, often holding vigil over Grazina's volatile dreams, the pages of *The Brothers Karamazov* ringed with mold and falling apart in his hands. He would turn a page and it would break right off, the book literally disintegrating as he read it.

How strange to feel something so close to mercy, whatever that was, and stranger still that it should be found in here of all places, at the end of a road of ruined houses by a toxic river. That among a pile of salvaged trash, he would come closest to all he ever wanted to be: a consciousness sitting under a lightbulb reading his days away, warm and alone, alone and yet, somehow, still somebody's son.

5

It was fast into October and the leaves fell steadily over the parked cars, filling the beds of pickups lined outside the VFW and clogging gutters with deciduous trash. Down the road, a single leaf, the ochre of a dirtied Van Gogh star, clung to a girl's hair as she bent to pour a stream of used cat litter into the sewer drain outside her house. In front of a row of track houses with broken down siding, a group of teenagers in hoodies selling dusters and Xannies were speaking to each other in hushed tones. A Camaro with no hubcaps was parked nearby, a faded Puerto Rican flag bandana hanging from the rearview. Down the road a stout white woman with sagging sweatpants that had *juicy* emblazoned on its backside was walking a chihuahua in the middle of an empty lot where a Citgo used to be.

At 16 Hubbard Hai stumbled on an old Schwinn from the seventies among the rubble in Grazina's basement. Somehow all it needed was air in the tires. The bike was so caked with dust he didn't realize it was silver-blue until he rode home one night in the rain and the sapphire shone under the streetlight, like a molting snake, as he let the wind know his unwashed hair and shut his eyes against the cold coming off the river, feeling almost clean.

Though it took some adjusting, he soon found his rhythm at work.

A typical morning at HomeMarket looked like this: You clock in at ten a.m., leaving you an hour to prep before opening. First, you turn on the heating wells under the counter and wipe down the grease and fingerprints on the sneeze guard from the previous day. As the wells warm, you refill all the napkins and plastic utensils by the register and dining room, then make a sweep of both the men's and women's bathrooms. When that's done, you start making the coffee by the soda fountain, marking the time on each metal tumbler with a Sharpie so customers know it's fresh, after which you'd switch it out every three hours with a new batch even if the tumbler's completely full because, as BJ said, "There's nothing Thanksgiving about stale coffee."

Then you take out the leftover tubs of mac and cheese or sweet potato pie, anything that was more than half full at last night's closing, and peel off the Saran Wrap. Then you take a knife and scrape the grimy top crust away, dump what's left into the food hoppers, give it a little stir, and after five minutes it'll bubble and steam with a just-made glow. Then you take that white Magic Marker and write the name of an employee on the little black sign in front of each item that reads MADE BY HAND TODAY BY: _____ . At HomeMarket, "made by hand" meant heating up the contents of a bag of mushy food cooked nearly a year ago in a laboratory outside Des Moines and vacuum-sealed in industrial resin sacks. Hai wondered if anyone ever thought they'd be eating leftovers at a restaurant. Or whether they knew that the FDA allows mashed potatoes to contain up to 2 percent rat poop and up to 3.5 percent insect "fragments." One time he spotted Maureen, out of sheer boredom, flicking a fly right onto a roasting chicken, where it sizzled and sparked before welding itself into a black nub on the crispy skin.

Next you head into the freezer, propping a milk crate behind you so you don't get locked in, which Sony said happened to him four times his first week and Wayne had to tape a chicken thigh on the door to keep it ajar. On the freezer shelf are rows and rows of vacuum-sealed bags labeled with various dishes. You lift the bag, big as a torso, of frozen creamed spinach and place it on a pushcart. Then you do the same with all the other sacks of food. One time, toward the end of a long shift, Hai needed more apple cobbler and opened the door to find Maureen pressing a slab of mac and cheese to her knee. "It helps my arthritis," she said, shrugging.

After you gather the sacks, you head out back to the insta-boiler, which is a huge cauldron of hot water with two hooks suspended above it. You clip a bag to each metal hook, and as they sway like concrete slabs you pull a lever to lower the bags into the boiling water, which is perfectly timed to melt the contents into "kitchen freshness." By the time you pull them out, cut open the top, and pour the contents into a metal loaf pan, the mashed potatoes are so luscious and fragrant with garlic, bits of parsley so miraculously verdant, you'd never guess it was reheated. Same goes for the supposed "soup of the day." One time Russia dropped his phone in the soup hopper and just looked at Hai and said, "I'll get it when we run out."

HomeMarket was not so much a restaurant as a giant microwave, though BJ kept telling the customers, "Look hard, folks, cause you won't see any Chef Mikes around here, okay? You know they have one at Denny's, right? They call themselves a sit-down restaurant but they got good ole Chef Mike fooling you. Everything you see here was made this morning by our very own Maureen." And she'd bow to Maureen like it's a play and Maureen would fold her little hands under her chin and do this little-old-lady smile she perfected, the one where you could barely see her eyes, they're so full of wholesome glee. Customers loved this and usually bought extra to bring home to their families, because who wouldn't want to support a grandmother who scooped your string beans with a shaky hand?

The one thing they do "make" is the corn bread, though the recipe is BJ's secret. The corn bread comes in giant bags of yellow mix that you're supposed to add water to and spoon into little loaf trays. But each Sunday, BJ stays back after the store closes and customizes her own mix, then dumps it all into a plastic drum to be used through the week.

Some people talk about how they'd never eat at a place after working there, after they see how the sausage is made, but with 60 percent off your meal, every employee ended up eating at HomeMarket. Even if you got sick of it, you find ways to switch it up. Wayne came up with a method to stuff the meat loaf full of mac and cheese, a hit with the crew for two whole weeks. Maureen combined her creamed spinach with the sweet potato pie and swore by it—though she was alone on that one. And whenever a tray came back—wrong order, mashed potatoes cold, green beans too mushy—you could take the whole thing and eat it in the walk-in fridge, standing there shoveling the slop in your mouth in under five minutes while a bulb flickers over your head.

The folks who made up the crew were just like people anywhere else in New England. Weatherworn and perennially exhausted or pissed off or both. Maureen was a retired elementary school hall monitor with the foulest mouth you've ever heard. She once dropped a tray of meat loaf and shouted, "Ohfuckthreedicksinabasket!" to which a man in a baby-blue turtleneck yelped and spat out his mashed potatoes. She seemed to Hai like the kind of person who puts her french fries inside her burger, which made him feel like he could trust her. She was on cashier, where she was a magician, her fingers flying over the screen faster than people could stand there, mouths agape, uhhhing through their orders.

There was also Russia, an eighteen-year-old kid who was actually born in Tajikistan. His father was a former major in the last gasps of the Red Army, and his folks arrived in the US seeking asylum after the Soviet Union fell. He was scrawny and hunched over most the time, a cuter version, Hai thought, of Gollum from *Lord of the Rings*. He had this Eminem buzz cut but colored anime-blue, and had a nose stud of Jack the Pumpkin King. Hai even asked him if he had a second shift at

Spencer's—but he didn't. He worked the drive-thru, which meant he'd walk around mumbling to himself, then shout "I SAID, DO YOU WANT KETCHUP?" at the top of his lungs every half hour or so.

There was the dishwasher girl, Amanda, who was there so rarely the crew referred to her only as "dishwasher girl." A high school junior who wore UFO pants and black eyeliner and wolf print T-shirts, she barely spoke and mostly chuckled to herself watching the mounted TV while she scrubbed away in the back. Most of the crew figured she was on some kind of downers—but the dishes were always clean.

Then there was Wayne, a barrel of a man from North Carolina who was "Chief of Rotisserie." He had a gift for it too. Despite BJ's claims about corn bread, the real reason this HomeMarket made so much profit was Wayne's chicken. "The chicken just feels different here, like different in your mouth," said one lady—a regular—who was chomping down on her half chicken right there in front of the counter. She dug into the paper bag and stood there gnawing on the side of this chicken, overcome by the power it gave her.

"Hey Sony," Maureen shouted, "come on out here and watch this lady eat chicken. She's a hoot."

"I got three kids, two jobs, and I'm going nuts. So thank you for this," the woman finally said, licking her fingers. "Y'all doing God's work." She tied up her hair in a ponytail, put a dab of hand sanitizer on her palms, chucked the bag full of bones into the trash, and walked out like she was striding on water.

One Saturday, just as they were lulled into a desert of a shift, three purple school buses pulled into the lot and about two hundred kids from a nearby Catholic prep school came pouring in, a sweatered sea of suppressed, unrepentant hormones. They had just come from their homecoming dance. Because it was a Catholic school, the dance took place at three p.m. in pure, sterile daylight. By the time they came in at seven thirty, the dinner rush was over and the crew was already prepping to close. The team was so slammed they didn't have time to get mad. BJ ran into the freezer and came out carrying three slabs of side dishes on her back like they were stone tablets. Hai spotted Wayne out back, bent over the utility sink and reaching into his pocket for blood pressure tablets. Russia was next to him, patting his back and handing him a Gatorade mixed with gin, while Sony was having a full-blown panic attack out front. He just froze up in the corner while a dozen kids shouted orders at him, his hands by the side of his face, so BJ sent him to the office to watch History Channel clips on YouTube to calm down. When it was over, the store looked like a tornado had ripped through it. Everyone stayed till ten thirty that night to clean up.

Before long Hai began to know which employee was behind him by their scent alone. The Johnson & Johnson baby lotion Wayne rubbed over the grease burns on his arms, the traces of whiskey coming through the Wrigley's Maureen chewed, the bootlegged Tom Ford (Tobacco Vanille) BJ wore cut with the strawberry Starbursts Russia was always sucking on. Sony, whose clothes, due to a faulty dryer at his group home, had the faint but consistent muskiness of damp fabric. These smells altered in intensity with each cigarette break they took. All this was mixed with the artificial flavors and aromas wafting from the vats of industrially produced food: diacetyl, acetylpropionyl, acetoin, and hydroxybenzoic acid, along with the metallic scent of colorings like Sunset Yellow FCF, tartrazine, Patent Blue V, and Green 3. Adding to this concoction was the char of chicken fat burning off the racks, re-leasing an endless stream of smoke not even the patented Hyper-Power HVAC could suck away. There was also the stale stench of dishwater and half-rotting food coming from the dishwasher station out back. By the third hour of any shift, a new odor—the only organic scent in the entire place—human BO, would start to emanate through the employ-ees' clothes. Mingling with the processed food and personal hygiene products, was the garlicky, tar-ish and vinegar scent of human work.

This was all compounded into a space no larger than 950 square feet, if you count the closets and freezers. In brief moments of reprieve, when there was no customer at the counter, Hai would poke his head through Russia's drive-thru window for a breath of air, only to inhale the car exhaust and motor oil that had pooled beneath the window.

There were times, too, when people were just people, which meant they were assholes. One day this family came in, a middle-aged father and two teen sons. You could tell right away they were in town because of the fancy tennis camp happening down the road in Glastonbury. The father looked like he'd been playing tennis since he was five years old, his resort-red face scorched save for two pale circles from his aviators, which he took off to squint at the menu, hands on his hips. While Maureen was taking the order from the dad, the taller son playfully elbowed the other one, saying, loud enough for Wayne to hear, "They *would* have a black dude roasting chicken." The boys chortled into their polo collars, pulled high to hide their moose teeth. The dad raised some sort of remote control to his neck, and it became clear he was one of those smokers who had his vocal cords chopped off. "Evan, what did we say about jokes?" he said in a digitized voice while suppressing a smile.

Hai was opening a box of ketchup packets on the nearby counter and clocked Wayne's face as he worked the rotisserie, whose eyes found the family, then flitted off them. BJ was bent over, scooping sides into their trays as if nothing happened.

"Is Uncle Ben the chicken guy or the rice guy?" the shorter kid asked his older brother.

"Hey, hey. Enough is enough," the man's voice said, his eyes passing over BJ to Maureen. "They're just stressed from the tennis. It's a pretty competitive camp."

"You can do better with 'em, though," Maureen said, eyeing the boys as she handed him the change.

BJ put their bags on the counter without a word.

The man snatched his dinner and pointed at Maureen. "Don't you . . . Don't you dare . . . tell me how to talk to my kids——" The device glitched and he had to keep pressing the button and wincing to finish his sentence. "And . . . wipe that st-stupid eyeliner . . . off. You look cheap," he said, his sons following him out. At the door he added, in a warped drawl that verged on Auto-Tune, "I'll be going to Arby's from now on!"

"The fuck was that?" Hai said, looking around.

"What the hell you think it was?" BJ ripped off her gloves and tossed them, missing the trash. "Wayne," she said real soft, her shoulders slumped.

Wayne just kept fidgeting with the rotisserie rods. "Wayne," BJ said again. "Look, I should've said something. I'm the manager. It's on me but . . ." She folded her arms and stared out at the passing cars. "I just got fucking thrown off by that robot voice, dude. I mean, I've never seen one in real life before. Felt like I was in some *SNL* skit or something and froze, okay?"

Wayne loaded a raw chicken on the rack, his head hung low.

"You know what, Wayne," Maureen said, "Russia can probably do the chickens too. You don't have to——"

"Maur." BJ turned to her, a gash of sweat lighting across her forehead. "I appreciate you. But this is not for you right now, okay?"

Maureen bit her lip and nodded, then scooted next to Hai and started opening a box of ketchup packets.

"I can take you off the chickens if it's easier, man," BJ said to Wayne. "It's not the first time I heard some shit like that and I know it's not the first for you neither."

Hai jumped when the chicken rod slammed through the metal eyelets.

Wayne turned to face them, breathing through his nose. "My father taught me this work." He said this softly but his bottom lip was quivering. "And he learned it from his own dad down in Carolina. And his dad before that. They were pitmasters. Now I'm no master, but this is *their* work. And I get to do it." He pointed so hard at his heart it left a greasy period on his apron. "I don't even have a *photo* of my granddad but I got this, you understand?" He glanced at each of their faces. "So nobody's getting me off this stupid-ass chicken line." He lowered his cap over his eyes, pulled a finished rack from the oven, the skins crackling, and turned his back to them, unloaded the rod, and started carving. And that was that.

BJ wiped her brow and looked down at her shoes, her toes wiggling inside them. "Get me a fucking lemonade," she said to Hai, who shuffled to the soda fountain as Maureen put her hand on BJ's shoulder and Wayne set another rack into the oven, the metal clanging like he was loading artillery. Wayne didn't laugh again for the rest of the day and they all felt it. He had a laugh that could vanquish depression in an elephant.

AFTER CLOCKING OUT, Hai went out back for some air and found Sony doing sit-ups on a piece of cardboard. Russia was perched on a milk crate by the door, his blue hair catching the sun as he bit into a sandwich he'd invented by stuffing crispy chicken skins into sliced corn bread slathered with hot sauce.

"They should put these on the menu," Russia said, admiring his creation.

"Maybe then you'll finally be employee of the month," Hai smirked.

"They should make me CEO. Then I can sell this place, cash out, and fire all of you bums," he grinned.

Sony was grunting through the sit-ups, his face scrunched up in the sun.

"How many of those you gonna do?" Hai asked.

"Fifty," Sony said, grimacing. "I can't try for the Marines, but I *can* try for the Honor Guard if I play my cards right. The Guard is much more competitive, actually."

Russia gave Hai this *Are you kidding?* look.

"But didn't you say you loved HomeMarket more than anything?" Hai asked. "You're not gonna retire here?"

"The military pays you three thousand dollars just to sign up. If . . ." Sony grunted as he came up. "If I can do at least fifty-five sit-ups, I'll be ahead of the other recruits. *The National Bugle* says most of them are overweight."

"You'll get three thousand working here, eventually," Russia said. "The army's a joke. You're just food for the military-industrial complex." Hai took another look at Russia and could imagine him listening to a lot of Green Day or Anti-Flag. "My dad was in the Red Army for just three years and my dude is *hardcore* fucked right now."

"They denied my mom's appeal, which means it's up to me to bail her out," Sony said on his way down.

"Wait, when the hell did that happen?" Hai untied his apron and faced his cousin.

"She called me last night." He sat up, breathing heavily.

"The industrial prison complex. Now *that's* a whole nother bitch. Everything's actually a prison, if you think about it," Russia said with an air of profundity. "My dad says that a lot." Then he took out a second chicken-skin corn bread sandwich from his apron pocket and handed it to Sony.

"No thanks." Sony continued his sit-ups.

Hai had always felt the military was a sham, even as most of his friends from high school joined, mostly skinny, pimply faced white boys from HUD housing with bad GPAs, swallowed up in fatigues and thrown into the desert, where they drank Red Bull and blasted Slipknot in their headphones while getting trigger-happy. He had overheard Wayne mention that out of every five hundred soldiers, there were most likely ten mass shooters. "What's an army anywhere but a bunch of state-sanctioned mass shooters funded by our tax dollars?" he'd said. "Do the deed as a civilian and you get the chair, do it as a soldier and they'll pin some tinfoil to your chest." He thought about repeating this to his cousin but instead just said, "You'd make a great Marine, Sony. Or whatever it is. If anyone can defend this country from evildoers, it's you, buddy."

Russia gave Hai a look he ignored. The sky was finally clear and blue, and crisp leaves were skittering toward them from the dead apartments as they watched Sony finish his sit-ups. It seemed the light wouldn't change for a while.

WHEN HE WAS YOUNGER Hai had wanted a bigger life. Instead he got the life that won't let him go. He was born in Vietnam, fourteen years after the big war everyone loved talking about but no one understood, least of all himself. The year was 1989, a year best known for the fall of the Berlin Wall and the Tiananmen Square protests. George Bush Sr. had defeated Michael Dukakis to be the forty-first president, and "My Prerogative" by Bobby Brown was at the top of the charts. It was the time of the floppy disk, denim jackets, leg warmers, Cool Ranch Doritos, and pasta salad.

In Vietnam, the Americans had left the fields a ruinous wasteland with Monsanto-powered Agent Orange, not to mention the two million bodies nameless and scattered in the jungle and riverbanks waiting to be salvaged by family members hoisting woven baskets on their waists full of sun-bleached bones. On top of that the country was fighting the genocidal Pol Pot and his Khmer Rouge, who were invading the western border. People starved, naturally, and scavenged for rats or stretched their rice rations with sawdust from lumberyards. Two years later, by miracle or mercy, Hai and his family arrived in snow-dusted Connecticut, their faces blasted and stricken, sleeping their first weeks on the floor of the Catholic church that sponsored them, between the pews, using Bibles for pillows. He was only two and remembered none of it.

He was raised by his mother, grandmother (rest her soul), and Aunt Kim, women spared by war in body but not in mind, and together they found a way to scavenge a kind of life in wind-blasted Hartford. Though he'd had his troubles, the boy couldn't say he had a bad life. After high school, he got into college—the first in his family to do so—enrolling at Pace University in New York, at the foot of the Brooklyn Bridge. Although he intended to study international marketing, at the last minute, for reasons unknown to him, he switched to something called general ed, which sounded more like the abandoned wing of a psych ward than a degree. By then he was already going steady for half a decade with the pills and spent most days in the library's basement, nodding off and reading literary periodicals and giant photography books. He once spent two hours out of his mind on a mix of cough syrup and oxy, staring at the Diane Arbus photo of the little boy clutching a grenade in Central Park.

By Thanksgiving, he was out of school and back in East Gladness, slumped on his mother's couch, New York City all but a faded dream. Even now he did not understand the chain of events that led him back to this dirty old town empty-handed.

ONE DAY, during breakfast a year after he dropped out—having seen him jobless and perpetually high, languishing for months at home—his mother had enough.

"You're on those pills again, aren't you? I just don't get it. What are they anyway, some kind of super Advil?" She was playing *Tetris* on her pink Game Boy and kept her eyes on the screen. For as long as he'd been her son, she was obsessed with *Tetris*. It was a hole she could crawl into anytime she wanted, right in her hand.

"They make things quieter."

"It's pretty quiet around here already, no? So quiet all the money's walked out the door and never came back. Just like your dad." She peered up at him, her fingers still jabbing the console.

"Whatever."

"Yeah, just like *whatever* in New York, right? How did that go?" she said sarcastically. "If I could speak English, I'd be speaking directly to the president, not any of you bums around here."

"Things happened that you won't understand." He spread cream cheese in thick gobs on his bagel, the codeine making his hands blur. "But at least I tried."

"I'm not going to fight again, especially not when you're high. I mean, look at you—you can barely open your eyes, Hai. I can't do this today, okay?" She set the Game Boy down. "I have enough to do."

"What, like level thirteen of *Tetris*?" he said, chewing. "You've been stuck on level thirteen for over a year."

"Because I have *work*." She stood, fuming. "I work for us. Just me. Alone. Remember?"

Then, in a surge of wild impulse, he removed a pamphlet from the copy of *Sula* he was reading and placed it in front of her.

"That a job application?" his mother said, eyeing it.

"I'm gonna go be a doctor," he said, chewing.

"A doctor?" His mother suppressed a laugh. "What are you talking about doctor? Of what?"

He shrugged. "People."

Her lower lip opened imperceptibly. "Please. And I mean please. Don't play games with me, son." She gave him a look, waiting for the joke to finish.

He opened the brochure's centerfold, revealing the bell tower on the campus green, its four turrets grand and regal as a castle. "I got into an MD program at this university in Boston," he told her, his chin high, expectant.

Ma held the page with both hands, as if it emitted its own light. "You're not on drugs right now?"

"I'm just tired. Tired but happy. I—I wasn't gonna tell you till I get my living situation all sorted, but—" He searched the floor, avoiding her eyes. "But I figured you'd like to know."

"This is real, then?" She stared at him. When he didn't blink, she shook her head at the pictures. "Well, look at that, there it is. God has answered my prayers. I knew it! Oh, this is such good news. Really? Hai?" She shut off the Game Boy and held his face in her sweaty hands. "Look, I know the past few years have been hard for you. It took you a while to get back on your feet after Bà ngoại died, but I always knew you would do something great. You're not like the other bums around here." She swept her hand across the room to indicate the whole town, knocking the bagel he was eating to the floor, cream cheese side down. "Are you sure, though? That you're *in*?" She pulled back a bit and studied him at an angle, her eyes mining him for the truth. Her boy, her only son. "But you don't *have to*, you know. Remember, I'm not like the other moms at the salon. You can do anything you like. You can work with me scrubbing old ladies' feet forever if you like, okay? There's no shame in that. As long as you can *work*, it's alright." She ran her fingers through his hair. "I don't want you to think you gotta be a hero. Just for me." But he knew this news had come as relief, a thread they could follow together even as they were spinning apart.

"I got in, Ma. It's still a long way from being a real doctor but I'm gonna do it. I'm gonna heal people." He glanced at his grandmother's photo on the altar. "Like they should've done for Bà ngoại."

"What about what happened in New York?"

"That was a fluke. And you know it." He picked up the bagel—there were only a few flecks of dust on the cream cheese—and kept eating. "This time it's for real."

"You know, I did eat durian all through my pregnancy with you—

and that gave you the good brains." His mother turned to Bà ngoại's altar. "Thank heavens, Mama. He did it. He's going to be a *doctor* and make people feel better, and we'll live in a real house. It's a long road but we knew he wasn't going to waste his life. Not like Kim's son, that poor little fool." She wiped her tears with the heel of her palms, lit an incense stick, and bowed deeply, the bead of ember trembling over her perm.

Five months later he was sitting in the same kitchen, a backpack and a suitcase tucked under his feet. The bus to Boston would leave in two hours, and the house was filled with that frenetic, fraught air that permeates when someone is about to depart for a long trip. There was nothing to do but tap the table and feel his heart pump as he waited for Ma to finish packing the coconut rice. Though it takes no more than an hour, she had woken at five, in the cold blue dawn, to steam the rice and boil down the coconut milk, which left her staring out the kitchen window for the rest of the morning until her son came down with his bags.

"You're going to be a great doctor," Ma said into her hands, head lowered. He stood behind her, the taste of vomit, even after mouthwash, still bitter on his inner cheek. "I'm alone here, but don't let that worry you. I know how to take care of myself. And Bà ngoại's spirit is with me." She looked at him. "You know, you told so many crazy stories as a kid, I thought demons were speaking through you. But then you got more and more quiet as you grew up, and now I miss it."

"I know, Ma." He wanted to put his hand on her shoulder but his arm wouldn't move. The past months had been the best he could remember. They had stopped fighting and the house was so dense with such feverish hope that he wanted to stand there long as he could, soaking it in.

She wiped her cheeks, avoiding his eyes. He knew she was anxious because she wouldn't stop humming "Happy Birthday." In the weeks after Bà ngoại died it was all he heard coming from behind her door as he lay awake in the next room staring at the glow-in-the-dark stars on his ceiling, the ones she helped him glue on for his seventh birthday.

His mother had cut out the brochure page depicting the grand bell tower and taped it to her desk at her nail salon in Bristol. Unable to pronounce the school's name, she beamed and pointed to the photo, announcing to her clients that her son was going to college in Boston, the big city, to be a doctor.

ON THE SIDEWALK outside their tenement condo, he fought back another urge to puke. His mother had offered to drive him to the bus station, but he wouldn't have it. There was nothing worse in the world than saying farewell at a bus station. You hug goodbye at the terminal, then sit on the bus staring at each other through the glass and feeling idiotic while the driver's inside taking a long dump or calling his wife, and after a while you have to look away and pretend to get something out of your bag only to look back and start the whole ritual of waving and mouthing "bye-bye" excitedly as you can so the other person won't be too sad. No, he called a cab and shelled out the twenty bucks to save them the trouble.

"I know this won't be like last time, okay?" his mother said, wincing. "And remember to find the Chinatown right away so you can get the good ramen." Her voice was muffled through the glass as the car pulled off. He knew she was standing in the middle of the road, growing smaller and smaller, wiping her face with her shawl, but he didn't have the stomach to look at her. A thousand sons must have been where he was now and turned back from their horses, wagons, rickshaws, cyclos, buses, schooners, trains, even dusty, sandaled feet. They must have offered a face reacting to their mother's shrinking form, a final enactment of separation, revealing to each other the cost this leaving imprinted on their brows. Instead, he ducked to unlace his boots, pretending to fumble with them, then tied them again, his head nearly touching the floorboard, out of sight.

Half hour later he found himself on a bench in Hartford's Union Station staring at his boots. He had popped two codeines in the cab and his head felt warm and empty at last, the world vignetted at its edges. It was mid-August, summer still full-on and the air humid and slimy. Spilled soda, reliquefied from the heat, had stuck to his soles and made smacking sounds as he fidgeted. Most people were returning from their final day trips before summer's close. He sat awhile trying to salvage what was left of his high. Before long the 6:45 Peter Pan to Boston pulled in. As people disembarked, the driver leaned on the bumper sucking a cigarette, sweat soaking through his shirt at the armpits. Hai checked the time on his ticket—6:45 p.m.—then laid the paper down on the bench, gently, as if it were weightless, as if it had no worth at all. Because it didn't. It meant nothing because Boston meant nothing. Because there was no medical school—not even an application. How *could* there be? He didn't even have a bachelor's to his name. The photo of the school bell tower was from a pamphlet for the Harvard Divinity School he'd picked up from the library after a Bible study group had dispersed.

Weeks ago, while ordering the bus ticket and wasting the thirty-five dollars, he foolishly thought he could go through the motions and something would just open up, that the "universe" would notice his efforts and offer a window he could climb through. How childish, how winsomely stupid, he realized now as he watched the bus pull out from the lot, its rear lights fading down the interstate, toward Boston.

Dragging the suitcase behind him, he left the station and entered the summer dusk. The sky was a deep red and garbage cans along the row houses reeked from weeklong heat. He made his way under an overpass where a man and a woman were arguing inside a dirty-blue tent that jostled with their agitation. Somebody owed somebody money, he gathered from the voices, which was always the case.

Doused in this aimless dread, his shirt collar itchy with sweat, he sat on a curb and tried to collect himself. Across the street, a group of skateboarders were throwing themselves down a four-step flight of stairs in a drugstore parking lot. Seeing them move made him want to vomit even more. He remembered Ma's rice cakes in his backpack, hoping they'd settle his stomach. There were four colors: purple, red, green, and yellow, all packed snug in neat squares in the Tupperware tray. On top was a garnish of salted peanuts and crushed cane sugar. He chewed quickly with shut eyes, too ashamed to see how pretty she had made it.

The rice was good, like always: not too sweet, chewy and soft, each grain plump and rich with coconut oil. He left the Tupperware on the curb and walked on, the city smoldering around him until he reached the interstate bridge and crossed it. Boats, packed with laughing families, fishing poles arcing from their decks, floated under him.

It was only when he got back to East Gladness that his stomach turned, and he leaned against a fire hydrant to puke, his mouth dripping over the pile of rainbow-colored rice on the sidewalk. In the commotion, a man whose hair and face looked like he'd just been electrocuted stopped digging through a trash bin and shuffled up to him. "Hey you gotta dollar? You gotta dollar brother. For something to eat?" He pushed the man aside by walking forward, wiping his mouth on his jacket shoulder. The man kept muttering behind him for a few steps until the sound of traffic drowned him out. He walked on, and after a while passed the old Kahoots nightclub, which was getting ready to open, the girls sitting in cars on the gravel lot doing their makeup under dash lights while glitter twinkled, like pulverized diamonds, across their faces. Crickets were singing in the cornfield to his right as evening settled over the valley. He walked another half mile until finally a brick building came into view. This was where he'd go, he decided, if only because it was getting dark and he was running out of roads to take.

The brick building had been an elementary school until an arson fire shut it down. Half the building had since been repaired and was now back in operation. A handful of cars were scattered across the lot as he neared the entrance. He peered through the window through cupped hands. Inside, a lace desk lamp glowed dimly on a wood-grain desk, giving the place a feeling of being far in the past. He pulled the door handle and an electric chime went off, the carpet suffusing the place with dense, cottony quiet.

The door behind the reception opened, revealing a woman with bleached bangs and a green cardigan. She stopped and gave him a once-over, her face softening. "You in a bad way, huh?"

"I could use some help," he mumbled, then put his knuckles to his mouth to keep it in, realizing he'd never said those words before in his whole life. But that's what you say when you come in here. There are entire places in this world built just so specific phrases can be said, he realized now. Phrases like "I hereby solemnly swear," "Do you have any last words?" "I want a divorce," "I want an abortion," "Congratulations, class of 2006," or "I do, I do, I do." In this building you can say "I need help" and they know not only exactly what you mean but also exactly who you are.

The woman scratched her nose and studied him behind her horn-rimmed glasses. "It's alright now. It's scary, I know. Here." She slid a clipboard and a pen under the glass divider. "Fill this out—but first go get yourself some water and settle down." She nodded to the cooler in the corner. "Take your time. I'll be here when you're ready."

He thanked her and sat down. For a scant, luminous moment he was filled with a displaced benevolence for every soul in their tiny town. That some selfless, angelic people had the good mind to turn a burnt-down school into a home for the words *I need help*. He took one more look at the cornfield standing in the warm, still night across the road, fireflies blinking through the dark, and filled out his intake for the New Hope Recovery Center.

THE FIRST PERSON Hai saw OD was somebody's dad.

He was twelve and had gone over to this girl Jennifer Knoxley's house to do a project for history class. They were in the living room cutting construction paper when her father came in very quietly, like a ghost was wheeling him in, and sat down on the couch. After a while his head tilted back and his mouth hung open, eyes rolled into their sockets. He looked like somebody had pressed pause at the peak of him laughing at the greatest joke he'd ever heard. This was the image imprinted on Hai's mind when he signed in at New Hope.

Every generation says this of itself, but these were indeed bewildering and unprecedented times he lived in, a time before iPhones were everywhere, and people still looked up as they walked, their heads filled with self-generated thoughts floating up from deep pits in the subconscious. A time when you still knocked on each other's doors, and if you wanted to talk to somebody, you had to call them, listen to their mother's breathing for a while, maybe the sound of her fixing a drink or shaving her legs, then meet up somewhere, one of you waiting about, shifting your feet and looking at clouds or trees or municipal architecture, cars passing, your dopamine levels higher for not having been depleted from blue-light screens throughout the day. A time when the drug dealer on the corner would, out of boredom, start balancing on a chain-link fence, the boy in him unable to help it, pants sagging from the effort, revealing his plaid boxers you can spot from the back window of the school bus. But then, slowly, one or two or seven of your friends will find the pills, and they will flood their young brains with artificial joy. And you will join them, running through the woods by the power plant, laughing at the immense night, your head levitating a foot above your shoulders. And their eventual deaths will not yet be used by politicians to gain traction with the base. It did not have a name, this slaughter, and yet your loved ones were being slowly erased, even teachers and lunch ladies overdosing overnight, then cremated without ceremony, their faces soon existing only in your mind. *Those were the times*, those who lived through it would say, years later, not knowing what it was they meant.

Though it was never his drug of choice, he was barely sixteen the first time he tried heroin. One summer night at a skate park on the outskirts of town, he sat huddled among three other skater kids in the valley of a half-pipe, the candle flame still in the humid air as the spoon sizzled over it, Fugazi's "Waiting Room" running on a loop from a stereo in someone's JanSport. The boys had removed their socks, turning their long, bony feet in the light, searching for a good vein. They preferred the feet because it was easier to hide the scars. Plus, they could feel the speed of the hot, acidic rush literally surging through their legs to the tip of their heads, some of them tracing the drug's ascent with their fingers as if pointing to ruined cities on a map. But the sensation, for Hai, was more like drowning in his own blood, his neck craning to get above the tide. Soon there was laughter everywhere in the dark, hands slapping bare skin. But a half hour later, the only sound left was Fugazi playing over their gleaming, shirtless chests, mouths gasping like shored fish as fireflies flittered over them in the greenish night.

Hai's crappy state-issued health insurance, good until he turned twenty-five, only covered three weeks in rehab—so that's what he signed up for. On the second day, dressed in newly issued white clinic pajamas, he decided to call his mother. They had confiscated his Nokia, so he was in an all-glass room the size of a closet where a landline was set up for patients to talk to family (and family only) in twenty-minute intervals.

"Ma?" he said, straightening up in the steel chair.

"That you, son?"

"Yeah, I'm calling from the dorm phone and——"

"You've made it. Oh, I was so worried. I mean, not worried but—— I'm sure you had a busy first night. Anyway, how is it? Did you see the bell tower?"

"It's amazing. Tall and majestic, just like in the picture. Even on a cloudy day like this, it glows."

"The dorms must be so nice. Did you have the sticky rice? How was it?"

He rubbed his forehead, searching. "Perfect."

"Wasn't too sweet, was it? My hand was shaky and I dropped a big chunk of sugar in." She laughed and he realized how much he already missed her voice.

"Not at all. I ate it all on the bus, actually. It's so pretty here, Ma. The lawns are greener than the lawn at our town hall, and you can see all these people everywhere—one guy was even Vietnamese—all of them future doctors, playing Frisbee in the courtyard. I never imagined doctors playing Frisbee."

"Friss-bee," she tried in English. "What's that?"

"Oh, it's uh . . . Sorry, it's that game when you throw the plastic disc? You know, like in Bushnell Park, when we saw those white people throwing them at that basket made of chains?"

Through the glass, a skeletal man in dirt-caked overalls, one strap hanging off his shoulder, was being led by two nurses toward the medical office.

"I remember," she said. "Who knew that would be such a popular pastime among doctors! See, you're already learning new things and it's only the first week. But——" She stopped, her exhale audible through the receiver.

"Ma, *I know.*"

"Really. Just don't push yourself. Take everything slow, okay? Don't read too fast. Pick up a book and then, after ten minutes, put it down and look out the window. Your brain is like a car, you have to let it—"

"Ma, I get it," he said, his voice more barbed than he intended.

They were silent a moment. "I should've told you when you were back in New York that you didn't have to plow through your studies. I know that's why you quit. I'm sorry. I want to do better this time."

"Okay, but look, I gotta go. They asked me to join them throwing the disc."

"Oh, of course, go, go, go. Throw it far but don't show off, you know? And no need to talk to me all the time. Just focus on yourself. I'll be here when you need me."

"Okay."

"Okay, lup yoo," she said in English. "Call me if you ever—"

He hung up before she could finish and sat staring at the laminated chart pinned to the cork wall: *7-Step Guide to Discussing Your Addiction with Loved Ones.* Underneath it, taped to the wall and decorated with clip-art flowers, was a piece of paper printed with the ubiquitous Mary Oliver quote hung on nearly every spare surface in the rehab—the communal fridge, the microwave, bathroom stalls, even the broken fire alarm by the detox:

> *Tell me, what is it you plan to do*
> *with your one wild and precious life?*

THE THING ABOUT THE PILLS was that he felt, once their magic seeped into him, like he was finally slipping naked into a warm, dry bed with thick wool sheets after days of walking soaked to the bone in rain.

While the first three days were by no means easy, the staff mostly left him alone save for mealtimes and check-ins from the house physician. Being on the slow-release stuff, he didn't have it so bad except for the headache and bone chills that gnawed at him the first nights, his pillow soaked through with dope drench. The meth fiends had it worst. One girl, a high school dropout from Hebron, had such hellish withdrawals, they let her sleep in an unlit room beneath a pile of blankets with cameras on her 24-7, in case she had seizures, which happened twice. Rehab, if nothing else, was a place to store yourself for a while. It was also, he quickly learned, a kingdom of boredom—but maybe that was the point, the *goal* even: to be with yourself, which was its own kind of hell. All the clichés about it are true. You wait around until whatever poison that's ruining you empties into the world as time. Then you fill that emptiness with more time. Talking, walking around the rec room, talking some more, listening to people "talk it out," painting watercolors of zoo animals, reading YA or science fiction novels (the only genres allowed). And after all that waiting you stand by the barred windows and watch the golden arches from the McDonald's across the parking lot light up, which means it's time for the nurses to switch shifts for the night, and an alcoholic with Down syndrome named Jordan is next to you pointing out the window, shouting, "It's chicken tender time! It's chicken tender time. Hey, guys, it's tender time."

The rooms are named after various genus of squash grown in New England, a laminated drawing of each type pasted on the doors. Hai shared the "Kabocha" room with a sex addict named Marlin, who was strapped to the bedpost with bungee cords to keep him from jerking off. He turned to Hai one night and said, quizzically, "Hey, man. I was wondering, how come I never see any Asians in rehab? I've been to, like, five of these joints and never seen one till now."

"MSG," Hai said, feeling crazy.

"What?" Marlin's eyes widened in the blue-wet dark.

"It absorbs all the poison. Why you think the government hates the stuff? They don't want you knowing the truth. Then all these places will be out of business. They make a big fuss about how it's bad for you.

Anytime the Feds say something's bad for you, eat as much of it as you can."

"Holy shit," Marlin said, sitting up.

"It won't work for your stuff, though."

"Yeah, no, no, I get that. I get that. And what about you? You couldn't absorb all your MSG or something?"

"I was adopted. Ate mostly waffles my whole life and now I'm fucked."

"Damn, dude." Marlin lay silent all night, this knowledge burrowing through him, his straps clinking as he tossed about.

There was a coterie of counselors at New Hope who huddled each morning in the rec room, nodding at their clipboards, then scattering like struck pool balls across the wards. Hai's was a guy named José with a greying handlebar mustache and a nose ring. "Listen, my guy," he said one morning during their one-on-one, "you're what we call clinically depressed, okay? That means you're down and out without ever needing a reason to be."

"So the clinical part just means there's no cause?"

José cocked his head and squinted. "Sort of. But don't worry, we'll get your meds worked out. While that happens, take this." He reached into his chest pocket and gave Hai what looked like a fortune cookie fortune, grease splotching the edges. Hai read it aloud: "Victorious warriors win first, then go to war. Defeated warriors go to war, then seek to win."

"Sun Tzu, my friend." José leaned back and grinned. "He doesn't miss, huh? And hey, don't think I'm showing you this cause, you know," he gestured at Hai. "I actually collect these." He nodded at an old Popeye's bucket on his desk filled with curling fortune strips.

"Thanks, but how about a brain transplant?"

"Sure, except your insurance probably won't cover it," he chuckled, twisting his mustache.

Besides Sun Tzu, Jesus was also at New Hope, lots and lots of Jesus, about fourteen renditions of the Holy Son, from what Hai could count, all hung in different shapes and sizes and various expressions of wounded exhaustion, staring down at him from the Cross while he ate his tapioca pudding in the mess hall, or while somebody wept or laughed—it was hard to tell after a while—in group sessions, their legs kicking, only one sock on. One time this retired math professor from the nearby community college on Suboxone had a breakdown and pissed all over the wall in the foyer, Jesus gazing forlorn at the darkened drywall as the staff dragged the screaming mathematician to Medical for tranquilizers.

Group session was, ironically, where the drugs were sold, since everybody was finally in one place at the same time. Before long the muffin-and-coffee table was transformed into a vibrant black market, though mostly for lighter fare brought in by the custodians: Zoloft and Xannies, the occasional Perc, homemade edibles.

The whole thing was no different from *One Flew Over the Cuckoo's Nest*, strangely enough, each patient dressed in standard-issue pajamas with a barcoded bracelet on their wrist (which the nurses scan each time they hand you a pill or when you take a tray of food at the mess hall). After all, a rehab, under God or not, was still a business. But Hai found the nurses to be good folks. Genuine, salt-of-the-earth women. No Nurse Ratched here. They all wore purple scrubs (a color purported to lower blood pressure) and were somehow always cheery, but in a depressive, sentimental way, like Midwestern moms whose children just departed for college. On the verge of tears but also quick to jab a needle in your arm without blinking, they roamed about, anticipating your needs before you could think of them. They passed you in the halls and said things like "How you kickin' today?" or "Can you feel the Lord smiling down on us? I can," or "Let me know if you want some hot chocolate, alright? I make 'em with the real marshmallows, not that freeze-dried crap." Or one of Hai's favorites, spoken by a nurse named Susan Bean (she insisted everyone call her by her full name): "Why don't you go ahead and turn that frown into a banana split for me?" There was another named Wanda, who spoke with a Spanish accent. Every time she took his vitals, she'd slip a Werther's Original in his chest pocket, give it a little pat, and walk away chuckling at nothing. You could go insane if they weren't so sincere about it. Most of them started as volunteers. Most of them had lost someone—a brother or sister or a husband or a child—who never made it to a place like New Hope. Or they did but it wasn't enough or was too late.

Inside those wide white hours, he often asked himself why he had deceived his mother in the first place. In the end, there was no good answer—only the image of her face brightening when he told her he was going to heal the sick, the cancer-riddled, the broken, the maimed, by becoming a doctor. After Bà ngoại died, his mother's light dimmed, and seeing her shriveled in the corner of the couch, her head down and lit blue by her Game Boy, playing endless *Tetris* day after day, her hair thinning, he figured he had to do *something*. You lose the dead as the earth takes them, but the living you still have a say in. And so he said it. And so he lied.

6

It was Hai's turn to close the store for the night. There was usually another crew member to help, but BJ had clocked out early to take her sister to a school play and it was Sony's turn to prep dinner at his group home, so Hai was alone.

After a brief rush of customers, mostly from the AA meeting at the Episcopal church on Mill Street, the place was empty the rest of the night. At one point the warmth from the heat lamps made his head heavy and he nodded off leaning against the counter. He woke, startled by the silence, and found that the stereo had been turned off. The clock on the wall above the drive-thru window read 9:16 p.m. and he had to shut everything down by 9:30.

He yawned, rubbed his eyes, and was about to look away when he saw someone walking past the drive-thru window. He rushed over and leaned into the night air, looking around. "Hello?" he said quietly. "Can I help you?" Only the crickets, lethargic from autumn's first chill, chirping weakly in the bushes. All night he had this strange feeling of being watched. But perhaps it was the withdrawals messing with his head. He shut the window and finished the rest of his closing in a daze. He had already brushed down the corn bread ovens, mopped the dining room and stacked the chairs over the tables, scrubbed the toilets, swept away the pubic hair around the porcelain, picked out the half-eaten meat loaf somebody tossed onto the urinal cake, taken out the garbage, careful to hold it by the top to avoid any rigs left over from addicts who used the stalls to shoot up, wiped down grease from the rotisserie, and wrapped the remaining four chickens in tinfoil. He moved about the empty rooms, careful not to look at the drive-thru again. All that was left was to clean the food vats and turn down the counter, but as he clicked off the lamps and heating hoppers, the front door opened.

It was a man in his late fifties wearing a lumpy brown leather jacket. He approached the counter, his face jowled and uneven, like somebody threw two black marbles in a bowl of mashed potatoes.

"We're actually closed," Hai said apologetically.

"You're not locked." The man glanced down at the cooling wells. "And looks like you still got grub."

When Hai asked him what he wanted, the man pointed at the creamed spinach without really looking, then the sweet potato pie. When Hai started scraping the dried crusts off the tops, the man stopped him. "Nah, give it to me as is. All of it."

"You sure?"

He nodded, the scent of booze wafting off him.

Hai filled the four sections of his tray to the brim with the two dishes and pushed it toward him. "It's on me," he said. "You're good."

"Thanks, bud. Oh," the man reached into his coat pocket and took out a piece of paper, "you mind if I post this on the corkboard over there?"

The poster was seeking information on a black sedan, and showed a heavily pixelated CCTV image of the car.

"You ever heard of anyone named Rachel Miotti?" the man said.

"She your daughter or something?"

The man reached into his back pocket and flashed his badge.

"Detective Lippman. Hartford County."

"Oh." Hai straightened up. "Something happened?"

"You could say that. She's dead." He made a vague slicing motion across his throat. "Seven years back now. Dragged out the passenger door of this sedan for almost five miles. Most likely by a john. I wasn't there that night but had to survey the strip the next morning. I was still on the beat then. It happened right outside here," he nodded over his shoulder, "and went all the way down Griswold to the dog run at Cook's Park. That's where the traces of her on the pavement ended." He shook his head, the black marbles gleaming on his face. Hai remembered now—the case was a big deal back when he was in middle school, the girl's mother appearing on TV almost nightly, her eye bags growing darker by the day. For years, Hartford County was either the seventh or eighth highest on the national murder list, and Rachel Miotti's death was the longest drag murder, by miles, on record.

"That car wash across the street was just an empty lot back then. Spillover parking for those run-down apartments out back. Junkies and working girls, mostly. But nobody deserves to die like that, you get me?" Cold now for years, the case was being reopened. "I'm retired but this one just stuck with me. Besides, it's something to do other than sit around on lawn chairs and watch the sprinklers in my yard go up and down." He smiled with only his eyes. "So can you keep a lookout and call us if you see anything?"

"Will do, Officer," Hai said, touching his cap the way he saw Wayne do.

"Good man. And thanks." He raised the tray, grabbed a spoon, and started shoveling the lukewarm food in his mouth as he walked out.

Hai watched him lumber toward a beige hatchback at the edge of the strip mall, then pull out. Maybe it was him he saw in the drive-thru. After locking up and shutting the lights, he took one last glance into the store, just in case, but it was all dark save for the exit sign glowing red above the back door. He shuddered, zipped up his jacket, and headed home.

The night was pitch and starless. All around him the sound of leaves, losing their hold on the branches, rustled unseen from gusts blown off the river. The sidewalk dropped off just as the sodium lamps stopped and the darkness spread out like a sea. As he crossed under an overpass, something flashed at the top of the concrete embankment. A man, wrapped in a sleeping bag, was texting on a flip phone. His face, lit blue and blasted, all teeth and beard, was so absorbed at whoever was on the other side, he didn't notice Hai's footsteps. As Hai made it down the road, the man started to laugh, and the voice, amplified by concrete, bounced across the night, making it seem like the valley itself was laughing behind him.

THE HOUSE WAS DARK and dead silent when he came in, Grazina long asleep. He ran his hand along the walls and by the bridge lights splintering through the house, made his way up the stairs and into his room. He hung up his jacket along with the cap and apron, peeled off his shirt rank with grease and Clorox, and removed his Nike military boots, the ones his mother bought him from the mall before he went off to college the first time, costing her half a week's pay.

He lay waiting for the dark to be truer than it was. Ever since he was little, it bothered him that you can never recall the exact moment you fall asleep, as though someone turns you off just before your mind fades, as if they knew you wouldn't choose it, that you'd stay awake if you saw sleep coming like the shadow of some colossal wave falling over you.

He wasn't sure how long he was out, but the first thing he noticed when he woke were the explosions. They sounded like thunder, but faster, tearing open the air outside. He thought of Grazina and realized, in his exhaustion, that he'd forgotten to check her pill tray to see if she'd taken her nine p.m. dose. He leapt from bed and looked out the window. There, across the river, on the far shore, were clusters of fireworks blasting though the canopies. Excited human voices broke off and flitted across the water, followed by barrages of Roman candles searing through the black, shot from a silo on the abandoned mill. Teenagers.

Panicked, Hai headed down the hallway. But when he got to the landing, he saw her standing there like a mannequin in her nightgown and nearly screamed. She was staring straight at him, hair disheveled and holding a spatula like she was about to swat a fly. The coyotes in the pines were going crazy as the fireworks went on, and their voices fell into the house as horrific shrieks.

He grabbed Grazina's hand and gently shook her. "Whoa, whoa. You're alright. Come on now. You're alright." She yanked away and shuffled, faster than he expected, into his room. She knelt on the carpet and started crying into the collar of her nightgown. When he touched her, she jolted and spurted something in Lithuanian.

"English, okay?" he tried. "Or else I can't hear you, remember? We're in America. No war, Grazina. No more war, I promise."

This time he was ready. He wrapped his arms around her, placed his hand behind her head so she wouldn't jerk about, and began to sing his grandmother's lullaby again, his voice raspier, thinned from a week of shouting orders down the line, the notes crackled as if cut with static.

When this failed, he switched to "Silent Night," but suddenly couldn't remember the words beyond the title, so he tried humming it. But this time she was off to nowhere-land for good, her eyes rolling wildly, face and neck wet with tears and sweat. "My brother, Kristof." She lunged forward, shouting at the desk.

With his arms seat-belted around her waist, a wild thought came to him. If she was that deep in the past, maybe he could reach her by going back there himself, something he did once or twice with his grandmother when she had one of her schizophrenic breaks. With scenes from *Slaughterhouse-Five* fresh in his mind, the soldiers, the ruined German landscape, he took a breath and made his voice deep and manly, rooting it in his gut. "Ma'am," he said, pausing to examine its authenticity. "Ma'am, don't you worry now. We're gonna go get your brother." He pointed at her chest. "But you gotta listen to me, alright?" He searched his mind, still foggy with sleep, for a military name and ended up blurting out the first one that came. "This is Sergeant Pepper from the United States Army, Second Division." He would learn only later that the Sgt. Pepper's Pizza in town had been named after a Beatles album. Having never listened to the Beatles other than a few songs that floated from the radio through the years, Hai had assumed it was the pizza shop's original name, short for Sgt. Pepperoni.

Grazina's head jerked up and turned toward this new, older voice, alert.

"Ma'am, we're under heavy artillery fire and need to evacuate this village now." He spoke quickly, his tone determined and grated, Bruce Willis–like.

She nodded vigorously, eyes clear. "Yes, yes of course, Sergeant."

"Your family, including your brother, is safe. They have already been moved to evacuation zone C, a camp for displaced persons outside of—" He knew nothing, he realized, of World War Two, of Europe, the world. "Outside of Gettysburg." Sony had rambled on about the Civil War during their shifts at HomeMarket, most of which Hai was able to tune out. But at least it was a battle. It was a war, something.

"Gettysburg?" Grazina's eyes flickered, trying to locate the village in her mental map. She nodded, her face pinched. "German, yes? Are we still in Germany?"

"I'm afraid so, ma'am." He gritted his teeth and gathered himself. "It's a small village. Occupied to store supplies for our next offensive on Hitler's front."

"Hitler!" she cut him off, then considered him with one eye, her way, he would learn, of measuring character. "Don't forget Stalin, Mr. Pepper," she said coldly. "There is more than one devil these days."

"Of course."

"Now listen to me, Sergeant." She drew closer. "You must send wire to my father. You say: his daughter, Grazina Vitkus, is healthy, not scared, and that her faith in God is strong. Tell him: wait for me in London. That was the plan before we left his bakery—to go to England, then find boat for America."

Flush with this new mission, she pulled his arm off her shoulder and staggered to her feet, nearly falling until he placed his hand on her back and steadied her. She faced him, her chin high. "I'm going now, Sergeant Pepper." She straightened the waistband on her underwear, smoothed out her nightgown as though it were a young woman's skirt, and gave him a military salute. "God bless you. I go now to Gettysburg."

Thrown by her sudden, sharp vitality, he clasped his hands together under his chin and pondered his next move. "Uh. You can't."

She was glancing around the room, and he wondered if she could actually *see* a road, or even a dirt path threading through a lush German countryside.

"We have to stay here, ma'am."

She ignored him. "The roads are clear. Farmer's roads. Dusty, yes, but good enough to go by foot. If we follow the tree line, the planes won't see. Now, which way, Sergeant Pepper?" She tilted her head back, awaiting his answer.

"You see this?" he finally whispered, as he made his finger into a hook. "This is a fishhook. It's how our defensive line is currently laid out across that ridge over there. Can you see the faint light from the officers' quarters between that bunch of trees?"

Grazina's eyes followed his finger down the unlit hall. "I see it, Sergeant," she nodded.

"Good." He would simply replace the Army of the Potomac's position with World War Two Americans, he decided. From the dregs of his mind, he recalled Sony talking about Union forces deploying a fishhook formation to successfully defend against Robert E. Lee at Gettysburg. "The fishhook, or S line," he told Grazina, "will prevent against flanking maneuvers from the Germans. Which means they can't surprise us from the side."

"I see it," she said. "The Americans, your men, got good brains. If the Germans come here," she pointed to the hook's inner curve on her palm, "the top of the hook will surround them from behind and they'll be finished." She looked at him, seemingly surprised that such military strategy would be so accessible to her, a teenager trapped in time. "War is a game. Just like *Price Is Right*," she nodded.

"Just like *Price Is Right*."

But how far would he play this out? To the bathroom? The closet in the foyer downstairs? The basement? Down the street? Where in the house—or rather, where in the past, her past—was Gettysburg?

She chopped the air in front of him. "But your men must *also* stop the Reds from advancing on the East! My mother said Vilnius has already fallen. That letter came four days ago but was dated all the way back in July!" Spit landed cool across his face.

"Okay . . . Just give me a sec. I mean—" He cleared his throat. "We must be patient and assess our options, ma'am." He put his hands on his hips and puffed out his chest but knew his face betrayed him.

She looked away into what must've been a smoldering landscape from 1944, the year, he would learn later, that she fled her home village of Bubiai when the Soviets advanced the final time. "Please, just call me Grazina."

"Okay, look, here's what we'll do. We'll take my jeep." Images of World War Two films he had seen on TV flashed before him: *Patton*, *Saving Private Ryan*, *The Great Escape*, etc.

Grazina scratched her chin. "So we're *driving* to Gettysburg."

"My jeep's right over there." He pointed across the hallway, toward the bathroom. The claw-foot tub should do.

"And what about air raids? The roads will leave us exposed."

"It's getting dark. I can drive with the lights off. We'll go slow. There's a moon." He peered at the ceiling, where an old water stain hung above them.

"I like your guts, Sergeant Pepper." But then she paused, stooped her shoulders, and examined him with a frown: his white T-shirt, still torn at the neck, his red plaid boxers, pale legs and knobby knees sticking out. He was caught—no uniform. The jig was up.

"You're too skinny," she said, shaking her head. "How are you going to fight with no meat on the bones?" She bent over and grabbed something from the box on the floor. When she lifted her fist to his face, he saw a pack of strawberry Pop-Tarts clutched in her hand.

"For the road."

"Good idea." He took her arm and led her, shuffling behind him, to the bathroom.

The fireworks kept on, their fiery blooms now muted through the frosted bathroom window. Grazina still flinched each time a big one went off. He pulled back the shower curtain printed with tiny yellow owls. There was a long crack of rust that ran the length of the old tub. He thought of removing her Shower-Aide, the white plastic booster chair, but, since it resembled the seat inside a truck, decided to leave it.

"Quick," he turned to her, "get in. We gotta move fast. Daybreak is in a few hours."

She clutched his arm and stepped inside, her free hand throbbing from the effort. Her other hand was still clutching the Pop-Tarts. He wiped away a streak of water in the tub's bottom, then directed her to sit down with her legs extended under the plastic chair. He climbed inside the truck and sat on the Shower-Aide, his back to her. "Alright.

You ready?" He adjusted an invisible rearview and fastened his seat belt. All those hours playing make-believe with his grandmother, building forts while her own brain was misfiring—though in another way—were paying off.

"You worry about yourself, skinny Pepper. This is the countryside." She gestured at a hand towel hanging on the wall a few feet away. "I'm not afraid to die here."

Hai pretended to start the engine. "Okay, we're going now. We're off!" He rattled the seat a bit and a few drops of water fell on his toes. "Can you feel it? It's bumpy."

"Of course. These roads have been ruined for years." She was shouting as though there were a diesel engine and rocks kicking at the jeep's carriage. "Nothing but dirt and mud since the czars. Peasant's roads. Honest roads."

It must've been nearly one in the morning. They rode on for a while without speaking, the countryside an indigo swath around them. A car drove past outside the house, the muffled yet distinct lyrics of "I Gotta Feeling" by the Black Eyed Peas seeping through its speakers. He looked ahead at the frosted window, which no longer flashed with fireworks, and listened to Grazina's slowing breaths.

There was a sharp *clank*. He turned around. Her amber bracelet knocked against the porcelain.

"It's a clear night. And there's a lake over there, Sergeant," she noted without interest. "It's dark but you can see it. Like a piece of the sky fell down." She looked up, scanning the ceiling as he drove on.

"I used to swim in Lake Rėkyva as a girl. With my brother." Another *clank*. "But that's all over. The water was bombed. The fish floated up, all fried and orange, rotting. Horrible. Terrible."

"They bombed a lake?"

"What, you think I'm making this up? The Nazis would bomb anything, even water." *Clank*.

This stirred something in him, and he realized now how odd it was that despite her derangement of senses, she'd managed to enter such a clear, lucid state of linearity as the one they were in now. But then again, he knew nothing of dementia, what wide, unbroken vistas it might hold.

He turned the invisible wheel in front of him, as though brushing something away. "Hey, why don't you take a nap?" This was his chance to close it up, to get her back to bed and finally hit the restart button. "I'll wake you when we're close."

"You're a soldier." She pulled herself upright. "And you want me to *sleep*? Even dogs know not to sleep during an invasion."

There was a crinkle of foil. Then a rough bark started scraping his mouth. "Eat," she said, jabbing the Pop-Tart at the side of his cheek. Cool bits of filling rubbed off on his skin.

"Lower," he said.

"What?"

"Lower! Yeah, mmph mmph." He bit off a piece, tilting his head back to keep it in.

"We can't have you hungry at the wheel. It's a long way, I can tell."

Grazina took a bite as well, her lips smacking loudly as she eased back in the tub. He shifted into third gear and the truck backfired before speeding up, easing through the liquid night ahead. He knew they weren't moving but could feel them getting smaller and smaller in the landscape as if he were outside himself, watching from the distance of years. He pressed his back against the seat and closed his eyes. He thought of his mom, his bà ngoại, Sony, Aunt Kim, the people he knew in town, all of them far in the future while he was still in 1944 with Grazina, three years away from when his grandmother would be born in Gò Công, Vietnam. So he started talking. To nobody. "Good night," he said. "Good night, everyone I love you. Thanks for coming. How many scoops of the mashed potatoes you want, ma'am? Careful, tray's hot. No, sir, our mac and cheese isn't gluten free." His mumbling sounded hollow off the tiles. And he could no longer tell whether he was talking or just thinking or passed out. But he kept on as fields of rapeseed unfurled under the starlight to his left and the moon hovered over his thoughts.

It wasn't until Grazina groaned that he saw the tub again. So caught up imagining the road ahead, he didn't notice the window in front of him had started to pinken with dawn. He turned around and found her asleep, her palms open at each side. A half-eaten Pop-Tart rested in the dip of her chest.

Quietly, he stepped out and went into her room, grabbed a pillow, along with her favorite green-and-white quilt. He took the pastry off her chest and placed it gently, so it wouldn't splash, into the toilet.

Grazina's head had slumped to one side, so he propped it up with a pillow, then draped the blanket over her chest and tucked it in along her length, covering her arms against the cold porcelain. That's when he clocked the piece of wood sticking out from behind the shower curtain.

The edge of a picture frame.

It hung on the wall above the tub but was hidden this whole time by the opaque curtain, which he pulled back. The black-and-white photo was set behind glass and was surprisingly large, about the size of a doormat. In it, a man and a woman, along with a toddler girl, are smiling. They're all dressed up for a party or some formal function. The monochrome hues and their style of dress indicate the fifties or sixties. The daughter is sitting in the man's lap. The woman's hair is fair and done up in a beehive. She is laughing, mouth open, all teeth and shut eyes in a room where voices must've been punctuated by clinking glasses. She is holding up a card with both hands that reads *$300*. A lottery? A raffle? It must be why she's laughing, why she looks so triumphant, as if all the world would cost no more than what she held in her hands.

He stood watching Grazina sleep under the photo of herself half a century ago, her face, the only part of her that wasn't covered, grey and compressed and smeared with strawberry jam. What did he know about her illness, after all, other than that four of the thirteen pills she took each day were supposed to "subdue" it, like some sort of criminal in her head? How could he have known that her brain was actually collapsing slowly inside her skull, how this made little holes, which then made new neural connections and scrambled old ones? It must be like water, he thought, as the morning rose up around them. It must be like the lake she had talked about. Diving under the surface until everything was muted and gauzed but still *there*. He listened to her wheezy breaths, and imagined a tiny fire scratching inside her. A little torch that forgot it was not supposed to burn underwater. Because to remember is to fill the present with the past, which meant that the cost of remembering anything, anything at all, is life itself. We murder ourselves, he thought, by remembering. The idea made him sick. And without knowledge of his own legs moving beneath him, he crossed the hall to his bedroom, fished the contact lens case from his jacket pocket, and, having been sober for forty-seven days, tossed the Perc and codeines back in one gulp, then returned to where Grazina lay slumped in the jeep.

"Good night," he said, but then saw her lips moving. "What's that?" He crouched down.

"I said . . ." She swallowed and blinked. "We made it."

"We made it?" he asked.

"To Gettysburg."

"How do you know?"

"Because I can see you. If I can see you, then I'm still alive," Grazina slurred, her voice thick with sleep. "Do you see *me*, Sergeant Pepper?"

A train whistle was blowing miles down the track. "Yeah," he answered. "You're right in front of me, right here in Gettysburg."

They watched each other in the weak light for what seemed like a long time.

Then she said, "So, have you killed anyone yet, Sergeant?"

Hai said nothing.

"Every soldier gets asked, I know. But a woman has to know." She was so still only her mouth seemed to move. "But really. Have you killed? There's no shame in it. Not in these times."

The pills were starting to take effect, vignetting most of his vision. He knew from experience that by the time they made it to his limbic system, all that would remain of the world would be a pinhole of light at the center of his consciousness, like a makeshift camera, making it dark enough for him to retreat into a hole deep inside him, curl in a fetal position, and rest. The fireworks were long gone, but he could smell the sulfur drifting through the cracked window. He looked down at his hands, as though the answer could be found there. He wanted to tell her that the body was just this stupid little shovel we use to dig through the hours only to end up surrounded by more empty space than we know what to do with. But the drugs were dissolving in him as hers were dissolving in her, and in this pharmaceutical stupor, all he could hear was the rush of static filling the room. It grew louder and louder, as if the whole house were one big radio left on a bad channel and he was standing inside it, waiting for a reason. *No*, he said to himself. *No, no, no*—and he covered his ears to keep it all out. Though it was only the rain.

Fall

7

He shoots the old lady and nothing happens.

He aims the gun at her mouth and pulls the trigger, and the words fall out of the world. Her hands cover her face as if to hold her skull in place. He aims at her chest and fires again, and she crumples to the linoleum, twitching. He listens for the slow groan underneath her robe and fires another slug into her back. Then waits.

Eventually, like always, she rises, her back arched like a puppet on strings. She crawls on all fours and lifts her wincing face toward his raised .32, then begs him to spare her family, her mother with gold hair who's still back there, through the rapeseed meadow, in the cellar of the hideaway house, crouched behind human-sized jars of pickled radishes and beets. He bites his lip and shoots her in the forehead. She jolts before doubling over.

He shoots her in the kitchen, in her bedroom, then the foyer. He puts his sights on her hunched back and fires as she sweeps the hallway. All over the house she lies, clutching her side, her blue robe billowing through the rooms as she dies. It's like he's aiming at pieces of the sky except he always ends up hitting a grandmother.

Because they're at war and it doesn't make sense. They are playing at real life but it's so much like hell it feels fake. She is his landlady. Sort of. She is Grazina Vitkus, and as the bullet hits her, she cries out, stumbles on the landing. But this time she reaches into the pocket of her nightgown, takes out her own pistol (a Walther P38), cocks it once, settles the nozzle where the boy's heart is, and pulls. He's hit in the chest during the commercial break of *Dancing with the Stars* and immediately winces before grabbing the nearby bag of unopened pretzels and hurling it at her. His head jerks back as he collapses on the musty carpet, writhing wildly, making blood-clotted groans while she laughs and blows smoke from her raised crooked finger like a James Bond villain.

Once he was assassinated from behind while eating breakfast. Her mouth fired a *bang* and the boy's face fell with a plop into the bowl, lukewarm, brain-colored oatmeal oozing from his temples. Because the Red Guard's coming and Stalin is killing thousands by the week. But the gulags won't have them, they've decided. Not if God and Mother Mary can help it. This is as real as it gets. This is East Gladness, Germany. This is November, and heat from their wounds comes out as steam between their fingers. This is nowhere in the middle of their lives, yet closer to death than they've ever been.

It is simply the way here, in this house beside a river marked only by what it makes disappear. He is Sergeant Pepper, Second Division, US Infantry. He aims for the mouth because it's the deepest wound he's ever seen. No matter how many years the body wrecks itself on the shore of living, the mouth stays mostly the same, faithful through its empty, eternal void. Some call this hunger. Others call it loss. He knows it only as the law. Whole nations have burned from this little oval ringed with teeth. Were we even human until God opened us here, His fingers singeing a place in the lower face so we can say, eyes narrowed at the embered new world, "The fuck?"

He aims for the mouth because it opens the way time opens—

whatever goes through never returns the same. Like a word. Like a you. Like I said, this is war.

AFTER THE NIGHT he pretended to be an army officer named after a local pizza shop to fight a war he knew nothing about, they began, at Grazina's request, to conduct shooting drills via mock gunfights. Whenever she slipped into one of her episodes, her eyes clouded with that faraway look, Hai would deepen his voice and bring out the sergeant. "I have no problem shooting Reds and Krauts. Just show me how," she said, hands on her hips, her nightgown blotched with Salisbury steak gravy.

These gunfights, a dream inside a dream inside an illusion, occurred around three times a week, where they'd fire at each other throughout the house, their finger-pistols locked and loaded as they crouched among the floral furniture. They were on an old dairy farm pasture, he'd tell her, or stopped over on the side of the road by a shelled village, a grove of pines, gunmetal light splintering through the eaves.

In this theater they made of her memories, the war was drawing to a close. If the Soviets had taken Vilnius, Grazina informed him, it meant the Germans were losing the Eastern Front, and it was only a matter of time before the Allies closed in from France. He nodded as if this was obvious to him. He was about to suggest they get back on the jeep when she stopped, looked around the room as if someone had just called her name, then walked into the kitchen, where she set out cups for tea as though none of this happened.

And like that it was over.

The house reappeared from behind their hallucinations, drab and musty as ever. It was like coming down from a high. Over cups of Earl Grey—which he found unbearable, like drinking hot perfume—she told him about her life, how much of it true there was no telling. She went on about her family in Lithuania. How her father was a baker famous in the region, his raspberry strudel unrivaled, capable of bribing the Nazis to spare his pastry shop when they rolled into Rokiškis in '39. "The Krauts smashed every window on the road. When my father saw them coming up the street, he ran to the back and dumped the chocolate rugelach—my favorite—into a sink of dirty water, covered them with baking pans. Then he came out with rye loaves big as babies and tossed them into the officers' arms. I was only twelve when I stood staring out the window as they marched by us—their arms full of bread after taking our country, their eyes watching me from under their helmets, this girl among prune cakes and cookies—and spared my father's windows." She spoke with a mix of pride and sunken rage. "Of course, we didn't know what they were actually capable of. What was happening in the ghettos. If we knew, we would have left like the others, the smart ones. You see, the Germans, they saw us as just Slavs, slaves, and wanted us gone, sooner or later."

"And what happened after that?"

"My mother was so scared, she became a Catholic. And then bombs. And more bombs. Boom, boom, boom," she slapped the table.

"And your father, what did he believe in?"

"No Catholicism, no Judaism for him. But he did convert to Alcoholism." She bit her lip and shrugged.

Her father, she explained, foolishly believed bread would spare his family forever. The Red Army, after pushing back the Nazis, invaded Lithuania in June of '44, just five years after the Nazis marched past the bakery. Two weeks before Vilnius was occupied, her father took her and her brother onto a train heading west into Germany, where they would hopefully sneak into occupied France, then perhaps London. Though the Germans might have had plans to exterminate them eventually, the Communists posed a more immediate threat, seizing private property and splitting entire families, deporting them into Stalin's working camps in the nether realms of the Soviet Union, many of whom would never return. "Like I said, there was more than one devil those days. You understand?"

He nodded, his tea cold. "A rock and a hard place."

"More like being crushed by two ballsacks filled with demon blood. You ever been crushed by a ballsack?"

"Not really."

"Stalin was worse for us only because he lasted longer. Ever heard of the pogroms? I regret nothing, Labas." She pushed up her glasses with her middle finger. When she saw him smile at it, she said, "My husband used to hate that, said it was just my excuse to flick him off. He wasn't wrong." She laughed and the glasses slid back down her nose.

He wanted to know more, at the very least to build out Sergeant Pepper's world, keep him believable and true when he needed him most. The longer Pepper existed, Hai realized, the easier it was to manage Grazina's episodes. It meant having a portal into which he could usher her when the present burned away, like the fog burning up now over the river as the first sunrays splintered over the mountains.

"You know what?" She held up a finger, as if testing the wind. "I do regret one thing. I never got to go to a Gene Pitney concert."

"A who concert?"

"It doesn't matter. He was born in Hartford, then became real big. When he finally came to town I had to do a fundraiser for the VFW. Thought I would have another chance, but that's how things go. You see people get big, then before you know it, they're washed away and it's all Duran Duran or whatever. I'm tired, Labas. Did I sleep last night?"

"I dunno. Did you?"

"I don't remember," she shrugged.

⌒

"I HATE TO tell you this, but Bugs Bunny is *definitely* sucking a dick," Maureen said, her lips pursed over Russia's tattoo as she studied it. It was a sketch of Bugs Bunny drawn down the side of Russia's upper arm, supposedly biting into a carrot. Wayne was the first to point it out. When Russia, withering, turned to Hai and asked if he also saw a dick, Hai tried to be diplomatic. "Honestly? It could go either way," he said. "I mean, with his cheeks bulging and all, I see what Wayne is saying. But I wouldn't, like, think of it . . . immediately, you know?"

"But you'll think of it sooner or later," Maureen laughed with her hand over her mouth. "Your Bunny's giving head. And you know? I think it's pretty cool."

"No, it's not, dude." Russia yanked his shirt over the tattoo, rubbing it like a burn.

"Why do you even have that thing anyway?" said Wayne, wiping down his butcher block.

"It was my nickname back in high school."

"Blow job?" Hai tried to suppress his laugh.

"Nah, man. B-Rab." Russia turned to Maureen as if she'd confirm this. "You know, Eminem's name in *8 Mile*? I used to memorize all his lyrics off the dome. I was a legend back in high school. The quarterback, Jimmy Nikels, when we made it to the state semifinals junior year, even asked me to hype up the team in the locker room before the game with 'Lose Yourself.'" Russia scratched his nose and looked at them sheepishly. "We got blown out but it was still dope as fuck."

"It's alright, man," Hai offered. "Your tats can mean B-Rab *and* be a sex-positive message. A double meaning. Most people have tats that are a bunch of stupid shapes or barbed wire or Chinese words they can't pronounce. But yours is sick."

"Who's sick?" BJ walked out from the back, her hands dusted with corn bread mix.

"Russia's dick," Maureen said. "I mean, his tattoo of a rabbit giving head."

"The fuck? Let me see?" BJ tried to lift his sleeve but Russia pulled away.

"Fuck out of here. I'm not a *museum*." Russia let out a sigh and turned back to the drive-thru window, where a customer was pulling up.

"Okay, since we're sharing, I got something even better," BJ said.

Hai stopped stirring the creamed spinach.

"Let me guess," Maureen said, smirking as she crossed her arms, "you got a Prince Albert."

"How the hell am I supposed to get that, Maur? No, man. Do I look like a penis ring person to you?"

"I thought a Prince Albert was a type of tattoo!"

A woman, in earshot from the dining room, stopped unwrapping her meat loaf and paused in her seat, her entire body listening. BJ loosened her belt, untucked her white manager's shirt, and unbuttoned it all the way to the top before turning to reveal her fleshy bare shoulder. At the center of the right shoulder blade was a dusky blotch the size of one of their chicken drumsticks, resembling a bad chemical burn.

"Am I supposed to be impressed?" said Maureen.

"Don't you see it? It's a fucking music note. As a birthmark. You know what that means? It means God marked me and I'm carrying out his work. And you know wrestling is ninety percent music, right?" She was nearly bent over, the birthmark shining with sweat under the halogens.

Maureen turned to Wayne. "Looks like Mexico to me. Don't it look like Mexico?"

Sony came over and peered over Maureen's shoulder. "It's more like Florida," he said in a rare divergence from his commander, "the third state to secede from the Union," and shook his head with disappointment.

BJ popped up and flung her shirt back on. "Okay, everybody get back to work! We're not paying you to have opinions." She buttoned up her shirt and fixed her name tag. "And don't forget it's Peace Treaty Day. And I want you and you," she pointed at Hai and Maureen, "to do the exchanges."

"What? Didn't I do it in the spring?" Maureen frowned. "I recall bringing back tulips with the cargo."

"That was two years ago. Sony did it last spring and fucked it all up." BJ was already walking away.

"Fuck me. Alright, come on, kid," Maureen said as she hobbled toward the back. "I gotta ice my knees before we hit the road."

The Peace Treaty, Maureen told Hai as they sat on milk crates in the freezer, a slab of frozen mac and cheese balanced across her knees, was a food exchange between HomeMarket and the employees at their arch rival, the Panetta down the road in Millsap. It was the only other fast-casual in a twenty-mile radius and had a notoriously snooty vibe. "They think they're better than us cause they have fucking *salads*. You kidding me? Who wants to eat leaves at a fast-food joint?" Maureen shifted the mac and cheese slab to one knee and grimaced. Back in high school, Panetta was the place where rich girls from "the Heights," wearing a uniform of Abercrombie sweatpants tucked into Ugg boots and puffer vests, would sit in a booth, look at you while sipping cantaloupe ice tea, then whisper to each other before erupting with toothy laughter.

Peace Treaty Day also gave each group of employees a chance to eat something other than what they served every day. "But the thing is," Maureen said, leaning forward, "their food is shit. *Fealthy* is what I call it. Fake healthy. They cut up two stalks of romaine, toss it into a bowl of mayo covered in bacon bits, and call it 'conscious crisps.' Don't that make you wanna punch a toddler?"

Hai thought about it and nodded.

"Just wait till you see 'em, stuck-up in their nutmeg aprons and T-shirts like it's a farmers market and not a franchise next to a Walmart."

Maureen shoved the mac and cheese to the floor, where it thumped like a dead body, and got up. "Let's go. Can you drive?"

Hai shook his head. "I failed my test four times."

"Jesus Christ." She gave him a once-over.

He braced himself for the expected comment about Asians and driving.

"You'll get it next time. Five's a lucky number after all." She walked out the freezer, adding over her shoulder, "I divorced my husband after five years."

Ten minutes later he was riding shotgun in the van, a black 2002 Dodge Caravan Passenger with *HomeMarket* emblazoned red on both sides. Sony and the dishwasher girl had already loaded the back with aluminum trays full of every menu item except pot pies, which they had run out of the day before.

Soon they were chugging through the back roads, taking the scenic route to stretch the drive. "The longer we ride, the longer I get to sit. Here, take this." She shoved an opened metal flask in front of him. It reeked of gin and something else. "Go ahead if you want. Three sips of this and my knees feel thirty-five again."

"No thanks. I'm allergic."

"To alcohol? That's a new one." She glanced at him with one eye. "Now, that a real situation or some gluten-free hipster thing?"

She took a swig, stuck her tongue out, and wiped her mouth with the back of her hand. They were silent for a while. Just the car puttering through stretches of rye and cattail marshes, past tracts of slate-like fields cleared for power lines, the mist burning steadily as the sun skimmed the knolls edging the valley. Then Maureen said, "I'm gonna tell you something that you might not be ready for."

He looked to see if she was joking, but her eyes were steady and red at the edges.

"You're green and you need to know some things, okay? All this knowledge is no good sticking on a creaky-kneed old lady. I might not look like it but I'm a philosopher, you know."

"What's a philosopher supposed to look like? Also, you're not an old lady."

"Oh, fuck off. This isn't a *date*, for God's sakes. You don't gotta butter me up, kid." She made a turn, then tapped the windshield with a nubby finger. "You know, if we keep on driving, like, past Millsap, past the Panetta, Hartford, then into New York State, Pittsburgh, all the way out west, and then beyond that, and if this van could swim and went out even further." She made her hand into a ship and sailed it toward his face. "Right out there, deep out in the ocean, you know what would happen?"

"We'd drown?"

"Guess again. With more imagination."

"Oh, I get it. You're one of *those*?" Hai leaned away and looked at her. "Like we're really gonna fall off the flat earth?"

"You kidding me? That's amateur stuff, friend. The earth isn't *flat* and it never was." She made her hand into a sphere. "It's *hollow*. And the entrance is in Antarctica. So if we keep going, we'll hit the big ice block down south. All roads lead to Antarctica. Literally and figuratively."

Hai thought about it, his head hurting. "I could use a coffee."

"Listen, before you go on and judge . . ." She gave him the one-eyed stare again, then went on talking about how the earth was inside some giant display case. "Like those model towns you see in museums? You know the ones. Except it's us, you and me, right now, riding in this shitty van to a shitty Panetta. Everything's a model. A simulation. The white coats have always known it too. They have formulas, algebra that can explain it now."

"I don't get it," Hai said. "What about that picture of the earth from space and all that? Neil Armstrong and Bud Lightyear and all them?"

"Buzz Aldrin!" she laughed. "Man, I forgot you're just a child." There was no free-floating globe, Maureen explained, because the earth was controlled by reptilians living underground, whose tunnels can be accessed only through a secret entrance on an ancient ice sheet on the "forbidden continent," and all the politicians—including every American president since Kennedy—have privately visited Antarctica to make deals with these lizards. For some reason, Hai hadn't pinned Maureen for a tinfoil hat. "What, you think they just all *love* icebergs? Even the goddamn Pope? Give me a break. They're checking out the entrance, maybe even going down there, snooping around. Why you think there's no country in Antarctica? Think about it now. Really think about it." She swallowed as they stopped at a crosswalk. An old woman with a headscarf was struggling against the wind, a tiny smudge of a dog in her arms. When they passed, she turned up her face and stared blankly at them with black eyes.

"The dinosaurs, they never died off, you get me? They evolved, just like us. Except they got a few million years' head start on us. Now they're intelligent lizards feeding off our negative energy," Maureen went on. "They've forced our world leaders to work for them, trapping humanity in endless cycles of war and death machines. Some of our leaders are even lizards in disguise. I mean, how else do you explain Dick Cheney? Now they can't wipe us out because they need us here to keep giving off bad vibrations. They feed on our suffering, ya know? We're nothing but a crop to them. They let us live our little troubled lives, let the sunlight and the rain make us grow . . . then, once in a while, they mow us down to keep their numbers up." She went on and on like this. Hai started drifting off, staring at the abandoned cars along the shanty lots, some so flat and rusted they looked like fallen trees. She turned to him, her eyebrows arched, and it took him a moment to realize she had just asked him a question he didn't hear.

"Yeah," he said without a clue.

"You really think so?" She slit her eyes at him and bit her lip.

"Most of the time. Yeah."

"Right." She nodded. "You're not as dull as you look, you know."

He had never heard of a lizard conspiracy before, but in a van cramped with trays of food, the overpowering smells of their twenty-one menu items mixing together, the world outside blurring by like a washing machine, amorphous and out of reach in its ruined stretches, it was hard *not* to believe her. It even made sense, in a way. Wasn't that how taxes worked? Aren't we alive just so they can skim our earnings off the top for as long as we live? But what would it matter if they *were* ruled by immortal dinosaurs hiding underground? He was not at war with them; he was only alive inside pieces of mistakes that gravity had collected into a life raft called the present. He was in a catering van, heading downriver, toward whatever iceberg lay ahead.

"It's a lot to take in at once, I know. But I'll break it down for you slowly. Through time." She reached over and patted his knee with a gentleness he didn't expect. That's when he saw the watch on her wrist. A *Star Wars* design with powder-blue bands, it had Han Solo on its face surrounded by tiny Chewbacca heads to mark the time.

"How does *Star Wars* fit in with hollow earth?" Hai nodded at the watch. Maureen stared ahead, keeping quiet. He looked out the window. They were passing a junkyard filled with car carcasses on both sides. The leaves had already fallen onto the shells of old sedans, some dating back to the sixties. The grass, high as the door handles, was still blue-green and weeks away from the moldy greys of winter. A yellowing fern had spent the summer prying through a crack in the floorboard of a taxicab and now swayed in the driver's seat like a person napping at the wheel.

"It was my son's. He was obsessed. We both were." She let herself chuckle. "The big man upstairs took him home in '99. Leukemia. Bad blood, they said. Funny thing is his deadbeat father always said that too. That my boy had bad blood. But he was talking about me. That he had my temper in him, which was true. Then my baby went ahead and really *did* have bad blood. What a joke."

"Sorry."

"Don't say stupid shit like that." Then in a mocking, Valley girl tone, she added, "'Oh, Maureen. I'm so sorry for your loss. Here's a Jell-O mold for your loss. Oh, Maureen, it must be so hard to lose your only child. We're so sorry.' Everybody's so sorry about what they don't know shit about."

Through the corner of his eye, he saw her shake her head, saying softly, "You'll learn not to get too worked up about me. My situation might be jacked up but I'm God-fearing and I respect people if they come at me straight." Her son loved Han Solo, she explained, and she bought the watch for him for his tenth birthday, over a decade ago. It didn't even work anymore. "He said Han Solo looked like a better version of his dad. I didn't want to believe it, but he was right. We used to——" She coughed into her arm, took out the flask, and was about to open it, then paused and put it back in her jacket. "We used to watch *Empire Strikes Back* together over and over. He said it was the best one."

"He's not wrong," Hai said.

"His name was Paul. Such a boring name, you'd think he'd get a long, boring life."

Maureen was still paying off Paul's medical bills. She had a town house off King and Main but heated only the kitchen to cut costs, where she slept on the floor in a sleeping bag.

They turned back on Route 4, and the gas stations and fast-food joints on the strip sparkled from a break in the clouds. Behind the strip, like a cardboard backdrop in a film set, was the Bowen power plant, its two water towers looming over the skyline. Beside the plant, in a grove of pines, was an unfinished SAM site built during the Cold War. In high school, kids would go there to make out, throw parties, do lines of coke off the old steel pipes while punk bands played in the concrete chambers with generators stolen from shop class. All this passed through his mind like projections from a slide.

After a while Hai said, real quiet, "Can I ask you something?"

"Normally I'd say no, but go ahead. Oh—that place over there has the best fried Oreos." She pointed with her chin.

"Where do you think he is?"

"Where who is?"

"I mean with Antarctica and the lizards and all that. Where does somebody like Paul go when they're done using his energy?"

"Ha! My baby's with God." She looked at him as though willing him to believe her, as though his believing would confirm its truth.

He turned his face toward the rusted power plant. "Right, that makes sense."

THEY PARKED IN the back of the Panetta, which, unlike HomeMarket, had a loading bay. Maureen took another swig from her flask. She wasn't exactly drunk but looser and warmer now. "You ready to party?" she said, tucking her hair behind her ears.

"Your eye shadow's running a bit," Hai said. "If you care."

"Oh, fuck's sake." She checked herself in the rearview and wiped her cheeks with her knuckles.

There were already two employees from Panetta waiting for them on the dock, a man and a woman who smiled too widely and in unison, like Wes Anderson characters. Hai trailed Maureen as she lumbered up the stairs. He noticed her red, swollen ankles, her heels sockless and scabbed with blisters. She headed inside and said to the workers, "It's unlocked. Get in there and do what you gotta do. I need a muffin."

The store was bustling with the early lunch crowd, most of them dressed either in full suits or business casual, office workers from the office park across the street that housed obscure insurance companies, tech services, or the occasional specialist in warts or Lyme disease. Everything in the place was neat and radiated politeness and order. The walls were lined with faux brick and decorated with high-definition stock photos of bread and vegetables. In the back row, where Home-Market had chickens dripping with grease, there were wire hoppers filled to the brim with bountiful varieties of freshly baked bread, spotlit by studio lighting. As they approached the counter, a blond woman with a yoga-instructor ponytail wheeled a baking rack filled with square croissants, so fresh from the oven they crackled as they passed.

"Give me one of those hand pie things," Maureen said, pointing to the croissants.

"Oh," the woman quipped, "those aren't ready yet." Despite Maureen's efforts, her eye shadow had smeared her other cheek, and she looked like she'd just been punched in the face.

"Would you just give it to us? We're from HomeMarket. Peace Treaty Day and all that. They look ready to me."

"I'm sorry, our pastries are baked hourly and come out very hot, and I simply *can't* serve them until they're ready. It's a safety issue." Then she added, more coldly, "Even if you're not a customer."

"Jesus Christ." Maureen went on her tippy-toes, wobbling as she peered over the tea displays into the hoppers.

Hai asked the woman if they had anything else like the pastries on the rack.

"Oh, you mean our pain au chocolat? Well, it depends——"

"What a name for a baked good," Maureen said. "You people are something else."

"Flat white at the register!" another worker shouted, setting a drink on the counter.

"What the hell did you just call me?" Maureen said.

"HomeMarket!" said a high-pitched voice from behind them.

They turned to find a five-foot-nothing man with a Pringles mustache rubbing his hands together and grinning. "You guys made it." He did a performative glance at his watch. "Only fifteen minutes late. But when in the service of peace, time, too, must wait. Am I right?"

"I want the chocolate pain," Maureen said, unimpressed.

"Of course." His name was Sam, and he was clearly the manager. "Shelly, please give our friends *four*," he raised his fingers to Shelly but placed them so close to Hai's face he could smell lavender hand sanitizer, "pain au chocolats, please." He pronounced it in French, then turned to them, his grin struggling to show through his overgrown mustache. "They're fresh baked, as always."

Shelly handed Hai the bag of pastries and promptly looked past them, calling for the next customer. Just then a man walked up behind Maureen and tapped her shoulder. She whirled around. "Nacho!" she cried, and started tucking what seemed like invisible strands of hair behind her ear.

The man let out a big laugh and pulled Maureen into his arms. He wore a cowboy-style button-up ringed with sweat at the armpits, his skin the shade of good scotch. "How you been, Mama? You look like you're thriving."

Maureen giggled and brushed his cheek with the back of her hand. "Now I am. And look at you. Florida gave *somebody* a little makeover."

Nacho smiled shyly and looked away. He was a big rig driver for Sysco, a distributor that provided restaurant supplies to a wide array of franchises, including both Panetta and HomeMarket. He was parked across the street to unload a sixteen-wheeler for a Subway inside the Walmart.

Maureen offered him a croissant, but he refused, saying he just had Chinese. "I'll meet you at the van when they're done," she said to Hai, then snuggled into Nacho's arms as they walked out, giddy with each other.

When Hai returned to the van the Panetta crew was already finished. The back was loaded with cardboard crates full of earth-colored biodegradable boxes tied with yellow ribbons. There was a piece of paper taped to one of the crates that had *Be Your Best Self* Sharpied in handwriting that can only be described as soccer mom Comic Sans. Maureen was right. These people were obnoxious. He looked around but she was nowhere in sight, so he climbed into the passenger and waited. After nearly a half hour, a white Sysco truck pulled into the lot. Nacho got out and helped Maureen down the passenger side, all gentleman-like. They hugged and air-kissed, and she hurried toward the van, grinning at the ground, suddenly lithe on her feet.

"That was quick," she said, breathing heavily as she closed the door. "They usually take forever loading their dumb salads. You wait long?"

"Not at all. Who's the guy?"

She waved at Nacho, who stopped on the truck ladder and waved back.

"Oh, Nacho? An old friend. Well, I'll just say it." She removed her cap and fixed her hair. "A friend with benefits. He's not bad-looking, right? A gas station ten with a good heart. What, you don't think I'm out of commission for a little joy yet, do you? His name's short for Ignacio. He said that nachos—you know, the ones you eat—were invented by some guy named Ignacio." She stared dreamily at Nacho's truck. "But he's so full of shit he probably pulled it out of his ass just to get in my panties."

"Guess it worked."

"Fuck you. We got everything?" She turned back and grabbed one of the boxes, squinting at the labeled sticker. "Oh, great, shit take mushroom salad? That's a hard pass for me. I take plenty of shits without them, thank you." She chucked it in the crate and fired up the van.

"At least we got these." Hai shook the bag of croissants, smiling.

IT WAS ALMOST three by the time they returned to East Gladness. Everyone helped unload the boxes, which, to no one's surprise, were full of salads. There were four tiny muffins shoved in the corner of a box of dressing packets. "I knew it!" Wayne said. "Every damn time. It's a scam, man. I don't know why we even do this shit anymore." And he proceeded to carve up a meat loaf for everyone while Russia started making his corn bread and chicken skin sandwiches.

Sony picked up a sickly green slice of something between two fingers, reading the label. "What's a hare-loom tomato?"

BJ peered over his shoulder. "It's when rich people think fucked-up-looking things are more special than normal stuff."

But the crew picked through the spread while tending to the sporadic stream of customers anyway. After cleaning the van of dressing that had spilled on the way back, Hai and Maureen sat on milk crates out back.

"Want me to get you a mac and cheese ice pack?"

"Nah, cum lubes up my joints. And Nacho had plenty." Maureen winked.

"You fucked in that truck?"

"It's got a bed, believe it or not. Oh, and he gave me some Purple Haze too." She nodded to a neatly rolled joint tucked in her apron pocket. A car pulled into the drive-thru. Russia's voice, cut with static, asked how the people inside were doing, and they answered with what they wanted to eat.

The sun had finally come out, cold and weak but making pretty shadows inside the hollowed rooms of the apartments across the lot.

"I just thought it would mean something," said Maureen, letting out a long sigh.

"What are you talking about?" Hai asked, not wanting to look at her.

"That it has meaning when somebody dies. That it leads to something. But it doesn't." Her voice sounded buried. "The only thing that's different is that I can't stand flowers now. All that color just pisses me off. Sometimes flowers just make you wanna quit, you know what I mean?"

"I think so."

She pouted her lips and drooped her shoulders. "Here." She nudged the paper bag of pastries with her foot. "Dig in. Good thing you didn't tell the others we had these."

Hai took a chocolate croissant, the size of his face, from the bag and pulled it apart, the gooey filling reflecting in the fading sun, and handed her half. "Have some chocolate pain," he said. "You earned it."

She laughed and bit into it, the flakes flecked across her lips. "Those fucking lizards," she said, staring at the bit of sweetness in her hand. "They don't know shit about this."

8

Grazina hadn't used her electric scooter in years, but Hai managed to drag it out from a pile of dust-laden coats in the corner of the screen porch. The scooter was hidden for so long Grazina had forgotten she had it until they saw a lady riding one during a news segment on the rise of diabetes and Grazina shouted, "Wait, I have one of those!"

A medical device that went no faster than eight miles an hour, the model was called the SpitFire 2, the *fire* part spelled out with flaming letters. It was like calling a catheter the Eternal Spring, Hai thought. He actually found it plugged in, probably charging for years, and spent half an hour wiping it down. When he finished, Grazina hurried over and hugged the scooter like it was a person. "Oh, thank you, Mother Mary," followed by something in Lithuanian. "I have car now. Finally, I have car like a true American."

"Close enough," Hai said, giving the tires a kick.

Minutes later, they were taking it for a test ride. Grazina was driving, wrapped in a plaid blanket that covered her head against the chill, as he stood behind her on the perch. It was Sunday and the streets were mostly clear. As they rode, slowly dodging the occasional pothole, Grazina pointed out the homes they passed in various stages of dereliction, naming the families they once housed, what they did, what they died of, where they came from. The two rode back and forth through the deserted blocks, Grazina squealing with delight each time she revved the handle and the scooter jolted. They went home only when her hands were numb from cold and there was nothing left to tell of the people in the gutted houses.

THE NEXT DAY Hai decided on a whim to make everyone at Home-Market his ultimate comfort food, Fluffernutter sandwiches. BJ was more bemused than interested in having any. "You work in a goddamned restaurant and you're making everybody eat school lunch." She shook her head. But amongst the tired, repetitive menu, the staff welcomed the relatively novel flavor of peanut butter and Fluff.

"It's about the ratio," Hai said, lining the sandwiches on a cutting board for Wayne to grill. "One-third Fluff, two-thirds peanut butter." It was after the lunch rush and things were slow. Sony was out back cutting tomatoes, and Hai could hear him humming "When Johnny Comes Marching Home," a Union Army drill number. After a while the song was interrupted by someone yelling in the dining area. Hai looked up. The man, judging from the logo on his polo, was on lunch break from the Nissan dealer nearby. "You smell like shit," he shouted at a woman sitting behind him. He had stood up from his meal to confront her. But the woman didn't move. Just sat there staring at one of Sony's origami penguins on the table. It took Hai a minute to realize she was a regular who went by Cookie. She'd come in once a week just about, asking for a cup of hot water and permission to use the restroom, which the staff allowed, figuring she was homeless.

The man turned to BJ, his face pink as ham and his wispy, thin hair coming off his head like cartoon steam. "How can you let someone like this in your business? It's terrible for your customers. She smells like *literal* shit."

Hai had the sudden urge to throw a corn bread at him. You get protective of your regulars, even if they don't buy anything. The woman was scrunched over in her seat, an oily brown coat draped over her shoulders with a matted ponytail poking out the back collar.

BJ asked the man, in her best managerial voice, to calm down, saying that he was free to move to the other side of the room, but he wouldn't have it. He got up and made a scene of dumping his half-eaten drumstick in the trash, then marched back to where the woman was sitting, standing over her with his hands on his hips like a dad in a bad play. "Come on, guys," the man said, exasperated. "I feel sorry for her too. I really do. I'm sure whatever she's going through is real. But you're really not gonna ask her to leave? I'm the one paying here."

The woman was bent over the table gripping an empty Poland Spring bottle. "You can't hurt me. You can't never hurt me. I've been through much worse than being yelled at," she said in a drawn-out monotone, staring at her scabbed knuckles.

The guy shook his head and walked out. He tried to slam the door, but it had pressure-resistant hinges, so it just shut behind him with a slow, tepid whoosh.

Soon the Fluffernutters were ready, and the crew all gathered around Wayne as he dished them out. No one noticed that the woman had gone inside the bathroom, all of them debating whether anyone would buy a grilled Fluffernutter if it was on the menu. The consensus was *no*. At one point the dishwasher girl had to use the restroom and banged on the door. When there was no response, BJ tossed her the key. Seconds later there was an air-splitting scream and everyone rushed to the bathroom. Dishwasher girl came bolting out, hyperventilating, her hands over her head.

BJ walked in and all anyone could hear was "Oh fuck, oh fuck. Shit, shit, no, no, no."

The homeless woman was sitting on the toilet with the lid still down, her head nodding back against a giant framed close-up of corn bread. There was an empty rig on the floor by her feet. Blood ran down her veined arms, phone cord wrapped tight around her bicep. BJ covered her nose and yelled for somebody to call 911. Wayne tried to get the woman down on the floor so she wouldn't fall and knock her head. Her mouth was open like a *Scream* mask. On the woman's thin, sun-wrinkled wrist was a bracelet made of lettered white beads strung with hemp, which spelled out MY BROTHER'S KEEPER.

Wayne asked Hai to grab one of her arms, and they started dragging her down the hall so the medics could get to her faster, BJ on the phone shouting directions to the dispatch. When they passed one of the counters, Wayne, trying to grab the ledge for support, accidentally pulled down a giant bucket of cheese sauce that was set out to cool, and the whole thing dumped on their heads. The cheese sauce, meant for pouring over the mac and cheese for extra creaminess after defrosting, went right into the woman's opened mouth. Luckily, it was lukewarm and didn't burn. Wayne, his face and hair plastered, started frantically scooping out the yellow goo from her mouth. "Fuck," he said, wiping cheese off her eyelids. "What the fuck is happening?"

The fire department came seven minutes later. They were just down the road and lately had been responding more to fent-dope ODs than fires and were ready with the Narcan. It took three long shots up her nose to get her back. Her eyes were fluttering like beat-up moths as they stretchered her away. She was waving her arms around and raging out, which he learned at New Hope can happen with Narcan. Maureen packed a bunch of corn breads in a paper bag and handed it to one of the EMTs, who had a mullet and a lip ring. She shoved it in her cargo pockets and said "'preciate chuh" as she carried the woman away, who was so plastered in cheese she looked like Han Solo trapped in carbonite.

The crew stood there a minute as the ambulance pulled off the lot, BJ wiping her face with her American flag handkerchief. Maureen, who had been clutching her Fluffernutter this whole time, dipped it into the leftover cheese on the side of the bucket, and kept eating.

"Really?" Russia said, watching her.

"I need to change the flavor in my mouth," she shrugged.

Wayne was sitting on a stool by the dishwasher popping a sheet of Bubble Wrap draped to the floor, which he always kept in his backpack. It was his way of de-stressing during breaks.

Hai headed out back for some air, cleaning cheese spray off his glasses with his apron. The sauce was gluing his hair into blobs as it cooled. He sat on the milk crate and tried lighting a cigarette but his fingers weren't working. He had the urge to pop five or six codeines just to sepia things out for a bit. Like putting yellow food coloring in the fish tank in your head.

There were footsteps behind him, then the sound of someone pulling up a crate and sitting down. It was Sony. They nodded at each other but didn't say anything for a bit.

"I saw your mom at CVS."

"What?" Hai faced him. "You talked to her?"

"'Course not, our moms are fighting. Just thought you'd like to know."

"Don't mention anything about me if you see her, okay?"

"Why?" Sony grabbed at a passing fly, then opened his hand—nothing.

"She thinks I'm in Boston," Hai said quietly.

"Then why are you here?"

"Cause I'm *here*. It's complicated."

Sony nodded anyway, which was his way. It was what Hai loved about him.

Hai must have been sweating, because when Sony took his finger and started tracing something on his cheek, it felt slick and wet.

"What you doing?" Hai pulled back.

"Just hold still. I'm writing something."

"What does it say?"

"Okay."

"Okay?"

"Yes. I wrote *okay*."

"Why?" Hai looked at him.

"Because I mean it."

Hai let his face say *okay*.

Once, when Hai was twelve and Sony was ten, they were at the playground near Hai's house at Welles Village. Sony was visiting for the weekend with his mom, and Hai was supposed to take his cousin to the park but didn't really want to. Hai had just gotten a Super Nintendo that week and wanted to spend the day playing *Castlevania*, so he sat on the swings and let Sony roam around the little playscape until enough time passed to go home. After a while Hai heard this commotion and saw Sony surrounded by three or four neighborhood boys. They were teenagers and always acted tough around the younger kids. Hai was never invited to play with them.

"Why are you such an offie?" one of them said. They had surrounded Sony, who was sitting on the ground with his legs splayed and looking up at them, bewildered.

"He's eating old gum from the slide," another one said. "Don't you know that's nasty?"

One skinny kid with a bald head kicked dirt in his face, getting it in his eyes, and Sony started to cry. Another one turned to Hai. "Hey, he your brother or something? Cause y'all look alike."

Hai shook his head and hopped off the swing and walked past them, past Sony crying on the ground. It wasn't until Hai was almost home that Sony caught up, his face dirtier, and told Hai about what happened to him as if his cousin didn't see it, as if he would've stopped it if only he saw. Hai couldn't look at the boy. "That's fucked up of them," he said without stopping. Outside the door, Hai made Sony wipe his face with his shirt before they went in.

"Turn the other way," Sony said now. "I need to get the other side."

Hai turned and offered him his other cheek. Sony wrote *okay* on this side too, Hai feeling every letter.

"There. Now you're double okay."

Hai put his finger on his cousin's forehead and wrote *okay* back. Sony grinned a grin that was supposed to be shy but was actually proud underneath.

THAT NIGHT, as Hai sat on the kitchen floor, the handheld radio crackling with the Lithuanian National Symphony Orchestra, broadcast from Boston, performing one of those melancholic, never-ending opera pieces, Grazina sat hunched in the chair above him, combing out rubbery globs of cheese from his hair. By now it was soothing to hear Lithuanian—not as white noise, but more like friends talking in the next room, inscrutable but warm and familiar.

"The Salisbury steak from Stouffer's is better than the one in the can from Hormel," Grazina said, her lips pursed. "Not by much, but it is. But the spaghetti dinner is on sale for $3.65 at Webster's." Grazina was tapping the orchestra's rhythm on his head as she worked. "You know, we are so lucky in this country. To be able to go to market and get anything we want to eat."

When he didn't reply, she leaned over. "Tough day at the office, huh?"

"You can't tell?"

She yanked a piece of cheese from his hair with a grunt. "Hold still, boy."

The image of the woman's bracelet suddenly flashed in his head. "Hey, you have siblings, don't you?" He remembered her pointing to a brother under the rubble during her attacks.

"One brother. Long ago. But that's another life." Her hand stopped on his head as the music kept on.

"What happened?"

She stood so abruptly he turned around. "Ah, we must be ready!"

"For what?"

"Sit, sit. Go on over there and sit, your hair is good enough now." She clicked off the radio and shuffled to the oven, opened the door, and lifted from it a cake frosted with chocolate.

"Here." Hai went to grab a pot holder but she stopped him.

"It's not hot. I made it this afternoon." She set it on the table along with plates and a knife. "See?" She nodded at the frosting. "It's Nutella cake. My specialty. Go put on the kettle for tea."

While he was prepping the pot, Grazina said softly behind him, "Happy birthday, Labas."

He paused, then remembered that she'd asked him the day of his birth the morning after they met. His eyes fell to the 9/11-themed calendar on the wall. In the square for November 15, scribbled in blue ink, were the words *Labas birthday.*

She pushed up her glasses with her middle finger and smiled.

"Oh, man. It's beautiful." There was a grain in his voice that quivered. "Thank you so much." He leaned forward and they hugged awkwardly, then he flipped the radio back on and the orchestra's final movement swept through the creaking house, muting the wide black river outside—and he was twenty.

9

S ince HomeMarket was the place for "Thanksgiving every day of the year," you'd think it'd be empty the day before actual Thanksgiving, when people would make their own versions of the menu items from scratch, surrounded by loved ones, but you'd be wrong. The store was slammed. It turned out a lot of people preferred to buy Home-Market's side dishes in plastic quarts to reheat the next day, probably claiming they made it themselves. This was in addition to the regulars: folks who had no time to cook, with two or three jobs, nurses on night shifts who slept during the day, veterans from the soldiers' home by the mill, maids who worked overnight cleaning the business park, and truck drivers who would spend Thanksgiving in the backs of gas stations, video-calling their families from oil-sticky laptops.

By noon the store was overrun. Five minutes after Hai brought out a boiling vat of sweet potato pie, Russia's spatula clanked the metal bottom and it was gone. They were so behind they ran out of boilers and had to heat the mac and cheese bag in the dishwasher's hot water rinse to get it started.

The corn bread ran out and Hai was hurrying back to scoop more batter into baking molds when he heard Maureen's gravelly voice behind him. "You know it's cake, right?"

"What's cake?"

"BJ's recipe? It's just cake." She was spraying the molds with a canister of cooking oil the size of a fire extinguisher. "She buys vanilla cake mix in bulk from Costco, right? Then mixes it into the company corn bread recipe." Maureen leaned in and grinned, the whiskey sharp under her breath. "That's it, rook. *That's* the big secret. Cake."

"Sounds pretty ingenious to me." Hai tried to wink but only managed to blink with both eyes.

"I could've been a manager too, you know." Maureen grabbed a metal spoon and started filling the tins with batter. She was offered promotion many times, she said, but turned it down. Managers get $15 an hour and Maureen was already at $13.50. "A buck fifty's not worth the headache, kid. Or the blame. Here, give me a hand."

They loaded the tray together and Hai set the timer. "Well, whatever's in it," said Hai, "BJ's recipe is pretty dope. Everybody's crazy about this stuff."

"*Dope* is right. Corn cake, as our dear leader has concocted it," she bent and scooped more mix into the vat, "is essentially a narcotic. It's all sugar, and my doctor says sugar spikes your insulin, which makes you hungry even if your belly's full of meat loaf. And hunger's good for business." She picked up a corn bread cooling on the rack and let it rest in her palm.

Hai poured in the water and set the mixer as Maureen rambled on.

She broke the corn bread in half and bit into it, dabbing her lips with her apron, and handed Hai the other half. "The reason why it's so good," she lifted her head, "is because it's a lie. And incredible things can come out of lies. Just ask good ole Uncle Sam."

"You're telling me this HomeMarket is the third-most-grossing because of sugar?" Hai swallowed.

"Listen, we deceive people by calling *this* bread. Bread sounds wholesome. You tell the public this is boring old bread, but then it hits their tongues and—*boom*—it's cake! And even if it's the shittiest kind of cake, which it is, they'd think they've eaten the best bread in the world." Sony rushed in to grab a finished rack of corn bread and headed back to the front. "But the question is . . ." She leaned in, her left eye bloodshot and smeared with eyeliner. "At what point, my friend, does the corn bread become corn cake? Can you locate the *crumb* where this deception happens?" She waited for an answer, her arms swaying at her sides.

Hai considered this. Indeed, at what granular material moment did bread become cake? Or was it always cake, falsely named to amplify bread beyond its potential? "That's kinda fucked," he nodded, biting into another one. "I can't tell."

"Once you realize they've lied to you, you lose faith in their fucked-up systems. Searching for another purpose, you start to root for outsiders. Underdogs. But then you realize the underdogs are nowhere to be found, the media has hidden them from you, the prisons and madhouses have locked them up, so you think you're the only one out there losing your mind when in fact there are many like you, trapped in this supposedly free world of work and sleep and endless fucking cakes."

She stopped to gather herself. His eyes started to burn, there was so much whiskey coming off her.

"Let me guess, this all links to the lizards living under the earth's mantle or whatever? Also, are you drunk? I mean, are you *too* drunk? You wanna go ice your knee in the freezer or something?"

She swatted at his chest, a cloud of flour floating between them.

"Me, drunk? What about you, with your pinprick little pupils? You don't think I know you're blasted yourself, Mr. Pill Popper?" He was making his way fast through the bottle of Dilaudid, and lately needed two pills just to make the shifts float by a little smoother.

"Listen here, this country," she lowered her voice, "was purposefully built on war. The reptilians shape-shift into politicians and celebrities, then use these puppets to start wars so they never run out of bad energy to consume. Don't you get it? War is fertilizer for their crops."

Usually quiet save for the occasional wry comment, Maureen was one of those drinkers who turned into a radio program half a flask in.

"But wouldn't scientists, like, be able to measure these bad vibes somehow?"

She laughed. "Oh, my poor naive little boy. Once upon a time, they also said women in Salem had to be burned alive because *science* said they were witches. And then that science became law. Now they use science to get people to bomb each other. Like I said, rook," she suppressed a smile, "everything in this world is *Star Wars*. Good versus evil. Dark and light. There's the Jedi and then there's the Empire. And in case you haven't noticed, I'm Obi-Wan Kenobi, and we're running out of time." She reached into her apron pocket, pulled out her flask, and shook it by her ear—empty. The oven beeped. Her eyes were watery. Another tray of cakes was done.

They blew through the service without anyone taking a break. Russia's voice had gone hoarse from constant shouting into his headset. And between the steam from the heating vats, the dishwasher, the ovens, the place must've been over a hundred degrees. At one point Wayne put his head under the sink faucet out back to cool down. Maureen's sports bra had soaked through her uniform. Sony pushed a stool under her so she could ring people up sitting down for the rest of the shift.

When things died down and the windows darkened, an elderly man with a cane came in, his spine a jittery question mark, and grabbed his steaming tray from the counter and just stood there wobbling a bit. He opened and closed his jaw as if warming it up, then raised his chin, and you could tell there was a Boy Scout somewhere inside him standing up straight. "I'd just like to say thank you for being open during the holidays. You folks, you're saving a lot of people from heartache, you know. From eating alone around Thanksgiving. And . . . and—" He bit down, chin juddering, then shook his head, lifted his cane in a kind of salute, and shuffled away.

The crew didn't believe they were saving anyone from anything— but each of them was filled with a rare and unnameable pride just to hear him say it. Wayne stood tall and tipped his cap, then carefully smoothed out his uniform, which was dappled all over with grease.

THE NEXT DAY, while reading in bed, Hai smelled something burning and left his room to investigate. He found Grazina in the hallway staring out the port window overlooking the river.

"Grazina," he said to her back, his hand hovering behind her. He bumped against one of the many boxes piled along the hall, and she turned around, wiping her eyes with her knuckles.

"Labas, that you?"

He paused, not sure whether to bring up Sergeant Pepper. "It's me. It's alright."

"Labas, please help me. Come here, boy."

She clutched his arm and held it to her side, then stepped into the window's light, where he saw that her face was someone else's. Her hands shook as they hovered around her cheeks. "Look," she said, dipping her head to one side, revealing a cluster of shiny, congealed hair. It looked like syrup had been poured on the side of her head.

"I was trying to curl my hair but it burned. I wanted to make it prettier. I look better with curls." She pointed to the curling iron on the floor. Hai picked it up, clumps of grey stringy curls glued to the prongs, which were still warm and had the sickening sulfuric odor of singed hair.

"Hey. Who's the president right now?" he asked, setting it down on the nearby mantel.

"What? Oh, Obama," she said, annoyed. "I'm not crazy now, I'm serious." She looked at him steadily. "Can you fix my hair? I melted her."

"'Course we can fix it. Hair grows back, remember? *You're* not burned, are you?" He scanned her neck and collarbones.

She shook her head.

Under the shaky vanity light, of which only one bulb out of four remained, Hai started giving the first haircut of his life. Grazina sat on the toilet seat, still and stoic, her lips upturned as the burned hair fell about her feet like dead insects. The clipper, which looked half a century old, buzzed dully as he went along, occasionally stopping when he paused to gauge his work. Soon her head came into shape, the forehead wide and framed under an inch of bangs. Yes, it was a bowl cut, the same one he wore himself, though a bit shorter by necessity, as some hair on her left side had burned nearly to the roots.

He stepped back and took stock of his efforts. "You look kinda like Julius Caesar."

She faced the mirror, turning to catch the angles. "I look more like a Boris," she frowned. "I was pretty once, you know. But what can you do?"

Once he had Grazina settled, Hai biked over the rail bridge toward town, the sky above him a unanimous grey. The streets were also grey save for a few crushed pumpkins here and there, burrowed through by squirrels or smashed by kids who stole them off front porches to hurl at telephone wires. Most of the houses in town were empty, the people inside now gathered at finer homes among their kin. By the time he passed Sgt. Pepper's Pizza, which was closed for the day, the grand opening sign long taken down, Sony was already waiting at the HomeMarket entrance. He was holding a plastic bag from CVS and standing like a tin soldier. "What you got your uniform on for?" Hai said, slowing down. "We're closed today, remember? It's Thanksgiving."

"This is the nicest thing I have. It has a collar." Sony pulled on the polo's neck.

"True. Well, Grazina will like it."

Grazina, upon hearing that Sony was alone in a group home, had invited him over for Thanksgiving dinner. There was a meal planned at his group home, but Sony wasn't into it since, as it turned out, there *were* addicts there after all. Folks with special needs like Sony were on the first floor, while the sober living program was on the second. And the dinner was in the cafeteria for everyone in the building, and a couple of the sober living characters made Sony uneasy.

"I brought Goldfish." Sony raised the plastic bag.

"Then I guess our Thanksgiving meal is complete."

Sony grinned and climbed on the back pegs, and they rode off. The river issued sheets of steam along its banks, gauzing the current from view. The boys didn't speak as they rode but Hai could feel Sony's grip on his shoulders as the plastic bag pattered against his jacket. When they got to the tracks, a freighter was coming toward them and they stopped, the train's force slamming the ground and up through the bicycle as the cars passed.

"So you're Sunny? Like summertime, yes?" Grazina said, turning from her pot of cabbages.

"Actually, no. It's an electronic company from Japan. Well, a TV they made, to be exact."

"Ah." She nodded to herself, tasting a spoonful. "That means you're expensive." Sony looked at Hai, a bit startled, then forced a smile.

"Labas, taste this. Isn't it perfect?"

"Perfect," Hai agreed, licking his lips.

"Fresh cabbages. Lucas brought them over, bless him, my dear boy. He left them on the porch yesterday, and with milk too. No hello, no goodbye. Just drop off and go. He's always so fresh with me, that one."

"Oh, really?" Hai said, going along with it. "Did he come from Paris this time?" He'd been hearing about Lucas lately, but unlike the daughter, Lina, Hai hadn't noticed a single photo of Lucas anywhere.

"No, no, no, he's around." She waved the spoon about. "He comes and goes all the time like a mouse, that boy. Sometimes he talks, sometimes you can't even hear him walk around."

Hai clocked her medicine tray on the counter, just in case, but everything seemed in order.

He poured Sony some grape soda and took the Salisbury steaks from the freezer. When he mentioned how many Stouffer's TV dinners he bought each week, Wayne had offered to make him homemade ones from leftover meat loaf at HomeMarket.

"Oh! These are the Salisbury steaks Wayne was making," Sony said. "Do you know why they're called Salisbury?"

Grazina stopped and put a hand on her hip, suddenly interested. "Why?"

"Because of James Salisbury." Sony sat up. "He was a doctor during the Civil War."

Hai said, "Can we not talk about war for once? It's Thanksgiving."

"No, go on. Please. I've been eating them for thirty years and no one ever explained this to me." Grazina wiped her hands on a rag, turned off the stove, and sat down. "This boy is very interesting," she said to Hai.

James Salisbury, Sony told them, believed that diarrhea, which was rampant among Union soldiers during the war, could be curtailed by consuming coffee and ground beef. "He also believed starches like rice and potatoes caused tumors in the digestive tract, and was the first advocate for a low-carb diet. So he created the Salisbury steak to prove his hypothesis." Sony lifted the ziplock bag of frozen steaks and marveled at it. "It's a true feat of Victorian-era innovation."

Grazina examined the steaks in the bag. "Huh. A kind doctor invented the best dish in the world. No wonder we love it." She turned to Hai, eyes bright. "Don't we, Labas? It's like the carrots! You can taste the goodness in the man's heart. Even a hundred years later." She leaned back and regarded Sony. "Thank you for the history lesson. God can be so good to us, yes?"

Sony chuckled nervously. "Well, I suppose. All things considered."

"You know my father invented fruit salad, right?" Grazina said, one eyebrow cocked with satisfaction. "But of course, the Reds didn't give him no credit. Wish we had some now."

"Your dad invented fruit salad?" Sony faced her.

"Of course. You think I tell tall tales? For what?"

When the meal was over, the dishes cleared, the table wiped and set for tea, Sony suddenly grew quiet. By now, Hai had learned Sony's rhythms through osmosis and could tell when he was drifting further into the sea of himself. Grazina, also sensing a shift in the air, poured the Goldfish into a bowl and sat down. "What's the face for, boy?"

"Hey, buddy." Hai leaned in. "You good? You wanna go back or something?"

Sony stared into his cup of untouched tea.

Grazina, catching on, finished chewing a handful of Goldfish and said, "You got the blues now, huh? It can happen on holidays." She scanned the tiny kitchen. "Great, and we're out of rolls to step on."

"I can just take you home and you can go to bed. It's no problem," Hai said.

Sony's hands pressed the table so hard there were heat imprints on the wood when he finally moved them.

"My mom's not getting out." He shook his head.

"What? How do you know?"

"I saw her a few days ago. I took the bus up to York Corrections after work."

"Why didn't you tell me? I would've gone with you."

He shrugged.

"How come she's not getting out?"

"Your mama's in prison?" Grazina put down her tea, eyes wide. "You *are* very interesting."

"I dunno why," said Sony. "They told me all these things, but I didn't catch much of it."

"Mommy's gonna be fine. Easy now." Grazina got up and wrapped her arms around Sony's head. "She's in American prison, after all. Not so bad, right? She won't die. You gonna hold her again, like this. You're expensive, and Jesus doesn't let valuable things go to waste."

"I would've helped," Hai said. "I don't care if our moms are fighting. We're cousins. Just tell me next time."

"You never helped before. How would I know you would now?" Though his voice was muffled in Grazina's gown, the words stung.

Hai cleared the table. Sony wasn't wrong.

"I should've made my honey carrots," Grazina pouted. "We could all use some about now." She then looked down at her waist and frowned, her palms opened at her sides. "Wait a minute, boys, how do I untie this thing anyway?" She let out a nervous laugh and tried again, but her hands only seemed to wriggle a bit and hover there. She stopped and looked about, confused.

Sony pulled the string on her apron knot and it came loose.

"Ha! Look at this one, Labas! A little genius, this boy."

BEFORE LONG THEY settled on the couch to watch a movie. Sony had brought a VHS of his favorite film, *Gettysburg*, starring Jeff Daniels, a movie he'd been watching since he was ten. This was actually his third copy, the others lost or worn out from being played on a nearly endless loop. Every time Hai visited Sony as a kid, it was on in the background like a kind of weather.

Sony was giddy as he pushed the tape in the old RCA and settled in between Hai and Grazina. "Do you know this is the battle that changed the course of the war?" he said as the opening credits came on. "And it was all an accident. Lee lost contact with his cavalry officer, Jeb Stuart, and wandered right into the Army of the Potomac. Can you believe it? The biggest turning point in the course of our country happened because somebody got lost." You could hear the smile in his voice in the dark.

"I believe it," Grazina said, grabbing a handful of Goldfish from the bowl.

The movie was over four hours long, and Hai could hear Grazina drifting in and out of sleep, snoring, then startling awake by rifle volleys and lunging at the bowl of Goldfish. Sony sat up the whole time mouthing the lines, grand speeches by grey- and blue-clad officers urging their "boys" to die in one bayonet charge after another.

"It's not so hard to kill," Grazina said sleepily when a Confederate soldier was impaled by a bayonet as he ran up a tree-lined hill. "You just touch something until its color changes."

It was such an odd thing to say that Hai bent over to check on her. "Grazina," he whispered.

"What?"

"Who's the president?"

She pointed at the TV. "Lincoln."

It was good enough. By the film's crescendo, she was passed out for good. "This is Pickett's Charge." Sony swayed in his seat. "Robert E.

Lee's biggest mistake in the war. Arguably. A suicide march against Meade's cannon barrage, the largest in the history of all Napoleonic-style battery engagements, ricochets heard all the way in Washington." He leaned forward, munching on more Goldfish.

"Let me guess, you're about to tell me this is where the picket fence came from?"

"No, the charge was named after one of the generals, George Pickett of Virginia. He never forgave Lee for ordering it. And for good reason. Pickett lost two-thirds of his division in just forty-five minutes. Lee was an overrated tactician, if you want my honest opinion. Not even close to Grant."

As the bodies piled up during the failed "charge," which to Hai looked more like a parade of bearded men walking slowly across a smoldering field and getting slaughtered in droves, Sony said, so quiet he barely heard it, "Everything bad always happens to the South," and crossed his arms and fell back on the couch, deflated.

"What you talking about? Hey—you okay? You're acting weirder than usual today."

"The South always loses. That's the rule."

"As they should. They were, like, huge dicks. Look." Hai gestured at the screen. "They walked across this big-ass field and got shot up just to keep slavery going."

Sony wasn't listening, though; he was drifting deeper into something. "My dad was a corporal for the South and they got smashed. Now he's in a shack in Vermont and all he does is listen to old records and cry to himself reading books about maps."

"You're joking, right? That's a whole *nother* war."

"I know. But the norths and souths are the same everywhere on the compass. It's just the rule." He turned to Hai, his mouth slightly parted. "Hey. You think my mom's gonna be okay? She's got nothing to do with any kind of south, right?"

Outside, moonlight broke through the clouds, making the abandoned houses through the window seem new and clean.

Out of desperation or stupidity, he couldn't tell, Hai pinched a single Goldfish and made it swim toward Sony, then toward where his head scar began. Sony fixed his eyes on the cracker as Hai made it swim down his cousin's scar river—just like the one running outside the house, the skin smooth and reflecting the light from the corpses on TV—all the way back to the nape of his neck, where it left the river, swimming around his head, past Sony's eyes, which had brightened with a mix of confusion and delight, and into Hai's opened mouth.

Sony giggled, covering his teeth like a child. "That's gross!"

Hai shrugged, chewing. "Tastes a lot better now, though."

They settled into the end of the film. After the credits rolled, and Sony was asleep, Hai slipped upstairs to call his mother. Alone in the dark, it was good to hear her voice. He was sorry he couldn't be there for the holiday, and she told him it didn't matter since they never celebrate anyway. But he knew his absence, like all the other times, hurt. She must've decorated so many women's nails with turkeys and bright orange leaves and pumpkins all week, her clients gushing about their big family plans. "I'm doing well, Ma," he said. "I'm making money too. As an assistant in a medical lab on campus. It's not much but it's something."

"I knew you would, baby," she whispered. He said he'd send her a check, which she refused, saying he should repay instead the money owed from his first time at college. And when she mentioned she had made herself rice porridge and was sitting by the altar "eating it with Bà ngoại," he couldn't bear it and made an excuse to wrap up the call and hung up.

He came down with blankets and made makeshift mats on the floor for him and Sony, who stirred, disoriented, then crawled down from the couch and stretched out. Hai laid Grazina on the sofa, removed her glasses, put her bottom denture in a glass of water, draped a quilt over her shoulders, and finally lay down himself. He stared at the ceiling. He could hear Sony scratching his head, probably running his finger through his scar, something he did in moments of idleness. Then Sony said something, just under his breath, either to Hai or to just give it to the air, he couldn't tell. "Why do I feel so terribly sad?"

That was it.

Hai kept very still, pretending to sleep. He told himself if Sony said it again, if he asked for anything else of him, anything in the world, he'd bolt up and tend to it, he'd throw himself at the boy and answer any questions he'd ever had. He would never walk past him while the bullies called him names again. But Sony didn't say anything else. And the night smoothed out into a quiet stillness, with only the wind creaking the eaves of the house. And Hai didn't know which of them fell asleep first, but he hoped it was Sony. He hoped it was his cousin with a river running through his head, full of Goldfish.

10

They are somewhere in Virginia. Outside the windows of Ma's rust-and-tan Toyota, foaming green pastures blur to deep golds in the late afternoon sun. At the edge of the fields is a mountain range that, according to the map at the last rest stop, is called the Blue Ridge.

"They have chicken coops in the front yard here," says Bà ngoại. She's clutching the handle above the window with both hands, a habit she picked up riding communal vans through rocky, unpaved roads in the Tiền Giang province of her youth. "An hour ago, the coops were on the side of the houses." As usual, no one's listening to her but Hai. His mother's driving, her sister, Kim, in the passenger, and he's in the back pressed to the door, Sony in the middle, their grandmother on the far side, and farther away still in her mind.

"I would free them if I lived here. Go out at night and cut the cages loose." She chuckles to herself and turns to Hai, her eyes wet for no reason.

"What's funny, Bà ngoại?" Sony says. "You have a joke inside you?"

She puts her arm around him and he scrunches from the touch. "Helicopters are funny," she says. "This one is driven by my daughter."

Sony wrenches himself free. "I'm gonna drive a helicopter one day in the army and take you around so you can see how they build chicken coops in Canada."

Bà ngoại reaches into her pajama pockets, removes two Halls cough drops, unwraps them, and shoves one into Sony's mouth. Then she looks over to Hai. "Open up."

Hai opens his mouth and she chucks it in, hitting his bunny teeth. "Home run! Home run!" she shouts in English, slapping the roof and laughing.

"What are you saying back there?" Aunt Kim asks in Vietnamese. She's eating pistachios and hurling the shells out the window.

"Would you stop littering?" Ma says.

"Oh, don't be so stuck up." Aunt Kim spits more shells out the window. "It's not littering if it's part of nature."

They're on their way to Florida, where Kim is going to scope out a nail salon to purchase. It's a big deal cause it means Kim and Sony would leave the family behind—and Ma's been nervous about it all week. As they were nearing Virginia, Sony had begged his mother to take the detour they're now on.

"How far away *are* we anyway?" Ma asks. "It's creepy around here." They pass a makeshift junkyard filled with broken-down carnival rides.

Tied around Hai's neck with a string is a GigaPet, a palm-sized device in which a pixelated "pet" can be fed and cared for until the battery dies, the rave of every preteen in 2001, which means he's eleven and Sony is nine. Which means it's August and the Twin Towers will stand for five more weeks in New York.

Aunt Kim unfolds a map and stares at it awhile. "I think twenty more minutes. Maybe less." Kim faces Sony, points a finger at him. "This place better be worth it. It's an hour out the way and your auntie is driving with a headache."

Sony nods vigorously. "It's very important, Mommy. I promise," he says in English.

The cough drop makes Hai's eyes water, and the gold hills start to smear as the car chugs down the one-lane road.

SOON THE TRAILERS and junkyards give way to a sleepy town laid up on a bank of hills overlooking horse farms and stretches of mown lawns big as municipal parks. Ma and Aunt Kim are trying to figure out the turns. The town center fills no more than a few blocks, which they circle, Aunt Kim scanning the house numbers. As they turn onto one of the streets, Sony shouts, "This is it! This is the street. Go to number eight, Auntie! Eight Washington Street."

They park on a quaint little brick-lined street with polished black lampposts, a coffee shop, a wine store, and a consignment boutique with a chalk sign set out on the walk claiming it *The cutest darn place for miles*. A young couple in their twenties stop to take a selfie with a Polaroid under a hanging pot of foaming mums. Everything is clean. The sidewalks, impeccably white, sparkle as the late sun washes over them.

Bà ngoại gets out and stretches her arms. "What are we doing here, guys? Is this Florida yet?"

"We're stopping here so Sony can learn something," Aunt Kim says. "And it better be quick."

"Is this a school?" Ma asks, frowning up at the high windows.

"You have to go in the back." Sony darts down the gravel drive toward the rear of the house. He opens the wooden gate that leads to the backyard and waves them through. The family enters what looks like a small vegetable garden, the names of local produce markered on wooden stakes. There's a shed where vines have overtaken the copper paint, the leaves motionless in the dead afternoon. Everything's still and silent save for their steps on the gravel.

"They have mint!" Bà ngoại says, pinching off a few leaves and cupping her nose with them. "And look! Eggplants!"

"This is somebody's house," Aunt Kim says. "They're gonna shoot us. I heard they can shoot you in some states without even asking."

"Don't be stupid. No one's going to shoot anyone. Hey," Ma calls to Sony, "hurry up and learn about these vegetables." She searches her purse for some gum. "I'm starving."

Just then the back door flings open and they all turn around. Sony is so excited he literally holds his head in his hands. A woman in a pantsuit with puffy blond hair appears. "Hello? Can I help y'all?" She scans their faces, blank as caught animals.

"Say something!" Ma hisses at Hai.

"Um, hello, ma'am," he tries in English. "We, um . . . we want to learn about, uh . . ."

"Oh! Of course," the woman chirps. "Don't be shy. Come on in, we're about to start in a bit." She holds the door open with a wide, impenetrable smile, her dangling earrings glinting like needles as they file through with lowered heads.

The entry door opens into a basement lined with fieldstone walls, the air drastically cooler than the heat they've been trapped in all day. It smells of dampness and Lysol.

The blond woman leads them to a counter. "So, three adults and two kids, right? That's thirty-two dollars."

"How much is it?" Ma asks Hai, digging into her purse.

"Three and two," Hai says in Vietnamese.

"Five dollars?"

"No, three and two. Here." He grabs Ma's purse, much to the clerk's surprise, and hands the lady two twenties.

"It's *that* much?" says Aunt Kim, glaring at Sony, who's holding Bà ngoại's hand and beaming.

"This place has ghosts," Bà ngoại says, her eyes tracing the ceiling.

The lady gives them blue stickers to put on their shirts. Bà ngoại puts hers on her forehead and convinces Sony and Hai to do the same. "This will ward them off. They'll think we're shamans."

The white lady then calls for someone named Carol, who immediately manifests from behind a curtained back room. A soft-spoken and cheery middle-aged woman with frameless glasses, close-cropped hair, and green cargo pants, Carol ushers them into a holding area where six other people, all adults, are lingering about.

Carol marches to the front of the room, clears her throat, and says, "Okay, folks. Welcome to the Stonewall Jackson Historical House and Museum! My name is Carol and I'll be your docent today. Your presence and support are very important to the preservation of history and her artifacts. But first," she gleefully holds up her index finger, "we're going to show you a segment of our award-winning short film on the man—and the legend—himself." She then twirls, in a full circle, and steps aside. A few seconds later the lights dim and a film plays on a TV mounted on the wall.

The film is about ten minutes long and talks mostly about this old man's life, the narration marked by dates, not of his military accomplishments but of the regular things he did every day: the path he took each morning to get to the Virginia Military Institute, where he taught, the gardening books he enjoyed, quotes from his letters to former cadets, foods he liked to eat, how his first wife, Elinor, died during childbirth, the baby stillborn, and his early years spent teaching literacy to Black families in Lewis County, West Virginia. This last bit was mentioned three times. The film ends with a slow zoom-in of Jackson's bronze statue at the University of Virginia, accompanied by sweeping violin music.

The lights come on and, with the images of Jackson's grandfather-like benevolence fresh in their minds, Carol directs them across the hall into a kitchen, where various foods are spread over every available surface: hand pies, dinner rolls, loaves of golden bread, wedges of cheese, fruit and vegetables heaped into wicker baskets or laid out on cutting boards—all of it bountiful, perfect, and fake, each item molded from bright, scintillating plastic.

"What's happening?" Bà ngoại asks in Vietnamese, loud enough for a few people to turn around. "They gonna cook for us?"

"This is a museum," Sony whispers in English. "To learn about Stonewall Jackson."

"Just be quiet, Ma," Aunt Kim hisses. "If you're hungry we'll get chicken tenders after." Aunt Kim grins at Carol, urging her to continue.

"Okay, so I'm gonna say right out the gate that the Jacksons *did* own slaves. But," Carol notes, her smile more a grimace as she pushes up her glasses, "we call them servants here—since that was how they were referred to by the Jackson family." She pauses and looks around the room. "We try to be contemporaneously accurate is all." The other visitors, all white, nod. "Two of the servants had even *asked* for Jackson to buy them. Which was very common," Carol emphasizes. "Jackson even allowed one of them, Albert, to work and give over his wages, thereby purchasing his own freedom in the end."

A woman in the group touches her chest with admiration.

While Sony is rapt with attention, Hai is bored out of his mind and wants nothing more than to get to a Motel 6 down the road and watch WCW using the free cable they don't have at home. He checks his GigaPet, but it's sleeping and doesn't want to play. "Useless," he mumbles, shoving it in his pocket.

In Jackson's study upstairs, Carol takes time explaining the types of furnishings used in the period: the oilcloth runner, the grass-weave mats rolled out for summertime, an original wall hanging, Jackson's chairless desk—the professor had poor digestion, she explains, and preferred to prepare his lectures standing up. Now here's the parlor where Jackson, against his austere Presbyterian beliefs, would be overcome and dance the polka to his wife's piano solo after dinner. Here the parlor chair facing a wall where the professor would sit to meditate and memorize his lectures. There the rug where he'd roll around playing with the children of his guests, for he preferred their company over the stale adults.

In his bedroom, the group is shown the toilet where the general would relieve himself, a four-post bed, a chair draped with a blue uniform and cap, the kind Jackson wore as a professor at the military academy before joining the Confederacy. At the corner of the bed is a small woven basket. Carol reaches inside and passes around laminated photos of Jackson, most of them showing a clean-shaven man, his pale eyes creating the curious mix of a mournful yet piercingly determined gaze. "He was mostly clean-shaven," Carol offers, nodding to Jackson's original shaving table, its mirror now holding the faces of the visitors, who take turns filling the oval that once held his face.

"Any questions before we move on?" Carol asks.

Sony shoots up a hand in the back but she doesn't see it. "Did he ever come back here after Second Bull Run?"

"You gotta speak up." Hai yanks on Sony's shirt. But Carol's already in the next room.

"Could you imagine living here?" Ma says, examining a polished wood sideboard. "How much *sweeping* you'd have to do?"

"I'd live here if my husband was rich," Aunt Kim says.

"And you can find a rich husband in Connecticut." Ma shoots her a glare.

Just as Ma and Aunt Kim leave, Bà ngoại grabs Hai's arm. "Hai, I need your help."

"What is it, Grandma?" Sony asks in English.

"What's he saying to me?" she asks Hai. "Never mind. I have to pee. Can you boys watch the door?"

"Okay, let me look for a bathroom," Hai tells her in Vietnamese. Before he could take a step further, she grabs a lidded earthenware pot from a wall shelf, clearly an antique, and puts it on the floor.

"Bà ngoại!" Sony squeals as Bà ngoại squats over the pot, the sound of dribbling filling the room, and faces the boys, her eyes shut with relief.

Hai covers Sony's mouth. As she finishes, a patter of footsteps approaches. "Hurry up."

"Get me that towel!" Bà ngoại says.

Hai hands her an embroidered cloth hanging on a rocking chair. She cleans herself, tosses the rag in the pot, and closes the lid. She's putting the pot back on the shelf when Carol circles back. "Okay, folks, so we're gonna come right through here back to the foyer—oh, oh dear! Here, let me get that, hun." She rushes to Bà ngoại as Sony and Hai back up against a wall. Carol takes the pot and helps her hoist it on the top shelf with a grunt. "Woo—heavy. They don't make 'em like they used to." She pats the pot on the shelf. "Now. Please don't touch the objects. They're *originals*. I know, I get it, it's tempting. History is fun." She turns to the boys. "Isn't it, guys?"

Sony and Hai both nod. Bà ngoại shrugs and gives them a wink.

After a brief stint in the dining room, where a table is set for an elaborate dinner, the tour draws to a close. There, on a side table beside yet another bowl of fake fruit, lies Jackson's leather-bound family Bible, the girth and size of a chopping block. "It was in here that he would pray each morning. And sometimes," Carol adds with a smile, "he'd even lock out his wife if she was late to prayer."

The tour ends here—on faith. Faith and nourishment, like how it began.

A minute later they're ejected into the gift shop, a tiny room renovated from some kind of ominous basement cellar. Among racks of both Union and Confederate military caps, you can also buy a pack of playing cards printed with every state flag in the Confederacy. There's also a slim graphic novel of Confederate leaders marketed to children seven and up. On one shelf, flanked on each side by illustrated biographies of Jackson and Robert E. Lee, are copies of Dr. Seuss's *Green Eggs and Ham*. Above that, a vibrant array of garden seed packets for cucumbers and pink asters. Aunt Kim bought a tin of Altoids mints by the register.

The door opens and they spill into the bright garden, the humid air filled with sweetgrass, dried hay, and cow manure from nearby farms.

A digital thermometer above the post office reads ninety-five degrees. The Virginian sun shimmers in Aunt Kim's auburn-dyed hair, now black at the roots at summer's end. "Did you boys learn a lot? Tell me, why was that man so important anyway? Or was it just cause he had a big house?" She turns to Ma. "Don't you hate it when they're famous just because they own something big?"

"He was a military genius," Sony chirps, "just like my dad."

"Your father's a bum," Aunt Kim snaps. "He doesn't even eat Vietnamese food anymore, you know that?"

"Looks like all that white man did was stand around and pose for photos," Ma says, opening the car door. "If I was famous for standing around with one hand on my hip, I'd never let anyone in my house—even after I'm dead."

From across the street, a pair of female cadets, their white uniforms bathed red in the shoulder-high sun, brush by, their heads nearly touching as they laugh at a tattoo on one of their arms.

Half hour later, the family's sitting on a curb in the McDonald's parking lot eating chicken nuggets.

"Happy birthday, boy!" Bà ngoại says, and dunks her nugget into Sony's BBQ sauce.

"Stop, Bà ngoại, no!" he giggles, turning away from her as she pulls him close. Ma and Aunt Kim are next to them, chatting between bites of Filet-O-Fish sandwiches about the nail salon in Florida, what it would cost, what it would mean to be so far apart from each other, long silences widening between their voices.

Hai stares across the vast highway, the cars blaring past on their way to September, to school and work, and leans into Sony, their shoulders imperceptibly touching.

"I'm glad we're out of that place," Bà ngoại says to Hai. "It was full of demons." She peels the blue sticker off her forehead and flings it into the breeze. Hai and Sony do the same as Sony smiles, a spot of BBQ sauce on his chin.

That's when Hai woke and saw Sony's face, stone-blue with sleep and moonlight, his steady breaths mixed with Grazina snoring nearby on the couch. It was Thanksgiving Day in East Gladness and Bà ngoại was long gone, along with that summer day so many years ago. But Hai whispered it anyway: "Happy birthday, Sony."

11

"Sergeant Pepper, it's time. You know what to do, yes?" Grazina's head cocked to one side, the bangs of her bowl cut damp with sweat. It was night, and they were sitting under the dining room table, back in the trenches. "Here." She pulled his hand to her chest, where a smooth, cold mass filled his palm. "I'm wearing amber. My grandmother's. With this we can make it through the dark. Amber is special stone, from the spirits in the forest—shh." She pressed her hand on his stomach and glanced around as if someone might overhear them. "Come, they're closing in," she whispered, lifting a page from a coupon catalog that was hanging down from the table. The moon coming through the various lace curtains had the effect of light falling through a canopy of trees.

Lately the medication's effects were waning and Grazina's mind started swaying earlier than the usual six-hour window. Her next doctor's appointment, her first since Hai got here, was in a month, and a van sent from the local hospital was to take her, and he was hoping they'd up her dose and get ahead of it.

Hai pretended to listen. "That's German all right. About fifty yards out to the left. An outpost. No more than three of them. Let's steer wide."

She vanished deeper under the table, and he followed. "Their voices are louder," she said over her shoulder. "I'm not scared. You scared, Sergeant?"

"I'm a long way from home."

"How old are you anyway?" She reached back and examined his hand, raising it to the moonlight.

He considered lying but told her the truth. "Twenty."

"Only three years ahead of me, then," she said. "I didn't know sergeants can be so young." She let his hand fall and searched his face.

"I'm a fast learner."

"I can see." She brushed her hair behind her ear and he thought he saw her smile.

"Come on." He ducked out from the table into the sweet-smelling night, tinged with wheat and tall grass baked from the day's heat, which he could feel, a week into December in New England, radiating from the earth as they staggered, hand in hand, through the meadow at the end of a horrific war and the start of their anachronistic adulthoods.

The cuckoo clock next to the 9/11 calendar read 4:51 a.m. "It's almost daybreak and we have to rest for the night. Here." He pointed to the pantry by the back door. "It looks like some kind of shed."

Grazina stopped, crouched low in the high grass, and poked her head above the swaying blades. "Most likely a hunter's cabin," she noted, raising her chin to see better. "But it's not the season yet. Might be empty. Worth a try, no?"

Above them, a plane, a real one, a domestic flight out of Bradley International, droned through the clear night, its engine humming beyond the warped windows. Grazina scanned the ceiling, alarmed. "What kind is that, Sergeant?"

He skimmed his brain for something suitable. "B-52," he tried, looking up.

"Will they bomb?"

"Let's go inside. Daylight's breaking over those hills." He brushed past her and waded into the high grass, the blades scratching his arms.

He held open the pantry door and Grazina went in. They sat on the floor; she leaned back to catch her breath, her blue face shining wet. He took a sheet of paper towel from a nearby roll and dabbed her cheeks and forehead. The plane was gone and the river could be heard again, which also sounded like wind through field grasses outside the hunter's shed. The past was synthesized into the now through visions forged in their brains. Grazina pushed aside a can of corn, then pressed her face into the hollow in the shelf.

"The Krauts must be sleeping," she said. "But there's a light from a farmhouse on that hill. Are they enemies, you think?"

"I think they're just people," he said to the back of her head, exhausted.

"They must be scared. They must have little ones. It's a big house. Oh, look—a fox!" She moved aside and waved for him to look. He pressed his face into the wall, and there, beyond the meadow, just before a huddle of trees, a small pool of water blinked twice from the animal's crossing.

"Lapės," Grazina said. "I've seen two since Vilnius."

The pantry's warm quiet made his eyelids heavy. He rubbed his temples and searched the walls for something to move the plot along and spotted a light switch and flicked it on. A bare bulb swung into view. Grazina flinched from the brightness and glanced around. She ran her fingers along the cans on the shelf. "What's this?" she said, picking one up.

"Green beans."

She frowned. "Where's my mother? Is she with the border agent already? I just saw her at the post office." She scanned the pantry as if they were in an open, public space, which made him nervous. Two timelines he could manage, but not a third. She said something in Lithuanian, then picked up a packet of penne, but was startled by the crinkling cellophane and flung it to the floor like it was alive.

"Who is the president?" he heard himself say. By now this phrase, lobbed at her in desperate hours of the night, had become more prayer than inquiry.

"Mama," she said, her voice shaking.

"Try again, Grazina. You can do it."

"My mama, she put my blanket in the cookie box." She studied him as if he were a stranger who had just sat down beside her on a bench. She bolted up and started moving cans and boxes from one shelf to another, knocking a couple off, barely missing her feet.

"Stop. Hey, we're in the shed, remember? It's a hunting shed, in Germany."

With both hands, she pushed aside a heavy bag of flour, a hole in it spraying the powder over their heads. Behind the bag was a large round tin box, rusted at the edges. She asked him to help her take it down. The box was hefty and furred with dust, the kind that won't come off when you blow it but sticks to your hands.

"Go on, open it." She nodded at the box, which looked to have once held those Danish butter cookies you get at Walgreens. Inside was a folded beige cloth. When he tried to lift it, he found it bigger than expected, and soon a king-size sheet unraveled across their laps, filling the pantry.

"Jesus Mary!" Grazina gasped and held the sheet to her nose, inhaling. When she looked up, her green eyes were wet with smile tears.

"Do you know what this is, Labas?"

Labas, he thought. *We're back. We're turning the corner. We can go to bed soon.*

"Can you tell me tomorrow?" He glanced around the pantry, making sure the German meadows were gone from his head as well.

"No, sit. Sit down." She smiled and patted the floor next to her. "I want to show you." Her eyes were clear and steady as she blinked away the tears. She unfurled the cloth, her fingers jittery, as if she were touching parchment from the Mount. "Look," she whispered.

All over the sheets were drawings. At one point colored in, the hues had been rubbed pale through the years, the stitching frayed. They seemed made in the hand of a child.

"This belonged to Marta the owl-girl," Grazina said real soft. "She was my best friend. She was an owl who was too fat to fly. She was closer to me than my own name. See? This is her house." She pointed with a crooked finger to a wooden cottage with a red roof, surrounded by plump tulips. Beside the house were a few spotted chickens and a small car. Marta lived here with her mom and dad and her little brother, Grazina said, the words coming out of her as if from a recording.

"Who made these, your daughter?" he asked. "They're pretty."

"Heavens no. My daughter is a much better artist. She doesn't know I made these. I used to have nightmares when I was girl, so I draw on my sheets to keep busy. My mother saw this and bought me colored pencils. I still do it now—seventeen and still drawing on my sheets." She chuckled, then shyly looked away.

"No, wait. What about Labas? Labas, remember? You're not seventeen. You're eighty-two."

But she wasn't listening. She pulled the rest of the blanket out of the tin, searching it for something. "This is the lake near the village. Marta used to swim here in summertime."

Hai stared at the faint blue oval lined with cattails and a few ducks whose color was so washed they resembled phantoms floating under the water.

"In Lithuania, you have to wait until August to swim and not be too cold. Here," she pointed at the shelf, out the shed's window again, "here in Germany, it's warmer." Marta didn't know how to swim until she was sixteen, Grazina explained. That's when this boy from her village began to teach her. The son of a miner, he was four years older and, with wide shoulders, a very good swimmer. When he was teaching her, his hands under the water were like two fish. Hai noticed her eyes were shut as she spoke. "The fish swam all around Marta—and she was very slow swimmer. She was only good at floating." This happened many times, she went on. Each time Marta swam with the boy, the fish would come to the surface from deep, deep in the water, probably from the very bottom of the lake, and start to bite. "But Marta never wanted to upset him. Since he was trying very hard to teach her." So Marta went on laughing along with him until there were hundreds of fish of all kinds, surrounding her. "Everyone loved the miner's son," Grazina said. "At twenty-one, he volunteered for Lithuanian Liberty Army and was about to bring great honor to the village. But one day, Marta and the boy swam one last time, two weeks before he was to go off to the front."

Hai hadn't noticed he was sweating until a drop fell from the tip of his nose onto the sheet.

"That last day, in September, it was very hot. By now Marta could swim good. She no need the boy's help." Grazina pressed on, telling how the fish came up again soon as the miner's son approached. "The fish, big as the forearms of farmers," she continued. "And Marta closed her eyes and put out her hands." Grazina stopped to mime this. "Then she swam as fast and as hard as she could, just like the boy taught her. She grabbed at the water in front of her, you know, like she was stuck inside a big garbage bag, until it tore it away." But only more water came, muddy water from the river bottom. And at last she broke through something hard and glided up to the light falling through the surface "like spears thrown by the old warriors in fairy tales." And she came to the surface and saw him, the miner's boy, whose name was Filip. "He was white like a summer rose. Very still and very quiet beside Marta, smiling at the sky." Grazina stared at the shelf while she said this. "A dead soldier who never killed anyone." Grazina touched one of the ducks on the sheet. "Marta ran home, fast as she could. Three days later, the priest made a beautiful, glorious eulogy about the brave soldier who had drowned before he could be a hero. And Marta sat in the third row the whole time, listening while the old miner knelt before his boy's coffin, crying like a toddler."

Grazina stopped and neither of them said anything for a while, the air suddenly dense, suffocating.

"And what happened to Marta?"

She stared at him hard and long. "Nothing."

"What do you mean? *Something* had to happen." He sat up, suddenly needing the end of a story he wasn't sure he wanted.

"How can I know what Marta knows? Some things belong to those who lived them." Grazina searched his face. "Who knows what happens to owls that are too fat to fly. Maybe they swim." She turned away. "She was just a girl from long ago. No one remembers her but me."

He knew enough to nod.

She lifted the sheet from the tin box. On the bottom was an envelope. Grazina handed this to him, the edges worn soft as tissue, and nodded for him to open it. He broke the seal, revealing a thin packet of hundred-dollar American bills. There must have been over four grand.

"Jonas left this for me before he went to God. He knew it would come in handy on a journey like this. Use it to take us to London, Sergeant. The border agents will be suspicious of a girl with this much money."

By now Hai had lost track of the timelines. "What do I do with this?" he said. He thought of Sony, of Aunt Kim's bail. He thought of everything, the envelope growing damp in his warm hands. He tried to put it back, but Grazina pushed it against his chest with a pleading look. "Take it," she ordered. "It's my money and I'll do with it as I like. In war, money becomes paper again." She held the envelope to his sternum.

As he wrapped the sheet around her shoulders, deciding that it'd be best to let her sleep where she was rather than risk more misadventure on their way to bed, she jolted up, searched the cramped walls, then took a box of plastic baggies from the shelf, examining the package. "Oh, God. It's Obama."

"Who?"

"The president's Obama, yes?" she said, her eyes cartoonishly open behind her glasses.

"That's right," he said. "And it's December 2009."

"Of course, Labas." She poked at the envelope in his hand, where her name was printed from an old statement from East Gladness First Eagle Bank. "What's this? Lina sent me a letter?"

Clocking her lucidity, he flipped the envelope over, hiding her name. "It's just my pay stubs. For taxes and stuff." He shrugged and tucked it into the waistband of his boxers.

"I remember the president this time, right?" She leaned back on the wall and sighed. "He has big smile, like you."

Hai had his head between his knees, unable to meet her eyes.

"Marta was a big owl. She couldn't fly, so she floated, like a duck," Grazina said dreamily. Her eyes were closed, her head resting now on his shoulder. Sleep pulling her down at last. "Words cast spells. You should know this as a writer. That's why it's called spelling, Labas."

After a long silence, from which he thought she had fallen asleep, she said, "I wish I knew you long ago. We would've helped each other. Wouldn't we?"

"We would."

Just as the blade of light under the pantry door started to glow with day, he shut his eyes and left the world for a while, the world their mothers brought them in, the one that they, in their hurry, barely survived. But he would survive, he decided once and for all, the money pressed against his wet skin. He was the richest he'd ever been.

12

They had just clocked out and were sitting out back, the cigarette a red bead passed between their lips in the cobalt dark.

It was one of those days where you work your skin off and have no desire, no strength even, to go home. There was a kind of luxury to be amongst this place of sweat and ache and yet sit and suck a cigarette down to its soggy nub and have no one tell you anything because you're off the clock. A dignified, defiant rest.

"Sick boots," Russia said.

"These?" Hai tilted his head and regarded his boots from an angle.

"Those the ones Nike made for the army, right? My cousin's friend had 'em when he came back from Afghanistan. Said he dodged so many RPGs, those things should be sponsored by the NFL." Russia laughed, his buckteeth flashing in the blue.

"At least he came back."

"At least he came back. He told us a story about it too, after a crazy meth binge one time. Like, this guy was tweaking for days, right? I'm talking just in a shed, without a bucket or nothing, for, like, two days. We were having a cookout, my cousin, Danil, and I. Well, not really a cookout—but a grill with some chicken on it."

"I get it," Hai said.

"I was flipping this piece of chicken and all a sudden this guy comes stumbling out the shed. And I'm looking at my cousin like, 'Yo, who the fuck do you have in your shed, dude? Like, there's a grown-ass man crawling from your toolshed.' And my cousin was like, 'That's Dumbass Rob.'"

"Dumbass Rob," Hai repeated, nodding. "Okay."

"Rob was one of those guys that was addicted to war, you know?"

"Addicted?"

"You know, those guys who can't get right once they come home, so they keep going back for another tour. To feel camaraderie or some shit. Rob was one of them. He was in this thing, Operation Phantom Fury, and everything. Anyway, Dumbass Rob is crawling toward us on his belly, like some freaky commando, his mouth all foaming, high as fuck. Like I'm talking psycho-high. Dude looked like *The Exorcist*."

Hai sucked the bogie and flicked it into the mist, where it sparked and faded. "So what'd you do?"

"My cousin saw me getting all shook, so he was like, 'Just flip that chicken, man. Don't sweat old Rob. He's good people.' So I'm flipping our chicken and my cousin is trying to stay cool but he's all fidgety and I'm like, man, is my cousin on meth too? Know what I mean? And now Rob's getting closer to us, like three feet away, trying to grab this plastic lawn chair. So my cousin holds the chair down so this guy can climb into it, which takes a long time, and I'm just standing there flipping these chicken breasts as the plastic chair clacks all over the place and my cousin just going, 'You okay, my man. You alright, Robbie. You're good, Robbie.' But Robbie was not good."

"You give him some chicken at least?"

"I took a piece from the grill, nice dark meat like Wayne does it, and blew on it to cool it and all. Then handed it to him with my spatula. He grabbed it and popped it in his mouth. Soon as he finished chewing Danil was slapping his face to get him out of it."

"How'd he even get in there—the shed, I mean?"

"Turns out Rob was an old high school friend of Danil's, so he let him use his shed to shoot up whenever he wanted."

Russia lit another bogie, cupping the flame with his palm. Hai watched him without him noticing. His face was sunken and glistening from the day's work, which made Hai want to wipe his brow clean and touch the back of his neck with his lips. The boy wasn't beautiful. Not even handsome in this gentle, dusky light. It was only that they were the same age, and that they worked there, shoulders touching through the steaming, aching hours, passing cigarettes back and forth in this lot, the filter's taste changing: slick and slightly sweeter from the blue Gatorade Russia sipped through his shift. Can camaraderie—the bond of working in unison—be enough to make you want to put your mouth to a kid with a busted face, to find him somehow more complete despite his unrecognizable beauty, the smell of his armpits seeping through his work polo, that garlicky, vinegary scent of humanness canceling the drugstore deodorant he wore to hide it? Yes, Hai realized now—it was.

Russia paused to text something on his phone, his lips resting in a pout, then went on. "He started telling us about this grenade launcher that blew up two dudes from his company. Can you imagine? Said the sand turned *black*. That's how much blood there was. But his head was rolling about and jerking while he talked. It was scary as fuck. So what I did, I just kept feeding him chicken. After a while he ate all the chicken, and Danil and I, we just stood there. And that's when I noticed his boots. The same ones you got on. I like the design. How it's soft where the ankle is so you don't roll it. It hugs you as you walk, doesn't it?" He stared at Hai's boots and smiled to himself. "Sony, your cousin, he's crazy about the army, huh? That kid's, like, *obsessed*."

"His dad was in it. Just like yours, I guess."

Russia cleaned his teeth with this tongue. "My dad's a big loser. Or should I say, *Major* loser."

"Major Loser." They laughed harder than the pun deserved, smoke rising from their throats and lacing the moment with beleaguered tenderness.

"An old friend of mine had these," Hai said. "When they were too small for him, he gave 'em to me. When those wore out, my mom got me the same pair for Christmas. When I opened the box, she was like, 'You know how many pedicures I had to do to afford those? Eight! That's sixteen feet I had to scrub just so you can cover two of yours.'" He shook his head and smiled.

"My mom left us a while back. But my grandma's been holding it down like a legend."

"How's Anna doing?"

He shrugged. In the gloaming, Russia's acne, which in the day resembled smeared blueberry jam, was now blending with the smoother parts of his cheek, like weathered cuneiform on old marble. It was almost unnoticeable save for the Band-Aid he had put on in the middle of his shift when the bleeding became too much, after a woman drove up to the drive-thru to collect her food and got upset, convinced that he had bled on her meal. The crew watched as he held his face with both hands and dashed, red with shame, to the bathroom. The bandage had since come loose, attached only by one end, and fluttered in the breeze as he paused to think of his sister, in rehab in New Hampshire now for two months.

Hai decided to keep his own stint in rehab to himself.

"They said she relapsed twice so far." His voice dropped, gone was the soft, sweet lilt. Russia was eighteen but still had the raspy timbre of adolescence, the kind of voice that makes you want to say *yes* even if he's just asking you the time. "But they said that's expected, I guess. Most of 'em need four relapses to get right. If they make it that far."

Hai didn't know much about Russia's situation but knew, like everyone else at HomeMarket, that the kid was working his tail off to put his sister through recovery. He also put in graveyard shifts at the FedEx warehouse loading trucks on the side, enough to keep her in New Hampshire one month at a time.

"You don't get scared?"

"I'm used to it." Russia bit his lip. "Anna's just like my grandma. She's strong."

They didn't say anything for a while, though for different reasons. The quiet settled over them and Russia sparked another cigarette, neither of them really wanting to go home.

"I keep thinking about this story," Russia said at last, "about this thing that happened back in this village outside Konstantinovo, where my dad was born."

"That why his name's Konstantin?"

"Original, right?" He smirked. "Anyway, there was this man who walked out one night to get a pack of cigarettes from the village store. When he didn't return an hour later, his wife came out to look for him. It had just snowed and everything was white and quiet. She followed his footsteps until they led to a wooden fence. But that's where they stopped. Right there in the yard. Just vanished mid-step."

"What happened?" Hai took the bogie from Russia's fingers.

"Nothing. That's it. My dad said the guy just disappeared. Like, they *never* found him again. Ever."

"You sure he didn't climb the fence?"

"Could've, but then where'd he go? That's it, dude. My man just poofed. I bet it actually happens all over the world all the time."

"Really?"

"People vanish all the time and leave no trace, even here in America, especially in the national parks. Shit, my dad used to tell me that story right before bed, drunk as fuck sitting on the floor. But it worked."

He laughed with all his teeth. "I was so scared my brain just turned off. I think of that story about once a month. Like, where is that guy now? Is he just floating somewhere in nowhere-land?"

They both nodded to themselves in the dark.

Hai finished the cig and tossed it. "You know they're talking about reinstating the draft, right?" Sony had told Hai about it earlier, grinning ear to ear. It was all the talk at his group home.

"Fuck 'em. The Feds just want free oil," Russia said. "But those boots *are* sick, though, no lie."

Russia pointed with his chin at the soggy leather wrapped around Hai's feet. "Shit, I might get my skinny ass drafted just to get a pair."

13

One afternoon, while Grazina was napping on the couch, a fresh twenty-three milligrams of Aricept deepening her sleep, Hai went down to the basement to pick out another book. When he surfaced, a paperback of Kawabata's *Snow Country* tucked in the waistband of his shorts, he found himself stopping before the kitchen armoire, the drawer opened. There, nestled among old coupon clippings, were three bottles of four-milligram Dilaudids. He had been keeping an eye out for them this whole time and had finally spotted them earlier that morning when searching for Grazina's reading glasses.

He stood listening to her snore in the next room, the house groaning from the gale blowing off the water, and waited, swaying on his feet, the bottles rocking as if in the hull of a great ship. He was down to nine pills from the first bottle, and this would hold him over the longer stretches at HomeMarket, build him a base from which the hours could be endured. Not unlike the way Wayne nursed his bourbon from his pistol-shaped flask between racks of chicken. *I'm no junkie*, Hai told himself now. *Junkies don't have control.* "I'm in control," he whispered down at his toes wiggling inside his socks.

On the morning he was discharged from rehab, the rain wouldn't let up. He hadn't slept the whole night, and just lay there with his arms on each side in the bleach-scented room while Marlin, the sex addict across from him, snored away. When the walls greyed with dawn, one of the nurses came in and touched his shoulder, her moonlike face hovering in the half dark. He could tell it was Marylyn by her platinum bangs. "Today's your day, bud," she whispered. "It's almost seven. You ready?"

"Can I get one more Werther's? For luck?"

"Oh gosh. That's Wanda's thing," she frowned. "I don't have a special thing. That's why I asked to be the discharger. This *is* my special thing."

"It's cool. I don't need it." He held the blanket to his chin, bracing.

"You're stronger now. And you'll be stronger tomorrow." She patted his pillow. "Come on, I have your things in the hall."

She handed him a plastic bag with the clothes he came in, all folded and laundered. "Go ahead and change in that bathroom there. I'll be right here."

He tossed his white pajamas in the biohazard bin under the sink and got dressed. He glimpsed himself in the mirror and saw something like a mannequin in the glass. So thin, so pale, cheeks hollowed out with shadows pooling under his eyes. He hurried up and got out of there.

They passed the unlit rooms where other patients were shivering through night sweats, their eyes roving under dope-sick fever dreams. In the admitting hall, Marylyn fetched his backpack and suitcase from the storage closet. "Everything should be in there, but go on and check just in case."

"There's not much anyway."

She handed him a clipboard with papers to sign, then led him toward the door and buzzed open the security lock. "Now, we know nothing's perfect. But I always say . . ." She paused and wrung her hands. "I always say I don't wanna see you in here again. Even though I know most of you, I mean . . . most people, they come back, you know.

Here, there's more details in these pamphlets—and the numbers you can call, even if it's late at night. We'll always be here if you need us. There's no shame in giving it another go, alright? Most folks *need* a few goes anyhoo."

"Okay."

"Normally I'd have tea and a Fig Newton for ya, but——"

"Oh, that'll be nice."

"No . . . I mean, it's all the way in my car, so . . ." she trailed off in a wilted voice.

"Oh, right. Yeah. That's okay——" he shrugged.

"Okay."

"Okay." He dipped his head, nodding.

They stood looking around, rain dribbling on the asphalt roof above them.

She cocked her head, then put out her hands, palms up.

Not knowing what to do, he waved—which felt insane since they were only inches away from each other.

"No, take my hands," she said. "We're gonna pray you out."

"Pray me out?" he asked, but held her hands anyway, warm and slimy with lotion.

"Dear Father, look down—no, close your eyes or it won't work. Dear Father, look down and guard this young man and forgive him his trespasses, for we are lambs of Your shepherdship and Your light is the lamp we carry through the darkness of this earthly realm ruled by the devil and his legions. May You lend Your strength to our dear brother here, who has been battered by the devil's magic, and send him home healed in the merciful good light of Your forgiveness, for they know not what they do. Amen."

"Amen," he repeated.

"That's my grandma's prayer. She was a preacher," she said, then added, "You know, you don't talk much, but I see you."

He had imagined these nurses would end up hardened from seeing endless hordes of ravaged human forms whose warped faces upon closer inspection often revealed a neighbor or a friend, but Marylyn was tender with him, with herself. This *is* her special thing, he decided: to send people home—whatever that meant.

"Somebody fetching you?"

"I'm close by," he said. "I can walk."

"Alrighty then." She raised her head as if to urge his to rise also, then turned and headed through the double doors, back to the ward.

HE OPENED HIS suitcase on the front steps. It was now mid-September, and the scent of summer decaying to mulch, the last spurts of grass growth, and phosphorus and motor oil on the pavement sharpened the wet air. All he had packed for his fraudulent college trip was the brown UPS jacket, a Carhartt hoodie, a couple hardback books, and an extra pair of jeans to give the suitcase some weight in case his mother had the wherewithal to pick it up the day he left. He put the black hoodie over the New Hope T-shirt they gave him, then the jacket over that, but left the jeans and books inside, shut the case, and slid it under a row of bushes by the entrance. He slung the backpack over his shoulder and kept walking.

The cornstalks across the road were a foot taller since he last saw them, but still green at the tips. Their ears, plump and heavy, bowed in the rain. He patted his jacket pockets until he found the half pack of Marlboro Reds his mother gave him before he left. He put one to his lips but, having no lighter, just sucked on it till the rain made it limp, then took it in his mouth, chewed, and swallowed before spitting out the filter. He raised his hood against the wind and pushed on, deeper into East Gladness.

AFTER WALKING AN HOUR, boots soaked through, he finally passed
the post office on Main and crossed the baseball field behind the
Salvation Army before reaching the entrance to Welles Village. Initially
built in the seventies as a neighborhood of double-unit ranch houses for
vets returning from Vietnam, it was now a low-income HUD housing
project you had to enter a lottery to get in. He'd lived there long as he
could remember but never recalled winning any lottery.

He cut through a backyard littered with spare tires and headed
down Risley, where their house was the second to last before the dead
end. But as the familiar smoke-stained vinyl clapboards came into view,
something took hold and he turned, as if on a track, and crossed another yard, ducking under laundry lines past a vegetable garden of withered stems, a silent chicken coop, then the wheel-less Camaro abandoned
on cinder blocks, before approaching a beige duplex browned with dead
moss.

His hooded apparition reflected in the kitchen window as he
knocked on the glass to the rhythm of "Skunk in the Barnyard."
Through the glass he made out a night-light glowing over a sink full
of dirty dishes. Hanging on the wall was a black embroidery stitched
in pink letters: *How Can I Be Hungry When I'm Full of Family?* A figure
stepped before it and the words vanished behind a huge white T-shirt.

The window opened and Randy was already grinning, his gold incisor sparkling under the gunmetal sky. The house smelled of sleep and
stale coffee. "My man! I got what you need!" Randy called everyone *my
man.* "Trust me do I got what you need." He pointed at Hai's face and
slapped the side of the window, his dimples deeper than Hai remembered. Randy was the type of guy who slapped everything around him
when he talked.

Hai gave him a mock-quizzical look. "You got what I need, right?
Then show me the goods, Mr. I'll-Be-in-the-NBA-by-Twenty-Two."

Randy leaned over, stuck his big head out the window, so close Hai could smell the Juicy Fruit he was chewing. "Don't mess with me today, okay? It's raining, it's nasty. My mom's back is acting up. I got what you need—if you need it. Don't be a punk-ass at my window."

"I'm fucking with you, Rand. I'm not having the greatest week myself here either, okay?"

"Why, what's wrong with you? Lose your library card again?" Randy cracked up, always laughing at his own jokes. Last summer, while on a mix of generic Perc and codeine, Hai had a bad trip and knocked on Randy's window crying hysterically that he'd lost his library card. Randy also liked making fun of him for reading books, since he believed, like a lot of folks in Welles Village, that reading is what schools *force* you to do, and that by the time you reach eighteen, you should be forever freed from the tyranny of printed words. A nineteen-year-old who still reads must be dumb enough to *willingly* refuse the wide-open book-free utopia of adulthood.

"I'll tell you later. Look, I'll take two oxys and two Cs. They're still ten a pop?"

"You got it, my main man. We'll get you right, don't worry." He tapped the sill, ducked inside, and disappeared into the back rooms.

Randy was known in Welles Village as the Candy Man. When Hai was a kid, each day after school he'd stop by Randy's window with the other children and knock to the rhythm of "Skunk in the Barnyard," which was the code. Randy would pop out with a shoebox full of Jolly Ranchers, Airheads, Fruit Roll-Ups, Welch's Fruit Snacks, even the fancy Pepperidge Farm Milano cookies he'd buy in bulk from their outlet factory in New Britain. One day, when Hai was in middle school, Randy showed him a new candy. So new, he said, that they didn't even have wrappers for them yet. "These are special," Randy cooed. "Don't you want to be the first to sample them? You can't get these at any store, my man." The candy sat in clear plastic, as if held up by air, like a magical force field. Some even had smiley faces or David Bowie lightning bolts printed on them.

Randy returned to the window with the goods. They gave each other a long handshake, inside whose grip the pills and Hai's two twenties, folded to the size of quarters, were exchanged.

"Just don't mix 'em this time, okay?" he said with a heavy sigh.

"Okay, Doc. Oh, actually," Hai shook the pills in his palm, "you got anything to hold these? I lost my film roll at the——" He nodded over his shoulder. "At the other place."

Randy dipped inside before coming back with a white contact lens case. "These should do. You can keep it too." He sensed a vague sadness—or was it pity?—in Randy's eyes. Hai must've looked rough standing soaked in the rain with the fucked-up bowl cut he gave himself in the rehab bathroom the night before. "Hey, you remember . . ." Randy said, scratching his beard. "You remember you used to run up to my window, each day at 3:40, right when the bus let y'all off, shouting my name? 'Candy Maaaan! Caaaaandy Maaaan!' You were Elroy's age, just about." He nodded toward his son somewhere in the house, then shook his head, deep in a memory while trying to say something. Finally he slapped his chest, sucked on his teeth, and smiled through it. "Fuck it."

"Sweet Home Alabama" was leaking through a neighbor's opened window.

"You've come a long way too, Rand. Not bad for a guy who couldn't make a single three-pointer all through high school."

Randy's reason for his failed basketball career was that he was a big man who didn't dunk. And the college scouts, mostly white guys in polo shirts with clipboards, expected him to be a three-point expert, which he sucked at. "It's all because of guys like Shaq and Shawn Kemp," he told Hai. "They fucked it up for dudes who finish with finesse!" The taller you are, Randy explained, the harder they expect you to dunk, and since he was a penetrating power forward with a preference for finger rolls, he never made it to the big leagues. Or so it went.

"Well, have you been practicing?" Hai asked, snapping shut the case with the pills inside. "Heard the Celtics could use a Cuban with a beer belly in his late thirties to make layups. With *finesse*."

Randy let out a laugh that was all tongue and teeth. "Get the fuck out my yard, little boy." They smiled before lulling to a deep, awkward quiet, their use for one another exhausted.

As Hai walked away, Randy stopped just before the window closed and pressed his mouth to the crack. "Hey! You gonna be fine, my man! Trust me, okay?"

Without looking back, Hai gave Randy a thumbs-up and kept walking.

He headed to the park to clear his mind, trying to gather the courage to break his mother's heart again. As far as she knew, he was nearly a month into becoming an MD in Boston.

He was sitting under a slide shaped like a blue hippopotamus, rain pebbling the plastic roof. He had known this park his whole life and, ever since he was little, would sit alone under this very slide and listen to the neighborhood flow past him. He'd stay here for hours some days, listening to people talk in hushed voices in the trees, lighters sparking here and there in the branches, their gasps and cut laughter snagged in the shadows. Once, after a blizzard, tired from making a one-section, enormous snowman by himself, he rested here and saw, at the tree line, a man kneeling in the snow while another man, standing, held on to a branch and searched the sky, saying the Lord's name over and over. To this day it was the strangest and most graceful prayer he'd ever seen.

The rain started to sound muffled, like it was falling inside a dream. He fingered the lens case in his pocket, then opened it and stared at the four tiny tablets (two blue, two white), a pair in each capsule. The codeine would get him through talking to his mother, would make her crying seem like it's coming from the basement of the world and not right in front of him. He nudged the pill, the smallest life raft he'd ever known, but finally shut the case. When he slipped it back in his pocket, there was a crinkling sound. Reaching deeper, he found a stray Werther's from Nurse Wanda. He put the candy in his mouth and sucked, savoring the caramel sweetness. He studied his warped reflection in the gold-foil wrapper. "What do I do, Wanda? I don't know what to do," he said, his voice drifting.

IT WAS EARLY EVENING when he woke. The sky still heavy with clouds but nothing coming down. He flipped open his phone and realized he'd been asleep almost three hours.

He crossed the Little League ball field, his boots sucking mud, and made his way back to the street. Nearing Ma's duplex, he noticed the living room light was still on and crouched under the window. The lace curtains were drawn but through the diaphanous fabric he managed to peer into the room. His mother was on the couch, her head bent over her phone, in her usual spot. Her body was more upright than before, her shoulders jerking as she texted. Next to her, on the side table, was a lit candle, the expensive kind that cost twenty-six dollars from Yankee Candle, the one you could only get at the mall. Her hair was tied back and clipped with something shiny, her face touched up with rouge, she was in an elegant blue linen dress that hugged her length—none of this she'd ever done when he was home. *You don't need to be beautiful to make other people beautiful*, she once told him, sucking on a cigarette and sweating in the back room on her break at the nail salon, her tiny frame engulfed in sweatpants and a Red Sox hoodie.

Now she looked healthy, content even—her gold hoop earrings

catching the candlelight as she beamed into her phone. A breeze shifted the curtain and he glimpsed her through the opening. How rare to see one's mother lost in such unfixed and unknowable contentment, so privately realized through a scarce, snatched freedom. He felt like a voyeur and yet, like a voyeur, could not look away.

How could he do this now? How could he go to the back door and knock—only to have her see him like this? How could he put an end, in a few short steps, to this version of his mother he'd never seen and yet had wanted, his whole life, to witness? And perhaps most sickening, how could he do it a second time?

The night he returned from New York, he had knocked on that very door. How could he have told her then that he had dropped out because Noah had overdosed, like nearly a dozen kids from his high school class, on a bad batch of fent-dope, and that a boy whose face she'd never seen had become the boy whose face he couldn't forget? That after Noah died, only eight months after bone cancer ate through Bà ngoại's hip and put her in an urn on the altar, college and books, grades and papers, seemed so minuscule, so exactly as Randy had said: "the driftwood of childhood"? On top of that he owed the school nearly twenty-five thousand dollars for defaulting on his scholarship. That night his mother nearly dissolved in front of him. "What do you mean you owe twenty-five thousand dollars now," she said, her hand over her mouth as if hearing of murder. "Isn't college supposed to help us? I don't understand. How can it bring more debt than we've ever had money?"

He just stood there, mouth agape, holding the box of Whitman's Sampler he had bought from the bus station with the chaotic delusion that it would blunt the blow.

Then, the catastrophe dawning on her, she bit her lip and pointed a finger an inch from his face. "I knew you'd fuck up—just like all the other *trash* around here. And I know it's my damn fault too. I chose to raise you in this town when all the other Viets went off to California and Texas. Everybody had the brains to go to better cities, but no, I thought only of my son, not wanting to uproot him again after coming all this way. So I stayed in this snowed-in hellhole." Her hair clip had come loose and her hair floated about her as she spoke.

"Ma, I tried. But things got tough. Things you won't understand and—"

"You were always a selfish child. Every time we got McDonald's you would eat my fries first, even when you had your own!"

"Really. We're really doing this? I'm a bad person because I was a *child* eating french fries?"

"It's a sign. I should've known what was to come. And why did I know this would happen? Huh," she said with a seething smile. "Even Miss Tran said so, you know. That you'd wash ashore like some dead fish. But I told her, 'Not Hai.' She said a pillhead won't last long in that city but I defended you, stupid me. I worked my ass off, fed you and clothed you all these years. For what?"

"I'm sorry your investment didn't *pay off*. I didn't know raising children was like throwing dice at a casino." They so seldom fought, the tiny apartment too small to hold festering tensions, that both of them were suddenly stricken by the blast radius of their words.

"That's right." She wiped her nose. "Curse your mother. That's what all that learning and wordsmithery did for you, huh? Give you just enough wit to shun your mother but not enough to take you very far outside this house, does it?"

"And what about you? What have you done after twenty years in this fucking country? All of you guys at the nail salon, you tell us kids to go out there and just 'succeed' like it's some random magic trick. But you, you've had twenty years to do what?"

"Don't." She knew where he was taking her, and she held out both hands as if holding back a boulder. "Enough—"

"You just sit there and scrub rich people's feet?" he said as his mother tried to turn away.

"Fuck you. I scrub feet so we can have this shitty apartment. You think I like bowing my head to white people like they were gods twenty times a day?"

The sight of her, so small and hurt, so bewildered and broken, sunk him—and in a rare surge of rage, he slammed the chocolates against the wall. His mother let out a yelp, covered her mouth, and ran upstairs.

"I'm sorry. Ma, please, I'm sorry," he cried after her, then stood with his face in his hands as her door slammed. They wouldn't speak for weeks, waiting for each other to leave the cramped rooms before passing like strangers on a subway car.

Through the curtain, her whole being now aglow, he watched her put down the phone and pick up the candle with both hands and inhale. Shuddering from this acid shame, he took in this view one last time before turning from the window, and headed back down the road, away from the dead end, until he cut clear through town, until the upper beams of King Philip's Bridge rose over the outskirts, which led him to stand, only minutes later, under its rail ties, and now he was here, in this house where Grazina was sleeping just a few feet away, and he was still in possession of his one wild and precious life.

The house was settling into its bones, and in between the cracking he heard his heart beating in its cage. Then, out of possession or abandonment, he took one of the bottles and cracked the lid open, placed the little white buoy on his tongue, and swallowed. He paused, thinking, then scooped the remaining three bottles in his arms and hurried back to his room, where he dumped them in the desk drawer and lay watching the ceiling until the darkness spun out around him, covering every distance, and he was warm as a blood cell being swept through the vein of a fallen angel, finally good.

THE ASHEN TOWN streaked across the murky windows of Maureen's Volkswagen as she yanked the shift into fourth gear and the car jolted down Orchard Street toward mud fields where deflated pumpkins, dusted with December frost and rejected by scavengers, lay strewn over the wasteland. Her Beetle was strung all along the insides with Christmas lights powered by the cigarette fuse. The bulbs were the frosted kind from the eighties and made the car feel both sleazy and cozy at once, an effect that imbued it with a strange yearning. Since it was Sunday during church hours, they had been the only car on the road since crossing the East Gladness town line.

"We're late," Russia said from the back, his head pressed against the glass.

"We'll be there in five." Maureen pulled the shift and the car rattled without speeding up, lightbulbs clacking the windows.

"You said that half hour ago."

"Any of those bad boys come through?" she asked Hai, who was scratching a stack of lottery tickets she had handed him a few miles back. "If we score big," Maureen said, "we can just turn the hell around."

Behind a line of elms, a pair of steel silos rose up from the muddy hills, their domes gleaming under the overcast. "That's it," Russia said. "Wayne said to turn right at the double silos."

"This better be fucking worth it." Maureen reached for her flask and swished the whiskey like it was mouthwash, before passing it to Hai.

This time he took an obligatory sip and handed it to Russia. "My dad's a drunk," Russia said, shoving it back.

"Guess you're not *that* allergic." Maureen winked at Hai. Warmed by the liquor, she swayed as they turned down a gravel path beyond the silos, the Christmas lights casting a sickly glow over their faces.

The path dipped toward the bottom of a hill where a gravel lot came into view. A few cars were scattered about, mostly pickups with raised axles plastered with mud. Wayne was already waiting when they pulled up. His arms were folded, his mouth lopsided, like someone was yanking it down with their finger. "Looks like we have a grumper today, guys," Maureen said.

Wayne banged on Maureen's window with the butt of some tool. Only when she cranked the window down did Hai see the black-bladed machete in Wayne's grip. "Come on, Maur. I said eleven a.m. You're all late." He pointed at an invisible watch on his wrist.

"It's Sunday. We hit church traffic," she lied. "You want me to run over little kids on their way to Communion? And the fuck you got a sword for?"

"I told you—we're working meat today." His breath vapored in the cold. He had a weeklong beard and his lips were cracked and white at the edges. The acidic wintry air, bleached with ozone and dead grass, mixed with the cut of manure and gasoline, blew into the car, stinging Hai's eyes. "I've been out here since seven a.m.," Wayne sighed, the curled white hairs on his temples flickering in the wind. "One guy already quit on us."

Maureen gave Hai this skeptical look, then said to Wayne, "Don't do this to me, Wayne. I've known you what, twenty years?"

"I've only been up north eleven years."

"You told us," she pointed at him with the flask, "that you needed help *packing* meat. Why do you need a sword to wrap up pork chops?"

When Wayne didn't answer, Russia pulled his hoodie over his head and tightened the drawstrings so only his nose showed. "I knew this was gonna be stupid."

On Friday, while they were closing, Wayne had asked the Home-Market crew if they were willing to make some extra cash packing meat at a warehouse an hour out east in Coventry. Wayne had been putting in days there to make more on the side during the holidays—

and it paid well. A few guys had caught the stomach flu last week and couldn't make the upcoming Christmas rush. And if they didn't meet their weekly quota, they'd lose the $1,500 bonus they'd each get at the end of the month. Only Hai, Maureen, and Russia agreed. They already handled raw chicken at the store—how bad could pork be, *the other white meat?* Since they weren't officially on the meatpacking payroll, the other workers were going to give the three volunteers a cut from their bonuses, netting $500 each for just a day's work.

They got out the car, wind biting at their edges.

"You know there's no corn bread in there, right, guys?" Wayne laughed and pointed with his machete at their black HomeMarket uniforms.

"There's blood on your fingers." Hai nodded at the purplish dust around Wayne's knuckles.

"It's called pork. Comes from a pig, you know? The one with blood and guts and brains?"

"This is a slaughterhouse, isn't it?" Hai said.

"It's an organic farm-to-store pork production facility," Wayne said through shut eyes.

"Holy fuckers!" Maureen leaned back on the hood. "I'm not stabbing any pigs with a sword, dudes. I'm *technically* a senior citizen—you know that, right?"

"The way I figure," Wayne tried, "is this: we split you all up so there'd be a regular butcher with you at each station. Then you could keep things to a minimum—"

"Butcher?" Hai looked away, everything around him awash in greys and browns.

"And what do you mean by *station*?" said Russia. "How many *stations* does it take for a pig to die?"

"Fast as you can cut the arteries."

Maureen didn't look like she believed him but started struggling with the cap on her flask.

"Here, use mine." Wayne took from his back pocket a gold flask shaped like a revolver.

"Your six-shooter, nice." Maureen pointed the gun down her throat and fired multiple shots.

"You can keep it for the day. You'll need it."

"It helps my knees. Gets bad during solar flares."

"The *sun* hurts your knee?" Russia said, straggling behind.

As they approached the barn's tractor doors, Maureen holding on to Wayne's shoulder for support, two men stopped talking to look at the crew in their black uniforms. Wayne tipped his cap and nodded at them. The cold and work had stiffened the men's clothes to shades of ash, as though they hadn't been butchering meat but fighting forest fires. One of them, who had an Eastern European accent and wind-pummeled face, raised his hand, clearly high on something. "You got us a squad, Wayne?" he said. "Good man. And look! You even got an Ornamental." He grinned with the few teeth he had. "Super nice!"

"You mean *Oriental*." Wayne turned to Hai. "Right?"

Hai gave Wayne a shove from behind and moved them along, too cold to bother.

The barn was made of concrete blocks topped with a sleek, weather-proof metal roof, which made it look more like a place that produced weapons for a proxy war. Wayne led them inside, where they were immediately engulfed by the odor of fresh urine and the deep iron of spilled blood. On both sides of a narrow corridor made of steel fencing were pens where enormous hogs stood cramped in mass contortions of peachy flesh, their nostrils, the wetness being all that caught the weak light, snorting the hellish air. Some were slumped in piles in far corners, their blistered, straw-flecked stomachs heaving as they breathed, pouted lips leaking brownish fluid and mucus.

The reason they were in pens instead of cages, Wayne explained, was to legally keep the coveted "Free Range" label on the packaging. But they were so crowded you could hear the crackle of their coarse hairs brushing against one another as they struggled to turn around, some crying out in crushed frustration.

"Jesus," Maureen whispered. "You're gonna kill all of 'em?"

"By Christmas," Wayne said, taking off his cap to wipe his brow, sweat turning the dust on his skin to mud.

"This is kinda fucked," said Russia.

"Kinda?" Hai said, kicking a few strands of hay by his feet.

The pork here was also "organic," Wayne told them. This meant the pigs were raised on organic corn, which, in the massive quantities they were fed, out of Rubbermaid troughs crusted with sludge, gave them acidosis, fermenting their blood to the point of requiring antibiotics. "I'm not saying I wouldn't feed it to my family. Shit, these things are huge and full of fat," Wayne said, looking around. "But it's not what people *think* they're getting."

These "people" included Linda McMahon—co-founder of WWE—who was currently running as a Republican for a Connecticut Senate seat. She was rumored to have ordered thirty of these hogs for a Christmas fundraiser she was hosting at her mansion in Stamford, where wrestling superstars were supposed to attend. "You know," said Wayne with a chuckle, "for some reason I can't imagine the Undertaker sitting down and cutting into a pork chop with a napkin tucked into his leather trench coat."

"Look," said Maureen with a serious face. "With my knees, I can't stab any pigs, not if they're *that* big. I can't get traction, see?" She jabbed her foot in the hay-strewn dirt and exaggerated its slide. Wayne removed his worker's belt and handed it to Maureen, who cinched it on without asking why.

"See that pouch in the front of your belt there? Those are dog treats, bacon flavored." Wayne winked. "When one of the guys opens the pen, your job is to lead the hogs to the slaughter tent out back. Use these treats and they'll follow you, no problem."

Maureen held up a treat and frowned at it before letting it drop back in the pouch. "I'm gonna need an Altoid for this. Russia, you still got any?"

Russia took an Altoid case from his back pocket and opened it. She shoved a mint in each of her nostrils and inhaled. "Hmm, cinnamon."

Russia and Hai did the same.

Wayne shook his head at them and started walking. "Pussies."

With Maureen at the pens, Hai and Russia followed Wayne around the barn. On the other side, hidden from the road, was a long tarp tent the size of a car wash, the sides covered all the way to the ground. It looked like the Civil War hospitals Sony kept talking about. As they approached, a swell of death metal music started filling the air. Hai could make out the Slipknot song once popular in high school as Russia nodded along in vague recognition. Wrapping around the tent's perimeter was a rust-thick chain-link that prevented hogs from bolting once they realized they were doomed for the chandeliered dinner tables of millionaires. The plastic sign, zip-tied to the chain-link, read MURPHY'S FREE-RANGE PORK. A FAMILY FARM SINCE 1921.

IT WASN'T UNTIL they got right outside the tent that Hai heard the screaming, more like preteen girls than pigs, but it was too late to stop as Wayne lifted the blue plastic and a waft of blood-soaked air coated his tongue with its metallic burn, as if someone had shoved a handful of pennies in his mouth. This, mixed with the mints in his nostrils, gave him the urge to retch.

"Holy fuck," he heard Russia say as Wayne closed the tent's zipper and their eyes adjusted to this underworld.

All along one side were hooks where the hogs were strung up by burly men with mustaches and beer bellies, the scene cast with floodlights clamped to ropes strung across the ceiling. Once the beasts were hung upside down, the machetes went to work, their black, corrosion-resistant blades dividing the air in great whooshes of violence. Wayne grabbed a brown rubber bib from a hook and tied it on, then slipped on thick rubber gloves that went up to his elbows.

The pork was expensive because it didn't come from the South or the Midwest, like most pork, but right here, in good old apple-pie-on-a-plaid-dining-cloth New England. Another reason was that the "farm" guaranteed the hogs would be "field killed," suggesting they would die where they roamed happily in lush meadows, their eyes holding the sight of green pastures as they left the earthly plane, when, in fact, their only access to the mud field, whose grass had long disintegrated from the trampling of a thousand hogs killed before them, was a tiny roofless pen on the side of the barn, so small none of the hogs ever used it.

"Here." Wayne handed Russia and Hai some sort of gun. "Follow me."

"We're shooting them?" Hai said, approaching the row of industrial meat hangers. "Wayne, are you serious?"

"It's more *humane* this way, kids." He gave the boys a tired, fatherly look. "What, you think we just stab these things to death? You'd burn your arms out after two or three kills. It's the twenty-first century, fellas. You shoot everything in the head."

He opened the small holding pen at the entrance and led one of the hogs out by its plastic collar, then took the gun from Hai's hand. "It's just a bolt, not a bullet. A little piece of metal goes into the head and knocks 'em out cold."

"Sounds like a bulle— Jesus fucking Christ!" Hai jumped back and clutched Russia's arm as Wayne shot the pig in the forehead. It immediately collapsed, thrashing and screaming in the mud.

"Usually they go out with just one," Wayne grunted as he jammed a knee on the side of the hog's face, blood foaming from its mouth now, and shot it again in the same spot. The legs went limp, then jittered as if being electrocuted. Wayne looped a metal wire to its hoof and pressed a button on a nearby machine that pulled the hog up by its legs.

Wayne handed Hai the bolt gun. Then, in one swift gesture, as if striking a match, he cut the pig's throat. A spray of blood flew over them. Russia looked about wildly, then fixed a ghastly stare at Hai, his mouth half-open, the pig's blood *inside* it and dripping down his chin. "Oh fuck, fuck. What do I do, what do I do, what do I do?"

Wayne stepped away from the carcass, grabbed a towel soiled with what looked like motor oil from a bucket on the floor, and wiped at Russia's face. There was a warm wetness on Hai's cheek, going up to his temple. Before he could touch his face, Wayne was dabbing his forehead with the towel, so hard he tilted back with each wipe. "You guys'll get used to it. This stuff's inside us too, you know. People love eating meat but they don't have a damn clue what it's about. It's alive. That means blood, piss, and shit." He laughed at his own words, then slapped Hai and Russia hard on their chests. "You'll both grow a third nut in a few hours—and you can thank me later."

How many people actually knew how a pig is killed? How much strength, adrenaline, it took—even a sinister kind of charisma? How it felt, weirdly, like combat? Maybe that's why so many guys drank on the job. Some have nightmares full of hogs, Wayne told them, the screams seeping into their sleep as they reach out to clutch their wives or sweat-soaked pillows in the night. In supermarkets, the meat looks so serene, placid, and calm, like something formed in a studio. Here—among Slipknot and the alloyed blood, breath, and gastric fumes bubbling from gashed esophagi, the grass dyed yellow with stomach viscera, these animals with faces so human, eyelashes blond and thick, so expressive it felt like they should have names, so much so that Hai had to look away as he pulled the trigger—the work was chaos.

He'd shoot, wincing as the hooves pounded the ground, as if the animal were launching itself upward, unaware that the bolt in its brain had most likely ruptured its cerebellum, destroying its motor controls. Then he'd shoot again. "Go, go on. Go on, hurry up," Hai whispered as Russia, eyes red with tears, pulled back the bolt, Rage Against the Machine now blasting from the stereo set on a cooler filled with Bud Light.

By the fifth or sixth pig, Hai learned to look not at their eyes, opened too wide, stunned at this terrible gun-wielding god suddenly before them, but at the ears, which, examined closely, resembled a piece of fabric flickering in the breeze. *That's it*, that's what he told himself while pulling the trigger: that he was stapling fabric. He was pinning death onto nothing. And it worked. Though he could still hear their torqued and anguished gurgling, which the heavy metal barely drowned out, this gave the killing enough distance for him to keep the line going.

For the next three hours, he and Russia took turns pressing the trigger to the hogs' foreheads as, one by one, Wayne bled them out a few feet away, the torrent flowing into metal gutters set on the field's incline to spill, like demonic runoff, into the river. Maureen would pop in once in a while and usher through a hog if the bolt line was moving fast; otherwise the hogs waited outside in the chain-link pen.

After a while Hai had to go out to get some air. The heat from the hogs' bodies had warmed the tent to the point where their shirts were drenched. The crew in the barn had a separate stereo, and something in Spanish drifted over the field above the cheerful sounds the hogs made as they left the cages, following the dog treats held out before them.

Hai turned toward Maureen. "You not quitting yet, are you?" She was slumped over a huge sow, almost hugging it from behind, supporting herself on its back. Her hair was matted to her face and she was bowled over, like someone about to deliver terrible news from the center of a natural disaster. "It's gonna be worth it, okay?" Hai offered. "One more hour or so, that's it. Then we can——"

She stared at him, blank-faced, before lurching forward to release a spray of vomit onto the hog's back. She reached down and gathered some dead leaves and half-heartedly rubbed the sludge off the animal. She waved Hai off, then wiped her face on her shirtsleeve, removed one of the Altoids from her nose, popped it in her mouth, and hobbled back to the barn.

He felt something in his pocket and realized his phone had been ringing. The whole time he'd forgotten it was there. It was his mom. There were already two missed calls.

"Ma?" he said, trying to smile as he hurried behind a nearby hay bale, out of earshot of the slaughter. "No, no, I'm not in a rush, just . . . um. Just out and about. I'm breathing hard? Oh, nothing, I'm just running errands. Being productive. You know." He tried to laugh. "You on break? Right. It usually picks up the week before Christmas, doesn't it? People need their red and green nails. And you do the best snowflake designs."

Wayne was coming through. A hog had run out ahead of him and he was struggling to catch it. The animal brushed against Hai and it screamed from the contact. "Hey, man, can you grab him?" Wayne said, reaching for its tail.

Hai covered the receiver and whisper-shouted, "I'm on the phone."

Another worker appeared, a stout man with tan features. Wayne thrust a bunch of fingers at the man's face, to which the worker replied with a flurry of signals before they both cornered the hog.

"You know sign language?" Hai said. But Wayne was out of earshot. "What? Oh, nothing. It was just a friend, Ma. Oh, *that* thing. It was . . . a pig. We use them for dissection. Um . . . supposedly their organs are pretty similar to humans', so the school has them for autopsies and stuff."

"Oh, poor things," Ma said. "You should pray for their souls after, okay? Otherwise their spirits will haunt you and shorten your life." Hai could tell she was standing up from her chair at the salon. "It's serious. Say a prayer for them, okay? Mr. Vu died after working all those years as an exterminator. He never prayed after killing those mice and croaked from a heart attack."

"He also had heart disease."

"Hai, please."

"Ma, I know. I'll pray, for sure. I'll do it, like, seven times."

"Eight. It's a more auspicious number."

"Okay. Hey, I gotta go. They need my help."

"Go, go. Of course. Call me sometime. Just to tell me if you need anything."

He hung up and ran over to Wayne. The pig had sauntered toward a shallow pitch of mud and had started rooting around in it, eyes shut and snorting with glee. It looked younger than the rest and probably had no idea its friends and family were being executed. Wayne regarded the pig, his face drooping to the side. Hai reached into his pocket and tossed a handful of dog treats, missing her mouth and landing on her belly, which was streaked with Maureen's dried vomit. The hog didn't seem to care. "We'll be done soon," Wayne said, catching his breath.

"I'm lying to my mom," Hai heard himself say.

Wayne peered at him from the corners of his eyes. "That her on the phone?"

"Yeah."

"I can tell." He took one of the treats and licked it. "Not bad. Kinda like smoked paprika."

"You can tell what?"

"That you been lying. By your voice. I'm a dad, remember. Or was. Or whatever. I know the sound of a kid lying out his ass even if I don't speak Chinese."

"Vietnamese."

He popped the dog treat in his mouth and swallowed. "Wow. These are nasty as hell."

The heavy metal music had stopped. The sound of men's voices behind them speaking low in the tent. There was a silence in its wake that sounded new. The pig was now resting on its side. "I got a son." Wayne squinted at Hai and suddenly looked ten years older. "And I can hear it. You boys all sound the same," he laughed. "*We* all sound the same." He nudged Hai's ribs. "I was you once, young buck. A hundred years ago."

"What's your son's name?"

"Knight. He's sixteen." Wayne shook his head as if his son's age was a rumor he wasn't willing to believe. "I named him after the knight—you know, in chess? I was high school champ back in North Carolina. The knight was my ace, my right-hand man, and I *killed* with him. Whoosh!" He made a slicing motion with his hand across his open palm, the pads so puffed and blistered you could no longer see his life lines. "I cut my little L and—*boom!*—out of nowhere your queen's all by her lonesome, ready to sing 'Goodnight, Irene.'"

"You gonna see him? I mean, for Christmas and all?"

Wayne was quiet a moment, then bent down and brushed the dog treats off the pig's stomach as if it looked indecent. "You know, I've been cutting up these hogs for three years now. I don't regret none of it. They were born to die. And I'm just a hammer. Somebody else is using the hammer, I know that. I just don't know if it's that dude up there," he glanced at the sky, slate grey and ambivalent, "or the motherfucker down here." He jabbed the ground with his boot. "But you see that tree there?" He nodded at a squat yew standing alone between two pastures beyond the silos. "My granddad told me when trees stand on their own, with no other trees around them, their branches grow wild like that. Branches twisted all over the place, like they're trying to grab at everything and nothing's around to hold on to."

"Yeah, I see it." Hai studied the leafless tree, its branches scattered as if frozen in the midst of waving for help.

"But when they're in the forest, with their people, you know? They all go straight up, reaching tall as they can. Isn't that odd? Probably bullshit, to tell the truth—but I believe it."

Before Hai could answer, Wayne took his wallet out his back pocket and showed him a photo: three black pugs sitting on a front stoop, pink bows on each of their heads. They regard the camera with tilted gazes, their large, orbular eyes preening and hopeful. "These are my babies now. That one with the lazy eye is Lisa, after Left Eye. That one's Rosie. And this little one, her name's Bethel, after my nana. They're everything to me." He smiled big at the photo, his blood-darkened thumb at the edge. "I don't have a photo of Knight, though. Not good looking at what you can't have, ha." Wayne looked at Hai like a man who knew people's secrets by heart, a mix of both fuck-you pride and damage.

"We done yet? I'm almost dead." Maureen came up from behind them. Followed by Russia.

It was time for lunch, Russia told them. The men were dispersing across the pasture. "They went out to grab KFC for everybody." He grinned with his buckteeth. "That's gonna hit the spot." Russia's arms were covered in blood, and when he saw Hai staring, he added, "The last one was kinda rough. The bolt got jammed after the first shot and I had to reload in between." He looked scraped out, his eyes sunken and spacey. Hai realized, for the first time, in the smoky light that made Russia's blue hair tinge silver with sweat, that the boy *was* handsome—but in the way that reveals itself only after you know a person for a while, the way a doorknob is polished to brilliance with use. Hai now found his buckteeth endearing, a reprieve after three hours of watching the yellow-mangled maws of hogs gritted into their ends.

Maureen took out Wayne's water gun flask, pointed the nozzle at her mouth, and pulled the trigger several times. Her eyes still closed, she raised her head to the sky and handed it to Wayne, who also shot himself in the mouth. He wiped his lips with his stained shirtsleeves and gave Hai this dismal, deflated look. He opened his mouth a bit, as if to say something, something he had been determined to say for a long while. But just as he was about to speak, a flit of light caught the filling in the dark of his mouth, held there, then was gone, and he turned away.

Hai drained the flask. The valley spanning before them looked totaled and endless.

"Look, it's snowing," Maureen whispered. "It's gonna be a white Christmas. It's always magical when that happens," she breathed and shook her head at the brumal light descending over the heather before them.

"Did I ever tell y'all about these hogs?" Wayne half smiled at the pig, now asleep at their feet. "Back in, like, the eighteen-somethings, there was this town called Berkshire."

"I know where that is," Hai said.

"No, not that place up north where rich people from New York go camping. I'm talking about Berk*shyer*. In England. This place had some of the finest pork in the world. And when England was trying to get into Japan—you know, to do missionary shit or whatever—they tried to win over the emperor by giving him these Berkshire hogs. Well," Wayne licked his lips, "the emperor was so amazed by the flavor of these hogs, so rich with fat, sweet and juicy, he flung his doors wide open. And that's how Christianity came to Japan. Through pork. That's why they call them 'emperor hogs.' My granddad learned about it when he was over there in the war. His name was Eustice. So they tried to make a breed of them out here in Connecticut."

"Sounds like a bunch of bull," said Maureen.

"If being called an emperor meant getting your throat cut in the name of Christ, then you can go ahead and call me a peasant," Russia said.

"Now the emperor is Linda McMahon." Hai stared at the hog's heaving belly.

A truck pulled into the lot. The KFC was here. The men, slumped on hay bundles, lifted their heads from their phones or from cupped hands. On the other side of the tent, on a tractor cart to be pulled to the processing plant down the valley, was a pile of freshly slaughtered hogs, their legs stiffening in the cold as the snow fell onto the hollowed cavities of their bellies, the flakes turning to rain inside the steaming walls of their ribs. Because that's what happens when you die—the world gets in.

"Look at her. She doesn't give a *fuck*," Russia said, shaking his head at the sleeping hog, snow glittering her back.

Maureen stared at the hog and sighed. "And all the devils besought him, saying, *Send us into the swine, that we may enter into them.* And forthwith Jesus gave them leave. And the unclean spirits went out, and entered into the swine: and the herd ran violently down a cliff into the sea."

"My name is Legion and we are many." Wayne winked at her and smiled.

The three of them must've killed almost fifty that afternoon in their station alone (Hai had lost count after eighteen). If Wayne hadn't been counting on them to get that bonus, Hai would've walked right down the road and hitchhiked back to East Gladness soon as he saw their faces. But what could he do? He was part of a team, and that meant something, didn't it?

He wondered how far the hogs' souls had traveled by now. He wondered if they'd ever catch up to the human dead, if there was even a difference between them. How silly, he thought, to believe souls go anywhere at all. Why should they? What if they just lay down like this pig here and decided enough was enough? What if the soul is just as tired as the body? Just as worn out from seeing its family get tricked into a tent with dog treats only to come out emptied, soon to be roasted by a political candidate who will spend 50 million dollars on a campaign she'd end up losing anyway? Where's the soul in that?

Half hour later, Maureen's sedan will putter through the cobalt hills, all three of them dressed in cutout black garbage bags to keep from soiling the car with their bloody clothes—no one saying a word. Russia will be snoring through his tied-up hoodie, the glass Christmas bulbs clicking against the windows at each turn. In the end, the butchers wouldn't make the quota anyway; the promised bonus would never come. Out of pity or guilt, Wayne will slip each of them a fifty-dollar bill during their shifts the next week, and each will nod quietly like it's some secret brotherhood. "A good man. You're a good man, Wayne," Maureen will say. And by way of reply Wayne will tap the visor of his cap before turning to carve his chickens in silence.

"I think she knows," Hai said now, the snow coming on heavy.

"Knows what?" asked Wayne.

"That we murdered her relatives."

"Don't say stupid shit," Maureen said. "The lizards will feel your negative energy. Here, clap instead. When I feel fucked up sometimes, I just start clapping. Like this."

Maureen clapped. And the blood on her hands, dried from cold, burst into purple clouds, which delighted everyone. And they all started clapping, the puffs of blood blooming before their faces.

"It's kinda like a gender reveal," Russia said, chuckling.

"What gender is purple?" Hai asked.

"Means you're screwed," Wayne said.

They all looked at him, the man who got them into this mess, and laughed uneasily. They laughed because they knew the blood on their hands wasn't theirs, and amid the laughter, and the purple dust rising over their heads toward the new year, Hai forgot to pray.

14

A low red sun skims the freeway grass in the distance. Sony and Hai are riding the push scooter in the McDonald's parking lot, where the family has stopped after visiting the Stonewall Jackson Museum. The summer air is warm and sticky in the breeze made by their movement. Hai stands at the rear, while his cousin is tucked between his arms in front as they rattle over the pavement. Somewhere behind them, the women are laughing. It will only occur to Hai, years later, when his grandmother is long dead, how easy it was for them to laugh, that it was almost a superpower, to crack up with faces so open they seemed on the verge of falling apart, and to do so without a touch of shame in a parking lot on the side of a highway in August with only a half gallon of gas in the Toyota, their bellies filled with french fries and chicken tenders and Dr Pepper, which they mistook for Coca-Cola but drank anyway, grimacing, the taste too close to a particular brand of cough syrup from the country they fled.

This laughter, clipped by traffic, buoys him, and Hai pushes harder. "Look, it's a spaceship! We're on a spaceship, Sony!" Hai makes beeping sounds into Sony's ear as the wind whizzes through the holes left from their newly gone baby teeth.

Sony shakes his head, eyes shut. "Don't say that. It's not a real space-ship. It's just a scooter. Don't make stuff up for the heck of it."

"I thought you liked space stuff. Or is it just the Civil War stuff now?" Hai stops pushing and lets the momentum roll them forward.

"I like NASA—the real kind, not make-believe like *Star Trek*. My mom likes make-believe, but I hate it. It makes things wobbly."

The scooter crawls to a stop. Sony turns around and Hai gets a good look at his cousin, the mole under his eye only an errant speck of black pepper. Sony clutches the Stonewall Jackson coloring book his mother bought him back at the gift shop. The book is big as his torso, which makes him look comically tiny, like he's wearing a sandwich board advertising Confederate generals. In three years, he'll be a head taller than Hai, but now he still looks the part of the little cousin. "Using your imagination makes you dizzy?" Hai says. "That's stupid."

"I can imagine things into other things—just not into fake stuff. Lying makes me dizzy."

"What about this Stonewall guy." Hai flicks at the book. "You really think he danced the polka every night after dinner like that white lady said?"

"She wouldn't lie. She's a docent."

Hai looks back at the women, their floral shirts merged into a sin-gular mass of deep gold in the oncoming dusk. "You'd get bored of dancing *anything* after two minutes. The lady isn't decent at all. She's full of shit."

"Docent. Plus, my dad even said so. If you lie too much, everything around you starts to look like you're drunk, like Mr. Phuong outside of A Dong Market, always talking to invisible elves. My dad knows stuff like that, classified stuff. He's the Stonewall Jackson of the South Viet-namese Army."

"Grandma said he was a janitor on a military base." Hai lets the scooter drop to the ground. Aunt Kim had bought it for him when they stopped in New York City's Chinatown two days ago. It's a knockoff, not the name-brand Razor scooter—which is all the hype—but it still cost eighty dollars. Ma had scolded him for accepting such a decadent gift. "Let the boy have something nice," Aunt Kim said outside the stall. "I won't be seeing him for a long time anyway." Hai watched Ma bite her lip and look away as the crowd on Canal Street swallowed them up, and that was that.

"My dad was a corporal and he even has a wound in his wrist from the Vietcong to prove it." Sony's face is scrunched up, his chin lowered.

"Let me see this thing." Hai grabs the coloring book and sits on the curb, flipping through it. Sony huddles beside him, relieved to move on to what he loves. The pages show Jackson in various pastoral settings, often with horses. The images are black-and-white, as expected. However, strangely, each figure's skin tone was already shaded in with a peach-like pink, making the faces look like they're peeking through the monochrome outlines, alive behind the paper.

"At least they give you a head start with the skin," Hai says.

"Faces are hard to color, that's why. Lots of tiny parts, like eyes."

Hai stops on a page showing Jackson sitting in his parlor smoking a pipe and reading a book while his wife, Elinor, crochets nearby at the fireplace. He hovers a moment, the shadow of his fingers darkening Elinor's smile. Strange new thoughts have been coming to him lately, mostly at night, right after the lights go out and his mother's TV hums with HGTV infomercials in the next room. In the dark his mind would snag on the features of some boy in his seventh-grade class: Chris, Nate, Tyler, Armando, Jason. But it wasn't exactly the faces themselves, though each had its distinct charm, a curious openness common to twelve-year-olds: Hai saw no beauty or prettiness in them, but rather a force-ful, brooding kinship to an amorphous *boyness*, that realm he was supposed to possess but was still partially hidden from him. Though it had no source he could name, there was something beyond reach, a gleaming heat, the way one knows, at times, where the moon hangs in the sky on an overcast night. Or a word existing before its definition— and like all things without meaning, it made no sense. It shook him with a hushed but stubborn haunting, his lids fluttering as their faces came closer, and he'd pull his blanket over his head to cover from the chill he made of himself.

"Wouldn't it be funny if it was another man sitting there knitting," Hai says with a laugh, his eyes trained on Sony, who's studying the couple.

Sony looks up. "That wouldn't make any sense." Then considers it, squinting at the image. "No," he shakes his head at last, decisive. "That would be weird. First off, they would most likely be fellow officers or instructors at the academy. Which meant Elinor would have to leave the room while they talked. That's what the docent said. She also . . ." As Sony drones on, Hai picks up a pebble and gently places it over Jackson's face, like a piece on a checkers board, then does the same with Elinor.

That's when they laugh again. Hai turns to see the women, mouths wide open with shut eyes, as they playfully slap each other's legs, holding their sides under a parking lot lamp that has just flickered on. Then he looks down at the two pink faces, each one covered in stone, and lets the women's voices wash over him.

HAI HAD FORGOTTEN to wash up before clocking out and was now wiping his greasy hands on his HomeMarket apron as he stared at the poster across the waiting room. It showed a child standing on a shoreline caught under a tsunami wave made entirely out of silhouette, as if the wave itself was cut out. The wave's shadow fell on the child, who was merely an outline filled with light. Below the scene was printed, in block letters, the command DON'T LET YOUR CHILD BE SWALLOWED BY

DEPRESSION. Underneath this was the name of a pill, Luminkind, that was to rescue your kid from this natural disaster of the mind. Hai wondered if he was too old to take something made for children. At what point does childhood sadness become adult sadness anyway? Does the tsunami get larger as the figure grows? Was his wave already twice the size of the one in the poster?

As he pondered this the door flung open, revealing a man dressed in a grey suit with no tie. He wheezed as he ambled toward Hai, his enormous face resembling punched dough. He had the wasted look of a public defender but was actually a psychiatrist, and this was his office. "Hey, you the father?" he said, then clocked Hai's youth. "Or brother or whatever?"

"I'm just—"

"Here." He turned to a nearby rack of pamphlets, arranged like rest stop brochures, each one relating to various mental illnesses. He picked two out, paused to think, then put one back. "Take this and read it and discuss it with him, okay? You guys have a long road ahead as a family. But this kinda thing happens. It's normal, okay? Super normal. Mark will follow up with booking his sessions. Any questions?" He was in his early thirties but had the voice of an old man, thick with spit. He was the only psychiatrist who both took Sony's state insurance *and* was in biking distance. "Now, the antipsychotics I gave him are gonna make him nauseous for the first two weeks, so make sure he takes 'em with plenty of food first, okay? Don't let the term scare ya. Sony's not crazy. He's a normal guy. Got it? Maybe a little extra normal." He tried to add a laugh but abandoned it and just coughed into his arm.

Hai nodded. "Thanks."

The man walked back inside. "Mark!" he shouted to a secretary somewhere in the other room. "Make him another appointment in a month, then shut it down. I'm done for the day. You wanna hit up Hairy Harry's?"

After some murmuring behind the door, Sony came out, his face unsmiling but placid. He was still wearing his apron and black cap. It almost made Hai laugh to see them, two fast-food workers in a shrink's office, like a *New Yorker* cartoon caption competition.

"So? You officially loony or what?" Hai said.

Sony shrugged, then glanced down at the pamphlet in Hai's hand. Hai saw the words for the first time: *Your Neuro-atypical Teen: The Next Five Years.*

Hai held it up for Sony to see, but he was staring at the ground, the bag of corn bread crinkling in his hand. Hai scanned the room, almost hoping there would be another poster that might instruct, through metaphor, what this meant, how big the wave his cousin was standing under. But the lights just hummed and Mark and the doctor could be heard shuffling toward the door, putting on their coats, so Hai just gave him a hug. Sony flinched and stiffened at first, then relented. They stayed like that a bit, then Sony, through an affected cartoon voice, the one he used when nervous, said, "Ouch. You're crushing me!"

"Good luck, guys. And stay safe!" the doctor called as they all walked out, the way you'd call to people as they got into their cars after a party. It was only five p.m. but the parking lot was pitch and shone with a thin layer of ice. Hai retrieved the bike from a nearby shrub and walked it over to the road.

"You didn't tell me this was why they put you in the group home," Hai said, climbing on. "I thought this was a therapist."

"It is."

"I mean for, like, sadness or whatever."

"It is."

Hai shoved the brochure into his jacket. "Never mind. It's okay, okay? Everything's normal."

"I have to take these," Sony said, shaking a bottle with the two sample pills the doctor had given him. "I'm kinda scared."

"I know." Hai felt his voice soften. "But you'll make it, I promise. They're doctors. They know what they're doing. They went to real college." It was hard for him to say what he felt were lies.

Sony shrugged.

Hai took a piece of corn bread from Sony's bag and broke it in half. "Want one?"

Sony took the piece and climbed onto the back pegs.

"You on tight?" Hai asked, chewing as he pedaled.

They rode past the houses with square-lit windows strung on both sides of the road and said nothing to each other for a while, only their breaths wafting up under the cones of light from the occasional lamp-post. Then Hai heard himself saying it. And he said it again, quietly at first, then louder as Sony's grip tightened on his shoulder. And Sony joined him as they said it together, speeding down the hill, back to East Gladness, its water tower belted with a string of colored Christmas lights in the foggy distance. "This is not a spaceship," they chanted. "This is not a spaceship! This is not a spaceship!" Until their voices broke off and they were swallowed by the oncoming valley and all was dark save for the faint blue etches of ice, crystal veins creeping across the road in their wake.

Winter

15

In somebody's life the train whistle blew through the late afternoon as it headed to Marlborough on the first day of winter. You could hear it standing in the parking lot of the HomeMarket, the blacktop dusted with frost as the last cars pulled out, the people inside full of hydrogenated oils and iodized salt after sitting all morning on warped church pews, nodding in and out of sermons they've heard a hundred times before. It was four days before Christmas and the winter light breathed around the store, which was still burning deep gold inside. Through the wide, daily washed windows, clear as air, a large woman in a manager's white button-up and bow tie flipped the sign from COME ON IN! to SEE YOU IN THE MORNING! before heading back to the counter. The crew took off their rubber gloves, untied their aprons, and gathered around her, their heads rapt in attention as she seemed on the cusp of making a speech of great significance, one that might report on the realignment of stars or announce the emergence of a new, benevolent epoch.

There were only three customers left inside, regulars known by name and gait. A pair of working girls in their forties, eyes smoked out with makeup and leather jackets zipped to their chins, were tucked in a booth working over a whole roasted chicken, their primary-colored nails gleaming between rib bones. Wayne had made it special just for them, rubbing it with rosemary picked from his windowsill garden at home and timing the roast ahead of their night shift along Route 4.

The last customer was a mechanic with a youthful face and battered, oil-clotted hands, whose sky-blue work shirt Hai always spotted the second he stepped through the door, the word *Tom* stitched over his heart. He sat alone by the dimming window over his usual: mashed potatoes and green beans doused with gravy. He ate with his head down, hiding the shiny, taut bump where his left ear used to be, stealing glances at the women picking the chicken down to bones.

The manager clapped her hands to get everyone's attention, the gold name tag etched with *BJ* catching the light as she moved. Her mother, in her seventies and stooped over a plastic table in a faux fur coat and red beret, had brought everyone a tray of her famous lasagna. The employees ate it standing, some with eyes closed and swaying slightly, which made the mother lean back and fold her arms, nodding with preternatural pride. She looked up at her daughter with something even more luminous, her mouth half-open as the woman she birthed now towered before the room corralled to attention. "All right, all right, all right," BJ said with a Matthew McConaughey drawl. "Y'all ready for the show?"

Maureen was chatting with one of the sex workers, so Wayne grabbed a corn bread from the basket and chucked it at her. "Shut it, Maur," he said as it fell to the table after hitting her chest.

Maureen picked it up and took a bite. "I didn't know this concert came with snacks."

"If you want more to snack on, just let me know." Wayne grinned at the women, who laughed into their jacket collars.

"You can do anything you want for a grand." Maureen winked at the women. "What you think, girls? Too low?"

BJ licked her lips and clasped her hands. "Remember, though, this is just a practice set. It's called a rehearsal, okay? So don't put too much weight on it and all that."

"You're doing great, Jean!" Her mother pumped her fur-lined fist.

"I didn't even start yet, Maman." BJ lifted a portable amp from behind the cooling vats and plugged it in, then unzipped her JanSport backpack, which looked more like a fanny pack in her hands. The zipper opened and out fell a pocket dictionary, along with a couple *Death Note* mangas. BJ snatched them and shoved them inside.

"A dictionary, huh? And what kind of grown woman reads coloring books?" asked Wayne, a plate of half-eaten lasagna in his hand.

"Do you know who else read the dictionary, cover to cover?" BJ glanced around the room. "Eminem. That's right." She looked at Russia, who nodded. "And don't sleep on *Death Note*. There's some good shit in there."

"You *would* be widely read," said Sony, predictably sincere. "All great generals are."

BJ switched on the amp and its static buzz filled the room. She removed her bow tie, wrapped it around her forehead like a headband, and smiled with all her teeth. The room grew quiet. The women in the booth sipped from their sodas, skeptically amused.

"You got this, BJ," Hai said.

"You can do it, baby," her mother chimed in. "You were blessed by *Him*."

BJ smiled nervously, then tapped the play button on the stereo with her shoe, and the heavy metal beat dropped. The restaurant bounded with thick, discordant guitar riffs, a dense, muscular drone of drums—and soon everyone's heads started to bob as if on puppet strings. BJ's mother snapped her long bony fingers, the fur jacket flouncing around her shoulders. She opened her mouth to laugh but only BJ's voice was heard through the speakers as she metal-screeched through a rendition of "Bodies" by Drowning Pool. BJ paced back and forth behind the counter as the bass raged on, the sight of their manager performing heavy metal behind the station where green beans and creamed spinach were usually served seemed conjured from a fever dream.

The crew had been hearing about her pro wrestling aspirations for months (and for Wayne and Maureen, years) and how vital an entrance song was to bolster a wrestler's persona—but none of them expected her to be even decent, let alone capable of sounds most of them had heard only on TV. Hai found himself flushed with a rare sense of communal triumph. He took two inadvertent steps toward her, as if toward a mystical source of energy.

"Okay," said Wayne, nodding along with his arms crossed. "Okay, so you're all right. Damn, this sounds . . . well, it sounds legit. Like," he turned to Russia, "like that crazy white music."

Sony was by the soda fountain, spellbound, mouth agape, his cup overflowing under the Sprite tab. He stared up at his Ulysses S. Grant thrashing her head to heavy metal. Even the beautiful mechanic, who Hai kept sneaking eyes at, pushed his plate of mashed potatoes aside to turn around, a smile eased across his lips. The working girls were shouting BJ's name, hooting between cupped hands, the tiny box of a restaurant in a strip mall suddenly a bizarre town square.

When the song was over, her neck drenched, her face a mix of happiness and relief, touched with the exuberance of accomplishment, taking in the dining room, her little planet spinning with the people who worked for and with her, BJ dashed from the counter and hugged her mother. "Vas-y, ma fille! Vas-y," her mother cried out into BJ's shoulder.

"Everyone listen up!" BJ cried. "On January eleventh. At Hairy Harry's bar on Churchill. I'll be in the lineup for the Valley Grand Slam Amateur Wrestling Association. So this was just a taste for you guys to get ready. It will be *for real* for real after New Year's, alright?"

"That was fantastic!" Hai reached up to hug her. "How did you get so good while working *here*? How did you have time to practice?"

"I love what I do, rook. Shit, I'm trying to be, like, the Steve Jobs of wrestling, you know?"

"Isn't that, like, the Rock or whatever?"

"Like I said," she patted Hai on his head like he was a little boy who had a lot to learn, "the *Steve Jobs* of wrestling. I'm here to change the game."

Hai went over to Sony to hug him but stopped himself, recalling something in the brochure about unprompted touching. "There's nothing she can't do," Sony said, enraptured. "She just makes magic. Hey, BJ!" He waved like a fangirl in the front row. "You're the general of magic!"

"Wait till you see my secret weapon." A knowing smile crossed BJ's face. "You'll see what I got up my sleeve at the match. It's gonna be epic!"

As the excitement ebbed in the room, Maureen waved Hai and Russia over to the register. She bent over and took something out from under the counter. "I want y'all to have this, okay? And you boys can share it if you want. It's for you both, really."

Before he knew it, Hai found himself holding what seemed like a plaster mold of a phallus the size of a middle school baseball trophy. Hai held it out in front of him. "It's perfect," he offered, "but . . . what is it?"

"It's R2-D2." Maureen folded her arms in admiration. "I figure since it was me who convinced you all to come help Wayne with those hogs, I just wanted to at least give you something. You know, as a thank-you."

"Dude," said Russia. "It looks kinda off, don't you think?"

Hai nodded to himself. "Six out of ten in accuracy."

"It's not finished, of course. Paul was making it for me before he got sick."

"Oh, I'm sorry," Hai said, turning it around. "It looks pretty close, actually."

"I have a completed one of C-3PO on my bed stand. It's papier-mâché, a tad skinny, and he didn't get to paint it, but you get the gist. I mean . . . I'm not gonna lie, it *does* look like a penis," she giggled. "Fuck, even the little wheels on the bottom look like shrunken balls. But if you squint," she closed one eye, "it's definitely R2-D2."

They stood a moment studying the object, their black uniforms making them look like undertakers inspecting an urn.

"It's all yours, rook." Russia tapped Hai on the chest and walked away.

Hai cradled the penis in his arms. "Thanks."

It was starting to flurry outside, flakes spinning in squalls through the drive-thru light. Not a single car could be seen beyond the glass, only a soft violet glow coming up from the earth, which meant the ground was already covered with snow.

A FTER THEY CLOSED and the parking lot emptied, the mini-concert all but a vague hum through their ears, Sony hopped on the back pegs of Hai's bike and the boys sped down the road toward the center of East Gladness, R2-D2 poking through the zipper in Hai's backpack. The pavement, warmed by the day's weak sun, had already begun to melt the snow into a wet sheen.

"Tonight's the night." Sony gripped his cousin's shoulder, his voice pitched with excitement. "I can't believe you found enough. How did you do it?"

In the commotion of BJ's rehearsal, Hai had forgotten about this secret mission they had planned after work, and let out a nervous laugh. "You think we'll have a white Christmas, Sony?" The brochure had mentioned it's helpful repeating names in conversation, that it'd be some kind of anchor for the "afflicted."

Sony removed his cap and held it out in front of him, letting the flakes blur into its bowl. "Yes," he said, breathless. "It *has to*, since we haven't had one in the last three years and it never goes more than three years. They won't let it happen."

"They who?"

Sony thought about it. "The generals."

"Robert E. Lee?" Hai dipped his head as the bike approached a small hill and they picked up speed.

"No, silly," he laughed. "The generals of history. And I'm one of their soldiers. See?" He showed Hai his cap. Before they left, Sony went to his locker and switched out his HomeMarket hat with his Union infantry field cap, fixed with a shiny golden bugle, he had bought on eBay.

"Why you wearing that thing anyway?"

"For luck. We're gonna need it tonight."

An icy gust blew up from the river and hit their faces, the boys wincing as they shouldered into the cold and the bike headed toward the lights in the distance.

BY THE TIME they made it to the strip mall, this one closer to the heart of town, the snow was done, leaving behind it a fog so dense the neon signs became smears of color suspended across the parking lot. Cold and wet, fingers raw, they walked the bike toward the lights as, one by one, the businesses came to view: a packy, the windows lined with wine bottles and liquor, an urgent care closed for the night. And there, in between a Subway and a hole-in-the-wall spot up for lease, was Bryon's Insta-Bail. Underneath the yellow-lit sign a banner read A WAY OUT IN 24 HOURS: OPEN ALL NIGHT.

It was almost ten p.m. when Sony pressed the buzzer and a man's frog-like face poked out from behind the glass counter. He studied them a moment, then waved the boys in and released the lock. The place was small but bright, like a drugstore in the outskirts of a distant and crumbling republic. There was a wood-paneled waiting room and a counter where the man sat chewing a sandwich. Above him was a poster of George W. Bush with a speech bubble that said, *Freedom ain't free.*

"Hey." Sony stepped to the counter. "I'm back. And we got it now. We can get my mom.".

The man held up a finger and winced as he worked to swallow. "Give me a minute. I got two bites left."

The boys stood, looking around the room, the sound of chewing and juices dripping on wax wrapper. The man took a final bite, sipped from a Subway cup, tossed the wrapper vaguely at a garbage can nearby, and wiped his mouth with his shirt collar. "Okay, who we liberating tonight, boys?" When he clocked the Union cap, the man's beady eyes, set deep in pink-raw skin, lit up. "Oh, right. You again. With the mom up in York Corrections?" He rubbed his jowls and nodded to himself.

"Yes, sir. Lê Thị Kim's her name. We can bail her out now."

Hai hadn't said a word this whole time. He'd never been in a bail bonds office, and it suddenly crushed him to think his cousin had been coming here for months alone with his useless little Civil War hat.

"Remember, five grand. No less. That's not including the fees, which puts you back half a grand more." The man leaned back and folded his arms. "I don't make the rules, capisce? If I could free everyone's mother for a nickel, I would." He couldn't help smirking. "I have a soft spot for single moms, you know. You her other son? Who did you guys rob to make this work, huh?" He winked at Hai and put up his hand. "No, no, no. Don't tell me! I'm not a lawyer." He slapped the desk and laughed. His thick glasses made it look like he was wearing googly eyes. Hai's head started to hurt. He felt like a reflection in a fun house mirror.

Sony turned his whole body to look at his cousin, whose hands were hidden in his UPS jacket. All of a sudden Hai couldn't move. Something had pinned him under the humming light. The man's labored breathing, which forced itself through a clogged nose, literally whistled as he inhaled.

"Show him, Hai. Show him what the old lady gave you." Sony tilted his head back and looked at Hai with lit desperation, as if looking at a map to a place he'd never been. "You said she paid you for taking care of her, right? And I'll reimburse you for this. I know you didn't want me to, but I will. Promise." Sony turned to the clerk. "I'm a man of my word, sir."

This was the plan—to finally bail out Aunt Kim with the $4,274 Hai took from Grazina's cookie tin. That, plus the one thousand and change Sony had saved up, would be enough. Hai shut his eyes until the sound of the ticking radio in the corner and the clerk's wheezing dissolved, and through the shadow under his lids, Grazina's head swam up to him, open and innocent as a lily, and he saw his own face reflected in her wide glasses. She was watching something over his shoulder, something he couldn't stomach to see: it was himself standing on the rail bridge on that rainy evening in September, the threshold of it all. Then he saw the bakery, the soldiers breaking the windows, a seventeen-year-old Grazina crying inside, surrounded by loaves of rye, the trains moving through kingdoms of ungodly death made by God's children. He didn't know his hands were shaking until he looked down and saw them.

"Here's my half, sir," Sony's voice said.

There was the sound of bills being counted.

Hai looked down past his hands and saw the crushed bread at his feet, the rain from the night he first met Grazina soaking through the rolls. Then he surfaced and nearly gasped realizing what he was about to do—and changed his mind.

The money was in two wads, one in each pocket. He put only one wad on the counter.

The man counted Sony's stack and put it aside. Hai was surprised how small $1,200 looked, no thicker than a Hershey bar. Next the man counted Hai's, then stopped, looked away at the wall, and let out a dramatic sigh before shoving the two little stacks back at them. "Not enough," he said with a face like he expected this all along.

Sony's shoulders wilted. "No, no. My cousin wouldn't get it wrong. He went to college. Sir——" And this was where Hai had to turn away. "Sir," Sony said, saluting the man, his hand trembling at the visor of the Union cap, the gold bugle blazing under the lights. "We wouldn't come here to mess with you. Please, with all due respect——"

"Okay, alright. Fuck me." The man picked up the two stacks and counted again as Hai stumbled toward the door, unable to meet Sony's dewy eyes.

"See? No. Still doesn't add up, brother." He handed Sony the money and told him, in a half-cheery tone, that he was only two grand off. "That's nothing. You'll get it in no time. Everybody does."

Sony turned to his right as if someone who would help was sitting in one of the waiting chairs. But no one was there. "Please," Sony said, his voice almost squeaking. "Can you please take it anyway?"

Hai walked back and put his hand on Sony's shoulder, gentle at first, then pressing down. "Come on. I fucked up, okay? I can't count."

"It's okay," Sony mumbled, looking down at his shoes. "Everyone has limitations. Even Lincoln." He handed Hai back the wad of cash.

"We'll try again, okay? You can help me count next time before we head out. I majored in general ed and suck at math. I'm sorry."

"Thanks for understanding, boys. I'm just the messenger. But hey . . . actually," the clerk leaned over the faded counter, "you guys know any- thing about astrology? I've been trying to get into it. My new girlfriend is *obsessed*. I'm telling you, broads with bangs love this shit. Look here." He showed them an entry in the *East Gladness Eagle*. "It says Aries will have 'an event that will bring renewed levity in your life by the end of the week.' But what the hell is a 'renewed levity'? Did mine expire or something?" He let out a nervous laugh. "Wonder if this thing can tell if the Bruins will make the playoffs."

Hai turned and walked out.

"Sorry, sir," Sony said, "but I believe only in history."

"You know what? Me too, brother," the man said, nodding. "Me too."

Their breaths smoked as they stared at the sodium lights criss-crossing the lot. Though it was still days away, the whole town had the eerie blank silence of Christmas Eve.

"I wish I didn't feel this way," Sony said.

"What way?"

"I dunno . . . like . . ." He shut his eyes, his forehead wrinkling as he searched.

"It's alright—"

"Like a loser," he said at last.

Hai flinched. Not because it hurt to hear but because he knew something like it was coming. Sony sat down on the curb and Hai joined him, their shoulders touching through their jackets.

"Hey, look at me." Hai cupped Sony's chin and met his eyes. "I'm a fucking loser too. Okay?"

"But you went to college—"

"No. Don't you get it? I dropped out. That's, like, worse than never going in the first place. I quit. I had the *chance* and I blew it. I'm a bigger loser than you or anybody else we fucking know. You, you at least have nothing to lose."

Sony frowned at this, more bewildered than hurt.

"Fuck." Hai kicked at a nearby paper cup. "I don't mean it like that. I just thought . . . I'm an idiot and can't count, okay?" He hid his face in his palms and had the sudden urge to scream. Not knowing what to do, he took out his phone and flipped it open.

"Who are you calling at this hour?"

"Just give me a sec. Here, listen to this." Hai played an MP3 of the song he used as a ringtone, the only song he had on his Nokia.

"What is it?"

"American Football."

Sony gave him a weird look.

"It's a band. And the song's called 'The Summer Ends.' I listen to it when I'm fucked up."

Sony listened to the tinny music, his head lowered and very still. "But it *sounds* sad. Why would you listen to sad things when you're already sad?"

"I dunno." Hai drew circles in the pavement. "Guess it gives the feeling a place to stand in. Like a little bus stop." The neon Subway sign switched off, and in the sudden dark he noticed the winter stars over the strip mall, clearer than they'd ever be in summer.

Sony tugged at his sleeve. "Look at this," he said as the song went on.

It was a photo. Hai brought it closer and saw his own face, then his mother's, Aunt Kim, Bà ngoại, everyone. They're standing on the tarmac of Tân Sơn Nhất airport in a group shot, moments before stepping onto the plane to America, for good. They're dressed in the garish floral patterns so common to rice farmers, the fabric bought from bolts of cloth in open markets, then sewn at home under a thunderous metal Singer machine left over from the French occupation. Their faces harsh in the noon light, unsmiling, worry crushing the features into knots. He examined the infant blob on his mother's hip sucking his own thumb, Ma no older in the picture than he is now—at the bottom of himself.

"You always carry this with you?"

Sony nodded, wallet in hand. In the photo, Sony is not yet born but two years away, a snapshot of his inevitable becoming, of them forever on their way to East Gladness, where he will be born a month too soon, so terrible was his eagerness to meet them, these losers.

He leaned in and Hai saw the stars reflected in the bugle on Sony's cap. "Isn't my mom beautiful?" Sony stared at the photo as if for the first time, his neck craning over Hai's arm so that his Adam's apple touched his wrist. "They're all beautiful," Sony's voice said. "Even Grandma. She's not old yet. And look at my dad, you see him? Look how short he is. I'm taller than him now!" He laughed, giddy with this precious fact. "My mom's up to his ear. But she's only up to my chest in real life. I mean, in this life, right now—"

"I get it."

Sony grew quiet, looked away at the dim headlights trailing off on the highway. The song was over. "But we're still losers. All of us. All we did was lose. Just like Robert E. Lee, my dad also lost his war in the South. My mom said Dad used to be taller, like me, but he grew short after all the fighting. War shrunk him up, and my mom lost her house, then her salon burned. And I lost her to York Corrections. And Bà ngoại's lost in heaven." His voice wobbled and he bit down on his jacket sleeve to stop whatever was coming. "We might be beautiful, but it doesn't matter when we're losers. We're short losers. Beautiful, short losers. And that doesn't do anything for anybody."

"Beautiful short losers." Hai nodded at the huddled faces staring back at them from the past. What good is beauty, any beauty, if nobody wins?

Sony carefully slid the photo back in his wallet. "Did you know . . ." He scooted closer and breathed into his palms. "Did you know my dad has a diamond in his hand?"

"Can you stop talking crazy—just for once?" Hai said, suddenly irritated. He blinked hard through his blurred vision and wiped his nose.

Sony grinned, this tidbit about the man he idolized coming through him with electric force. He licked his lips and talked about how his father, a soldier in the South Vietnamese Army, was at a jeweler picking out a ring for Aunt Kim when a Vietcong car bomb went off at a noodle stall next door. How after the explosion, his father shielded his eyes from the smoke and saw the back of his right hand sparkling through the dust. A diamond, big as a pea, was embedded into the top of his hand. He then wrapped the hand with his overshirt, and by the time he made it back to the field hospital at base camp, the rag had buried the diamond so deep that when the nurse was dressing the wound in fresh bandages, his hand no longer caught the light. The diamond lodged deep inside him. "When I was little," Sony shook his head at the stars, "whenever I was having a bad day, he'd take my finger and run it over the hard bumps on his hand and say, 'Your daddy's made of diamonds, son. You don't have a three-star-general dad. You have a diamond-general dad.' That would always make me feel better."

One day, Sony went on, his voice wistful and soft, he and his dad were walking to the library, where the boy would get lost for hours in the Civil War section of American history. Though he left with another woman after Sony was born, his father managed, once in a blue moon, to come back and see his son.

The handful of neighbor kids recognized Sony and went over, calling him the usual names. *Hey, crackhead, you know God split you in the wrong spot, right? Do you put your head in the toilet to take a dump?* They cackled like hyenas, and Sony's father, having learned English to work on the army base, heard every bit of it.

"At first he just tried to speed up and he grabbed my hand and we ran, but the kids followed us. Finally my dad turned around and showed them his hand. He said he had a diamond in his hand from the war. That the war gave him diamond hands. And he let the kids touch 'em. They were quiet for a long time as they rubbed the diamond bulging under his skin. One of them asked if my dad killed anybody, and Dad said it was between him and Jesus, and the kid understood in his heart what that meant, and the boys whispered to each other and backed off a few steps. Then they just stopped and watched as we kept on walking. After a while my dad started humming this song in Vietnamese. And I held on to his hand, sometimes rubbing the diamond under his skin, until the library appeared." Sony's brows arched, lost in the memory's wide undertow.

"Your dad's the best," Hai said. "I wish mine was like that."

"It's okay. Not everyone can be an officer in the army. Besides, car bombs are actually very rare, and the chances both our dads would be in one would be next to none."

Hai flicked Sony's cap. "Let's get going, soldier."

By the time they rode away from the strip mall, the only light left was Bryon's twenty-four-hour Insta-Bail. Sony had forgotten his backpack, along with his new meds, so they rode back to HomeMarket to fetch them. Later that night Hai would sneak into Grazina's pantry and slip the two bundles of cash back in the tin box. But now, as they approached the store, Sony seemed to have forgotten about the failed mission, giggling to himself each time they hit a bump. "Look!" He laughed and pointed at the HomeMarket sign, part of which had blown a circuit. They crossed the lawn on the median, and the grass, stiffened from frost, snapped under the tires as they headed toward the word HOMEMAR hovering red through the mist.

16

W hat is it?" Hai said. "You alright? You want me to make you some hot milk?" He had just gotten out the shower and found Grazina sitting slumped over at the top of the stairs.

"It's Christmas Eve, Labas."

In the house's unchanging light, each day resembled the other, and he'd forgotten all about it.

"I don't understand," she said, resting her chin on her palm. "I feel so heavy. It's supposed to be Jesus's birthday. But I feel strange, Labas."

"Your new haircut's not so bad, really. It's like mine. We're twins now." He forced a grin at her.

She touched her bangs. "No, it's good. You did good, boy. I just feel . . . I don't know. Sometimes, I get like this. And . . . I want to climb inside the TV and just stay there." She paused, her eyes searching. "That sounds crazy, yes?"

"You're just clinically depressed," he heard himself say. "Means you're sad without a reason."

Her forehead wrinkled at the idea. "No, I didn't outlive Stalin to be *depressed*." She shook her head defiantly. "You kids blame everything on feelings. Do you blame starvation on feelings too? Floods? Earthquakes?"

"Look, I have it too. It's just like weather. Like clouds and rain and stuff. They go away. But some of us spend more time in London, you know? Or Seattle. You're just raining right now. Remember? What about the rabbits and the light inside the carrots and all that?"

She nodded. "I guess I'm raining on Christmas Eve, then."

They were quiet a moment, then her shoulders flinched. "Oh Jesus Mother Mary, we have to go see Lucas today! He's expecting us at five. It's Kūčios—I almost forgot."

Hai blinked at her. "What?" This whole time he had thought Lucas was made up, or at most a scrambled figment of her youth, another dementia-riddled apparition. On every photo on all the mantels and walls, there was never a Lucas, never a son. Only a blond girl, Lina, her school portraits, from kindergarten to college, fanning above the defunct fireplace as an accordion of time. Hai sat up. "What are you talking about?"

"Yes, every Christmas Eve we have a dinner with lots of fish. Kūčios." Grazina grunted to her feet and shuffled to her room, grabbed a piece of paper from her nightstand, and handed it to him. On the back of a used envelope was an address for a condo in Manchester—a well-off bedroom town twenty minutes by car across the river.

"Wait, you're serious? What do we do now, then?"

"Don't worry." She crossed the room and opened the lowest drawer on the dresser. "Here, put this on."

He unfurled what appeared to be a nurse's scrub top.

"It was Janet's. It's big on you but it should work. Go on, good. Wait . . . There you go." She helped pull the scrub over his head, eyeing it on him.

It was two sizes too big, the seams draping over his shoulders, but he managed to roll up the sleeves and make it work.

"You look the part. Here, just take the name tag off." She removed the pin tag printed with *Janet*.

"What am I supposed to say? Which hospital do I even work for?"

"New Cross, in Bethlehem. And don't worry. I'll tell them you're new. My son, he respects Asians. Says they make good doctors. Lucas is a genius in brains but not so good in human relations. But he'll like you better than Janet. He thought she wore too much perfume." She sighed, her eyes in the distance. "He's so fresh, that boy."

She looked like she was about to crumple again, so he did a little twirl. "Hello, ma'am," he said in an official-sounding voice. "I'm here to be your nurse-slash-chauffeur for the night. May all your Christmases be filled with fish and cooka."

"Kūčios." She laughed and hit him on the arm. "Now help me find my owl sweater. I got it in London on my anniversary in 1986. And with my own money too."

HALF HOUR LATER they were in the kitchen, onions sizzling in butter on a skillet. The day was windless, chilly, and overcast, which meant snow ahead. Grazina, engulfed to her chin in a lumpy wool sweater knitted across the chest with a huge white owl, the sleeves rolled up, spun about the tiny room with nimble, youthful footing—muscle memory aided by a double dose of Aricept. Her hands danced over the burners, chopping and stirring.

Hai sat sipping coffee and nibbling a Pop-Tart while reading *The Brothers Karamazov*, the worn paperback cover translucent against the words beneath. "What's a samovar anyway?" Hai put down the book.

"Some kind of Indian pastry, yes? Jesus, I used to know. But that was a long time ago." Grazina scrunched her nose and removed her glasses. "Look in that drawer there. My husband used to keep a dictionary for his crossword puzzles."

It was dusk outside when she finished. The cuckoo clock read 4:05 p.m. Grazina wrapped the steaming casserole tray filled with green peppers stuffed with fish covered in tomatoes and onions. "Lucas's favorite. An old recipe from my baba," she said. But Hai remembered stumbling on the recipe weeks earlier, cut from a Betty Crocker cookbook, tucked into the first magazine in the stack on the table.

As she finished up and wiped her hands, Grazina stopped and just stood there, so still Hai put down his book and looked up.

"I almost forgot to call Lina." She shook her head. "Oh, I never forget on Christmas Eve." She picked up the rotary phone on the table, dialed a number, and waited, the veins in her hands shifting as she held the receiver. It went on ringing.

"Maybe she's out," he said. "You know, getting last-minute presents and stuff. People do that all the time."

"That's right," Grazina whispered, staring out the window. She let it ring a few more times before hanging up.

"Should we bring dessert?" he asked, still unsure whether Lucas was real. "I still got a bag of corn bread in the freezer. It'll thaw by the time we get there."

"Good idea. We can't be good guests with just one tray of stuffed peppers. He has kids, you know." She opened the fridge and handed him the bag. "It's Christmas, Labas. Can you believe it?"

"It's Christmas," he said.

"You sure it's fourteen?" Hai said, staring down the hall on his tippy toes. They were standing outside the condo of a gated community called Colonial Green, the lights from the cab that dropped them off fading down the bend.

"It's been fourteen for over ten years. I think."

He watched her eyes, which seemed clear. He had given her an extra half dose, just in case.

"And it's your son, Lucas, right? He's a person. You've seen him?"

"Don't be stupid. He came out of *here*." She pointed between her legs. "Why wouldn't I see him?"

The casserole was cold under his hands. "Here, let's try this." He pressed every doorbell in the building, all six of them, and waited. Seconds later the lock buzzed and they hurried in from the cold. On the second floor, they found number fourteen, faint music seeping through the door. Grazina knocked, her blue-veined hands making no sound against the music.

"I'll try again."

"You sure he called that cab for you? *You* didn't call it? Not even by accident? Did you call it yesterday, maybe?"

Grazina's head floated back, her mouth parted. "Oh God, oh God." She put her hand over her mouth and looked at him with red-ringed eyes. "I'm not sure. I don't know now." She shook her head.

"It's okay, don't cry. Hey——" He pulled her into him and she said something in Lithuanian against his shoulder.

"Mom? You're here."

In their embrace they hadn't noticed the door opening.

A paunchy man in his sixties with a sad-brown cardigan smiled and rubbed his grey neck-beard. The two let go of each other and blinked at him in their oversize coats. Hai gave an awkward wave, then thrust the casserole at the man, who tucked his chin, as if being handed a piece of shrapnel, and gently pushed it back. "Um. We have plenty of food, actually. Here, come on in. It's freezing. Glad the taxi found you okay."

Grazina pushed up her glasses and wobbled inside clutching Hai's hand.

The condo was spacious, the ceiling vaulted with polished oak beams. Everything was lit by dimmable sconces hung on the walls. There was so much *space*. That's what wealth is, he realized: to live in a house where all the tools of living are out of sight. There were no brooms or mops or laundry baskets, no endless trays or cubbies for receipts, bills, or pills and keys. Everything, from the counter to the furniture, the side tables to the credenzas—all of it was there for decor, for the pleasure of the eyes and access of the body. Nothing was in the way. It reminded him of homes he'd seen in pharmaceutical commercials.

Grazina stopped and looked around. "Very modern," she nodded. "Very nice. See, Labas? Science can do incredible things." She beamed at her son, who rubbed his elbow and looked to the kitchen, where a woman and two children, a boy and a girl, appeared.

"Oh, look at you, Grazina! You're fabulous." The woman scuttled over and gave her a hug, her arms encircling Grazina, Hai noticed, without actually touching her. She turned from cheek to cheek, making loud smooches, her red lips nearly a foot from Grazina's face. "And you must be her aide. Oh gosh, you're so *young*. I was in the Peace Corps in Malaysia, you know, and I was so *jealous* of the ladies there. But oh, what am I doing? How are you?" She smiled with every tooth. "Here, let me take this." She took the casserole, lifted the foil with her pinkie before forcing her wince into a grin. "Hmm, looks great."

"Tilapia-stuffed peppers," Grazina said to Lucas. "For Kūčios."

"Coochie," the boy whispered to his sister. He was around fifteen, scrawny and cursed with a face whose features were all pinched toward the center, as if molded out of clay by a toddler.

The girl was slightly younger and had seemingly no chin to speak of. She stepped behind her mother and covered her nose. "She smells like pee."

"Abbey," her mother said. "Be respectful. That's your grandmother. Come on, the ham's about ready, isn't it, hun?" She headed toward the kitchen, where she set the casserole down on the counter behind the coffee machine.

Hai held Grazina's trembling hand as they went, moving slowly, as if through an unlit room. "Josh, when was the last time you saw Granny anyway?" the mother said, lighting three tapered candles. "It must be nearly five years now, it's so fast. Only when you're busy, of course. Like we've been. I don't even know *how* to relax anymore. Even on the holidays."

"You're just overstretched," Lucas quipped from the kitchen. "You've been doing the PTO meetings, latchkey club field trips, board of ed." He turned to Hai. "Clara basically runs the school system here."

Clara, who appeared a decade younger than her husband, tilted her head and pouted. "It's true, I guess. And it's not like I get a dime for it either." She sipped from a glass of port and regarded her children.

She was the kind of person who would say "You look tired," her head tilting with feigned concern, and mean that you were actually ugly. Her hair was the shade of red he had only seen in magazines. Simply nodding and staying silent would go far with her, Hai decided. He smiled and placed the bag of corn bread on the table.

"You don't look like a grandma anymore," the girl said. "You look like Regis Philbin."

"On crack," the boy added in a whisper, as they chortled behind their glasses.

"Guys," Lucas called from the kitchen. "Let's try to be a bit mature for one night, okay?"

"What did he say?" Grazina asked the little girl sitting across from her. "He make a joke? He's funny boy. Like his grandpa. Always in good spirits."

"Oh, he's full of it, this one." Lucas had come in and ruffled Josh's hair before setting down a bowl of brussels sprouts. "A real Jerry Seinfeld we got here." The boy swooned from his father's attention, the candlelight dancing on his incisors.

Lucas, who was clearly the cook, set the table with chicken roasted with thyme and half a ham glazed with honey, its edges crusted black. Cranberry juice was served in a crystal pitcher.

Grazina explained that Hai was newly appointed on her case as Lucas nodded in somber approval. Then they ate through a drone of unbearable small talk. The son had a habit of positioning his mouth before the plate and shoving crumbs into it. The food was pretty-looking but everything tasted mostly of butter and nothing else. Hai suddenly ached for BJ's mom's lasagna, or even the creamed spinach or the mac and cheese from HomeMarket, which Russia always topped with extra bread crumbs.

"Now, tell me something, uh——" Lucas pointed at Hai with a stout pinkie.

"Labas," Grazina said. "His name is Hi, so I call him Labas."

"Oh, how fun. Labas," Lucas nodded. "You know what, tell me this: How come so many live-in nurses are from the Philippines? Do they have a partnership with American hospitals or something? I read somewhere in *The Atlantic* that they're doing that now. Like an internship or something?"

Hai reached for the cranberry juice and drank, biding his time as the table waited for his answer. "Well . . ." He wiped his mouth and coughed into his hand. "I can't speak for other Filipinos. But when I was a kid, I used to watch this cartoon called *Captain Planet*." The family leaned forward, rapt, sensing some mild intrigue about to be delivered via exotic anecdote from the cultural source itself. "And there was this one kid who looked kinda Asian, like me. I guess he might very well be Filipino."

"Right," said the mother, nodding.

"And the kids on the show would all raise their fists to the sky, and they'd each have a call based on one of *Captain Planet*'s themes. Like fire, wind, water. Well, the brown kid, he always said 'Heart,' which confused me because it wasn't a natural element of the planet. But I misheard it as *health*, like you must be in good health if you wanna protect the world. So I wanted to be a doctor for as long as I could remember, but," Hai shrugged and forked at a piece of meat, "a nurse is as close as I've gotten." He scanned their faces as he chewed.

"Lame," said Josh, waving a drumstick around. He looked eagerly now to Grazina, as if the two were to be the source of the night's entertainment.

"That's it?" Clara frowned. "A *cartoon* decided your career path? That's kind of . . . reckless, don't you think? Better not happen to you, miss," she said to her daughter, "with your *Last Airbender* nonsense."

Grazina took her fork, a piece of brussels sprout caught in it, and tapped the glass. "We should do Kūčios prayer, yes? Lucas, you remember?"

"Let's not this year, okay, Mom?" Lucas said. "That's all that old fish stuff. It's Christmas Eve. We're *finally* having you over after the big renovations. You don't have to do that whole old country spiel."

"You renovated?" Grazina looked around. "I guess so, huh."

"She's getting worse," said the boy with real concern.

"Don't be rude. I wanna hear this coochie prayer," his mother said, her pearl earrings dangling as she straightened up and took a sip of wine. She was the only one not drinking cranberry juice.

"Clara. Let's not poke the bear, please."

"She smells awful. It's, like, *actual* piss," the boy whispered, loud enough for everyone to hear.

Hai wanted Grazina to fire off one of her vinegary remarks, something smart about Stalin's minuscule scrotum or a cutting comeback on the boy's birdlike features—but none of it came. Grazina only cocked her head, as if listening to something far away, and mumbled in Lithuanian. Then she started to clap, laughing.

"I honestly didn't know it was gonna be this bad, hun." Clara's face grew taut. "Let's just get on with it, please? Will you just ask her the thing?" She tossed her napkin on her plate and took another swallow of wine. Whatever mask she developed had dissolved to bone-like indifference.

"In a minute. Hey, Hello, whatever—Labas—can you take Mom to the bathroom and, you know, get her sorted, please?" He let out a sigh and looked away as Hai guided Grazina down the hall.

"This better be the last time, Lucas," Hai heard Clara say as they closed the door to the powder room.

"Hey, how are you feeling?" he said, real soft. "Who's the presi—?"

"Nobody."

"Okay. Try again."

"Am I here? Am I still here, Labas?"

He held her hand. "Look at me. What's going on, really? Do you still see me?"

Her milky eyes scanned the room before settling on his chest. "Yes, oh of course, I see you. I see you, Labas."

"Then we're still here, right?"

She slumped on the toilet, the owl on her sweater scrunched. She stared at her hands in her lap, finally herself, and looked more lost than he imagined a person could ever be.

He ran the faucet so they couldn't be heard.

"Fuck 'em, okay? They're just a bunch of fucks."

She jerked at the sharpness in his voice. "What you talking about?" She forced a smile. "They're good people. Smart grandkids. My Lucas, his beautiful wife. Look at this home—have you seen one like it?"

"Look, can you make it back out there, or should we just ditch 'em?"

After a while, she nodded. "I can do it. But can I get a cough drop first?"

He unwrapped one from his pocket and slipped it in her mouth. "Cherry."

WHEN HE OPENED the door, Lucas was there waiting. "Hey, Mom." He bent down so he was eye level to his mother, his face now open and soft. "You doing okay in there?"

In *there*, Hai thought, as if she were in some kind of box.

"Listen, I'm glad you came tonight. It's important to me to see you on Christmas Eve, you know that. And the kids really appreciate it too."

"You guys miss having this old coot around, huh?" Grazina smiled weakly at Lucas, who took her gently by the hand back to the dining room.

"We're all refreshed!" Lucas announced as they took their seats.

"You going to the Lithuanian mass at St. Peter's tomorrow?" Grazina asked. "Your stepfather used to take me——"

"Oh, come on, you haven't gone in years yourself. Even when Jonas was still alive. Now . . ." Lucas inhaled and removed his glasses, putting them neatly on the table. "I wanna tell Josh and Abbey something. Something about our family, our *roots*. Since you wanted to do Kūčios and everything. And it's important," he made an effort to look at his children, nodding at their blank faces, "for their grandmother to be here when they hear it." He made a steeple with his fingers and spoke low into it. The candles, halfway burnt, danced on either side of him, casting stark shadows across his thick face. "You see—Abbey, Josh—your grandmother was married to a war hero once." His hands floated over the table. Clara got up and went toward the kitchen, and his eyes followed her.

"Go on, I'm just filling up." She shook her empty glass.

"Your real grandpa was not that old kook who used to come over and read in the corner like a piece of driftwood. You guys remember, right? With his hunchback spine? All he did was read and read, but what did he do for you, Mom? Huh?" His voice was barbed—gone was the gentleness he showed a moment earlier.

Grazina's head was so low her chin nearly touched the table.

"Nothing. That's what happens when you do nothing with what you know. It's like filling a car with gas and never having the balls to turn the ignition." He nearly spat the word *balls*. "No, my father, your *true* granddad, who I was named after, Filip Lucas, was a soldier in the resistance. He fought against Stalin *and* the Nazis. And he died for it." His face intensified under the candlelight.

Clara returned with a glass brimming with something deep and red. "To the heroes," she said dreamily, and took a swig.

"Lina, your aunt, she was old hook spine's kid. But me——" he leaned back, the steeple dissolving as he folded his arms, "I'm a soldier's son. You guys come from courage, class, and discipline. That's why Lina ended up a drunk in Texas. She got the kooky genes, right Mom?"

"Don't be so hard on her, Lucas," Clara said. "That *poor* girl. She had a good heart. And she tried her best . . . While she could." She gave Lucas a knowing look.

Grazina jerked back as if waking from sleep. "Of course, of course, dear. My son, Lucas," she said to Clara, "he's so smart. So fresh too. Like his father. Good brains. Scientist."

"I'm a *pharmacist*, Mom. I take pills," he said to Hai, "mostly statins, and put them in a box at Walgreens."

"But you're a soldier on the inside," Josh said, his face finally serious. "And so am I." He wiped his greasy lips and lifted his bony chin. For a moment all they could hear was his nasal breathing.

"My dad was also a great swimmer." Lucas turned to his mother. "He would've been in the Olympics if not for the war. He even taught Granny here how to swim. Didn't he, Mom? Didn't Dad teach you how to swim?"

"In summertime, yes. We swim in Lake Rėkyva." Her head didn't move as she spoke.

Hai trained his eyes on Grazina, willing her to look at him, to give him the bridge they could cross together—but she wouldn't do it.

"He was shot on the Eastern Front. But not before putting me into your grandma's belly. Tell them, Mom. Isn't that why Jonas wouldn't call me his *son*, even after forty years?"

Grazina nodded.

"The old man was ashamed." Lucas leaned back, satisfied. "And why wouldn't he be? Raising the son of a hero while having a wino ESL teacher as a daughter." He put up his hands. "Sorry, I really don't want to go overboard here."

Clara's eyes were crystalline with delight, drinking it in.

"But that's why I'm going to take care of you, Mom. Your son comes from men who take care of their families." He nodded slowly, collecting himself. "There's this place, okay, just fifteen minutes from us. Called the Hamilton Home. The best of its kind. Fit for the mother of a scientist."

Hai's ears grew hot. Grazina finally turned to him, her face dull and wiped away. Hai took another cough drop and placed it on the table next to her hand.

"Ah, you want to put me away already." Grazina chuckled nervously. "And what about the house—"

"Oh, Mommy." Clara reached over, reeking of booze, and squeezed Grazina's wrist. "We'd sell it and use the funds to care for your many, many needs. We'd repurpose that little ramshackle thing and make you *comfortable*."

"And there'd be people just like Hello over here. Except more. You can have a dozen Labases. It's what Dad would do, I know it," Lucas said tearfully, without tears. "I mean, your husband's pension only gives you, what, four hundred a month?"

"But the house is paid off. And I live there for almost fifty years. Your father . . . I mean, Jonas—"

"Look, Grazina." Clara put down her glass. "Really, you did a *fine* job with what you had. I just want to say that to you. Mother to mother. And Lucas is a wonderful son. I just . . ." She paused, searched the table for her children's faces, then pushed on. "I just think it's been so *hard* for you. Getting older all alone and all. My mother at least had her father's estate. You need rest. I don't want you feeling abandoned. No one deserves that. And that house, oh God, it'll probably need to be *gutted*—that is, if the city won't tear the whole block down. But Lucas and I will take care of it. We're not going to abandon you ever."

"Just think about it, okay, Mom? I have the paperwork done already and you just have to sign. I'll bring it over in a few weeks after I figure out the deposit."

Hai leaned back in his chair.

"I'm sorry," Clara said to Hai. "This must be so strange to you. Thanks for bearing with us." She made a laugh and it hung over the table among the animal carcasses, the chicken ribs and pig bones strewn with gristle and fat. "That sound like a plan, Grazina?" Her voice was the pitch one uses to praise a dog.

Grazina nodded weakly.

"Oh, wonderful," Lucas said to his mother. "I'm sure we'll discuss the details down the line, but that's great, just great. You're making the right choice and we're so relieved for you. Merry Christmas, Mommy."

"Merry Christmas, Mommy," Clara said, smiling at her husband.

NEITHER OF THEM spoke for a long time during the ride back. It was that vast emptiness one feels after any gathering, where the muscles still throbbed with people's voices, energies both expelled and unspent, and the cab became a kind of cradle lulling them to stillness. The driver had put on Sinatra's "My Way" and was now humming softly as they floated through the snow-white gloom. The tray of stuffed peppers, still full, sat like a cinder block in Hai's lap. The roads were nearly empty and the blue dark was filled with that rare silence amplified by new snowfall and the absence of people. As they reached Main Street, passing lampposts glowing from lighted wreaths, a tinny speaker tied to the traffic light blared holiday songs over whitened sidewalks. In the windows of squat houses, the front yards the size of rich people's carpets, plastic snowmen and Nativity assortments, paled by years of sun, glowed in yellow orbs against the ashen realms of night made darker behind the glass.

He couldn't tell if Grazina was asleep. When they passed Route 4 and the HomeMarket strip mall, the only thing lit was Sgt. Pepper's Pizza. Hai saw the owner, slumped at the counter, resting his head on his palm, his green turban the only color under the lights. He had opened on Christmas Eve, perhaps hoping that other closures would increase his traffic, but it looked like he'd been sitting idle for hours, his arms stuck to the counter.

"Good night, Sergeant Pepper," Hai said as they passed the pizza shop.

Grazina poked her head up and looked over at Hai. "Good night, Sergeant Pepper," she whispered to his back. Then, after a long silence: "Hey, Labas? What does your name mean? In your culture. You never told me."

"It means 'the sea,'" he said, still looking out the window.

And that's how he felt then, drifting through the wide-open waters of East Gladness.

Soon the cab stopped at 16 Hubbard Street, its dilapidated familiarity somehow soothing. Grazina took the bottle of sparkling cider Lucas had given her and handed it to the driver, "Merry Christmas, sir," and quickly turned toward the house.

"Oh, how kind of you. Merry Christmas, guys," the man called out, lingering a bit before sputtering down the street.

Grazina walked straight for the door as Hai struggled to catch up. Inside, she flung off her jacket and made a beeline for the stairs. He set the casserole down on the dining table, strewn with pill bottles, and followed her up. "Hey, you alright? Hey!" He followed her into the bathroom, where she turned on the water. Steam pouring forth. The roar of pipes. She tried pulling off her owl sweater, but it kept catching on her chin and she grunted in frustration.

When he tried to help her, she snapped, "I can do it! I can take off my own damn clothes. I don't need your help, boy." She heaved again, but the sweater was caught around her chest and wouldn't budge. Finally she stopped, stood there with steam filling the room, her arms at her sides, the sweater wrapped around her head and face, part of her bowl cut poking through. "Please," the muffled voice said.

"Raise your arms. Yeah, like that. There."

Grazina stepped out of her underwear, removed her bra—no shame or fear between them now. She tested the water, then stepped in, her arms jerking at the effort. He put out his hand and she grabbed it before lowering herself. When the warmth rose to her shoulders, she turned off the faucet and leaned back with shut eyes. She took a bar of soap and scrubbed vigorously along her arms and shoulders, then her neck, her fingernails making red streaks on her skin.

"Stop, stop it. You're gonna scratch yourself."

"They say I smell like *piss*. So I'm gonna get clean. See me? I bathe like everybody else, don't I?" The soap slipped into the water, and as she frantically searched for it, her bottom dentures fell into the water with a plop. "No, no, Jesus Mary." She gasped, covering her mouth with both hands, her eyes clenched.

"Just stop. Please stop this." Hai clutched her arm as she tried to wrench free, but he wouldn't let go. He could feel her heart working through the pulse in her wrist, and held tight.

"Just relax. We'll find it later. And you don't smell. You're clean, Grazina. You're a clean person, okay?"

She stared at her stomach, floating just above the waterline. "My body is a nightmare." She regarded him with vacant bafflement. "Is my body a nightmare?"

Steam, illuminated by the bridge lights outside, wafted up and veiled her face.

He shook his head. "No."

She dipped her chin as if to coax him to tell the truth.

"I have nightmares nearly every night and I've never seen you in them."

She regarded the boy with something he couldn't place, the way you look through the window of a room entered for the first time to see what's outside. "Can't you undress for once?" she said sheepishly. "You're always seeing me naked, like I'm some patient."

Without thinking, he took off his nurse jacket, then his shirt, his pants, and finally stepped out of his boxers. He stood, his hands tucked in his armpits. She looked at him for what seemed like a long time, but he didn't move. There was so little to hide from each other by then, their bodies finally scraped clean with each other's gazes.

"I saw you long before—you know that, right?"

"What do you mean?" Hai sat down against the wall.

She nodded toward the window. "Long before you tried to jump, I already saw you. Soon as you came on the bridge, I had a feeling you were in trouble. Nobody walks over a beautiful river like this, and in September, without looking up. Not even once. So I went out to make pretend I was doing laundry."

He studied the tiles between his feet, little blue flowers painted on each one. "I'm sorry."

"For what?"

He shrugged. "Being stupid."

"I'm the stupidest of them all." She paused to swallow. "I raise my kids, I feed them, I make stuffed peppers, then one day I'm far, far away from everything and everybody. They belong to somebody else. They don't know me. *I* don't know me. I just . . ." She shook her head at the murky water. "I don't know how this happened. I escaped the tyrants in Europe and I had everything I ever dreamed of. It all vanished so fast. But how?"

Hai looked around. The dingy bathroom felt smaller, more stifling than ever. He wanted so badly to give her an answer—a reason. "Was there, I dunno, anything else other than this house and your kids? You just went to work and came home and cooked stuffed peppers for forty years?"

She blinked away the tears and inhaled. "I managed people at Woolworth's—women. But it's not all that. Often they cry and I sit there, listening, sometimes for hours."

"But what about a passion, a thing. Don't you ever want, like, a thing?"

"I had a life, Labas." She paused and thought about it. "It started on a burning hill. Then it went down that hill and did like this," she drew a line across his face with her finger. "Flat. Kaput. Nothing. Just days and days, and sometimes a little bump. And that's enough. The Lord gave me peace and it's good."

"Tonight was peace?"

She swallowed. "To be alive and try to be a decent person, and not turn it into anything big or grand, that's the hardest thing of all. You think being president is hard? Ha. Don't you see that every president becomes a millionaire after he leaves office? If you can be nobody, and stand on your own two feet for as long as I have, that's enough. Look at my girl, all that talent and for what, just to drown in Bud Light?" Water dripped from her nose. "People don't know what's enough, Labas. That's their problem. They think they suffer, but they're really just bored. They don't eat enough carrots."

He looked at her and sighed, exhausted.

"You really gonna go to that place they set up for you?" he said.

She twitched from the question like it was a pebble lobbed at her forehead. She widened her eyes, the irises clear, undarting. "Hey, Sergeant Pepper. Are the Nazis above the hook line yet?" She pointed a dripping finger at the toilet. "I was just sleeping in this jeep. It's so—"

"Come on. I know you're still with me." It was the first time he held firm with her.

She fell silent and stared at the ceiling. "Labas?" Her voice wobbled, the voice of somebody looking down from a cliff. "Labas, I'm scared to die. I want to live a little more, just a few more years, if God wills it. I know it will be a good rest when we go—but—oh, to taste freshly brewed tea, with a spot of cream. I still want that. Especially when it's cold outside." There was no telling if it was her younger or older self who thought this, and he was too tired to press it, to figure it out. What did it matter which timeline they were in? It was all one skeleton anyway.

"It must be Christmas now," he whispered toward the sky. "We still have the casserole you made for Kūčios. You want some?"

She looked around the tiny bathroom, but there was no clock. "Sure, let's have some." But he didn't move. And neither did she.

Then she reached out and brushed aside his bangs. "Tu esi mano draugas."

"That some sort of Christmas prayer?"

She shook her head.

"Then what'd you say?"

She stared at the water, saying softly, "You are my friend."

17

I t's basically a pizza bagel. Any of you brainiacs confused about that?"
BJ held up the brochure and pointed with an overgrown fingernail at
the cheese-oozed pizza printed across the center foldout. HomeMarket
headquarters wanted the pizzas added to the menu by next week, and
BJ, stuffed into the driver's seat of the catering van, was briefing the
crew on the new product.

"Not exactly Thanksgiving-themed, is it?" said Wayne from the
back.

"Paul and I had pizza the Thanksgiving my husband left us," Maureen offered. "The best Thanksgiving I ever had." She was beside
Wayne and looking out at another mist-wet night in East Gladness.
Sony was in the middle row by himself and Hai was riding shotgun.
The van was parked in the back of Hairy Harry's, a dive bar surrounded
by rye fields off I-84. Despite the brooding evening coming on around
them, the crew was giddy—they were about to see their manager fight
the biggest match of her life.

"But that's like going to a Chinese buffet and getting chicken tenders." Wayne clicked his tongue. "Who the hell would buy pizza
from us?"

"I wouldn't mind," said Sony.

"Long as I'm not the one making 'em," said Wayne.

BJ turned around. "Headquarters did one of their surveys last year and it turns out kids love pizza bagels. Apparently, our clientele is aging and we gotta switch it up." She cracked her knuckles. "We're gonna split the job between the drive-thru and the dishwasher. And we're gonna master these little pizzas before that skinny-ass regional manager comes back next month."

"This mean we're losing money?" Hai said. A light rain was sprinkling the windshield.

"Of course not!" BJ jabbed Hai on the shoulder. But she quickly hid her eyes by pretending to search her pockets for something. "It means we're *expanding*. Companies like us can't just sit by and let Pizza Hut do all the talking. Here, Sony, take this and study it over the weekend. You have a photographic memory, right?"

Sony slipped it into his chest pocket. "That's what my grandmother said."

"Oh shit!" BJ's cell phone was open; the blue light filled the van. "My boy Rob just texted. That producer I was telling you guys about—DJ Red Card—is literally inside *right now*, at the bar. Wow." BJ pinched her temples. "This is my fucking chance, dude. I gotta ace it tonight. You guys get it? Any wrestler that this guy makes an entrance song for takes off! He's like the Dr. Dre of entrance songs."

"Hold still," Hai said, reaching for BJ's makeup case on the dash. "Let me fix this one part." He took the brush and dabbed a bit of white on BJ's face, which was done up in a monochrome plaster reminiscent of the Insane Clown Posse. "There. Now you're good."

In an hour, BJ would be in a wrestling ring set up on the dance floor of Hairy Harry's, performing as "Big Jean" for a one-on-one match with Miss Magician, a fifty-two-year-old grandmother and fan favorite, in one of six matches in the annual New Year Grand Slam, sponsored by the local rock station PWR 89.7.

DJ Red Card, who was also an unofficial talent scout for the WWE, BJ explained, was famous for showing up at random shows and putting up a red card when he was impressed by a certain wrestler. "Then he goes backstage and offers you a recording contract. So I gotta *kill it* tonight."

Just then the windshield crackled with bits of ice. The rain had turned to sleet. BJ dipped her head and winced at the murky sky. "You freakin' serious right now? Come on. Snow? Snow!" She turned to the crew. "The biggest night of my life and it's gonna fucking freezing-rain on us." It was the second week of January and the snow had been coming on and off. The ground was paper white for a few days but had since browned to muddy slush. "See? This is why there's no good wrestlers coming out of Connecticut. Soon as we get our shit on, there's a fucking nor'easter. Every damn time."

"It's okay, dear," said Maureen, sensing an emergency. "It's just a squall. It'll die down in ten minutes. You can tell by the way the flakes spin." She traced them half-heartedly with her finger.

Hai took a Dilaudid from his jeans pocket and popped it in his mouth. "You want one?" he offered BJ. When she shook her head he slapped the second down his throat.

"You got this." Maureen reached from behind and massaged BJ's shoulders. "Big Joe is gonna make her claim to fame in this year of our Lord 2010."

"It's Big Jean. I already told you." She wiggled out of Maureen's grip. "Just make sure you do your part, okay? You're my pinch hitter."

"Wait," said Wayne. "Maureen's wrestling with you? She's barely five foot two!"

"My driver's license says five four."

A shadowy figure loomed up to the driver's side and knocked on the glass.

BJ rolled down the window, revealing a Jim Carrey–looking white guy smiling through a pornstache, his narrow face shrouded in a hoodie. "Sup guys, I'm V-Bean, your MC for the night. Short for Vanilla Bean, ha-ha."

"I figured," said BJ, unimpressed.

V-Bean took out a clipboard and started writing. "I'm guessing by the face paint that you're wrestling tonight? Can I put you down for . . ." he leaned back to look at something on the side of the van, "Deez Nuts?"

"The fuck you talking about?" Flurries were catching and melting on BJ's knitted brows. A gust of wind blew fast-food wrappers against the van.

"It says 'Deez Nuts' on your van, my dude."

"She's a woman," Hai said.

V-Bean narrowed his eyes. Wayne opened the sliding door and examined the spray-painted graffiti. "It does say 'Deez Nuts,'" he confirmed, and shut the door. "Those damn graffiti kids on Route 4."

"For what it's worth," V-Bean shrugged, "it's a pretty dope wrestler name. It's bold, you know. Like you don't give a fuck."

"Except I do, man," said BJ with a sigh, then thought on it a bit. "You really think it's good, though?" Her knuckles gripped the steering wheel. "You know what? Fuck it. Put me down as Deez Nuts. The universe is telling me something."

"Right on, man. I got you." The MC offered his fist for BJ to dap, but BJ was already rolling up the window.

"Deez Nuts," Hai repeated, letting it roll out slow. "You sure about this?"

BJ was texting on the flip phone. "I'm trying to get Rob to tell me how many people are in there already." Cars were pulling into the lot now, people talking excitedly as they huddled toward the bar dressed for a night out, mostly biker guys with girlfriends in sweatpants and white boys dressed in Carhartt hoodies and baseball caps of defunct lawn care services.

BJ dropped the phone while texting. "Fuck me. These buttons are terrible."

"Her fingers are too fat. Like mine," Maureen whispered to Wayne. "That's why you gotta get a BlackBerry."

IN THE BAR'S KITCHEN, which was cleared to serve as a makeshift locker room, hulking wrestlers sat on stools wrapping their hands, their bodies shining with oil and sweat, globed muscles gleaming under fluorescent lamps, the air a mix of Old Spice and BO, latex and leather, Hai sat beside BJ, keeping her company and calming her nerves. She'd been sitting on a whiskey barrel near the janitor's closet with her headphones on, going over her sequences. She was supposed to win tonight, at Miss Magician's insistence. Magician had remained undefeated for over two years, and this win would introduce Big Jean, or rather Deez Nuts, to the community. They'd apparently been working on it for months. BJ went over and peered through the curtain draped across the kitchen door.

"One, two, four, five . . . maybe six."

"What are you counting?" Hai said.

"Black people," said BJ, peeping from behind the curtain at the crowd. There were about sixty-five people in the bar now, most of them standing a few feet back from the stage in clusters, hands in their pockets, bobbing their heads to the eighties rock blasting between the matches. The first two sets had already gone and BJ was up next.

"There's only four," BJ said.

"I see six, I think." Hai searched at the faces. "Did you count Wayne?"

"Yeah. And that's an Indian couple." BJ let the curtain fall and groaned. "Fuck. How are there only *this* many Black people at a wrestling match?"

"Are you kidding?" said Hai. "It's an amateur wrestling match. In a dive bar where biker gangs make drug deals."

"They don't even look like they're from East Gladness," BJ sighed.

"Well, I see Russia with one of his friends and . . . oh, looks like Cherry came too." Cherry was one of the sex workers at the rehearsal. "So you got support. Don't worry, okay?"

"Hold on, are my mom and dad out there?" BJ moved the curtain and searched the crowd until she found Ruby in her fur coat sitting along the wall, hands folded in her lap like she was at Sunday mass. Beside her was a man with a majestic grey beard and leather jacket.

V-Bean came up and tapped BJ's shoulders. "Yo, Deez Nuts, you ready, man? I have you coming on hot in five."

"Is DJ Red Card still on the floor?"

"Don't worry. The guy sees everything. Just do your thing and be chill."

"Wait, where'd Maureen go?" Hai asked, looking around. "Isn't she part of your set?"

"She's in the bathroom getting ready. She's a real artiste when it comes to what she does, trust. We got this."

Hai was glad to see a calm come over her.

"Now go out there and enjoy the show, rook." BJ tapped him on the chest and winked. "We're about to make Stone Cold Steve Austin look like Mr. Rogers."

V-Bean took the stage, extended both arms, and shouted into the mic, "Ladies and gentlemen! Aaaaaare you ready to SMAAASH??? You ready for New England's second, and I say SECOND, ranked amateur wrestling show to ever grace the valley with more homegrown talent?" The crowd, noticeably drunker now, jostled to attention. A few beer-clutched fists shot out from the front row. "Alright. Now put your hands together for . . ." He fumbled with his piece of paper, tilting his head to catch the handwriting. "Oh yeah! Make some noise for . . . Deez Nuts!" A few people looked at each other with raised eyebrows. DJ Red Card, a chunky white dude whose bald head was hidden under a Kangol hat, flashed a smile at a nearby woman and shrugged before taking a sip from his Solo cup.

But the crowd cheered in earnest as the guitar in Drowning Pool's "Bodies" ripped through the smoke-machined air and BJ swaggered through the curtain in a taxi-yellow velour sweat suit. Hai, Sony, and Wayne looked on with bated breath as Hai realized, with sudden dismay, that BJ looked like an unhinged Big Bird from *Sesame Street*. It turned out two teenage boys a few rows up had the same thought and were now shouting into cupped hands, "Go get 'em, Big Bird! Yeah, go Big Bird."

Still, BJ held her own, growling to the entry song she had recorded in the HomeMarket office. Some girls in the front had even let go of their boyfriends' hands and started bobbing to the bass. Sony, wearing earbuds to dull the noise, nodded along, wide-eyed and awestruck. His general was actually *glowing* onstage, the sweat dripping from her nose and chin like literal diamonds.

Much to the crew's relief, perhaps even surprise, the audience was eating this up. BJ then made her last circle around the ring, when something no one expected happened. BJ grabbed the microphone from V-Bean and urged the crowd to clap along with her. "Now I need you to get ready for a special treat from my main girl, Maureen! Are you ready for something fucking special?! Some once-in-a-lifetime exclusive?" She jabbed the mic into the crowd as they roared with a collective *Yes.*

Then the song was cut. The crowd murmured with confusion. Maureen stepped through the curtain wearing an Irish saffron kilt.

Pulling her suspenders tight around her shoulders, she took a deep breath and raised a banjo from her hip and started plucking away, doing a jig down the aisle that, with her bad knee, looked more like a walking seizure. The crowd seemed to have taken a step back in unison. A woman in the front row lunged toward Maureen as if to help her but then, realizing she didn't know how, sat back down. Maureen began moving about a mile per hour down the aisle.

"The fuck is this? Dude, *tell me* this is a joke," said a white boy to his friends, relishing this unintentional farce.

"What the hell is going on?" Wayne turned to Hai.

"It sounds like bluegrass music. Played by Maureen," Hai said as the crowd started to boo.

"She never told me she played the *banjo*. It's kinda sexy."

Hai spotted DJ Red Card, whose eyes were shut in laughter. That's when the boos grew into a deep and resonant roar, rooting into the floors and felt through the soles of everyone in the bar. BJ, sensing this, waved her arms to cut the track, but somehow it kept going. A balding biker in a silver ponytail was the only one rocking enthusiastically. Maureen, oblivious to it all, played on, her cheeks jiggling to the plucked chords as she hobbled around the outside of the ring, while BJ did some half-hearted taunts on the turnbuckle, the boos intensifying.

All this was made worse by Miss Magician's legendary entrance, which began with an eternal twenty seconds of blackout, the anticipation mounting through the building before Metallica's "Enter Sandman" slammed right into its chorus as a pandemonium of lights tore through the smoky room, searing everyone's eyes. The bar's roof almost lifted off with cheers as a toned and tanned grandmother, whose government name was Nora Jiménez, stepped through the curtain wearing a cape of sequins and a pink magician's top hat studded with jewels, which she then removed with both hands and placed on the head of perhaps the most adorable eight-year-old girl within fifty miles. The place erupted. A sideburned biker wiped away a tear, thrust his Bud Light bottle into the air, and shouted, "That's my fucking mom! Fuck yeah, Mama!"

The match went on as expected. Most of it was BJ and Miss Magician trading backhand chops to each other's chests and one of them pulling the other into the ropes, then clotheslining the other in slow motion. This was considered "light" repertoire, Hai learned, which avoided body slams and was common when working with older wrestlers with back problems. All this while Maureen paced back and forth outside the ring, strumming her banjo like a displaced panhandler. It ended with BJ missing an elbow by nearly three feet. Miss Magician, who was thrown against the ropes but too slow to get to the elbow in time, collapsed anyway, as if she'd been struck by a poltergeist before crumpling into a heap of glitter. BJ then attempted her finishing move, the "Bahama Bomb," which required carrying the frail Nora Jiménez across her shoulders in a fireman's carry, then slamming her spine down between BJ's legs. But since this move would certainly put Nora in the hospital, BJ had Miss Magician kind of slide, slow-motion, off BJ's shoulders, anticlimactically rolling the grandmother off her arms and onto the mat. It was less of a slam and more like laying a drowning victim by the side of a pool. BJ then went on all fours to pin her, covering Magician's body almost completely—without putting any weight on her—as the ref counted the pinfall.

It was terrible. Everyone immediately resumed booing as BJ's music came on. She had not defeated a long-standing powerhouse, but rather destroyed, in bizarre fashion, an elderly and beloved local icon. Afterward, the only sign that Deez Nuts had ever been in the ring at all was a cluster of sweat droplets and glitter, around which coiled a single saffron ribbon that had come loose from Maureen's kilt.

⤙

BJ PRESSED HER head into the steering wheel as Hai sat mute beside her, the heat from her body steaming up the windows. The bar's neon signs purpled the van's interior. "Tell my parents to go home, man. Tell them not to wait for me," said BJ to the floor.

"I'll do it." Maureen, eager to get away from her role in the disaster, dashed out of the van.

"And tell them I'm sorry," BJ called, but she was already gone, gingerly dodging ice puddles across the lot.

It wasn't until her mouth said *sorry* that BJ lost it, her shoulders jerking as she cried. Hai placed a steady hand on her back. Her white-and-black face paint was melting; what once looked like Big Bird had devolved into an underworld Ronald McDonald. The van shook with BJ's crying and the rosaries that Maureen tied around the rearview mirror began to sway. "The entry fee was three hundred dollars! I could've bought my sister a new coat and boots. She needed new boots."

"It cost money to get on that stage? I thought it was a local display of talent."

"It's a ring. And yes, it's a competition. You pay to enter a pie baking contest, don't you?"

"Look, it's alright. You . . ." Hai searched the blurred window for the right words, "performed. You did your thing. People know you now. Isn't that the point?"

"They know me as a joke." A bright lace of spit had stretched from the wheel and was dripping on the leg of her yellow suit.

There was laughter outside the van, coming from a group of kids walking by on a smoke break. "Dude, check it out. It's Deez Nuts." The windows were too fogged for them to notice anyone inside. One of the kids squatted outside the van and posed by the graffiti. "They call me Deez Nuts. Aka Hillbilly Big Bird!" Their cackles erupted before fading toward the venue, where the muffled bass of the next entrance song was already picking up.

"Look, just don't worry about those——"

"Oh shit. It's DJ Red Card. He's coming over here. Fuck, fuck."

"What? How do you know?"

"Look!" BJ wiped at the windshield. "He's walking over. With fucking Maureen!"

"The hell?"

"Get back so he can sit, go, go. Make room!" BJ grabbed Hai by the collar and basically threw him into the back seat as the passenger door opened. Maureen ran a hand through her red hair and adjusted her suspenders. "I found this kind gentleman who wants to talk to ya." She winked at BJ, whose mouth was half open. DJ Red Card stepped out from behind Maureen and fell into the passenger seat with a grunt.

"I'm gonna go fetch the others," Maureen said. "You two get to know each other." She winked again and walked away. Red Card pulled at his white turtleneck sweater and said it was hot in the car. The immense turtleneck, Hai realized, was to hide a massive skin rash.

"Look," BJ said, seeing her chance at redemption. "I know that shit looked wack and weird as fuck. But I have a reason for it all, okay? I even had a vision board and everything for this show, and I just——"

"How much?"

"What?" BJ glanced back at Hai. "What do you mean?"

"How much you want?" Red Card spoke in an affected, subdued whisper, like a man who had survived getting stabbed in the throat or, as Hai soon realized, like someone imitating Don Corleone in *The Godfather*.

BJ mulled it over and shrugged. "I dunno. I-I-I never thought about it." BJ sat up and blinked. "I mean. I never considered how much a manager would be. I guess . . . I guess I'll take whatever the standard is——"

"You fucking with me?" Red Card leaned forward. "I said, how much you *want*? Like, how much you need? Are we a bunch of amateurs here or what?" He glanced back at Hai, then let out a big sigh and shifted to remove something from his pocket. "Here, there's a deuce and a quarter ounce. I also got nickels but you look like you could use more than that." In his palm were two baggies of weed, one larger than the other. "Like I said, how much you need, my man?"

Hai leaned back as BJ's face fell.

Red Card, clocking this, regarded her from across the cab, his shock melting to sincere, open pity. "Awww, man. You thought I was talking about a *deal* deal. Oof. You mean to tell me that shit you did was no spoof? That wasn't no Weird Al Yankovic shit? Damn." He looked out the window and shook his head.

"Are you signing *anyone* from tonight?" BJ asked.

"That skinny kid who went before you, Young EZ? He's got it. Kid's got that Rey Mysterio high-flying vibe but with a pretty face. Plus he's rolling eight hundred deep in MySpace friends. So yeah. Him for sure."

"That's Mitchell Kelleher. His dad owns the Ford dealer in Millsap. He's fake as fuck. What I'm doing is real, man. It has roots."

"Listen, buddy—or ma'am—I don't make the rules. You think I make money off this shit? Why you think I'm in here trying to sell you trees? This isn't no *American Idol*. Sob stories don't work in this business."

"Just give me the fucking deuce." BJ handed him a twenty and Red Card slipped the baggie into her chest pocket.

"Listen, friend," Red Card said, resuming his *Godfather* tone, "don't hate the player; hate the game."

He then patted BJ on the shoulder, threw up a peace sign, and hopped out.

"Yeah, happy New Year to you too."

"Yeah, happy New Year to you too!" Hai added more forcefully.

BJ looked at Hai, exhausted, then wiped her nose and started the engine.

THEY WERE DRIVING BACK, the fog thickening by the minute, as if it knew to take over the town soon as people left the roads and shut themselves in. BJ was rubbing the music-note birthmark under her suit like it was a fresh wound as they stopped at the light, the only car on the road.

Wayne exhaled. "Well, I'm ready to go home, put my feet up, and have a Twinkie."

Maureen sat up, her eye shadow so blotched it looked like she was wearing makeup for a panda costume. "You know in another universe tonight never happened, right? I've been looking into this. It's called the Mandela effect." The Mandela effect, as Maureen explained, is when a large part of the population remembers something that never actually happened, at least not in the current universe.

"Oh, please," said Wayne, hugging Maureen's banjo case. "The last thing the poor girl needs is more of your flat-earth shenanigans. In *my* universe there's this interesting thing called physics."

"Like C-3PO, for example," Maureen went on. "In my timeline, the one that I belong to, he was all gold. Did you know that? He didn't have a silver leg like he does now. Now his leg is silver like they forgot to finish painting him. Where I'm from, George Lucas had the good sense to paint him all gold."

"Maybe they made it silver for disability representation," Sony said, looking out the window. "My counselor says that's starting to—"

"The point is, he was *never* all gold in this universe. It's fucked up. I was ejected into this universe, probably after a mass extinction event. It happens to a lot of us. Paul's still alive in the original timeline, and my husband . . ." She cut herself off and turned away.

Wayne squeezed her shoulder. "For what it's worth, it was all gold in my timeline too," he whispered.

BJ stepped on the gas. "Okay, then. Is there a universe where you *don't* wear suspenders?" She was looking at Maureen through the rearview. "Why didn't you tell me you were gonna dress like some redneck grandpa?"

"This was what my granddad wore when he played the banjo, the one who taught me this thing you so desperately wanted in your little charade. It's also ergonomic. OSHA." Maureen's voice was barbed for the first time. Under her breath, she added, "You wouldn't know, since we had three violations this year alone."

"Alright, alright, come now," said Wayne. "We don't gotta make this worse for each other. It was an okay night."

"Actually, why did you have the banjo in there in the first place?" Hai asked, genuinely puzzled.

BJ inhaled and trained her eyes on the road. "The banjo," she let out a heavy sigh, "has roots all the way back to the Middle Passage. Before all those bluegrass folks used it, it was an instrument from West Africa. Did anybody know *that*? Huh? Exactly. When slaves in the cargo holds started dying on their way to America, these slave traders figured out that if they just played the fucking banjo, it would keep the stolen people's spirits up long enough to make it through the journey. So they played it all across the ocean to keep their cargo alive. Before it was bluegrass or low-grass or whatever, it was African. My mom taught me this. *That's* what I was trying to do. And I asked Maureen to join me cause she plays a mean-ass banjo. I was trying to give these wrestling heads knowledge." She spat into a drink cup and scowled at the road. It wasn't clear if she was about to scream or cry again.

"Fascinating," said Sony, nodding to himself.

"I told you it was a good idea," said Maureen. "And I happened to already know this little tidbit about the banjo before she asked me." She started rubbing her knee. "Now my cartilage is down to zero. Listen, you looked like a real star out there, okay? No one can take that away from you."

"I *am* a real star," said BJ.

They took a left onto Route 4, starting the long straight shot toward HomeMarket. Maureen patted BJ on the shoulder. "You're just ahead of the curve, is all. You did good, kid." Then, deciding her part was done to satisfaction, she grabbed at the bag of Doritos in Sony's lap. "This one's Cool Ranch, right?"

THEY GOT TO the HomeMarket and BJ cut the engine. The restaurant was dark and the only cars in the lot were Maureen's and Wayne's.

"Now I need some St. John's wort," Maureen said, buttoning her coat. "I'm getting depressed."

"You and the whole world," said BJ.

"No, really. I can feel it coming. It starts in my shoulders and makes its way down."

"How far down?" said Wayne, nudging her with his elbow.

"Further than *you* could reach."

They all sat for a moment, none of them really wanting to get out.

"I'm ordering a pizza," BJ said decisively. Everyone murmured in agreement.

"Let's try them for once." Hai pointed at the Sgt. Pepper's across the way, the shop blazing like a crash-landed spaceship. BJ called the number and put in an order for two large special pizzas, no mushrooms (for Maureen), extra cheese (for Wayne).

As they sat waiting, held in the van's warm lull, the only sound the occasional rustle of somebody's jacket, the misty parking lot an immense sweep around them, Hai considered Maureen's multiverse. He wondered if there *was* another timeline where he was also sitting in a van in a parking lot at the beginning of a new year. If there was also a group of people waiting for a pizza after a long night of disastrous adventure. If wrestling and novels were merely the result of people trying to cast yet another universe where they're the more heroic, patient, and capable versions of themselves. He wondered if they looked the same—if his mother was still lying on the floor next to her bed, staring up at the ceiling with the same dreams she had in this world. He thought of Grazina, who must be falling asleep now before the TV, an empty tray of Stouffer's in her lap, and Aunt Kim in her cell at York Corrections, her bunkmate snoring beneath her. He thought of Bà ngoại and Noah, both ashed to atmosphere. He thought of the hogs he had put to death a few weeks back, their huge eyelashes fluttering to their final thoughts.

"Pizza's coming!" BJ jabbed a thumb at the windshield. A figure was walking out from Sgt. Pepper's, a thermal bag hoisted over their shoulders.

"I'm starving," said Sony, sitting up.

Once they neared the van, the delivery person slowed, then stopped about ten feet from the bumper. It was a young woman wearing a UConn hoodie, her hair tied in a ponytail under a red cap. At first her shoulders started to shake, vapor blowing from her mouth. Then she removed the pizza box.

"The hell is this?" BJ threw up her arms. "Hey! What gives?"

"Maybe she's scared?" Hai offered. "You wanna go out and give her the money?"

BJ sighed and was about to open the door when the girl flung one of the pizzas hard as she could at the car. Everyone screamed as it landed, cheese-first, on the windshield. Then she did the same with the other pie, this one folding like a glove over the side-view mirror.

"No wonder they don't have any fucking customers!" shouted Maureen.

The girl marched over to BJ's side and started shouting. Up close, she looked no older than fifteen. Though her voice was muffled behind glass, the crew caught most of it. It turns out she had lost it when she realized she was delivering pies to HomeMarket employees. "Is this some kind of stupid joke to you? You put up a huge sign for pizza bagels this morning, like you aren't already robbing us of our customers with your nasty chicken? Now you want to take away the only fucking thing we sell? My dad worked his ass off to get this dump!" The thermal bag fluttered in the wind as she spoke. "You're a dumb fucking franchise. You don't even have green tea! None of this even matters to you. We only got one place. Ever." Her voice cracked and she had to stop herself.

The crew stared, blinking. The girl was gonna say something else but glanced away, at the lurid void across the road, the river lying somewhere behind it.

"Go eat your stupid bagels." She flipped them off and hurried across the lot, the empty bag flapping behind her as she ran.

"Alright," Maureen declared, "I'm fading. That's a sign for me to hit the hay."

"And I'm overdue for my insulin shot," Wayne added.

With that, she and Wayne got out and lumbered off, their good-nights growing fainter as they reached their cars. Before her Beetle pulled off the lot, Maureen rolled down a window and shouted, "Your mom and dad were happy, BJ. I saw it with my own eyes. That's all that matters." The car sped off before BJ could answer. She sat there staring at the pizza glued to the windshield. "Fuck it." She opened the door, grabbed a slice off the glass, examining it. "Still good. You want one?"

"Sure."

"Sony?" She handed each of them a lukewarm slice, and they sat chewing in silence.

BJ held the slice away from her face. "This is actually not bad. It's kinda, like, pretty good even. Damn." Hai and Sony nodded in agreement.

"You know what my favorite kind of light is?" Hai said after a while, chewing and staring at the Sgt. Pepper's sign.

"What kind?" said BJ.

"The one that comes from a microwave left open in a dark room."

"Say again?" BJ looked at him over her pizza.

"I can't explain it. But it's the kind of light that makes you think about people. You feel both lost but also at peace with everything, and it makes you want to call somebody on the phone for no reason."

"Why the hell are both of you so damn *weird*?" She took a final bite. "We need to all get the hell out of this dead-end town. Is there a light that beams you out of here?"

Sony turned to his hero with a hurt look. "But I love it here. East Gladness is the best place on earth. We have two McDonald's *and* a GameStop. Who can say that? Only New York City, probably. But it's too noisy and dirty there. We also have a higher life expectancy than all of Mississippi." He turned to Hai. "Seventy-four point six years. And besides, when I needed a place to stay, the town gave me a room at the Meyer's Center. No charge."

"Are you kidding me? *This* place?" BJ stared out the window. "Where some girl gets dragged from a car for, like, ten miles and nobody knows who did it, even with all the fucking cameras? This place that snows for seven months and summer is twenty-four seven swamp-ass and a shit ton of mosquitos? Where the concerts are packed with white kids with glow sticks and the wrestling shows are full of diabetic hicks? Where nobody appreciates real, authentic music and technical grappling?" She was near hyperventilating. "I'm not gonna stay here forever. I'm—" She stopped, her head completely still. "The fuck is that?"

A warped-looking shape had appeared at the edge of the parking lot and was now moving toward them. The snow had frozen to a fine powder and blew across the pavement in a monochrome tundra as the figure, which looked more like a giant worm, its belly dragging along the ground, came closer. A shock of hair spilled out of the wormlike torso, but no features were distinct enough to make out. Hai leaned forward. "Is that real?"

"What can it be?" Sony said.

BJ narrowed her eyes. "Looks like a coyote caught in some kind of trash bag. Don't get out. It could have rabies."

The thing kept shifting and gyrating, then collapsed, curling into itself with an anguished thrash.

"We should call animal control," said Sony. "Right?"

"Hold on. Shit's heading to the store." The animal hugged the glass wall and made its way to the entrance, where it crumpled into a fetal position by the front door.

"Great. A coyote's blocking the doorway," Hai said.

Sony looked to BJ. "You're the manager. It's your duty to clear the path. We'll help you, of course."

"I dunno," Hai said. "Like you said, it could have rabies."

"Alright," said BJ, gathering herself. "Sony, give me one of those catering trays from the back . . . Yeah, that one. Now, when I go out, you guys file in behind me, you hear? Don't do shit until I say so."

Moments later, BJ, crouching from the wind behind the huge aluminum catering tray, still dressed in her taxi-yellow suit, face full of chipped paint, led their way toward the coyote, Sony and Hai flanked on both sides like some postapocalyptic SWAT team. When the animal twitched, BJ stopped and banged on the tray, making hooting sounds to scare it off.

"Maybe it's hurt," Sony offered.

"It's probably half-frozen." Hai clung to BJ's sweat suit.

When they got close enough to see how large the thing was, much larger than a coyote, they stopped. "Oh shit," BJ whispered as the shock of hair rose from the fabric, which appeared to be some sort of sleeping bag, and the pair of human eyes blinked at them over the zipper. BJ dropped the tray and ran over. "It's a dude! I mean, *you*—you're a person!"

The man, his bearded and filthy face gnarled from cold, said something unintelligible and tried to sit up, but fell on his side. He was in bad shape, his lips dead purple. BJ took out her key bundle and quickly opened the door. She then bent down and scooped the tiny man into her arms and carried him in the store as Sony ran ahead to flick on the lights.

BJ set the man down in a dining booth, where he stayed curled up and shivering. It wasn't until the lights hummed on that Hai got a good look at him. "Wait. You're the dude under the bridge. You're the one on your phone laughing all the time."

"I usually make it through a night like this no problem." The man felt for his lips with both hands, making sure they were still attached to his face. "But my second bag, the good one I keep on the outside, blew down the embankment into the river. I tried to chase it but twisted my ankle. You . . ." He struggled to sit up but couldn't. BJ pulled him to a seated position, his head lolling like a rag doll's on the seat. "You spotted me. Thank God. I mean, thank *you*."

"We got any carrots?" Hai said, remembering Grazina's theory.

"I've never seen a single damn carrot in here," BJ said. "Go grab some corn bread."

Hai took some leftover corn bread wrapped in plastic on the counter.

BJ instructed Sony to fill a pot with warm water for the man's feet. "You just hang tight, my man. I'll fix you some of our hot chocolate. I would get you real food, but it'll take forever to fire everything up right now."

The man waved her off. "It's alright. I just want to be warm for a little bit. Then I'll go."

"You stay long as you need. Here." BJ removed the man's bag, untied his soiled, frozen boots, and wrapped his rootlike feet in her yellow jacket.

Sony came back with the pot of water. They sat watching the man eat, his fingers shaking. He bit into the corn bread and his face opened, a discernible personhood unfurling through the matted hair and beard, like a blooming diabolical flower. He looked up at each of them. "Wow, this is amazing." He shook his head, crumbs in his beard, then put another piece in his mouth.

"BJ made it," said Sony, eager to point out the masterwork.

"You made this, my man? Damn." The guy nodded. "Right on, dude."

"Sure did." BJ nodded, her head tilted slightly as if someone were whispering some secret good news into her ear. "It's my recipe." Hai thought he saw her eyes glisten, but it could've just been the light. Underneath her jacket she'd been wearing a black HomeMarket T-shirt that read *HomeMarket 5K Walk for Domestic Violence: Summer 2003.*

"Fuck it, you know what?" BJ said, standing up. "I'm gonna go ahead and fire up this grill and we're gonna eat like champions tonight. Sound good to you, boys?"

"Jesus. Really? Bless you, brother. God bless you all," the man said, and stuffed the remaining bread in his mouth. "Wait a minute." His eyes widened and he pointed to BJ's peeling face paint, finally noticing it. "Who the hell are you anyway? Some kind of vigilante?"

"No." BJ stood up and put her hands on her hips. "I'm the fucking manager."

18

Hai found an extra pepper grinder at HomeMarket earlier that morning and locked himself in the bathroom, grinding his pills into two heaps of powder in the contact case. Now he's sitting in the waiting room again, a line of Dilaudid dissolving fast in his bloodstream. He was at that point, early in the high, when his hands buzzed with a radiant warmth, as if his fingers were made of light.

This time the psychiatrist's office was more barren, the walls somehow further away. He could hardly look around when the door flung open and a man's voice called Sony's last name, to which his cousin bolted upright.

"You coming?" Sony asked, his face pale and stricken.

"I guess?" Hai followed him through the door, into a larger room with lights bright enough to conduct autopsies under. A woman's face floated into view, a pulled-back ponytail revealing a spray of pimples across her shiny forehead. It wasn't until she jabbed Hai's chest with her finger that he noticed her uniform, the badge gold and gilded with *County Corrections: Est. 1963*. Sony flinched when her cuffs rattled against the metal hooks on her belt loop.

"You okay there, friend? You're shaking and it's making me nervous." She leaned to check Sony's face, his eyes shut. "I have to pat you down—that gonna be a good idea, or should I get some help?" She said this looking at Hai.

"We're okay, ma'am. My cousin, he's . . . he's special-needs, that's all. He gets nervous."

"George, can you do him?" She nodded at the male guard.

Hai and Sony stood, hands raised, still in their HomeMarket aprons, the black fabric splotched with sweet potato and dusted with flour.

"What's this?" Pinched between the woman's fingers was a pink origami penguin.

"It's for my mom," Sony said, eyes still shut.

The guard behind Hai gave his shoulder a light tap and cleared his throat to indicate he was done.

"For your mom." The penguin lay on its side in her palm. "Well . . . go on and take it to her, then. She's in eighteen."

She stepped out the way and the boys headed down the row of booths, their cell phones left behind at the metal detector. The booths were separated by metal privacy sheets, and they didn't see Aunt Kim until they turned into her cubicle and her face suddenly appeared a foot away, gaunt and sullen. Aunt Kim seemed surprised to see Hai. She covered her mouth and looked away, then back at him. "You look so much older, Hai. God, it's been two years already, huh. Wh-what are you doing here?"

The boys sat on the plastic bench bolted to the floor. Aunt Kim instinctively reached for her son's hands but banged her knuckles on the telecom grid. Hai wanted to evaporate, to let Sony do this alone— what did this have to do with him anyway? He had only agreed to come because he didn't want Sony taking the one-hour bus ride after work alone. He could've stayed in the waiting room and at least enjoyed the high coursing now through his veins.

"How are you, Aunt Kim?" Hai said, his Vietnamese somehow strange to him in the concrete walls. "We wanted to come because it's Tết."

"Oh heavens. It is, isn't it? How did I forget? How did I not—"

"It's just another new year," Hai said. "The Tiger's overrated anyway. How long have you been in here?"

There was another guard standing by the door behind her. Only one other booth was active, so far down the line they heard only the stifled chatter of a man and woman, most likely lovers.

"It'll be a year in June. Con trai tôi okay không? Hãy cho Dì biết sự thật nghe." She looked only at Hai.

"Nó vẫn tốt chu. Dì đừng lo. Con coi chúng em mà."

"Do they give you noodles in there, Ma?" Sony asked. He was running a finger up and down the scar on his head, soothing himself.

Aunt Kim forced a smile, pleased by this question from a boy who rarely asked how anyone felt. They fumbled with small talk, their voices dropping each time the keys on the guard clinked when he shifted his weight. Aunt Kim told them about her days there. How the prison reminded her of an indoor courtyard, like the one from her childhood apartments in Vietnam. How the women milled about on little islands of alliances and friendships, playing cards, braiding each other's hair, watching *The Ellen DeGeneres Show*, some just sitting for hours slouched against a wall, waiting—her eyes fixed on the middle distance as she spoke.

Hai noticed her features, crushed at their edges, not sharp like her usual self, her hair frazzled and streaked with hundreds of white threads that fell wildly around her shoulders. Gone was the steely, biting wit and angular countenance he once knew. She had always been the rebel of the two sisters.

"At first everyone thought I was Native American," she chuckled. "I guess I'm the first Vietnamese they've seen in here."

"What did she say?" Sony asked in English. He had a knee pressed to his chest and was picking at a hole in his apron.

"Your mom gets confused for Native American in here," Hai told him, and Sony nodded without looking at her.

"How's *your* mom?" Aunt Kim asked, sitting up. "She doesn't know I'm in here, does she?"

Sony and Hai looked at each other and shook their heads.

"Good. Last thing I need is to have her realize the bad daughter's the one in jail. She still have that key chain I got her? The Louis Vuitton one?"

On Ma's key chain was a pendant the size of a matchbook meant to resemble a miniature Louis Vuitton clutch. It swung on the knob each time she opened the door and came home after work. It even had a latch you opened, though you couldn't put anything in it, pointless as something in a dollhouse.

"I bought it for her birthday before I left for Florida, before our big fight." Aunt Kim shook her head, smiling. "She always wanted a Louis Vuitton bag and I meant to buy her the real thing. I walked into the LV store in the mall, after saving for months, took one look at the price tag, and knew I could never get it. I was so embarrassed, I walked around picking up the smallest things I saw, until the items got smaller and smaller and I got near the register. By then all the staff seemed to know I didn't belong there." She gave the boys a shriveled glance. "Finally picked up the key chain from a pile on the checkout counter. Do you know how much a key chain costs at Louis Vuitton? Two hundred and fifty dollars. Probably the most expensive key chain in the whole world." She licked her chapped lips. "I'm stupid. But at least I can say that. That I got your mom the most expensive key chain money could buy. And she loved it. The whole week she kept saying, 'You got me *real* Louis Vuitton!' Well, what can I say? I did."

"It's still on her chain," Hai assured her. "Even now."

Aunt Kim nodded. "Hey, sweetie," she said to Sony, her voice shifting, "you wanna go get your cousin a soda from the machine over there? He came all this way—"

Hai reached into his pocket for cash, but Sony was already on his feet, glad, it seemed, to have a task other than staring at the floor. "Ma'am, yes, ma'am," he said with a military salute, and dashed off.

When Sony was out of earshot, Aunt Kim dipped her head toward the intercom and rubbed her temples. "Listen." Her eyes were squeezed tight. "I need to clear something with you."

"Auntie," Hai leaned forward, his breath fogging the glass. "I know you and Mom aren't talking but I promise you, she's not mad. She's just—I dunno—lost."

"Her? Lost? Look at *me*. I'm in a boat at sea with no oars. That's what it's like not being near him. I want to know how he's doing but I'm too scared to ask. Each time he comes we just talk about the war stuff he likes or he just goes on and on about this chicken job." She leaned back and shook her head. "I just . . . Why can't he be a math genius or something, you know? Isn't that what the illness gives other kids? Makes them some kind of prodigy? Something useful?"

"It's not an illness. And he knows more about history than anyone I know. He's smart. Way smarter than me and I'm not just saying that."

"I know, but . . . Oh, fuck me." She covered her face with both hands. "What have I done? I'm gonna pay for being such a shitty mom. He just seems like he's full of secrets. How did I give birth to a *stranger*? All these years and I still don't know that boy."

"Stop."

"Listen, though. I just want to tell you this. And please, please, keep it between us." She glanced down the row of empty booths, blinking through wet eyes. "Sony's dad, Minh. Well . . . he was an odd man. Sony worshipped him, though—and I should have told you this a long time ago." She lowered her voice to a near whisper. "But Sony's father, your uncle Minh, is dead."

The plastic bench creaked as Hai leaned back. "Like *dead* dead?"

"Almost four years now."

"Are you kidding me? Uncle Minh?" Hai whispered.

Sony's dad was found in a forest outside of Brattleboro one February morning, Aunt Kim said. His car was parked a little ways into the trees, after a trailhead. The car was charred to a crisp, having burned for hours during the night with nobody knowing. "They said it was a gas leak in his tank that lit up when he was smoking. He had a habit of stopping by the side of the road and smoking and sulking, even when he was with me. But I—I don't know . . ." She shook her head, her face doubtful and adrift. "He'd been—"

"And you never told my mother?"

"She doesn't talk to me. And I'm in fucking *prison*."

"So Sony has no clue? None?"

Her silence said *Yes*.

"What am I supposed to do with this?"

Sony's footsteps approached, the twist of the soda bottle opening, the Sprite set down on the counter. For a moment the fizz in the bottle was the only sound, the couple down the aisle long finished with each other.

Aunt Kim smiled with only her mouth. "Go on, drink." She nodded at Sony. "I made you get it cause I knew you were thirsty."

This made Sony grin. He sat down and drank with both hands. "You're always thinking, Mom," he said in English. Then, "Hey, you think I can go see Dad next month? I have three vacation days now I can use. He wrote about his new job at the post office last month, and I wanna see him in uniform. The Postal Service changed it to white shirts last year."

Aunt Kim wiped her nose with her sleeve. "I dunno. We should let him work. Remember, he also has that wife. And her kids."

"Maria owns the biggest Mexican restaurant in Vermont," Sony went on. "He told me all about that too."

"Can you just hold off a bit?" She said it with a bite that jingled the guard's keys. "Can you at least wait till your mother gets out of here first before you see that man, who's free and living his dream life out there?"

The guard glanced at his watch and announced that they had three minutes left.

Sony's eyes were down. "I'm not gonna hate him just cause you do."

"I didn't *get* to be young, you hear me? You have your schooling. Don't you want to get some kind of degree? Get a piece of paper and be something for talking about all that Civil War nonsense all the time? I . . ." Aunt Kim glanced away and took a deep breath. "I never got to study hard and fail a test, then go to the library with my friends to study again. To improve. I don't have any second chances. Just you. That's it. You're my second chance." She stretched her arms, the tan oversize jumpsuit making her seem like a very old child. "I had you at seventeen. And right away I went to work at the Colt gun factory along with your father." Sony could only understand a portion of the Vietnamese, but he didn't need to. He could see it. He had instinctively shielded himself with a cupped hand to avoid meeting her eyes.

She let her arms drop. Hai grabbed the Sprite and drank as the guard cleared his throat.

"Your father was not a good man." She lifted her chin. "But he loved you. I won't deny that."

"I'm training to be a guard at the Tomb of the Unknown Soldier. It's even harder to get into than the Marines, and I'll—"

"Time!" the guard said. "Wrap it up, nine-two-four."

It was only then that Hai saw the number stitched on his aunt's chest.

"I made this for you." Sony dug into his back pocket and showed his mother the pink penguin in his palm. She watched the paper bird lying on its side, her eyes soft and warped. "It's a pink penguin. I'll pass it to the guard and they'll put it through the X-ray and you can have it to-morrow."

She nodded. "It's beautiful, baby. Hey, hey, look at me now. You're stronger than you think. You hear me?"

Aunt Kim stood just as the guard opened the steel door leading to general population. "If your mom asks, tell her I'm okay," she said to Hai over her shoulder. "Tell her I'm still in Florida and I got a big car and everything, okay? A Honda. You tell her I have a Honda, and you—" But the door shut behind her and all of a sudden the only sound in the room was the Sprite fizzing between them.

THE COUSINS STAGGERED into the frigid night as the fourteen-gauge metal doors closed behind their backs. They stood in the immense quiet engulfing them, the sky above smeared with stardust. The prison was surrounded for miles by a pristine winter wasteland, full of pine forests and marshes and protected preserves—an earthy scent came off the nearby trees and filled the air. Everything the prison produced and used was now sealed away, not even the scent of Pine-Sol and Clorox from the scrubbed halls had made it past the gates.

"There's more stars than I remember," Sony said.

Before Hai could answer he was already crossing the lawn toward the parking lot. The wind was cutting as they huddled together, following the barbed-wire fence toward the bus stop, their aprons flapping like friars' robes in a medieval fable.

"What time does it come?" Hai asked as they sat shivering in the glass vestibule.

"9:02." Sony flipped open his phone. "So a half hour."

Hai took out his copy of *The Brothers Karamazov* and thumbed through it, the book now half its original thickness. He had gotten to the part where they were carrying the boy Ilyusha's adolescent coffin through the run-down church to be buried, and stopped weeks ago, unable to continue. "You know," said Hai, "Dostoyevsky named the protagonist, Alyosha, after his own son, who died of epilepsy when he was only three. He made him the goodest person in the book and . . ." Hai shook his head, not knowing where he was going with this.

"Hey. When you become a writer, would you—"

"I'm not a writer." Hai shoved the book in his jacket. "It's just a thing I used to say. I'm fucking around, okay?"

"Well, you can learn, can't you? That's why you went to college, to learn things fast."

"Sony." Hai stared hard at the woods across the frost-covered road, the spaces between the birch trunks so dark they seemed filled in with Sharpie. "Look, touch me. Go ahead. Grab on." He held out his arm and Sony squeezed it, cautious. "Harder. See? That's the only real thing about me, that I'm sitting here next to you at this bus stop. That's it. Everything else, what I do, what I've done, the goals and promises, they're all, like, ghosts. For most people, their ghost is inside them, waiting to float out when they die. But my ghost is in pieces." He pointed with his chin at the scattered trees. "It's all over the place, caught in all the spots where I snagged myself. You get it?" Hai paused. He had actually never verbalized this before, and the sudden clarity made him queasy. It lay before him like a perfectly dug hole, the edges immaculate and sharp. "I don't have nothing left. Don't you get it by now? Not even something the size of your little paper penguins. So quit going on with this stupid college shit."

Hai instantly regretted what he said. "Hey, I don't mean to creep you out. I'm just tired. This is a weird place." He bent over and hid his face in his hands.

"But I don't get it," Sony pushed on. "Isn't it a dream of yours?"

Hai wanted to say more, to tell him everything, but he didn't have the strength. "Your mom is gonna be fine. And that's all that matters."

Sony took a swig from the Sprite. "But you can't control your mind.

Even if you think you should, you can't." He was whispering now—and for some reason Hai was afraid to see what his face looked like when he was saying this, so he kept his eyes down. "My mind only pulls in certain things," Sony went on. "Sometimes I want it to pull in something else. Like my counselor dates, or the names of people I keep forgetting, or how somebody is feeling about CNN or the Patriots, or Wayne's windowsill garden he loves so much . . . my mom. Your mom. But those things don't come over and choose me. They leave me out of it." He zipped his coat up to his chin. "Sometimes I want to think about being good. But it doesn't choose me. It just doesn't. I'm no good at goodness."

"That can change," said Hai. "It's called growth, learning. People can—"

"But truths don't ever change. Only lies do."

"Did some dumbass general say that?"

"No, BJ did."

Hai accepted so much in Sony, he realized, that he wouldn't in anyone else. The boy could say anything and he'd take it seriously. Sony could strangle somebody with his bare hands and Hai would sit down beside him at a bus stop and be convinced there was no other way, shovel in hand.

Sony was trying to figure something out. "Would you ever write about me, though? Like in a story or something?"

"I don't know."

"Well, if you do," he laughed nervously, "don't put my mole in it, okay?"

"Okay." Hai nodded, but his mind was somewhere else. "Hey. Do you think a life you can't remember is still a good life?" The question sounded almost silly aloud. "I mean, like—"

"Yes," said Sony.

"Why's that?"

"Because someone else will remember it."

With that Sony swiped his hand at the air in front of them—so fast that Hai jerked back. "What was that?"

"A fly." He brought his fist to Hai's face, then opened his hand. "An imaginary one."

"Did you get him?"

"No." Sony shook his head, looking around the immense night. "He got away."

IT WAS ALMOST ten thirty when the bus dropped the boys back in East Gladness. After he rode Sony home on the bike pegs, exhaustion seeping in his marrow, Hai crossed the park through the baseball diamond, the mud so thick and deep he had to walk his bike the rest of the way. Only when the dead end appeared, and with it the smog-grey house, did he remember why he came.

He dropped the bike and sat on the curb across the street. The house was still, the lace curtains diffusing the lights with its dreamy gauze. He had promised Grazina he'd go see his mother that night to wish her a happy Lunar New Year. "Go, go," Grazina had said. "Go hug your mother and say thank you. Believe me, just say thank you. You don't have to explain anything."

He was to fill her in on his big life out in Boston. He had even invented an anecdote about dissecting the liver of a hog using what he saw at the butchery to render it with verisimilitude, down to its twitching hooves. But now, as he stood shivering across the street from the house they shared, the will to face his mother suddenly drained from him. Devoid of conviction needed to give the performance its veracity, he decided, at the last minute, to call her instead—and so he dialed the number he knew by heart, the big rigs blaring behind the highway fence as the phone rang.

"Ma?"

"Oh—it's you!" she said, surprised. A faint shadow in the upstairs bedroom filled the frame. She must have been sleeping and was now sitting up in bed. "It's so late. Are you up studying?"

"Well, I just . . . I just wanted to say happy Tết. I figured since you're alone and all, and I—" He caught a voice in the background, a woman's, pitched by a question, and he realized his mother had suppressed a laugh when she picked up.

"You there, Hai? I think the signal's bad—there's no tower by this stupid highway."

"I'm here." He swallowed, scanning the window. "And yeah, I'm in the medical school library. It's open all night. Hey, I'm sorry I didn't call earlier. I just . . ." He sat down on a soggy couch on the curb, yellow foam bulging from its sides. "I just got caught up."

"Oh, it's nothing."

"I just wanted to be the first to wish you happy New Year. So happy New Year, Ma."

"You too, son. Did you cut some of your hair today?"

"Fuck," he said in English.

"Don't say that in a library! What kind of doctor swears like that?"

"I'll cut some tomorrow. I promise."

"I cut a piece this morning, the size of a thumb. We have to let go of the bad energies from last year, you know. You have to take that weight off. And there was a lot of weight."

He nodded at her shadow in the window.

"Hey, Hai?" Her voice was breathy. "I wanted to tell you this while you were here, but I just—I dunno—there was a lot going on and—"

"What is it?"

"I'm just really proud of you for taking this chance. At everything. I mean, not just taking it. But you made your own opportunity. You went out there and strung it together. You know, all my life, after you were born and your father left us, I kept thinking something else would come, and it just didn't. I always thought it would stop for me like some boat while I waited on the shore with my son and my mother, our bags all packed and ready. But it never came for me and . . ."

"Mom don't."

"No, let me finish. I never tell you anything and I need to say this. The truth is, it never came for me, okay? Sometimes you have to be lucky but also very brave. And I wasn't either. But you *are*. You made your own way with just your mind. No one helped you—I know that, okay? Just know that your mother knows that."

There was a long pause as they let the words hang in the street between them.

"I'm trying," was all he could manage, the cold damp of the couch seeping through his pants. He heard the woman talking in the back, and in the window a fainter shadow approached his mother's silhouette. "Hey, is someone with you? I thought I heard—"

"Oh." She forced a chuckle. "It's just Ms. Do. You know, from the salon. She also lives alone, so we decided to keep each other company today. It's less grim this way." Ms. Do's shadow sat down next to his mother's.

"Good luck in your studies, Hai!" Ms. Do called out. "We're all very proud of you."

"Please tell her thank you," he said.

Through the downstairs window, he spotted the night-light his mother kept on the kitchen counter. Underneath it, in a ceramic cookie jar the shape of a monkey, was where she kept her tips, folded into hundreds of cigarette-like rolls and packed stiff in the jar. How many times had he woken in the immense and throbbing silence of predawn, crept into the kitchen to lift the monkey's head, and taken out a few rolls before heading toward the Candy Man?

"Oh, actually, I wanted to ask you this thing," his mother said. "What's the difference between Suz-anne and Susan anyway?"

His mother, like her coworkers, used an American name at work. It was believed that the more "familiar" the name, the more tips you'd get. For years, she went by Julie, then Stacey, but after a while felt the long *e* sound at their ends sounded too childish, so lately went by Susan.

"I dunno. Which one you like better? But yeah, they're two different names. I think Suzanne is a bit older sounding, like from another era."

She thought about it. "That's what Ms. Do said too. She goes by Lucy. But I like Suzanne. It goes up at the end—don't you hear it?"

"It definitely goes up."

"I knew you'd get me." She laughed brokenly.

"I love you," he said in English, his voice somehow strange to him, the Dilaudid fading fast.

"Love you too. Well, I better go, okay? We've been drinking Ms. Do's Hennessy and my head's spinning." The edges of their shadows touched as they laughed.

"Okay. Happy New Year, Ma."

"Happy New Year, my son."

Before he could see their figures move, the bike spokes whirred beneath him and he was already halfway down the block, the night breeze cool and soft on his brow. He rode for a while through the dew-slick streets, the February trees like wooden sculptures carved from another time. Soon the storefronts dropped off and he entered the sunken quiet of suburban roads—the lights still on in one, maybe two rooms in each house. There's a way an old Connecticut town feels when you pass through it at night. Hollowed out, blasted yet stilled into a potent aftermath, all of it touched by an inexplicable beauty, like the outside has suddenly become one huge living room. And you feel you can sit down underneath the sincere light of a streetlamp and no one would bother you, no one would tell you to leave, because they know you're staying for a reason. That you're bound by your debts, by blood or sweat and the cars sprayed silver with hoarfrost along streets named after white millionaires no one remembers. How boring, he thought, to be yet another boy wanting to rid himself of the hometown dust clinging to his clothes, setting out like a spark flung from his mother's cigarette. He floated through the empty streets, eyes watering from the icy wind. He passed houses filled with warm light and imagined the people inside, his head growing blurry with the thought of them huddled in their tiny parlors full of furniture and voices breaking through the raiment light of TV commercials, the news, its endless reel of abjection, their bodies kept, for now, from the intolerance of daylight and its procession of work and misgivings. Shot through him were fantasies of being amongst them all. He imagined all the boys he wanted to know lying sleepless in their cramped and cluttered rooms, the curling posters and chipped trophies, the endless cords to defunct video game consoles, all of it once the feeble altar of teenage triumphs, now the detritus of adolescence. He wavered through the blocks, searching each window for a face and, finding none, lent his face to the overcast sky, a bowl so emptied it was hard to imagine it held anything at all, let alone entire flocks of geese. By the time he crossed King Philip's Bridge, he was delirious with want for everything unreachable. Entire lifetimes seemed within his grasp, and producible within this one, then vaporized with his breath fogging over his head. The bridge lights smeared everywhere as he called out, in a voice so shrill it jolted him out of his pilled stupor. "Bà ngoại! Uncle Minh! Where are you?" he shouted in Vietnamese as he pedaled. "Uncle Minh, Bà ngoại! Are you there?" He wanted to plunge his bike forward and ride all night toward the horizon, looking for them. If he pedaled hard enough, fast enough, he thought, he could tear through the film of time that held him in place, reaching lateral escape velocity, and find them both sitting alone at the McDonald's parking lot in Virginia, a half-eaten chicken tender in Bà ngoại's hand, grinning at him. "Grandma!" he cried in English, as he dropped the bike in front of 16 Hubbard and staggered toward the door. "Grandma, come back!" It wasn't until the sky flipped in front of him that he realized he had slipped on a patch of black ice and the streetlamp, the last one left on the block, was blazing down from above.

He lay there awhile listening to the river, its low rush along the banks, the periodic gurgle as the waves swirled around an inlet. It must've sounded like this for thousands of years, the only constant thing, no matter how much people polluted it. No matter how much waste was dumped into its depths from the chemical factories in Springfield or Manchester, how many bodies it swallowed and spat out, clean as teeth, this sound of its flow toward the sea remained unchanged. He heard the screen door unlatch, swing open, then footsteps crunching over.

"Who are you? Which camp you come from?" Grazina's floral nightgown splayed across the snow as she knelt and put her hand on his forehead.

"My name's Hai Sergeant Pepper," he said, looking up at the streetlamp, "and I'm taking us to America."

"Are you wounded?" She felt around his chest for holes. "Oh Mother Mary, he's been shot."

"I'm okay." The pills were making him feel like a boatless anchor at the bottom of the sea. "I just . . . I just can't quit it, Grazina. I don't know how to quit it, oh man." He broke into a silent sob and rolled over, tucking his knees to his belly. "I can't quit."

"Of course you can't quit! You're the American army. There are no quitters here, yes?"

"I can't stop—oh, I'm so fucked. We're so fucked."

"Okay, okay, wait here. I know what will help." She shuffled back to the house and returned moments later holding something with both hands. She slipped it through the collar of his zipped jacket, and soon the handheld radio crackled to life as a swell of orchestral music—cellos, strings, flutes, and clarinets—swept out from his chest.

He listened to the score as it merged with the river, his breath tightening across his ribs.

"There, there. Easy now, soldier." She dried his eyes with the hem of her nightgown, the tulips darkening. "It's just a flesh wound in your eyes. But your blood is clear, see? That means you have a clear conscience. Now this, this is Lithuanian National Symphony Orchestra. They air it all the way from Vilnius, bless their hearts. The music will make you feel better, trust me." She placed her ear against his heart and listened, nodding. "Don't worry, Pepper. God won't let good people die. Not tonight."

He dug in his jacket and fished out his pocketknife. "Listen, I need your help with something, okay?"

"You know I can do anything, Sergeant."

"I need you to take this," he handed her the knife, "and do surgery on my hair. Here, just this part. My mother said it would take all the weight off."

"I'm no nurse but let me see." She drew closer, ran her fingers through his bangs, flipped open the blade, and cut. The strands of black hair vanished in the wind as the band played on.

It was late and the interstate across the cornfields had hushed save for the rain's steady drone on tarmac. He let the water drip from his face into the sink and gathered himself. In the next unit, someone was watching *American Idol*, the applause seeping through the vent as he regarded himself in the motel mirror, his bangs cut short and revealing his high forehead.

He stepped out of the bathroom, into the thirty-nine-dollar room at the Motel 6 off Silas Deane Highway, where a man was lying naked on the bed, smiling awkwardly at him. The boy hovered a bit, unfamiliar with desire's choreography in late-night motels. But the man took his hand and drew him in until he was stretched atop the man's bristled chest, their arms hooked like the necks of swans.

The boy watched as the yellow streetlight filled the hollow where the man's missing ear once was—lighting it like a gold coin. The man was just back from Iraq, he had said when they got into the room, his tone apologetic. For a while they lay side by side, the cigarette burns throughout the sheets scratching their arms and legs, the rain drumming the gutters above, both of them ejected onto the shore of something too massive to define, stranded now in each other's arms.

As the man drew close, the boy spoke to the little coin. "Okay,

okay," he said, without knowing what he was affirming. His nerves so newly opened under the man's sweet heat, he hadn't noticed his error, so he paused and moved his head to the man's other side, the one that could hear, and began again. But as he did this the man's back tensed, the corded muscles suddenly torqued under the boy's hands.

"No," the soldier said, putting a wide palm against the boy's tiny cheek, fixing his face before his. The rain outside sounded, somehow, like fire eating through dried leaves. "Keep talking into the other one. I like your voice better in the other one."

"But there's nothing——"

He gently cupped the boy's back to the coin, which had now grown dim. The man's Maybelle auto repair uniform was draped on the chair, the word *Tom* stitched in red cursive on the chest. The boy read the name aloud to the coin and discovered what the man's own name did to the bones in his spine, how the vertebrae seemed to gorge with the single syllable as they found a rhythm to work. Tom the regular. Tom, who came in a week ago and sat hiding his ruined ear as he ate the plate of green beans and mashed potatoes and gravy the boy had prepared.

The boy focused on the ceiling, cream and spotless save for a single brown halo from what must've been hundreds of people lying where they were now, smoking and thinking, the circle murkiest at the center, then fading into pale yellow rings as it waded out. What you see might not always be what you feel. And what you feel may no longer be real. Somewhere inside him the boy believed this law was what turned the planet on its axis.

After, both of them sitting on the bed, their bodies dew-wet as they dressed facing the blank wall, he asked the soldier if he ever considered getting a prosthetic ear, recalling how his mother once gave a pedicure to a woman with a missing calf. The boy stared into the cavity of his boot before sliding his foot inside.

"They don't make 'em in Dominican yet," the man grinned. The ones the VA offered were either too dark or too light. "But they'll have one soon." He raised his hand, as if to touch the hollow, but scratched his chin instead. "What are you reading there?" He nodded at the paperback the boy was tucking into his jeans pocket.

"Just a novel. About an old war."

"Could probably tell you a couple things about that."

"I bet. Wanna get some pizza? I know a place that just opened."

The soldier regarded him with puzzled relief—then laughed a laugh so big and ripped open, the boy heard the tiny scream inside it. "I could eat," he said, nodding to himself. "I could eat."

They rose from the bed, the room somehow emptier than it was before. It was late, but not enough for anyone to look for them—and neither of them moved for a while.

The man stood, his frame pillared and austere, a soldier again; then he gave him this crumpled look—as if the boy were an arrowhead freshly pulled from the man's side.

On the wall, their shadows were so faint they could be mistaken for smoke as the sound of TV applause seeped through from the other side.

IT RAINED ALL WEEK, then cleared. March arrived with cold, sun-washed days, dark-green water sliding past the bankside oaks dusted with frost. It was well into 2010 and the shine of a new year marking the first decade of the new millennium had already dulled, pocked with dispatches of horror. The massive Chilean earthquake from February had left a humanitarian crisis, and the Red Cross sent a lady with pink earmuffs each day during lunch rush, asking customers for donations. The country was still gutted by the recession, and Obama's popularity was already waning from his push to bail out corporations that were "too big to fail." In Cyprus, three men were detained for stealing the corpse of their former president, and eleven endangered Siberian tigers, of which only thirty remained in the wild, had starved to death in a Chinese zoo. The detective on the Rachel Miotti dragging case, face bloated with bloodshot eyes, had returned once more to question staff and customers—to no new leads.

Because his mother worked six days a week in Meriden, in the opposite direction of East Gladness, Hai was able to avoid running into her this whole time. He still rode his bike with his hoodie up just in case. But one Tuesday night, while on a run to grab Pedialyte for Grazina's upset stomach, he spotted her in the CVS half hour before closing.

He looked up from the shelf and saw her distinctive L.L.Bean fleece jacket, decorated with blue and red flowers, the one he had gotten for her fortieth birthday. Her head was down, looking at a bottle of shampoo. He quickly maneuvered to the opposite aisle and stood very still. She took a few steps closer to him, then stopped to read a text on her phone. Through the thin shelf between them, he could hear her breathing, the clinks of her earrings as she moved her head. It was the closest they'd been in months. "Ma," he wanted to say, with nothing to say. "Ma, Ma, Ma." But he stood stock-still. When she made her way toward the back of the store, he bolted to the register, checked out, and flew home on his bike.

At 16 Hubbard, Grazina was getting worse by the week. She'd turn to him while they were watching *The Office* and seemingly pick up a conversation from decades ago, much of it scrambled, like someone turning a radio dial to a random channel. "Did . . . you get out and get the rest of it?" she asked him with gravity. "Did you get the deposit for Lucas's dance classes? Well, she must've filled out the carburetor to get it, don't you think?" She'd also started crying out of nowhere—not big sobs but quick spurts of tears that abruptly ended, sometimes with an eerie chuckle, the memory gone but its sadness remaining, like smoke from an invisible fire.

The only thing that stayed constant was HomeMarket, which went on operating like it did the year before, and most likely the year before that. It was slower the first two months since people were sticking to their New Year's diets, but by March they came back strong, as expected, and the mac and cheese would have to be refilled by one p.m.

There was also the nor'easter that trapped the crew one night after the dinner rush. Within a half hour they were all in the dining room surrounded by burning candles, waiting for power as the snow climbed a full foot above the windows. The only customer with them was Cherry, who was withdrawing from heroin, not by choice but because her dealer was in the pen, and Wayne had to wade to his car in the blizzard to get his pistol flask to hold her over. When that ran out Maureen passed around a metal Yoda tumbler filled with chilled whiskey while singing, in a scratchy drawl, the opening to what sounded like an old Irish folk song. "That song saved my life, if you can believe it."

"Oh, for fuck's sake," said Cherry, grabbing the tumbler from her. "And I'm Princess Diana in witness protection."

ONE DAY HAI was sweeping the dining area when this man came in looking agitated. His head was bald and exceptionally small compared to his body, so that, when not looking directly at him, it resembled a raised fist in the corner of Hai's eye. The fist-head floated toward the counter, where he stood waiting with hands on his hips. When no one noticed him, he dinged the metal bell nonstop.

"What can I do you for, bud?" said Wayne, wiping his hands on his apron.

"First . . ." The man spoke as if his nose were being pinched. "Remove your soiled gloves before wiping them on your damn uniform. And second, where are the pizza bagels?"

Wayne looked around like the man was speaking to someone else, then realized. "Oh. You're the RM. Hello, sir. Um . . ." He read the plastic name tag on the man's shirt. "Mr. Vogel! I'm Wayne. I think we met last summer when you came through." Wayne extended his hand, which was ignored.

"Where's BJ?" The man lifted his chin and the fist rose above his shirt collar. He seemed like the kind of man who wore his Boy Scouts uniform for his senior yearbook photo.

"I'll get her," Hai said, and leaned his broom on the wall.

Hai knocked on the office door and poked his head in. "Some kind of manager's here and he wants you."

"One sec." BJ was hunched over the tiny keyboard, uploading a track to her SoundCloud. "Wait, a *manager*?" She swiveled around to face him. "You mean a blue shirt?"

Hai nodded.

"Fuck." She wiggled herself out of the chair and hustled to the front as Hai followed behind.

"Hey there, Mitch! What's going on, boss?" BJ extended her arms wide and greeted the RM with her pitched customer-service voice, the one she used when someone plopped an undercooked meat loaf on the counter asking for a refund.

"Don't *hey there* me. How come the pizza card isn't on the menu yet? We launched *weeks* ago."

"Well, we got two posters in the drive-thru and they're selling pretty good. We just haven't had an electrician come fix the light behind the card, see? My guy had to reschedule when that snowstorm blew in."

Vogel stepped back, uneasy with BJ towering over his five-foot-three frame. "That's no excuse. If it's not up there, they won't point to it. What kind of promotion doesn't have any pictures of what's being promoted? Pictures get their salivary glands going and they order more. Images increase counter turnover by twelve percent. You should know that." He made his voice travel so the other employees could hear. "What kind of ship are you running here, Cheryl?"

"It's Jean," she mumbled. BJ had a habit of touching her hair, as if patting it on the back, when she was nervous.

"That's funny cause your *file* says Cheryl." He stretched the name so it lingered in the air. By now Maureen, Sony, Russia, and Wayne had gathered around the counter. Vogel leered at BJ and pressed forward with his scolding.

"Can we do this, like, in the back?" BJ asked. "What if a customer comes in?"

"Don't worry, big girl." Vogel grinned like a fifth grader who had just hit you with a spitball. "I locked it on my way in. Sit down, Cheryl."

BJ fell into the metal dining seat as if released from puppet strings. There was a current of uneasiness in the crew seeing BJ treated this way. Vogel started pacing back and forth before the front counter, his thumbs hooked in his pants pockets.

"Listen, kids," he breathed through his nose. "While your manager here," he put *manager* in air quotes, "is throwing grandmas around in leotards . . ." He glanced at BJ. "I saw the flyer outside for your little bar fight. Posted on company property, by the way. Well, while she was doing *that*, a brand-spanking-new McDonald's just opened on Mercer and Cumberland, a seven-minute drive from us. Know what that means, folks? You there," he nodded at Hai, "you know what that means?"

"More burgers?"

"Are you remedial or just being a wiseass?" Vogel's bald spot was growing red as he spoke.

Hai shrugged—a part of him had this wild urge to be fired on the spot.

"It's *competition*. A McDonald's within a five-mile radius from a HomeMarket will decrease sales by 7.4 percent. Monthly. It means we're fighting for our lives here!" He shouted this part so loud Russia dropped his drive-thru headset. "Every store on the Eastern Seaboard that Bill"—this was the other regional manager—"oversees is scrambling to keep up. And guess what? The store in Redding increased meat loaf sales by fifteen points. All while you chumps put on sideshow fights for dropouts and drug addicts." He watched his words enter BJ, whose forehead was now lit with sweat.

"It's that cold case," BJ said, looking around for help. "Customers don't wanna go in here knowing that girl was picked up in the lot across the street and murdered all through town, and that fat cop keeps coming in, asking everybody questions. It leaves a bad taste in their mouths."

"With all due respect, Mr. Vogel . . ." Wayne stepped out from behind the soda machine. "Redding is a more conservative county, and from what I hear, conservatives will eat more meat loaf than liberal folks." With that he took a step behind Maureen, who took another step to the side to avoid him.

"Conservatives eat more meat loaf?" Mr. Vogel said, his eyebrows so high they nearly sat *on top* of his fist-head. "You're telling me *meat loaf* is political?"

"We *are* in a historically blue district." Maureen nodded vigorously.

"Well—" They all turned toward Sony, who was standing behind BJ. "Actually, there's an argument for meat loaf being, at the very least, fiscally conservative." He wrung his hands. "After all, like the Salisbury steak, meat loaf is made from leftover animal protein, sometimes from multiple animals and their end-parts. This is also true of sausage. Historically, hamburger was a way of salvaging leftover meat. One could make a case that meat loaf is a right-leaning dish only because cultural conservatives tend to be fiscally so as well, though not always—"

"That is the *stupidest* thing I've ever heard. And what is this crap?" The fist pointed at the tray of fresh-baked corn bread cooling in the pan. "There's a *sheen* on the crust. That means there's too much sugar." He picked one up, turned it in the light, then pinched the top crust and dropped it on his tongue, swallowed, and winced. "Jesus! This is basically a muffin! How? If you wanna sell muffins, go to Dunkin' Donuts with all the other community college moms."

"But sir," Sony saluted the man, who took a step back, looking at BJ for an explanation, "with all due respect, it's the best-selling item we have. It's also a special recipe from BJ herself and——"

"Can you shut it?" BJ called out. "Just let the man finish. That's an order. But yeah," she added, folding her arms in wounded pride, "our customers swear by our corn bread."

The fist threw the bread, baseball style, into the trash. Russia tiptoed toward the bathroom, and Wayne, spotting an opening, headed toward the back door, fishing for the pistol flask in his back pocket.

"First off," Mr. Vogel said, "corn bread isn't calculated in sales since it comes with every meal, so that claim can't be proven. Secondly, why are *you*——" he pointed a crooked pinkie at BJ, "adding sugar to my corn bread? You want our customers to get diabetes?" The pinkie had a long nail, and Hai wondered if the guy had taken a bump of coke in the car beforehand, which would explain this impressively sustained burst of energy.

"That's enough," Maureen said weakly, but no one heard her.

"And what the hell is this?" He gestured at the nearby "Employee of the Month" wall. "Why are there mug shots on your HomeWall?"

"That's a professional basketball player," Sony added.

"Sony." BJ covered her face with her hand.

Vogel suppressed a disbelieving laugh, then stood blinking at Sony. "Alright, alright. Wow. This is *truly* insane. I can't believe Bill missed all this. BJ. In the office, now. Please." For the first time since he got there, Vogel seemed genuinely sad and bereft. His agitated charade had dislodged the few reddish strands of his balding comb-over. Tamped down with drugstore pomade, they now hovered above him as if he were underwater. "And you," he said to Hai, "get rid of those scraps of paper on the tables. What were you doing, sweeping *air* this whole time? There's trash everywhere."

"Oh, that's not trash," Hai said.

"That's . . . that's my origami." Sony tensed up.

"If it's not relevant to HomeMarket, it's trash." He walked over and snatched them one by one off the seven dining tables and tossed them into the bin. "Now open this godforsaken place already," he shouted as he closed the office door.

Sony rushed over and picked his penguins out the garbage, Maureen helping him. Hai was too angry to move.

"Why would he do that to my penguins?" Sony cried, earnestly confused.

"It's alright," Maureen said. "Here, this blue one will be pretty good once we get the sweet potatoes off."

Hai went over to the office door and pretended to fiddle with the punch clock as he listened in. The door wasn't closed all the way, leaving a pencil-wide crack.

"Hey, man. Look," Vogel said. He started to sit down but changed his mind. Hai could hear BJ's labored breathing. "You cool? Hey, I'm sorry about the Cheryl thing. I shouldn't have . . ."

"I'm fine."

"Look, you know I had to do that, right? I respect you—really, I do. You've been with us since, what, right after 9/11, right?"

"Sure."

"And by the way, I was doing *you* a big favor, Cheryl. You know that? Cause next month . . ." he lowered his voice to a whisper, "you're gonna have to let go at least one from this crew, maybe two."

BJ was silent, but her chair creaked.

"And what you're gonna do is you're gonna blame it on me. Bill's doing the same spiel in Worcester. You can just tell 'em, whenever you're ready, that big ole Mr. Vogel from evil headquarters made you do it, okay? Attagirl." He let out a heavy sigh. "This way, you'll keep your costs down and morale high. They've even mentioned this method a couple times at headquarters. Let us RMs be the bad guys."

"Thanks?" BJ mumbled.

"And before you ask, it's nonnegotiable. I need it done. And it's not just your outfit either, it's all of them except Redding. Remember, we're in a recession."

Hai turned away just as the door opened and the blue shirt darted out. He didn't know where to go and didn't feel like talking to BJ, so he opened the walk-in fridge and stepped inside. He sat down on a crate of lettuce and caught his breath. He didn't know how long he was in there, but at one point the door opened. It was Maureen. In the half dark, lit only by a night-light, she didn't see him and headed to the corner, where she stood leaning her forehead against the wall. Not knowing what to make out of this, Hai stayed still. When she didn't move for what seemed like a long time, he finally said her name.

Maureen startled around. "Oh, it's you. Why didn't you say anything? Why you in here anyway?"

"Why are *you*?"

She had this pained blue gaze, her usually blasé demeanor far away.

"Hey," he stood up. "That guy was a total dick, but BJ'll be fine. And Sony will make new penguins. Hey, hey . . . what's the matter?"

She didn't say anything and just looked at him funny, her eyes filling. "I'm a little nervous."

She half turned toward the sacks of BBQ sauce on the rack. He was surprised by the fear in her voice. "I have this lump . . . in my chest." She touched her right breast. "And I know what it is. My grandma had it and so did my aunt Patty and I just *know* it. I knew it for months." She shook her head, the white roots of her dyed red hair showing.

"You can get it checked, right? Don't people put 'em in that panini-press-looking thing?"

She nodded vaguely but looked like she couldn't see him clearly. She was going to say something, but a shaft of light cleaved the room in half and the door opened.

"What you guys hiding for?" Russia said. "Dude's gone." He grabbed a huge sheet cake on the rack, rimmed with pink frosting. "Come on, we got a birthday booking at twelve. Remember?"

Maureen and Hai followed Russia out, where he placed the cake on a counter and lit the candles before carrying it out front. Wayne, Sony (somewhat recovered), and BJ, her cap back on, her manager's bow tie cinched up, led the procession, clapping as they staggered out from the kitchen, singing "Happy Birthday," their faces lifted into masks of glee as they crossed the rubber mats and onto the warm brick tiles of the dining room, where a family had gathered around a girl with a pink crown on her head, the wax number 6 hovering toward her as she shrieked with pristine delight, scanning the crew's faces, then turning to her parents—no older than twenty-five—regarding them with what looked like the *invention* of gratitude, unbridled to the point of levitation.

Russia set the cake down, Band-Aid hanging from his cheek, and the crew swayed as the song emptied out of them, the applause rising and falling, the father shaking BJ's hands, conspirators of this tiny miracle of joy, as MGMT's "Electric Feel" came through the speakers, and underneath that, under the giggles, the clicking of plastic forks as they're passed around, and the footsteps of each worker returning to their stations, the mounted TV in the corner, its voice announcing, *Multiple suicide bombings, including one at a hospital, have killed at least thirty-three and wounded more than fifty people near Baqubah, Iraq.* And everyone kept on working, and the family set down the pink-wrapped gifts around their girl as Maureen stood watching the family eat cake through an opening in the stainless-steel machines that made up what was called "the back of the house." And winter was over.

Spring

20

One night while riding over the rail bridge after the dinner shift, Hai noticed the house was completely dark. It was not like Grazina to leave the lights off, not even when sleeping, and for the first time 16 Hubbard looked like the other disemboweled buildings on the block. He let his bike fall in the front yard and rushed inside. The living room was lit by slivers of streetlight, and it was so cold his breath hovered before him as he stood, listening for movement. If someone had broken in, and was still hiding, calling out would be a bad idea.

Slowly, he made his way to the kitchen, careful to avoid the creaky spots on the floor, his fingertips tracing the walls as he went. He took the pocketknife from his backpack. At the bottom of the stairs, he tapped the handrail with the knife's handle and waited for the air to change. Still nothing. He could hear the river from an opened window in the bathroom, but after climbing the stairs, he found the room empty. Everything steeped in blue. Curtains fluttered here and there in the hall. He checked her room, which was vacant and horribly quiet. The bed unmade, sheets bundled in knots, the row of wooden owls on the dresser waiting mute and undeterred by their owner's absence. His room, too, was untouched.

"Grazina," he called, slipping the knife in his back pocket. When there was no reply, he flipped on the lights. Sometimes, when she was deep in a spell, a change of light would jolt her out of the past. He ran back downstairs and turned on every light, calling her name, panicking now. Images of her roaming the streets, or by the riverbank, over the bridge, flashed in his head. Having checked the basement, he went back to the front door and found her shoes, an old pair of sun-faded loafers, untouched on the rack.

Before long he was back on the bike, riding up and down the empty streets, the houses with their ransacked doorways gaping like open mouths as he shouted her name into their black hollows. He rode until the pavement became mud before finally turning back. He twisted his head about, undone, scanning the trees, then up to the mountain with its radio tower blinking red.

Back in the kitchen, he picked up her rotary phone. Calling Lucas would be risky. If he knew Hai had lost his mother, it would all be over—kaput. His hand on the receiver, he shouted her name one more time. When only the river replied, he turned the dial.

"What do you mean 'where is she'?" Lucas spat.

Hai could feel a vein pulsing in his temple. "Well, she's not . . . I don't, I don't . . ."

"You're calling from my mother's phone and you don't know where the hell she is." He sounded like he had just stood up and was breathing hard.

"No."

"And you're her nurse. What kind of racket is this, huh? How much are they paying you? Am *I* paying you? She's in the *hospital*, for Chrissakes. How do you not know that?"

For some reason he looked over his shoulder. "How? I mean, what?"

"She fell this morning and called me in her maniac mental state. Missed all her damn pills. Where the hell were you anyway?"

"At work. I mean, at the . . . clinic, where my boss was picking up supplies. Uh—a new walker—I had no idea. She was fine when I left, I promise."

Lucas was thinking, calculating, his breaths fast over the receiver. "I found her in the pantry with her chin bleeding," he said. "She kept asking for you, calling you Dr. Pepper or whatever. Look . . ." He sighed the way people do in movies when they're about to say something hopeless. "She doesn't have long. This brain thing, I'm sure you know, is fast. In a year she won't know who anyone is. Six months after that she'll be dead weight in a wheelchair. I'm trying to keep my distance, to protect myself, but I'm still her son. Look, how 'bout this—just make her comfortable until I work out putting her at the Hamilton Home, alright? Can you do that for me, my man?"

"Yeah," he nodded. "I'll make sure she won't fall again."

"Oh, she'll fall again. That's bound to happen. Just make sure she's in one piece for me. For now, just tidy up the place and call me, you have my number, call if you see any leaks. The house isn't worth squat if it's mold-infested. Not that it's worth much now," he mumbled. He told Hai that Grazina would be ambulanced back from the rehabilitation center in a couple of days. Hai could hear Clara in the background asking if "that's the boy" and hung up before they could say anything stupid.

He stood in the unlit kitchen, the faces—humans in family portraits, and owls—all staring at him like an audience in a carnival. Then he opened Grazina's medical bag on the dining table, put on the seafoam nurse's jacket, zipped up his UPS coat, and headed out. The night, with its sinister neon and greenish lights of bars and loading bays, empty car washes, smeared by as he rode. Dollar General, Burger King, Super 8, the water tower with its gleaming satellite dishes, and the power plant, its flares winking like monstrous eyes.

IF IT'S YOUR turn, and you never want it to be your turn, you'll be wheeled in, always wheeled in, by people young as your children, maybe even grandchildren. You will slide through the Cloroxed halls, whose walls are painted with placid teal or dishwater grey to induce a sense of sedation. The linoleum, too, though warped and shiny to the point of seeing the twisted faces reflected above it, mouths open in soundless half screams, is blue. So blue you'll have the feeling of being swept away, because you are, into a current of corridors intentionally too narrow to turn around in. Only the beige floor moldings reveal how long this place has stood, how many gurneys, wheelchairs, EKG machines, IV stands, stretchers have passed through, holding both the living and the newly stiffened, moving through these halls at all speeds, streaking the corners black, the marking of time's passage here. You will see those shriveled into their eighth or ninth decade bent in chairs or beds, left in the hallways for hours to stare, baffled, at the ceiling fan or a spot on the wall, some heads swiveling at each passing shadow, calling the name they once gave to a son or daughter, faces they haven't seen in months, years.

There are even doctors among them, lawyers, custodians, minor pol-iticians, bureaucratic functionaries, pilots, bakers, and barkeeps, varied stations of life now equalized in the only true egalitarian wing of the American dream: the nursing home, where the past is nothing but what it's done to you. Where "a home," like this one, is often a place to hide the aging body, the crepe-paper skin, the wounds weeping with yellow sap, anemic bruises that stay for weeks, bloodshot brown eyes. How is it that we have become so certain that the sight of years, the summation of decades, should inflict such violence on the viewer—including family—that we have built entire fortresses to keep such bodies out of sight?

As he passed the halls, Hai became aware of how far he had strayed from the "outside world," like a shade passing through a circle in the nether realm. The TV room lit white from the shadows, commercials flickering over half-empty pudding cups and plastic pink tumblers of water, a few runny noses or dewy eyes gleaming silver. Same with the mess hall, where wheelchairs were parked around small tables, some with hushed chatter, others seated with stopped faces. And one, a man in an Air Force cap, talking energetically at the air. All this while the greenish uniforms floated about, mechanically repositioning limbs, as if rearranging furniture, under the constant drone of four TVs, each running CNN except for the one airing a dog show, much to the delight of the woman clapping beneath it. This "facility," state-run and underfunded like many others, wasn't even the worst of them.

He only had to approach the front desk, ask for Grazina, flashing his scrub jacket, and the lady with a perm simply nodded down the hall, her jaw working a piece of gum. "It's 217. Follow the signs to physical rehab. Just make sure you're out by nine. Janitor's coming."

The rehab ward was mostly empty. Unlike regular hospitals, with ERs, trauma docs wheeling bodies with open wounds through double doors, families huddled around coffee machines in step-down units, it was eerily quiet here, the same quiet, strangely, of living rooms of people who live alone, though everyone's here together.

On his way he found a woman who must've been in her eighties lying on a gurney in fetal position, her arm under her head, as if waking from a nap. "You wanna come to the party?" she said as he approached, her eyes tracking him. Hai looked around the half-lit hall, certain that there was no party and most likely hadn't been one for months. He passed two nurses sitting outside a patient's room, keeping vigil over who knows what. They stopped their hushed Spanish to stare at him. He kept on and turned into room 217. With a single step, it was dark everywhere and he had to pause at the entrance to let his eyes adjust. Soon the green blips on the machines came to view. He approached the bed where an arrangement of bones was twisted in its sheets.

"Grazina?" he whispered, reaching toward what appeared to be an arm. He touched it and knew something was wrong. You bathe somebody enough times, hold their hand as they climb into beds, tubs, chairs, scooters, and you know every crease and fold marking their body. He gave the hand a light squeeze and knew it belonged to a man—who didn't even notice his presence—and let go. That's when he saw the curtain. He pushed it aside and stepped through.

There she was, lit dimly by whatever light was coming through the window. She looked a petalish thing, her limbs lost in a swaddle of sheets and towels. Her puffed white hair now matted around her temples and forehead. The rise and fall of her stomach told him she was asleep.

Hai knelt and touched her forehead with the back of his hand.

"Hey," he whispered, wiping a few strands out of her eyebrows. "Grazina, you there?"

At first only her fingers stirred, then the winced-shut face relaxed, its eyes opened and blinked out the window. He said her name again, leaning closer. She turned and looked at him with an expression so plain, open, and unwritten, he almost thought he had entered the wrong room altogether.

"Grazina? You with us?" He waved his hand before her face, but she stared past it.

He could tell right away that something was different—her pupils at once dilated and glazed with a milky film. He had of course seen her dim before, but this time she seemed fully opaque. When he touched her arm she pulled back and hissed something in Lithuanian.

"It's Sergeant Pepper," he tried. "You gotta use English with me, okay? Listen." He managed to hold her thumb. "London's only a day away. We're so close. I told you I was gonna get you to America and we're doin' it. You believe me, don't you?"

She glanced around, her mouth open. "Who are you?"

"I'm a specialist," he said without thinking.

"In what?"

"Human relations."

He thought he saw her nod. "Willem."

"No, my name is Hai Sergeant Pepper. US Army, Second Division, remember?"

"I saw him last night." Her eyes finally fixed on the boy's face, but there was not much behind them. "What'd you do with his dustpan?"

"What about his dustpan? Do I even know this guy?"

"He was on fire. From chest up." She gestured at her heart. "I saw him run into a house to burn up. He burned up in Sigi's house while I was down here."

"Down where? Here?"

"This basement. Tell his mother, will you? She's with group D."

"Okay, group D. I'll tell her when I go back up."

She looked to her right, where the curtain was drawn, and reached for it. "How do we open this door? Can we go out this way?"

Hai pulled her hand toward him. "There's no way out. You have to stay put for now."

"Am I in the upper rooms yet? It still hurts, even up here."

"You're on the first floor of a hospital."

"I'm not in heaven? I'm still downstairs?"

"You're still downstairs. We all are."

"Why does God kill us?" Her face threatened to break.

He was surprised by the suddenness of her anger.

"Why would the weatherman lie to us like this?"

"What did he lie about?"

"I took everyone to Missouri, you know."

"Yeah? Okay, for what?" he said, his voice tender and affording, trying his best to follow.

"When I worked at Woolworth's. My biggest achievement was organizing a trip to Missouri. We wanted to see the big arch. St. Louis."

The bones in the next bed coughed, then repositioned himself on the mattress.

"Hey . . . You tell me a story now, Sergeant Pepper. Tell me something about you, brave soldier." She turned to him with glassy eyes.

"I don't got a story."

"When the bomb siren went off, we ran to the shelters. Sometimes we stayed many nights with oil lamps and candles. The people down there, they passed the night telling stories." She smiled at this memory, a streak of clarity in her voice. "You know so much about me, but I don't know about you. Tell me about your life. About America. What state do you come from, Officer? They have many states, yes?"

He thought for a moment. Then remembered the pair of ceramic owl salt and pepper shakers he grabbed from the kitchen table to cheer her up. He took them from his coat pocket and stood them on her blanket. Two owls on a field of snow.

"I had a friend once," he said, so soft it came out as a whisper. He waited a long while, then, "We can call him Noah." He listened to the name leaving his mouth. "Like Noah's ark."

"Like Noah's ark," Grazina nodded.

"Here's Noah," he said, shaking one of the owls. "And here's a younger Sergeant Pepper. They lived in a place with lots of snow."

Grazina's eyes followed the owls as he moved them along the blanket.

"So on summer evenings, when summer finally came, and the full moon lit the fields so silver, you could squint and it would still look just like it did after snowfall. On those nights, Noah and I would run together through the tobacco, like this. And there was this mighty clear sky full of stars that made you stop and look up, your head empty as a ladle as you tried to locate yourself inside an immeasurable universe. And no one knows where you are and you feel, for a tiny second, that you have no parents, that they never existed at all, which is impossible and shameful to love, but I did. I loved that feeling."

He told her of their friendship, of the days driving aimlessly in a truck through a town far, far away from Europe, from Germany, called East Gladness. How they'd walk for hours through the pines, the back lots of that rusted strip of earth, singing in adolescent voices that crackled like wartime radios. About the pools of clear water that rose over the cattails and sweetgrass in the junkyards after a storm, how once they swam in a shallow tub made from rainwater collected in a dent on the roof of an old school bus. And the water was so clear, so sweet, your skin looked truer than it did on the surface, warped and magnified by the tiny current they made from their scavenged laughter. He told of Noah's barn, where they knew the wrong inside them was the only thing that made sense of where they grew up, where the gods, after flipping the table from losing their bets, left them alone to make a fugitive life. That a boy beside a boy could form an island called "okayness." "With him," he said, "it wasn't that I was happy—but that I was okay. And okay was even better than happy because I thought it had a better chance of lasting." He turned and was startled to find her staring right at him. "Okay is underrated. You know what *underrated* means, right?"

"More than what the Lord planned," she said.

"Yes. And we were very underrated. But we were also very okay."

He stood the owls back-to-back. "We'd sit for hours like this under a metal slide in the park and talk." The boys had this way of knowing what the other was thinking without ever using words. "Because it's like that when you're fourteen," he said. The superpower of being young is that you're closest to being nothing—which is also the same as being very old. "You can ride a thought in and out of somebody, and it'll do so little damage, you think anything's possible. You can say things like *I want to be a gay father with a wife and kids,* or *When I'm high enough I start to feel sorry for straight people, they always seem trapped on front lawns,* or *When I'm sixty-five, I'll be happier than my dad.*"

Grazina looked fondly at the two owls, the faint light touching their heads.

"Do you ever think you'll have kids?" he mimed the right owl's voice.

No one in his life knew he had such a friend until now, until Sergeant Pepper told her. Somebody goes ahead and dies and all of a sudden you become a box for them, he thought, you store these things that no one has ever seen and you go on living like that, your head a coffin to keep memories of the dead alive. But what do you do with that kind of box? Where do you put it down?

"I'll have a daughter," the left owl said.

"A daughter?" The right owl leaned to one side. "Hmm. I always thought you would want a son for some reason. But it'd be cool to see you teaching her to shoot bottles with one of those pink rifles from Walmart. I'd watch you both and be that worried gay uncle." The right owl laughed.

"But I don't want her to be shooting anything," the left owl said.

"You wouldn't? *Really?*" Hai looked over his shoulder, as if to find Noah's back pressed against his. "Maybe she'll be a painter. Didn't you always want to be a painter?"

He looked down at his hands. The owls were both lying down now, separated by a circle of air.

"Where's Noah now, Sergeant?"

Hai dipped his head. "He was storming Normandy, like J. D. Salinger did, and was wounded. We enlisted together. To be heroes of East Gladness. Then he took medicine to make his wounds go away. He wanted too much of one feeling—and I guess his heart gave out because of it. I don't think we're made to hold too much of any one thing." Hai regarded the dead owls in his hands.

"Of course not."

He wiped his nose with the sleeve of the nurse jacket as he thought about that time, a time he barely remembered. He had dropped out of school in New York not because he was getting headaches from reading too much, as his mother had thought, but because one day Noah stopped breathing and a week after that was lowered in the cold November ground. What could he have said to his mother about a boy she'd never met? To even tell of it would reveal how he had chosen his sadness over her joy, over her pride in him making it to college after everything, after the war, the refugee camp, the abusive husband, the dead mother and estranged sister. But he had come home—he had given up—only because he wanted to be near her, New York being unbearable in grief, its massive and unending throb of human magnetism making the vacant parts in him more vacuous than he could bear.

"I'm sorry," Grazina said from the depths of the medical bed.

"Don't be."

"I'm sorry they sent you to war. Nobody should go to war. Boys should be owls running in snow fields. I'm sorry you had to find me." She touched his arm, her grip warm and stern. "So you're a liggabit then," she said, sniffling.

He looked at her hand on his sleeve. "What?"

"You're—" she gestured at him, "a liggabit. Boy and boy, girl and girl. I see them in newspapers. Liggabit community."

"Oh—oh, you mean LGBT?" He wiped his eyes and let out a single disbelieving laugh.

She shrugged.

"Yeah, I'm a liggabit."

"A liggabit soldier," she said, her head slipping to the side. "Must be rare."

"Sure."

A brightness had pooled at the corner of her eyes as they started tracing something on the ceiling. She was fading again. He didn't know what to say, so he took her cold hands in his and said the only thing that came to him. "Tu esi mano draugas."

She blinked.

"Hey, Grazina. Hey." He leaned forward. "Tu esi mano draugas . . . Please." He patted her cheek. "*You are my friend*. Right? Did I say it right? Am I doing it right?"

She turned to him as if following a sound in the room. Then, deep under her breath, she started singing "Silent Night." Her lips so still it was like a music box was playing inside her.

"Wait a minute. Who are you again?" She started to reach for something in her lap, then seemed baffled at her hand.

"I'm Labas. It's——"

"And who am I?"

"Grazina. You're Grazina Vitkus."

"I don't know who I am. Wait a minute. How can that . . ." And like that the world was falling away in slabs, rinsed and pooling at the periphery.

"You're you, okay. You've *always* been you." He was starting to shake.

"But am I still me if I don't remember who I was?"

"I don't know!"

"I can still hear the river from here," she said. "It's saying I did a good job. It said I did good."

"But I'm not good." He said this to the back of his wrist to steady himself. "I'm a horrible son, do you know that? I was never a good son."

He tried to will her back to the present, but when her eyes grew blank and unseeing, he couldn't take it anymore and got up. He floated through the halls, the porcelain owls clutched in each fist, her voice thinning behind him. The nurses, busy on their phones, didn't even notice. By the time he got to the parking lot, he had a delirious urge to scream. He made a snowball and threw it far as he could and watched it hit a parked car with a silent white puff. He wanted to touch something until its color changed. Only when he tasted the salty snot did he realize he had fallen to his knees and was crying. "Please leave me alone. I'm sorry, okay?" he shouted at the ground. "Noah, Grandma, I'm sorry you had to die when everybody else fucking lived! But it's not that great here, okay? It's as shitty as it was before. Trust me."

The metal door behind him clacked open. Footsteps in the powder. "Hey, man, you gotta get out of here, you hear me? Get the hell up." It was a security guard. He looked genuinely sorry for the boy curled in the snow. "There's people sick inside, man, and people who gotta work. So whatever you got going on, it can't be here."

Hai rose and brushed himself off. "Sorry," he blurted, without looking at the guard, and made a beeline toward his bike. Fingers shaking, he zipped up his UPS jacket, the same jacket he had found hanging from a nail in Noah's barn the day of his funeral, having ridden his bike through mud-frosted roads to get there. Because Hai was not invited to see the coffin. Because to Noah's family he never existed. He was locked inside the head of the cold boy in the pine box.

He glanced at his hand and saw that he had dialed Sony's number on his cell. He put the ringing phone to his ear as he picked up the bike. "Sony, that you?"

"Hey, you okay? You never call after five p.m."

"I'm good, man. I'm real good. Listen," he said as the guard went back inside, the snowed-in quiet spreading around him. "You wanna watch *Gettysburg*?"

"Now? It's almost nine and I . . . I have work tomorrow—"

"C'mon. Please? I wanna see it with you. I wanna see Pickett's Charge again. I—I think I know why they did it. Why they crossed that big-ass field."

He could hear Sony thinking. "Alright, fine. Can you get here in a half hour?"

Since it was after hours and visitors weren't allowed, Hai and Sony sat on the floor in the lobby of the Meyer's Center, their backs against the wall, staring at the corner-mounted TV playing the warped VHS of *Gettysburg*, a box of Goldfish between them. It was the scene when Colonel Chamberlain's Twentieth Maine was about to make its famed stand on the Union's far left at Little Round Top. "Chamberlain was a professor before the war, with no military experience," Sony explained. Hai had downed three painkillers on the ride over and was hardly following, but had made it to that juncture in the high where everything sounded unassailably true. "But he had the wits to judge the Confederate volleys. That's because he was a rhetorician. It means 'the strategy of words'—I looked it up. Rhetoric is like a battlefield, but in the mind. About positions and counterattacks. Isn't that right?" He cupped a handful of Goldfish to his mouth and chewed.

"That's right," Hai said as Colonel Chamberlain unsheathed his saber, its flash lighting across the faces of the men he was sending forth to die. "The sentence is the end of the line," Hai said. "And there are no other flanks. It is naturally vulnerable on the right side. Because that side must be open in order for the other sentences to continue. But the left margin is closed."

"That's right," Sony said, turning to him as Hai watched the Twentieth Maine pour down a forested hill. "Napoleon would use rivers and mountains to protect one of his flanks so he only had to defend the one." He placed a Goldfish in Hai's half-opened mouth. "But tell me more about the battle line of the sentence," Sony said. "It's interesting."

But Hai had already lost the idea, the line broken, and just shook his head real slow until they were lulled back into the movie, their faces sick with the Union blue glowing from the screen.

Hai was actually *there* the day Sony first became enamored of the Civil War. It was like witnessing Larry Bird pick up a basketball for the first time, he thought. Hai must have been eight or nine. Each year, on Memorial Day, a marathon of war movies would be shown on one of the four channels picked up by the tinfoiled antennae on their Sony Trinitron, transmitting an endless loop of carnage, the wars occurring often out of chronology, the bodies interrupted only by brief credit rolls and commercials for vacuum cleaners and used car lots.

The film depicted, from both sides, the three days in July 1863 when the pivotal battle took place on the outskirts of Gettysburg, Pennsylvania. As soon as the movie started, Sony was hooked. He left his bowl of Kraft Mac & Cheese untouched, scooting closer and closer to the TV until his face was inches away. He sat running his finger down the scar in his head, back and forth, so oddly quiet Aunt Kim had to come to check on him, once, twice. She walked up and was about to tap him on the shoulder, but then stopped and regarded her boy, who was finally doing a normal-boy thing—watching a war movie with such devotion, it was the closest he came to peace.

The other film often shown on Memorial Day was *The Green Berets*, where an aging John Wayne is seen emptying his M16 into hundreds of North Vietnamese rushing to overtake an American firebase during another civil war. Hai didn't know it then, but with not enough Asians to fill the number of corpses the film demanded, white actors wore black makeup as yellowface during night battles, the crude paint streaked with sweat shimmering across the screen as they died, in comically exaggerated throes, piling in heaps around sandbags stacked about the base, shot from a distance that would hide their whiteness but not far enough to frame the three million dead Vietnamese throughout the war. The film was released in 1968, before the war even ended, the deaths on-screen predicting the deaths in life.

Hai stared as *The Green Berets* played on, Sony beside him searching the corpses for a face. "Is that us?" Sony said, his seven-year-old finger pointing at a mangle of limbs. "Is that us?"

What does it do to your mind to see "your people" die so vastly that you can't even tell that they are *not*, in fact, your people at all? Hai thought, looking back. How easily a face is disfigured in the abstraction a pile of bodies so naturally makes. After a while, it was not the dead but merely death itself that Hai saw folded into this scene of American triumph. Was this why, watching *Gettysburg* for the first time, Sony sympathized with the Confederacy? With the butternut- and grey-clad men who were, like the "Vietnamese," dying in hundreds, mowed down in scene after scene by cannon and musket fire, their uniforms, like the Vietcong's, made mostly from civilian clothes worn to rags, their bodies turned, it seemed, to laundry? And yet, unlike the "Vietnamese" in *The Green Berets*, the faces of Confederate soldiers in *Gettysburg* are clear, the camera lingering on their agonized expressions, casting their human deaths as felt losses, full of pathos. The illusion was made possible by the very fact that the "Vietcong" bodies were captured in passing, transient, blurring themselves toward death—and not, like Robert E. Lee or Joshua Chamberlain in *Gettysburg*, zoomed in and fixed to a distinguishable lived life.

"Is that us?" Hai heard his voice say, back now in the group home lobby. "Is that us, buddy?" He nodded at the white men crumbling in the 1863 scene from the 1993 film.

Sony searched the screen long and hard.

Hai thought of that time they visited Stonewall Jackson's house. How no one told them during their tour that in 1909 the house was bought by the Daughters of the Confederacy, the organization that helped erect Confederate statues all over the South. And although it was the general who was featured in the tour, his face repeating throughout the halls, it was the unseen presence that was most felt. Inside each room, from the fancy set table to the kitchen counter, the knife left on the cutting board beside a sprig of green onion, through the spotless banisters and dressers, the commodes that must be emptied, underwear washed and dried, and then, outside, among the verdant vegetable and flower beds around the property, the carriage that must be driven and tended to, its wheels oiled, horses fed, was the unmarked presence of Jackson's six slaves, who Hai later learned were Albert, Amy, Emma, and Hetty, along with her two sons, Cyrus and George. Like the fake Vietnamese in *The Green Berets*, they were everywhere yet nowhere to be found.

The pills were blurring his edges, making his skin feel permeable and possible. He was sitting with his cousin watching his favorite movie, which was fast becoming Hai's as well. *Is that us?*

But who was *us* if everything, in the end, as Maureen pointed out, was corn cake, even when they insist, rhetoricians that they are, that it's bread?

"So why did they cross the field? Didn't you say you had a theory?" Sony's face was open and expectant.

Hai watched the technicolor ruins smoldering before them. "You know what? I totally forgot, buddy. I had the answer in my head the whole way here, and now it's all gone."

"Oh yeah . . ." Sony nodded knowingly. "That happens in war all the time."

21

He stood in the unlit living room back at 16 Hubbard, gathering himself, the Dilaudids down to a quarter bottle. Somehow he made it home and two days had passed. Somehow he called out of work, twice. Normally the TV would be on, humming with the eleven o'clock news or reruns of *The Young and the Restless*, Grazina talking to the characters like they were guests in the parlor, but now the quiet was immense and amplified by the scratching of a mouse somewhere in the kitchen.

Hai climbed the stairs, eyes lingering on Grazina's blow-dryer hung by a nail on the wall. He walked into her room, picked up random items on her dresser. A porcelain powder jar, a makeup case, the foundation long dried and scraped clean, a half-eaten box of Walker's Shortbread cookies, the endless bottles of medications. One of them was filled with baby teeth, most likely from her two adult children. There was also a photo of her and her husband, her daughter on her hip, staring into the camera from the steps of the rail house. Next to that was a single wool glove surrounded by cough drop wrappers. All this, the debris of her living, somehow made her absence feel absolute and stifling. She was everywhere and nowhere at once.

A sharp agitation coiled through him. He thought of the stupid pizza bagels and how the Sgt. Pepper's pizza shop would be destroyed because of them, the corn cake, BJ's futile and ingenious scheme, the fake school in Boston, the fake life in East Gladness and the true lies that did nothing but prolong their nights in this crumbling house at the edge of the world.

He placed another pill on his tongue and lay curled on the floor beside Grazina's bed, waiting for sleep to rise from his feet to the tip of his mind as the day fell away like a photograph snatched by wind.

IT WAS ALMOST three in the afternoon when the hospital van pulled up. He rose from the floor, wiped his eyes, and hurried downstairs. An icy wind had blown out the sun and the street was a sick monochrome. An aide in blue overalls, who could have easily been a janitor, pushed Grazina, slumped in the wheelchair, down the walk. Hai watched from a sliver in the curtain and opened the door as the wheelchair tapped the front steps.

"This your . . ." The man looked him over, mustache twitching. "This your grandma? She's supposed to be dropped off here—was told there'd be somebody to take her in. Are you . . ." he checked the notebook in his chest pocket, "Lucas Vitkus?"

"That's my uncle. You can bring her up."

The man picked up the wheelchair, carried it up the steps, and placed it in the sunroom. Grazina moaned, her head unmoving. "I'm home? This Hubbard Street?"

"Sure is," said the custodian. "Go ahead and sign here for me?"

Hai scribbled on the clipboard and the man left.

Grazina cocked her head, dazed. "You have anything to eat?"

"Of course we do. But how you doing?" Hai squeezed her hand. "They treat you alright in there?"

"I'm not dead." She winced a smile. "But I don't wanna go back, Labas. It's too dark in there. They have no lights, and my owls." She struggled up from the wheelchair and shuffled inside. "Oh God, my owls." She grabbed a plastic barn owl from the fireplace mantel and pressed it to her cheek, cooing into it. "It's much better with them around." Her hospital gown drooped from her bony shoulders—she seemed to have lost ten pounds in four days.

"Here, come sit down," he said, pulling out a chair. "I'll put on some tea."

While Grazina sat staring at the tablecloth, he emptied the contents from a paper bag onto a plate and set it before her. "Corn bread," Grazina said cheerfully, and bit into it. "Thank you, Labas. Thank you. Oh, she's perfect, this batch."

"You can thank HomeMarket."

"Yes, HomeMarket. They still good to you, boy? They give you raise yet or what?"

"No—but I never asked. Should I ask?"

"Ask what?"

"About raising it—maybe to $7.50 an hour?"

"Who was in it?" She peered about the room as if following something he couldn't see.

He put the cups on the table and drew closer. "Never mind. Listen, you wanna take a nap or something?"

"Me or you?" she said, still chewing.

"We can both take one. I could use it."

Grazina shrugged.

The kettle started to whistle. He poured the tea. She took the sugar spoon and rubbed it along her teeth but stopped when the metal clanked against her molars, then held it up and frowned.

"Hey, don't do that. You'll chip a tooth."

"No I won't. But . . . but I . . ." She stopped. "What was I saying?"

"I dunno. You had a spoon in your mouth."

"I have to brush my teeth. They didn't let me brush in there. I kept telling the little girl at my bed to get me a toothbrush, but she only spoke Croatian. So it was all kaput." She looked up at the ceiling. "Looks like Timothy fixed the roof. We didn't have a . . . well, it was an older car, so it broke down. Nissan—Japanese stuff. No good." She placed the last piece of corn bread in her mouth and stopped. "Labas? Am I going crazy? Or is everything still?" She stared open-mouthed.

"No, no. You're just having trouble remembering, that's all."

She gave him a warm, doubtful smile.

"How about this. Let's go watch the Easter dinner tape again, okay? We can finish it this time."

Grazina had showed him, a couple months back, a home video of an Easter dinner at the very house they were in, the band of Scotch tape on the VHS reading *Easter '89* in black marker.

Before long they were slumped on the couch as the room filled with voices that once filled the room. The decorations and furniture in the video remained identical to how they were now, down to their exact orientations. The only owl in the grainy film, however, was a woven tapestry hung next to the TV, the same RCA model with wood-grain panels.

The camera, which was held by her husband, Jonas, was pointed right at the TV from the couch, the same one they were sitting at now, so that the exact scene they lived in was doubled behind the screen—only the room was brighter in the video for having been newer, the objects less dusty, luminous with human use. Grazina sat nodding and mumbled names as faces flashed by: Ludva, Markus, Daiva, Sigitas, Patrukas, Lina, Darius, so-and-so who moved to Missouri, someone else who died of pancreatic cancer, another gone back to the old country. But mostly she was indifferent, as if naming streets on her way to the doctor's. The bowls of food floating from smile to smile, the glasses of wine, skipped through the warped film.

Then, at the stove, with her back turned, the back of whose head Hai could recognize now from across the river, was Grazina. "Say hello! It's Easter, it's Easter!" Jonas said from behind the camera, followed by something in Lithuanian. Grazina turned around, shy but happy, quickly stepping aside to showcase the potato latkes she was cooking, the gleam in her eyes sharp and capacious—the personality inside them overflowing. "Here's Mama making her famous pancakes!" The camera panned down and revealed Lucas, in his forties, planted on the same chair Hai had sat on earlier.

She started pointing to something on the screen when there was a knock on the door.

Hai flipped off the sunroom light and peered through the curtain. It was getting late. On the steps was an official-looking woman clutching a folder—never a good sign. Behind her was Lucas, his thinning, cotton-candy hair shivering in the breeze. Hai opened the door halfway and the woman, seeing him, stopped mid-step.

"Out of the way," Lucas said. "Where's my mother? Ma? You in there?" He brushed past the boy into the house. "It's time to get you somewhere *safe*." His voice had altered, Hai noticed, pitched with performed distress. Lucas glanced around the corners of the sunroom, searching.

"Sir, who—may I have your name?" said the woman. "And what's your relation to Mrs. Vitkus." She was handsome and tall, with the presence of a CEO, but in a lumpy sweater.

"No relation," he said. "But I live here. She asked me to live here."

The woman jotted this down and stepped inside. "Okay. And you do realize Mrs. Vitkus has a medical history. And that she suffered a bad fall here last week? Which means this space is no longer safe for her. And whatever you two have going on, I think we need to—"

"I take care of her. I do my best and I have a job. I'm not a bad person—and she's not crazy. She's—"

"No one said she's crazy." The woman stood taller. "And we'll do the proper evaluations to know where she's really at."

"Look, she doesn't want to go to a *home*. She already has one and you're standing in it."

Grazina let out a distorted cry from further inside the house. Hai rushed to the kitchen, where he found her sitting in the chair behind the dining table stacked with magazines, barricading herself from Lucas.

"Ma, seriously. I'm gonna get you some help. Remember, *I'm* your son. The scientist." He was clutching the table so hard his fingernails whitened.

"Ma'am, are you doing alright?" The counselor came in. "Do I need to call an ambulance?"

"Let's just go ahead and do it now, Tonya. Call the ambulance, maybe even the cops." Lucas glared at Hai.

"No!" Hai ducked under the table and put his arm around Grazina. "What are you doing? She clearly doesn't wanna go. You can't just take people against their will like this."

"Don't you dare touch my mother." Lucas was spitting at this point. "I'm the guardian. I also have power of *attorney*. And she needs to go. For her own well-being," he added. The nursing home counselor stood at the threshold, thinking, her eyes flitting across their faces. The Easter video was still running, its voices leaking into the kitchen.

"Sergeant Pepper," Grazina said, her voice wavering. "Sergeant Pepper, help me. They're going to take me to the camps. Pepper, please."

"They won't take you. They can't violate your basic human rights." Hai said this loud, directed at the nurse. "The international code for displaced persons during wartime," he mimed, "as signed by the Geneva Convention, article 11.5, section 12, states that no refugee shall be taken against their will by any representative of any belligerent state other than their own. All other authorities are null during wartime as protected by international law. Which was all made evident at Nuremberg," he added, spouting the last dregs of his World War Two vocabulary.

Grazina nodded. "Please, Lucas, listen to the sergeant. Be a good boy." She spoke to him in the tone mothers use to put their sons to bed. "I'm not crazy, I promise. I was making it all up, okay? It's just a game, really. I still have all my brains. I make it up because I'm lonely old lady."

"What's going on here?" The counselor looked to Lucas, whose teeth were the grey of loaded dice.

"Sergeant, please . . ." Grazina shut her eyes and grabbed the boy's arm, tears running down her cheeks. "Don't let my son call me names anymore. Please. I don't smell like piss. I'm a good person. I'm clean."

"Lucas." The counselor took a step toward him. "What's she talking about?"

"Are you kidding me?" he stammered. "I've never ridiculed you and you *know* that. And what the hell is this Dr. Pepper crap you keep spouting? This fucking kid is messing with her mind. Can't you see he's manipulated her? She's never talked like this before." He pointed at Hai's face. "You weasel your way in and—"

"Lucas." The woman put her hand up. "Let's regroup, okay?"

"Of course." Lucas straightened up and picked something off his shirtsleeve.

As the counselor turned to speak to Lucas in hushed tones, Hai slipped the salt and pepper shaker owls from the table into Grazina's hands. "You ready for a special mission?" he whispered. "I've already loosened the pins for you, and you know what to do, right? Just like our training. On my mark, okay?"

Grazina nodded.

"Okay, guys." The nurse faced them.

"Get out of my house, you Nazis! They already killed my cousin in the raids. Why do you torture us simple peasants?" Grazina cried. "Why do you come to take over my country?"

"That's it!" A vein pulsed on Lucas's forehead. "Call the police. I've—"

"Now!" Hai cried.

Grazina, in what appeared to be slow motion, chucked the owl salt-shaker at the cabinet above the counselor's head—where it shattered. She did the same with the pepper grenade, which bounced off the cabinet and exploded onto the tiles. She then lifted the lid off the clay sugar jar on the table and flung fistfuls of sugar at them.

"Let the devil take you, cowards! I curse you! I curse you with holy salt!" The kitchen was small enough for the sugar to burst and ricochet with surprising violence.

The counselor shielded herself with the clipboard and hurried away, calling for Lucas, who ducked out behind her.

"Now shoot 'em," Hai shouted.

"With what?" Grazina asked.

"Your pistol, remember?"

Grazina raised her finger-pistol and fired. And Hai did the same. "Bang bang. I'm hitting them in the balls," she said.

"Good, me too."

"I gave you a chance, now I'm coming back with the cops!" Lucas shouted as they headed out. Hai ran to the front door and locked it, then stood guard as the car sped off.

In the kitchen Grazina sat back in a heap. The sugar, mixed with sweat, had coated her hands with white crystals. She shrugged at Hai, then started licking her fingers.

"They're gone." He pushed the table out of the way and dragged her chair out of the corner, then grabbed a wooden owl from the china cabinet and placed it in her arms. "There, just hold this and calm down a bit. Just breathe for me, alright?" He took a second owl, this one made of resin, and sat on the floor by her feet, cradling it in his lap. They sat rocking the owls as the heaters clicked on.

"Where'd you get these, Sergeant Pepper?"

"America."

"Ah—that's why they have more open faces." She examined the owl as if it were alive, turning her head to see its features. "Americans are optimistic. It shows in how they make their owls. The Romanian owls, like that one there," she nodded at the case, "the one Lina got me when she was exchange student, have tiny eyes, skeptical."

"Hey, who am I right now?" He wanted to check in to reorient himself. "Am I Sergeant Pepper or am I Labas?"

He thought he saw her eyes flutter. She tilted her head as if listening to voices in another room, but the Easter video was long over. Then, rocking the wooden owl in her arms, she got up and opened a drawer in the china cabinet. She placed on the small table a mason jar filled with what looked like pebbles, then sat down and pushed it toward him. "My husband—he collected these."

"I know, he was a hoarder."

"No. These things," she tapped the table with her forefinger, "these came from inside him."

Hai put the owl down and picked up the jar, the yellowish stones shifting as he turned it.

"In old country, they had to bury the horses with big stones from the river. No time to dig holes with Russians coming. When horses were killed by air raids, we kids would go out and find stones. I never thought humans can make stones from the river inside them. But they said Jonas had too many rocks in his organs. This whole time he was burying himself. I thought he was getting promoted. He was conductor for Amtrak, and he was making more salary, watching our children grow, going on trips, picnics at the Lithuanian camp in the summers in Massachusetts, but he was slowly covering himself with stones. Just like he covered the basement with garbage." She held the owl at arm's length, frowning, then brought it to her chest. "You never know how big a horse is until you have to bury it."

But Hai's mind was snagged on something else. "You said to the nurse that your cousin was killed in the raids—but wasn't it your brother?" He studied her face, then decided to ask what he'd wanted to ask for some time. For weeks he'd had the nagging feeling she'd been embellishing a minor diagnosis into a pageantry of chaos.

"Grazina, are you making this all up? You can tell me if you are."

He said it so gently that she turned her whole body to face him. A thin, nearly imperceptible smile crept along her mouth, then vanished. "Stouffer's," she said.

"What?"

"We're down to two Stouffer's." She patted the back of the owl's head. "Now, don't think too much about the stones, boy. They'll just weigh you down."

Just then the cuckoo clock went off; a headless owl emerged from the door and swiveled as it chirped above them.

"I guess Stalin's invading Vilnius again," he said, nodding toward the sound.

"No." Grazina was looking out the window at the bridge. "That's 6:43 p.m. The time Lucas was born."

APRIL CAME ON. The steam, which all winter had covered the top half of the windows of HomeMarket, dissolved as the outside temperature slowly equaled the inside—cause for Wayne to look up in the midst of carving and shout "Spring's here!" before returning to his knife work, now whistling as he went. In a stretch of brown pasture along Route 4, migrant farmers had begun planting sweet potatoes, calling to each other in Spanish across the wind-swept dust. One of them, a woman in overalls and ponytail tied through the loop in her cap, had fingernails painted turquoise blue, likely at one of the three Vietnamese nail salons in the five-mile radius. Some of these potatoes will be shipped to the plant in Missouri, where they'll be mixed with other spuds from Louisiana and New Jersey, then cooked down in 150-gallon vats to be shipped back to the HomeMarket down the road from where they were grown, as Grandma's Sweet Potato Pie.

In the days since Lucas and the nurse left, Hai and Grazina would peek through the curtains half expecting the medical vans to come charging up the block. But it had been two weeks, and so far the road to their dead end sat still and empty.

Grazina also lost a tooth. She held up a Fig Newton to Hai's face one morning at breakfast, the snaggled incisor sticking up from the cookie like a tombstone on a plot of earth. "Now what?" she said with delight. It was not only her teeth—it seemed her mind was loosening too, the sundowning getting worse. One time at HomeMarket, Hai picked up his cell to the sound of Grazina sobbing about a flood, saying the water from the river had seeped through the back door into the kitchen. Outside the store windows, the rain was a bright curtain of water. He hung up and rode home so fast he nearly slid off the muddy embankment at the highway overpass. When he got in, sopping wet, Grazina was sitting at the kitchen table reading a magazine, dry as stone. "Why you early, Labas?" she said, without looking up from her 1986 issue of *Better Homes and Gardens*. He took a deep, patient breath, then turned around and went back to work.

And Maureen's lump, to everyone's relief, turned out to be a cyst, a warning of potential malignancy in the future—but not yet, not with the green season on the cusp of breaking open and the days about to melt into a stream of hours under fluorescent lights, time so vast and empty, pulled forward by the promise of summer, longer days and more light to live by.

But then came the morning when Mr. Vogel returned. Wayne caught him coming in and gave him a polite "How's it going?" to which Vogel answered, without slowing his stride, "Monday." BJ was in the office fiddling with time sheets, her head bobbing to the bass of her new entrance song, when the RM opened the door and slammed it shut behind him.

The crew, sensing danger, hushed themselves and tried to eavesdrop, though nothing could be heard. Two minutes later, the door swung open and Vogel walked out, his fist-head red like it just punched a wall. He got to the front door, turned around, and pointed at BJ, who was lumbering out of the office, her face drooping. "I gave you three weeks, Cheryl. Three!" For some reason he put five fingers up when he said this. "So now I did your job *for* you. So don't ask me, *How come I can't be a regional manager? Why do you guys always skip me for promotion?* It's because you have no discipline, Cheryl." He bit his lip, then, noticing the three identical headshots of Samuel Dalembert on the "Employee of the Month" wall, snatched off the latest one, crumpled it into a ball, and flung it in their direction. "Now tell them what I told you and get it over with." He turned and left. A customer who was about to come in but instead got caught behind his diatribe pressed a hand to her mouth and backed out.

The place was empty. Somehow even the TV was off.

"Tell us what?" Maureen said, touching the spot where they'd just drained her cyst. "I don't like secrets, they give me palpitations."

"Also, who the hell is *Cheryl*?" asked Wayne.

"Shut the fuck up, Wayne." BJ gave him a look you could collect debts with. Then she told Hai to flip the sign to CLOSED and called everyone to the front.

Sony emerged from the back, along with Russia and the dishwasher girl.

BJ pulled her pants up by the belt, took out her American flag hankie, and patted her shiny forehead. "A while back Vogel told me I had to let somebody go." A collective groan spread though the room. "Was supposed to do it weeks ago, and—well, I dunno. I thought we could've proved to them we'd be alright but . . ." She trailed off, her hands lost in her pockets and her eyes shut. It was the first time Hai had seen her so bereft, lacking possession even of her own size. There was a long silence before she broke it.

"It's Sony," she said at last, giving the boy a half glance, then looking down and away. "He said something about the origami penguins being a waste of time or some shit. I dunno."

Hai could feel the heat crawl up his temples. He thought he heard Russia and Wayne say *fuck* in perfect unison. "But what about his mom? I mean, my aunt. He's my cousin." Hai stepped forward. "They can't just do that. He has to get a package or something. Does he get a package?"

"The hell you think this is, FedEx?" BJ kept patting her face with the handkerchief. "There's no packages here, not for part-timers."

Sony stood still as a cut flower beside the soda fountain. Hai heard him mumbling something before he realized his cousin was reciting the names of Civil War battlefields. "Shiloh, Fredericksburg, Antietam, Second Manassas, Murfreesboro . . ."

"He's getting sacked cause of penguins?" Russia said in disgust. "What a dick."

"Look, maybe he can have one or two of my shifts," Wayne said from behind them. "I'd give more, but I got . . . my kids and my dogs and all that." He gave Hai this knowing, withered look, then pulled his cap over his eyes.

"What if he takes my spot?" asked Maureen. "I was offered, in secret, the store manager job at the HomeMarket in the airport last month. Before my operation."

"They filled that two weeks ago," BJ said.

"Okay, so get this." Russia took off his headset. "You take one shift from Wayne, and I'll give him half of mine. We can make it—"

"No," Hai said, "we're not touching yours. Not with your sister and shit."

"Only for a little while," Russia said weakly, but you could tell he was relieved.

That's when Sony bolted for the door.

"Oh, come on," called Wayne. "Don't act like you're in a movie!"

Hai ran after him, but when he got to the entrance there was a crowd of twenty or so customers huddled outside. They had all just gotten off the shuttle from the nursing home in Millsap. It was Senior Monday, he remembered, and was now surrounded by grey and white perms and sweater vests. "Where you going? Sony, stop!" he shouted over their heads, but Sony was already rounding the corner outside.

The customers, impatient from waiting, filed through the doorway, pushing him back. Hai ran toward the lockers to grab his stuff, but BJ stopped him.

"Can you just ring up five or six orders so we don't drown here? I get it, I get it. But I'm down a man as it is and that fucker Vogel's still around and I don't need him coming back and seeing this damn line."

Hai started ringing the customers up, his fingers trembling over the screen. After a number of them had their orders in, he rushed into the walk-in fridge and called Aunt Kim. A corrections guard answered and told him it'd be about five to ten minutes before they could get her on the phone. Hai stayed on the line as he punched out and gathered his stuff.

Soon he was riding out the lot, the air crisp and fragrant with pre-spring clarity. Blue and white hues smarted across the sky, and the wind came off the hills in waves, buffeting his bike as he struggled down the busy thoroughfare. He was riding up and down the roads, standing up on the bike and peering into the distance for Sony's black cap, when the line clicked and Aunt Kim's voice came on.

"I need your help. Sony's gone and I'm scared he's gonna do somethin' bad."

"What do you mean *gone*? Where's my son?"

"He got fired and just left . . . I dunno."

"Trời ơi chết cha rồi." Her voice slowed, realizing something.

"What is it?"

"He's going to Vermont. What a fucking idiot! For God's sakes. What have I done?" She was talking to herself now, near tears.

Hai assured her he was going to fetch him way before he'd get to Vermont. "I tried calling him, but he's not picking up. Maybe you can try?"

"There's something else you need to know." She went on and told him about how she'd been writing letters to Sony from prison. "Except I've been doing it as his dad. All this time, for four years—even before I was locked up. I've been doing it with this shitty Viet-English dictionary. And he believed it because his dad also had shitty English." She was crying now. "I told him, as Uncle Minh, that he could come up and work with me at my wife's taco bar if he wanted."

"What the hell is wrong with this family? Why does *everything* have to be a lie?" A semi blared by and Hai was shouting over it.

"What family are you talking about, boy? This isn't a damn *family*. Are you living in a fantasy? You've let that American bullshit rot your head in. Who the hell got the time to sit down at a dinner table with you and be a family?"

He scanned the road for his cousin and saw nothing. "Sorry."

All this time she was writing to her son, making up a future for his father while the man was a pile of ashes. "I know it's horrible and I feel awful, I really do." She blew her nose. "Can you just please get him and bring him here? I'll tell him everything. I'll make it right, I will. I promise." She instructed him to follow the railroad; Sony always wanted to take the train north to see his father and had been studying the Amtrak maps.

Hai hung up and plunged the bike toward the tracks at the end of the county road, where it turned into a gravel slope toward a rock quarry that fed into the tracks. He looked both ways down the ties but couldn't see his cousin. He knew the river where he'd just come from was south, so he headed the opposite way. He stood up on the pedals and humped the bike over the gravel ditch beside the tracks until, among the brown-washed April landscape, a wavering black speck came into view.

"Sony!" he screamed. "Sony, stop!"

Hai gained on him, yelling the whole time until he saw the thin frame turn around.

"What the hell are you thinking?" Hai said when he caught up. He was bent over catching his breath.

Sony's face wore the eerie calm of an NPC in a video game. "They don't want me no more. So I'm gonna go up to see my dad."

"You can't go to your dad." Hai paused to think. "I mean, yes, but not now. We can take a bus or something. We can talk about it first."

Sony shook his head and kept walking. "There's nothing to talk about."

"At least get out of the damn tracks. Hey——"

"There's nothing to talk about when this country's falling apart by the seams and I'm out here trying to preserve this, our Union." Sony gestured wildly with his arms, his face flushed. "And you know what those rebels did in Kansas, don't you? They went out and whipped up their own militia and put holes in the city hall with ten-pound cannons. That's no way for a country to be, General Hai. There's no proper decency out here anymore."

"No, there's not. You're right. Look——"

Sony turned and walked on.

"You can't go, man. Please." Hai let the bike drop. "Your dad . . . Your dad's not up there. The letters you've been getting from him are from your mom. All of 'em. He's dead, okay? Your mom told me. Your old man, the diamond guy, he's gone and—" Hai saw a flash of clouds, a blue sky, the sun, then realized, with the track trestles hard against his back, that Sony had just punched him in the mouth.

Sony stood over his cousin and looked him dead in the eyes, unblinking, his apron flapping in the wind. "I know."

22

Sony was breathing heavily, his face both calm and stricken at once. Hai picked his glasses from the gravel and put them on, the taped left arm completely broken off. He wobbled back to his feet and studied his cousin, the mole under his eye, as if for the first time.

"The fuck was that? You can't hit me. You're autistic."

"I'm sorry, I had to make a statement."

"Yeah, and people usually do that with words." He spat on the ground and touched his cut lip. "And what do you mean you *know*? What the hell do you know?"

"You're bleeding."

"Answer the question."

"I'm not an idiot, Hai. My dad died three years, seven months, and fourteen days ago. He burned up inside his '98 Nissan Maxima. I read all about it online. They even have a printout of the article at the group home in my file. They declared his death due to misadventure. I didn't know people can die on adventures. I didn't know," he stopped and swallowed, "that smoking a cigarette by the side of a road was considered an adventure. But now it's my turn to go on my own adventure. To see him at last, after all these years." He straightened up, puffed out his chest, and saluted. "This is Private Sony Minh Le of the Seventeenth Connecticut Volunteers reporting for duty." His bottom lip was quivering.

Hai had the sudden urge to grab him and steal the poor delusional boy away from himself. But he took a breath and tried again. "You can do all this later, okay? Your mom is scared shitless for her little soldier—who's very brave, of course. We all know that."

"Finders keepers, liars weepers. And she shouldn't have lied anyway." Sony removed his HomeMarket hat and flung it into the brush. He then took from his apron pocket the Union cap and pulled it over his eyes. "Besides, I have to get the diamond." The diamond trapped inside his father's hand from the explosion in Vietnam. A diamond that size, the size of a pea, Sony explained, would be worth over two thousand dollars. "There's this quantum theory I've been looking into," he went on, "specifically something called the Golden Triangle. It's in *Heroes*, you know—have you watched it yet? Never mind. It posits that my dad is still alive somewhere. And if I enact myself finding his diamond, I can introduce a line of action into the universe wherein I can eventually go see him the moment his car ignites—but in a parallel dimension, of course, which will eventually ripple back to this one and alter the course—"

"You're finally insane." Hai wiped his bloody lip.

"Not yet."

"There's no way the car will still be there. It's been *years*. And why didn't you go before, right after it happened?"

"The letters started coming." He looked away and whimpered. "And I just . . . I kinda went along with it."

"Let's just go home for today. You can sleep with me at Grazina's. We'll watch *Gettysburg* again all you want. We'll stop at CVS and I'll get Goldfish, a family-size box and everything." He reached out but Sony pulled back and Hai flinched. "Don't hit me again. I'm high and can't really see straight."

"Diamonds are forever," Sony said softly, caressing the spot on the back of his hand where the diamond was on his father's. "BJ told me that. A diamond can survive a fire. She told me that when I started. No one gave me a job cause of my brain problems, but she did. She believed in me." His eyelids flickered. "She said, *Anybody can become a diamond. All they need is a bit of pressure.*"

"Please . . ."

"A soldier—" Sony winced and corrected himself. "A *career* soldier needs a foundation of courage, duty, and sacrifice."

"But you *don't* need that crap. It's just bullshit the commercials say to convince you to go to war. Let me tell you something, okay?" Hai glanced back at the tracks to make sure a train wasn't coming. "You say I'm so smart, right? Cause I went to college and all that? Then listen to me." He put both hands on Sony's shoulders. "Most people are soft and scared. They're fucking mushy. We are a mushy species. You talk to *anybody* for more than half an hour and you realize everything they do is a sham to keep themselves from falling apart. From prison guards to teachers, to managers, psychiatrists, even fathers, anybody—even your stupid generals. People put on this facade of strength. They act like they have a purpose and a mission and their whole life is supposed to lead to this grand fucking thesis of who they are. But what happened, huh? Robert E. Lee sent all those people who believed in him across a half mile of hell because he was too scared to say he fucked up and had no cavalry. His generals told him to fall back to the mountains, but he wouldn't listen. You told me that, right?"

"He also had dysentery," Sony mumbled.

Hai clutched Sony's shoulders, as if steering a ship. "They're just scared somebody will look at them bad and judge 'em. Scared somebody will see through the fake-ass armor they've wasted their whole lives building. And for what? To have fucking dysentery while a bunch of people who think you're some god walk into a wall of bullets? Don't you see it? We all want some story to make it bearable so we can keep living long enough to work our asses off until we're in the ground, like Grandma. Like your dad. Like . . ." Hai sucked on his bloody lip. "Look, being fucked up is actually what's most common. It's the majority of who we are, what everybody is. Fucked up is the most normal thing in the world. You're both fucked up *and* you're normal, got it?" He searched Sony's face to see what his words were doing, not sure if he even believed them himself. How come every time he said anything important, it felt like it was coming from somewhere else, from a cesspool collected from shitty movies at the base of his skull?

"*Everyone's* scared," Hai continued. "It's just like those stupid corn breads we give out every day. They all have this thin golden-brown crust, but ninety-nine percent of those things are just soft, mushy cake with a shit ton of sugar. So you don't have to be *anybody's* soldier. You can be a person doing what you do every day and that's fucking enough. Don't you get it?" He was nearly doubled over now, his arms still on Sony's shoulders, catching his breath, then pushed on.

"People aren't so bad. They're just wounded little kids trying to heal. And that makes them tell each other stupid stories," he said softly. "Would you just stand in your skin with me and stay? Just for a bit, while I sort this out? Will you stay? Please? I can't do this anymore."

Sony reached up and touched the brass bugle on his cap.

"You're so much better than me, Sony. That's the truth. I look up to *you*. You're, like, the goodest person I know. You're Alyosha." Hai's bottom lip was doing something weird, and he had to put his fist over his mouth to steady it. He looked at the boy's face as if waiting for a dice to finish rolling. "You're still gonna fucking go, aren't you?"

Sony swayed side to side, then stopped, gave Hai this mournful, sheepish look, and nodded.

Hai took a long look down the tracks, at the new spring heat rising weakly over the iron ties, enough to warp the faraway bits of East Gladness into a mutilated dream. "Alright." He bit his lip, his head hung in defeat. He was in too deep and had to follow through now. "Let's go to Vermont, then. How bad's my mouth, out of ten?" He turned to show the side where Sony hit him.

"Six," Sony said, and shifted his eyes to the ground. "Sorry."

Hai picked up the bike and nodded over his shoulder at the pegs. "Get on, Private. The Union's not gonna save itself."

If they were going to cross state lines, he had to bring Grazina with them. Too risky to leave her alone in her current state. The trip also had the added benefit of dodging social services if they ever came back, buying them time.

Maureen's car was in the shop, so they decided to try Wayne, the only other employee who owned a car. BJ never had a car and was dropped off each day by her mom.

"Hold on a minute," said Wayne. "You're both going to Vermont to look for a pea-sized diamond that was jammed *inside* his daddy's hand?" He adjusted his cap and scratched his chin.

They were deliberating by the dumpster out back. BJ was pondering the ground, brainstorming. Hai was surprised at how readily she agreed to help with what sounded like a near mythical quest.

"Would you drive if we covered gas?" Hai said to Wayne. "And throw a little on top of that?"

"So, let me get this straight. You want me to drive you two and pick up some demented white lady you've been living with this whole time and go to Vermont to look through burnt dirt for a lost diamond to free this boy's mama from jail?" He put his hand on Sony's shoulder and squeezed. "I respect what you're going through and all, I do. But I'm not gonna be Morgan Freeman in *Miss Daisy* driving around crazies when I got bills to pay. Plus, I'm already driving five hours to see my girlfriend in Lancaster this weekend. I love you all. But I'm sorry, my guy."

"What's Miss Daisy?" Sony said.

"Okay, I got it." BJ clasped her hands under her chin and eyed the cousins. "Here's what I'm going to do for you. And it's just cause that douchebag fired you without my consent." Her nails had been bitten down to the nub. "If I put in for a pickup of creamed spinach—which we *do* need—at that HomeMarket rest stop outside Thetford, then I can authorize the use of the catering van *and* keep us on the clock during store hours." It was a bit past three p.m., and Thetford was only two and a half hours away and just north of where Sony's dad was. "We'd be back before closing."

"Thank goodness. Alright, chicken's not carving itself." Wayne headed inside. Just then Maureen came out the back door.

"What's going on? Half the store's out here."

"What's going on is you're going to Vermont," said BJ.

"Delivery?"

"Sort of," Hai said.

"I'm gonna be in the van with *him*," BJ pointed to Sony, who saluted her, "and *him*, who's supposed to be babysitting some crazy landlord. Don't ask. I need somebody to make sure we don't become another one of those unsolved mysteries around here. Plus, it's on the clock. You in?"

Maureen shrugged. "Beats standing around on my jacked-up knees."

"Get your coat and meet me out here in five. And tell Russia and dishwasher girl to load those cooler bins in the van with ice." She gave Hai a double take. "What the hell happened to you?"

"I got punched in the face."

HALF HOUR LATER they pulled into the driveway at 16 Hubbard. "Back in a sec," Hai shouted as he ran inside.

Grazina was sitting on the La-Z-Boy watching *The Young and the Restless*. "Labas, you get that new pizza from your restaurant today?"

"No, but I can get you some tomorrow. Hey," he came over and held her hand in both of his, "we have to go on a little trip, okay?"

"Really?" Her eyes widened. "To see Lucas and Clara again? Aren't they a nice couple?" She was woozy from her dose of Zoloft.

Hai reminded her about his cousin Sony and said they were going to go up to Vermont to see his dad for a very important occasion. "It'll be nice. Vermont has all these pretty trees."

"Not till May it doesn't. I did go there years ago, to a Lithuanian music camp. Mountains, biggest I've ever seen." She gestured at them like they were across the room.

"Great, so you know what I'm talking about." He started packing their things, filling her plastic medicine organizer and adding a few extra pills in case. He took some Pop-Tarts and a bottle of water, grabbed a blanket from the couch, and stuffed them all in his backpack. Then he got Grazina dressed. "Here, your favorite owl sweater." He put it over her head and helped her into it, then fetched her Woolrich chore coat from the sunroom, buttoned her up, and wrapped her head with a scarf. "Good, you got your glasses? Where are your glasses?"

Grazina stared at him, blinking. "I dunno—oh! In microwave."

"What?"

"I was making tea."

"Okay, hold on." He grabbed the glasses from inside the microwave and put them on her face. "There, you ready? Good."

When they climbed in the car, Maureen glanced back, surprised that this landlady actually existed. After everyone shared hellos and snapped on their seat belts, the van started chugging down the potholed roads. BJ was driving, Maureen up front, Sony alone in the middle, and Hai and Grazina in the back, all of them huddled together like some ghoulish family vacation.

Hai stared out at the river rushing by, the waves swollen and globular, the water higher now with the upstream thaw. It felt good to sit and look out a window, to be driven somewhere and float over the blasted landscape he'd known for so many months only by bicycle.

Grazina seemed lucid enough for now. Hai noticed her being more self-conscious lately, offering sanguine smiles when a thought fell away from her mid-sentence. "You alright?" he asked her as the van merged onto the interstate. She shrugged and pushed her glasses up her nose and stared out the window. Once in a while BJ would glance at them, half expecting Hai to explain their situation.

"This is just like *Star Wars*." Maureen giggled from up front. "I swear it's like that all the time now."

"What do you mean?" said BJ.

"Well, you got a kid trying to get some jewel from his dead dad. Sorry, hun," she said to Sony. "It's kinda epic, don't you think? Darth Vader, Anakin Skywalker, a cosmic quest to save Princess Leia trapped in the state pen—all that stuff." She sighed and checked the time on her dead Han Solo watch. "It's a beautiful thing. A kid looking for his people."

"Long as we keep it more *Star Wars* and less like *Die Hard 2*." BJ gave Maureen a look, then glanced at Hai through the rearview. "I'm just saying, this is kind of wild. What if this old-ass lady dies in this van or something? What am I—and you know it's gonna be me—what am I gonna say to headquarters?"

"She's not gonna die," Hai said from the back. "She just has memory issues. You don't die that way."

"Oh! How lovely!" Grazina suddenly sat up. "Why don't we keep talking like I'm not here. Like I'm meat on a hook. How nice, huh? I'm not slow, you know. My brain is just on and off." She looked over to Hai, stunned at her own brashness.

He squeezed her hand.

The van was quiet for a bit. When they crossed state lines, and made steady distance through the country roads north, BJ cut the silence. "Hey, guys, actually, can I ask you something—you know, since I'm driving anyway and risking my career, my livelihood and all?"

"Don't tell me you're getting cold feet." Maureen turned to her. "We're already past the airport."

"I just wanna try this one thing . . . I promise, it won't be too much trouble. It's just—" She paused to think.

"Just say it," Maureen said. "Didn't know lesbians beat around the bush so much." She looked around and cackled, realizing her own joke.

"So I know this guy Kenny. His cousin's a scout up in Toronto—you know, Canada, Bret Hart country. Anyway, you all cool if I stop by and drop off my tape? He's a couple miles ahead in Springfield."

"We're trying to get a secret diamond and you wanna network?" Maureen said.

"You should do it." Sony poked his head around BJ's seat. "You deserve this. We can knock two thirds with one stone."

"Two birds," Grazina said to Hai, gladdened by her ability to correct this.

BJ took the tape from her coat pocket and held it up. "I'm gonna make this worth it. Don't worry."

"This was your plan the whole time, huh?" Maureen said with wry admiration.

BJ grinned as she veered off the ramp toward the Springfield exit. The city's ramshackle skyline rose from the horizon, ambered from the afternoon light. "Whoa! This is where half the rifles were made for the

Union Army. That's why it was called the Springfield rifle." Sony pressed his face against the glass, as if someone on the street might be spotted carrying one of the rifles.

"Like I said," Maureen picked at her nose and watched the city come into view, "everything is *Star Wars*."

THEY PARKED IN the lot of the Cracker Barrel where Kenny worked as a server, and were now waiting for him to come out during his break. "See that place over there?" BJ pointed across the street to the Blue Chickie, a regional chain. "I heard one time, down in Virginia, one of their workers had a heart attack, right? And they were so slammed they just dragged this dude into the walk-in fridge and left him there till the shift was over. Like, two employees just laid him down and went back to work."

"Damn," said Maureen. "He die?"

"Must have."

"Pepto-Bismol," Grazina mumbled. She'd been so quiet her voice sounded new in the van.

"What's that, ma'am?" Maureen turned around. "You need something?"

"It's Italian for 'abysmal,'" Grazina said. She turned to Hai. "We waiting for the boy's father now?"

"We're waiting for BJ's friend. It's a pit stop."

"A what?"

"A pit stop," BJ said. "And he's not my *friend*. I barely know the dude."

But this "stop" turned into an hour of sitting in the lot before a dumpy guy in a grease-stained apron finally came scuttling up to the van and took BJ's tape. "No promises," Kenny said with a blank face, "but I'll see what I can do." BJ pumped her fist as she watched him go back inside, the tape bulging from his back pocket. "One small step for mankind, one giant leap for pro wrestling."

Hai watched the Blue Chickie sign spin on its axis as the van lurched back on the road, and thought about that man in Virginia, lying very still on the floor of the walk-in fridge, his soul hovering above him waiting for his shift to end so he could go home. For some reason this reminded him of those emperor hogs, so named not to signify the act of ruling—but to feed the ruler with their lives.

The sun had plummeted into the horizon, making peach-red smears over the hills. The dash clock read 7:01 p.m. Grazina was dipping in and out of sleep. In the van filled with the warmth of bodies, the chilly April night seeping through the windows, Hai let the glass hold up his head and watched the scraps of light across the fields from shanty houses, gas stations, and half-lit strip malls morph into blobs of color as the window began to fog.

After a few miles BJ pulled into a motel off the interstate. "Where are we?" Sony asked, rubbing his eyes.

"Sign back there said Nowhere, Massachusetts," said Grazina, pulling the scarf around her head.

"*Northampton*, Massachusetts," said BJ, getting out.

"Says no vacancy, hun," Maureen sighed.

"I'm gonna ask anyway."

"Why are we here? Brattleboro is only an hour away." Sony turned around to Hai.

"Yeah, and what diamond are you going to find in the dark?"

BJ's demo drop-off had pushed them back, and the stars were already shivering above them.

"I brought a flashlight." Sony took out what looked like a Swiss Army knife contraption and, pressing a button on it, lit a beam of light the size of a toothpick.

"We gotta wait till tomorrow," Maureen said. "Plus, my knees are dying."

Maureen saw a flicker of worry on Sony's face and reassured him that they'd make it first thing in the morning just as BJ came out from the office in a huff.

"They're full," she said, getting in. "Lady said there's some sort of festival to celebrate *asparagus*. Apparently it packs the town every year for the whole damn weekend. Whitest shit I've heard of in a while, that's for sure." She stared at the motel marquee. "But I called Wayne to clock us all out. He'll clock us back in tomorrow when he's in."

"Are there any Stouffer's?" Grazina said. "I'm starving."

"I could go for some Hooters wings," Maureen said. "Wouldn't it be awesome if they had a Hooters but it's all grandmas over fifty-five?"

"I'd go," BJ said, looking for the gearshift.

They chugged down the road to another motel, and when that one was also full, the crew stopped at a 7-Eleven for snacks and gas. Maureen got a roll of scratch-off lottery tickets. Then they drove a bit further, BJ sipping a slushy while a bag of Cheetos was passed around.

"I can't sit in here much longer," Maureen said finally. Everyone agreed they had to stop for the night—but where? They were debating whether it'd make sense to drive all the way home and just try again early the next day when Hai spotted something in the distance ahead.

It was a barn, unlit and alone in a vast field. Having worked on tobacco farms through his teenage years, he knew the shape and feel, the clean edges, the looming frame, of these sheds that littered pastures all along the Connecticut River Valley, and could spot them even in the dark, like living creatures slumbering across the landscape. He knew, too, that most farmers lived several miles from their barns, some even hours away, and that it was likely idle enough to stay the night.

They agreed to stop at the dirt drive just to regroup and think, but when Grazina opened the door and started wandering toward it, they all left the van and followed her in.

"When I was girl," Grazina said, stepping into the barn's cool dark, "I used to sleep in a barn like this, in summertime. At Baba's house in Bubiai." She scanned the rafters. Light from the street filtered through the slats just enough for them to see.

"Look," Sony said, "there's hay too. Just like in the cartoons."

"Well, it's not very warm—but warm enough." Maureen was already testing out the hay pile with her hands. "It's soft too," she added, sitting down and wincing as she rubbed her knee. "But this is kinda crazy, guys. Are we really gonna do this? Sleeping in a barn? I feel like I'm back in high school after a shitty dance."

"What kind of high school did you go to?" said BJ, who had suggested they sleep in the van. But Maureen's knee needed to stretch out through the night or it'd lock up come morning.

Hai flipped open his phone and scanned its light across the interior, revealing a cluster of wheeled metal dumpsters. He reached into one of them and scooped up a handful of sandy clumps. Bringing them to the light, he recognized bulbs of garlic, their stems still attached, left to cure in huge bins throughout the barn. He turned to tell the others and saw them settling in, exhausted. BJ had found an old couch along the wall and was lying down with her hoodie pulled over her head, texting on her phone.

"It should be pretty safe here." Hai walked toward the hay piles and closed the tractor doors they had slipped through.

Maureen turned over on her side. "Smells like an old horse."

"Old and weird," Sony added, sniffing the air. He had been quieter than usual, other than his burst of excitement when they passed Chicopee, where he went on and on about the Ames Company, producers of standard-issue officer sabers for the Army of the Potomac. Hai was about to lie down when he remembered the backpack with Grazina's pills in the van. He asked Sony to come with him to fetch it.

They left Grazina lying beside Maureen and walked back. The spring air touched their tongues with scents of alfalfa, sweetgrass, and wild thyme. A stand of dogwoods, furred with buds and silhouetted against the streetlight, swayed from a breeze coming off the hills. Hai got in the van, Sony next to him in the back seat. It felt like a good place to be still for a while, the only sound the occasional semi coming off the interstate to park in one of the cutouts along exit ramps for the night. That and the branches clacking here and there across the fields.

Hai grabbed the backpack and hugged it to his chest. He popped two Dilaudids, chewing to get their magic out quicker.

"When I was little, far back as I can remember," Sony said, his voice eerily distant. "I used to have this dream, you know. I dreamt I was flying over East Gladness. It's always at night and I can see the little streetlights flickering between the leaves and I'm flying but I don't hear any wind. Sometimes the dream starts with me high up in the sky. Sometimes I'm on my way up, sometimes I'm coming down. Sometimes I'm over the water tower or the power plants or the big Walmart off Route 7. And for some reason I know—you know how you know things in dreams without nobody telling you?"

"Yeah." Hai turned to look at his cousin.

"Well for some reason I knew that the people inside every house in East Gladness, and even beyond that, all across the county, were really penguins. Birds with wings that don't work. Their rubbery feet shuffling through the little rooms below. And I would just keep soaring. And the thing is, in the dream I can never tell if I'm also a penguin or not. And every time I try to put my hands out in front of me I don't . . . I don't see nothing. But I must be something else since I'm flying and all, and penguins, their wings don't work. I just can't tell if, according Darwinian evolution, if the penguins ever flew, whether their wings worked once before, long ago, or were they, like, a hundred years away from working. I wonder if I'm just floating up there alone, the only penguin with wings. And I don't know if I'm ahead of everybody or behind them. You know what I mean?"

"But whatever it is, it's a good thing, isn't it—to have wings?"

"To have wings you need to want to go somewhere. But it feels wasted on me, you know? In my dreams and in real life, I always wanted to stay in East Gladness. I hated going to Florida, you know that?"

"I can imagine," Hai said, the penguin still flying in his head.

"You know my dad wrote to me once." Sony leaned back and stared at the peeling ceiling. "He told me about all the trees and the plants up there in Vermont. And even though I knew it was my mom the whole time, once in a while I'd wake up in the middle of the night and pretend it was real. That it was him."

"I think your dad would've written you anyway."

"It was nice to be awake in the middle of the night in the group home. I wasn't used to the room so I imagined I was in another place reading my dad's letters. I'd always read them soon as they came in the mail. But then, at three in the morning, I'd read them again, this time with the flashlight, and pretend they were really his."

"I guess both your mom and dad were talking to you at once."

"Yeah, the best of both worlds." Sony grinned woodenly at the ceiling. Then he turned to Hai and said, "Hey, can you say something interesting? I don't feel like going to bed yet."

"Okay . . ." Hai bit his lip and traced his mind. "Okay, how 'bout this. You remember that one summer—I must've been, like, ten and you were eight—and we rode that paddleboat, trying to go all the way to Canada?"

"The time we took a road trip to the Great Lakes together," Sony said, real quiet. "Everyone was there. My mom, Grandma, and my dad. And your mom too. We rented a cabin on Lake Michigan, right? It looked like Abraham Lincoln's cabin, and when I asked my dad if it was, he said it was the exact cabin Lincoln was born in. But I knew he made that part up."

Low voices floated out from the barn's mouth where the others were.

"Why did we go?" Sony asked.

"To Lake Michigan?"

"To Canada."

"I remember seeing the yellow paddleboat on the beach, and as we were trying it out, you said you wanted to see if we can make it to Canada. I'd never been to Canada. Still haven't."

"It's right above Vermont," Sony said.

"After a while we were in the middle of the great lake and the shore was so small and everyone was in the cabin, everyone but your dad. He was this tiny speck swimming toward us. It was like some duck flapping toward our boat. And we didn't even care. We just kept paddling." Hai shook his head in fond disbelief. "Were you scared?"

"I wanted to keep going. It was a paddleboat, but it felt so big, like we were on this huge ship, and I wanted to go to Canada."

"All of a sudden there was this slap on the boat and it leaned to one side, and your dad was right next to us clinging to the base and catching his breath. But, you know, the weird thing was, he wasn't mad at us, remember? He kinda had no reaction at all. He just said something like, *Come on, guys, you've gone far enough.* Then he sat down next to us, his feet in the waves, and we just drifted for a while without saying nothing. And I remember feeling kinda weird, how quiet we all were. Just the waves tapping on the plastic boat and your dad, the adult, seemed relieved to be floating with us, like he didn't wanna go back either. Then you asked him. You remember what you asked him?"

"I think so." Sony was caressing the scar on his head now.

The murmurs in the barn had died down and only the dark mouth remained.

"You said, *Ba, do you see Canada from here?* And it was like your voice woke him up from a long dream and he said, *Yeah, yeah, it's just up there, son.* But I looked and looked and all I could see was more water, all the way to the edge."

"Yeah, I remember now."

"But why would he lie about that? It makes no sense." Hai's hands were vaguely in front of him now, and he made an effort to gather them back to himself.

"Maybe he did see it. We don't know that." Sony was holding his cheeks with both hands and watching the ceiling like he could see through it.

Hai had the urge to tell him about the afternoon he stood on the beams of King Philip's Bridge last summer, all that rain on his face— but thought better of it. "Come on, let's get these back to Grazina. She needs another dose before bed." Hai got up, but Sony didn't move.

"I'll meet you in there," Sony said without looking at him. "I just wanna be here for a while. It's kinda nice."

"Okay."

"Okey dokey," he grinned, but Hai couldn't see his teeth flash in the dark.

BACK IN THE BARN, Hai gave Grazina her last dose, then broke a Pop-Tart in half and placed it in her palm. He then tucked her blanket along her length, laid his UPS jacket across her chest for good measure, and stretched out between her and Maureen.

Grazina stared at him, hay clinging to her hair, chewing. "You still working on your little novel, Labas?"

"In my head I am," he lied.

"Good boy." She finished eating but seemed lost in thought.

"What you thinking about?" he said.

"I should've known all along that you were liggabit."

"Really? How so?" he whispered.

"You ask so many damn questions. Normal boys don't ask so many questions." She chuckled and turned the other way. "Good night, Labas."

"Good night." And soon the jacket over her body rose and fell with steady breaths.

BJ was already snoring softly a few feet away. When he heard Maureen shuffling behind him, he offered her a Dilaudid from his stash.

"Look at you," she said, yawning and extending her hand. "You're like a Walgreens over here." She slapped the pill into her mouth and rubbed her knee. "Thanks, hun. Oh, nice shirt." Maureen nodded at his T-shirt, the one he had gotten from rehab and had been wearing most days under his uniform. "*A New Hope*. My personal favorite, if I had to choose."

"Uh. This is a very, very different new hope," he smiled. "But hey, I was thinking of something I wanted to run by you. What if . . ." His eyes sifted the slats for starlight. "What if the reptiles aren't actually bad at all? Like, what if they're here as a safeguard, just so we don't all kill ourselves, you know?"

"Go on," she said without moving.

"Maybe it's their job: instead of getting us to kill each other, they're actually down there stopping us from nuking everybody. And once we evolve beyond that, and get to a higher realm of thinking, they'll bring us with them to a new place. A place only the good ones get to go."

"Nice try, mister. But now you sound like a cult leader. Why don't we stick to corn cake for now, yeah?"

"But——" Hai bit his lip and watched the dust motes floating through a shaft of moonlight. "Does it matter if the reptiles suck all his energy if, like, overall, after everything, Paul still had a decent life? That you gave him a good life, even with the monsters underground?"

Maureen was silent for what seemed like a long time, then exhaled and said, "When you're somebody's mother, nothing's good enough. Good and bad doesn't exist."

"But isn't *Star Wars* all about good and bad? You keep saying everything's——"

"Go to sleep and stop fussing about lizards. They're probably draining our ether as we speak, and I don't got much to spare as it is."

"Okay." Hai's glasses, with the one lost arm, slipped off his face. "Good night, Maureen."

He sat up from the hay and cocked his head, listening. To make sure it was real.

Then it came again. Someone whistling outside the barn, distinct and clear—and close.

The others were still asleep. Maureen was snoring lightly, her back rising and falling. Through slats in the barn, the near-white fog was so thick it seemed illuminated by artificial light. What time was it? How long had he been asleep? He rose and crept out of the barn's mouth, looking around.

It was both late and early, the dark untouched by dawn. The whistling went on in uneven intervals, as if someone was forgetting the melody and had to stop to draw it up again. He wandered away from the van, toward the meadow, where dew, freshly gathered upon the weeds, sparkled around his feet.

The nearby highway was empty. He looked about in the absolute stillness, his breath sounding larger than the life it worked to keep. That's when he saw the greenish light flake ahead of him, like unearthly strobes flaring through the bracken. As he headed toward it, hands outstretched through the mist, the emerald lumens shifted and bloomed above the branches like tree-high northern lights merging into a globular mass. The sight made him turn his head toward the barn, where his friends were locked inside the world of sleep, to make sure he hadn't stepped into a portal.

He pushed on, waving away low branches until he stumbled into a second field, where it all came into view. He didn't notice his knees had touched the ground as he stared up at the thing gliding past him. An enormous ship, an ark made with features fashioned from a primitive century, pulsing with a sickening green light as if cast from melted glow-in-the-dark stars, swam soundless over his head. All around him the trees, without wind, leaned to one side, and long grasses were pressed to the ground, as if the ship emitted a silent propulsive force.

He searched the hull and decks for people, but none could be seen. The ship kept moving but its sails were still and drooped. When it touched the tree line ahead, the branches never cracked or fell away. Soon the hull was devoured by a forest that stretched to the foot of the mountains. And before long only green streaks could be seen, obscured behind increasing canopies as the ship sailed off. That's when the whistling returned.

He scrambled to his feet and swung his head toward the sound.

In the path the ship had come, he saw a figure slowly drawing up to him, moving with a precise, clean gait, its footsteps sucking mud.

When his eyes adjusted, the outline of an immense black hog, tall as a child, came to view.

With his hand shielding the light fanning out from behind the animal, a light that seemed to have no source, he saw that the hog was actually a deep chestnut brown, with a spot of cream above its left eye the size of a church wafer. As if in greeting, the pig started to whistle a tune he quickly realized was the start to "Silent Night." He walked toward the song until he was just a foot away and could hear the animal's massive lungs working underneath.

"Hello," he said, his hand reaching out, and found himself cupping the hog's chin. Through the warm skin he felt the song swelling past the animal's hidden teeth.

"I don't know how to be," he said, his own harried plea scaring him. "How do you stay here? How does anybody stay here?"

He recalled the story Russia had told him, of the man who walked to the store for a pack of cigarettes and never returned. Is it possible for a hole to be cut open and for you to step inside it—not to be destroyed, but simply gone? Where on earth was elsewhere possible? Is that what the pills do, in the end? Is that what was happening to Grazina? The brain's derangement of itself to other reckonings? Is it possible to be a hog in a field left behind by Noah's ark, whistling "Silent Night," and not be the loneliest thing in the universe?

"Don't let the emperor get you, buddy," he said as the whistling dwindled to an airy whir.

The hog's eyes roved, as if searching for a crack inside the boy, a way in.

Then Hai started to sing along. And as he did the hog shifted on its hooves, and its eyes rolled back, revealing two white pool balls before slowing to a stop, like a statue that suddenly remembered it was made of stone. Hai bent close enough to feel the beast's breath on his face.

"I'm sorry, Bà ngoại," he said in Vietnamese. "I'm so sorry. Sorry, Noah. Sorry, Ma. Sony, Aunt Kim, Uncle Minh. I let you all down. I tried my best, but I don't know how to be here."

He peered into the hog's barely open mouth and saw a fractal of the green light glowing there. And it was the light of morning coming through the barn slats. And he felt a radius of warmth on his skin and turned to find Sony's face, inches away. He was blowing on Hai's cheek the way one blows on a window to write on it. "You were mumbling. And you looked very sad," Sony said, "so I'm giving you an *okay*." And with his finger Sony wrote the word *okay*.

"There," he said, satisfied. "Just like new."

"Labas." Grazina stirred next to him. "Is it tomorrow yet?"

"I think so," Hai said, looking down at himself, still here.

23

The scrap of light crawled over Maureen's face like a moving scar and startled her awake. She blinked at Hai a few times, took a swig from her flask out of habit, wiped her mouth, and said, "Why am I lookin' at you?"

Hai nodded over at Sony, who was already up and ready to go.

"Oh yeah. Diamond crusade."

The crew filed into the van and drove another hour in a post-wake-up stupor, this time with Maureen at the wheel. Grazina's head rested on Hai's shoulders as he watched Vermont float by, the land misting under telephone towers as the sun rose, goat and dairy farms unfurling around them toward mountains hung on every horizon. They passed Brattleboro, a sleepy town not yet wakened by the spring thaw, then drove further north, the air growing thinner, and at one point a thirty-second flurry ignited before the windshield, causing everyone to look up at the sky and wince.

Finally, after a long stretch down a single-lane county road, Sony sat up. "This is it," he said, staring at the map he'd printed out and kept folded in his apron. "This is where he's at." He pointed to the brown recreational sign that read DEVIL'S LEAP STATE PARK.

"Didn't know the devil can jump nowadays." Grazina peered out the window. Hai had doubled her dose before they left, and she was suddenly alert as ever, eyes darting quick at the passing landscape.

Maureen pulled into the gravel easement on the road's shoulder. Devil's Leap was not a major park but more a small hiking loop for travelers to stretch their feet or let dogs run about or for loners and middle-aged dads who stuffed their pockets with Fireballs to get away from their families for a few hours. The brush was overgrown, and there wasn't even a signboard with a trail map.

"We have to keep going," Sony said, pointing to the gravel drive leading further into the park.

After a few minutes hugging the winding path, then stopping so Maureen could pee behind a fallen oak tree, they arrived at the supposed spot: a clearing in the brambles right before the path turned.

"This it?" Maureen asked, searching the leafless branches.

It was further in, Sony told them, where his dad's car went off the road.

"How'd he run off the road going five miles an hour?" BJ said from the passenger.

Maureen swiped her on the knee. "Hey, stick to body slams, detective."

They parked the van and got out, Sony leading the way. Hai asked Grazina if she wanted to stay back, but she shook her head and forced her way to the front, trailing Sony.

The police tape was long gone and there was no sign that anything had gone through here save for the vague opening in the brush which, after more than three years, was already covered thick with new growth. Young saplings, pulled by spring sunlight, poked their heads here and there around the scarred plot of earth.

Then Sony stopped. And because they were walking single file, holding each other's shoulders to keep steady, Hai saw only the back of

Sony's elbow shivering as he removed his Union cap from his head and pressed it to his chest.

"What is it?" BJ said, pushing up front. "Oh, oh shit, he's not kidding." She covered her mouth and stepped aside, her head turned away. "Whoa."

Sony pushed forward.

There wasn't a car—not even a charred skeleton of metal like Hai had thought. Instead, there was a circle of blackened leaves and dead sticks, more a space where a bear had napped than where a car once burned. You'd miss it if you weren't looking. However, it wasn't the circle but what was inside it that pinned them all in place.

There, lying at the far end of the burn site, nearly unrecognizable, was a half-seared headrest, its metal rods still attached like impossible bones. It was made of cloth that the flames mostly burned off, leaving the cushioning exposed and spilling out like yellow fat cinched with melted polyester.

Sony knelt in the dirt, then placed his soldier cap on the wounded side of the headrest so it sat at an angle. The others watched on, keeping a respectful distance. He lifted the headrest with both hands and stared into it as though into a face, one hand smoothing out the crinkled cloth where the burning stopped. "I miss you so much, Ba. I won't ever do anything to make you not proud of me. And I won't forget you long as I live." He stroked the headrest. "I forget many things, but I'm learning to be better, I promise. And I promise I'll never forget who you are and everything we talked about." Seeing his cousin kneel at the tiny circle where Uncle Minh died, Hai's chest started to tighten, and he scanned the treetops for a place to put his eyes. A few birds, returned from the winter south, flitted between massive oak branches.

Maureen came up behind Sony, untied the black apron she'd been wearing, and, juddering on her bad knee, wrapped it around the headrest and over the Union cap, leaving an opening in the front and knotting the bands at the bottom so that the whole thing resembled a newly born child. She patted Sony on the back and mumbled something, to which Sony nodded. The whole thing resembled a Nativity scene in a dystopian movie.

Hai could tell, from the faint throb in Sony's neck, that the boy was trying hard to hold it in. BJ's shadow slid across the dried leaves and covered Sony like a cape. She cupped the boy's head with her hand, as if to hold him in place, before reaching down to hug him. He turned into her embrace as Maureen took the headrest into her arms, bouncing it like a living baby. Hai came forward, his mouth partly open, and threw his arms around the huddled group, his face buried in BJ's enormous back as the branches clicked above them in the spring gale. These people, bound by nothing but toil in a tiny kitchen that was never truly a kitchen, paid just above minimum wage, their presence known to each other mostly through muscle memory, the shape of their bodies ingrained in the psyche from hours of periphery maneuvering through the narrow counters and back rooms of a fast-food joint designed by a corporate architect, so that they would come to know the sound of each other's coughs and exhales better than those of their kin and loved ones. They, who owe each other nothing but time, the hours collectively shouldered into a shift so that they might finish *on time*, now brought to their knees in a forest to gather around a half-burnt headrest of a Nissan Maxima on a Tuesday in mid-April, their bodies finally touching, a mass of labor cobbled together by a boy's hallowed loss—on the clock.

BJ was saying something into Sony's ear now, her jaw and temples working the syllables—but in the huddled mass it seemed she was speaking to Hai and Maureen as well, all of them merged into some HomeMarket Frankenstein in the middle of the forest. Which was how it must have looked to Grazina, leaning against a tree a few feet away. "All my fucking life," the HomeMarket monster said, its voice muffled in flesh and clothes, "I tried to convince everybody that I was stupid. I convinced myself too. But I'm a smart person. I'm a daughter," the monster said, "sister, a wrestler. And so are you. You're fucking great, Sony. You're an amazing person, okay? You're the best soldier I ever had. Don't let this shit turn you into anything else. Don't let whatever your father is or was knock you down on the mat."

Underneath BJ's voice was another one, indecipherable at first, but Hai soon made out the names, names he had heard many times before. Sony, nearly buried by his coworkers, sniffled and continued chanting. "Is the Corps at the ready?" he cried at the ground. "And Armistead's Virginia battalion? Wilcox's Alabama boys? And now, Mr. Davis, are your Mississippians ready? General Anderson, is our right flank on its mark at the line, and your skirmishers out ahead? Alright, then, all of you, on the double toward that group of trees!"

BJ glanced at Hai, puzzled, and Hai could only shrug as Maureen clutched the headrest to her chest.

"Gentlemen!" Sony's voice took a deeper drawl now. "Are you prepared this day to give your life for what you've been defending? For you will take my Twenty-Fourth Virginians over that ridge, and we will push the blueberries back across the Potomac and into Mr. Lincoln's backyard. For the enemy is on his heels today, this day of our Lord April twelfth, 1863." Sony turned to grab the headrest baby from Maureen and lifted it with both hands above his head, the way Rafiki did to Simba in *The Lion King*.

BJ and Maureen took a step back, the HomeMarket monster breaking apart, falling to pieces.

"Gentlemen, fix bayonets! And . . . on my mark . . ."

"Charge!" Grazina lunged from behind them all and raised her fist in the air next to Sony's headrest.

Everyone followed suit and shouted *Chaaarge!* But only Sony ran ahead. He broke into a dead sprint and dashed about fifteen yards into the forest, then wrapped himself around the trunk of a birch and crumpled around it, his shoulders jumping as he wept.

The others stood and watched, letting him go through it. Maureen started swaying gently, cooing to the headrest in her arms, the whole scene so weird and heartbreaking Hai bent down and retied his boots just to do something.

After a while BJ said they might as well try to find the diamond. But there were leaves everywhere and the understory was already seasons thick, the leaves mulching the layers to soil. Sony, his face raw and red, got on his hands and knees and frantically swept away armfuls of dirt and debris. "It would have fallen around here, guys. Please, it would be right here on the driver's side, where his arm was. The diamond was in his hand." But they had stopped even before beginning in earnest, BJ giving a twig a final, obligatory nudge with her shoe. Grazina had already sat down by the base of a nearby tree, the scarf wrapped tighter now around her face as she blinked behind her glasses. Did any of them actually believe it would be here? Was it *ever* here?

It turned out Sony's father, Hai learned much later, was not a soldier in the South Vietnamese Army at all, but merely employed in the laundry room of a US Army base, collecting the gunsmoke- and sweat-soiled clothes of GIs, their underwear and tank tops, uniforms that stank of liquor and gasoline, marijuana and shrapnel dust, dioxin residues. It was how he acquired the commando uniform he wore, green beret and all, to Sony's seventh birthday party, the photo of which Sony tucked in his wallet and religiously stared at on his breaks. The one he would show to customers, telling them his dad was a commando in the war for southern freedom.

Even worse, Hai learned that Uncle Minh's wound wasn't from a terror attack from the Vietcong at all—but a grenade from an American soldier's belt loop that he'd forgotten to remove, which snagged on his watch, releasing the pin as he was turning the pants inside out to be washed. At least this was how Aunt Kim would tell it.

Hai said, "You can go home now, buddy. You did it."

And BJ grabbed Sony under the armpits and pulled him to his feet, then she turned around and hoisted him on her back, like a body slam that wouldn't finish. "Come on, no good general leaves a soldier behind," she said, and started carrying him toward the van. All around them the woods seemed to be breathing. "You sound like a TIE fighter when you cry," Maureen said to Sony, "it's kinda neat."

The rank-and-file group stumbled out the trees in a daze. Grazina, who'd been mostly quiet, went over to Sony and gently squeezed his foot. "This . . ." she gestured to the forest, "is not new. It is same story. Okay? Don't be too sad, boy. You still have your hands. And with these what you make is yours."

A woman in neon-green yoga pants with her hair in a ponytail jogged by with a blue-eyed husky in tow. "Spring's here!" she shouted, too loud for the distance between them, then took a performative inhale. "You can literally *smell* the growth. Enjoy your hike, guys!" Her ponytail bounced ahead, the dog clicking after her. Soon the van pulled away from where Sony's dad died, Sony sitting still and not looking back.

When they hit the highway toward Thetford to finally pick up those two bags of creamed spinach, Maureen started to hum a little song. Sony's head was pressed against the glass—the headrest, still dressed in cap and apron, tucked under his arm, Grazina now beside him.

The roads were carless save for the occasional wheel-less tractor sitting in an overgrown front yard. New buds alighted along gnarled oaks, yews, and dogwoods, each branch tip offering a thumb's worth of lucent, just-touched green, as if adorned by swarms of baby crickets. Soon the leaves will quicken and the treetops will foam across the ravines into an astonished presence of green. The clean prosperity of spring. In all of Hai's enormously tiny life here in this valley, he'd never witnessed the budding of April blooms. It always seemed the trees were barren for months of ash and pewter greys, and then, as if overnight, the new, card-sized leaves would unfold, fluttering in the morning breeze, open and fat and already done with arrival. But this morning, for the first time, he saw the *becoming* of the season—and it looked to him false, the tips too hearty and dense against all that dead wood, as if placed by an artist with tweezers and superglue in a futile attempt to cheer up the world.

But it didn't matter. Because Maureen had started singing—she was not drunk or high, but her eyes were shut and her head swayed—interrupting herself to tell them her father had taught her the song at her niece's funeral when she was a girl back in Wilkes-Barre:

> *Of all the money that ereeee I've had,*
> *I've spent it innnn good company.*
> *Of all the harm that ereeee I've done,*
> *alas it waaaas to none but me.*

Her voice cracked and shook as if she were singing from the back of a carriage, but enough of it came through as the false spring ignited all around their little van, still tagged on the side with *Deez Nuts*. And they drove on surrounded by a pandemonium of clean light.

> *For all I've done, for want of wit,*
> *with memory now I can't recall.*
> *So fill to me the parting glass.*
> *Good night and jooooy be with you all.*

Then she stopped, remembering something. "Here, you have it." She turned around and handed Sony a used scratch-off ticket from last night. "They were all busts except this one."

"Oh. Oh, geez," he said. "Thank you. What did we win?"

"Just another ticket."

"Nice." He slipped it in his chest pocket and gave it a pat.

"Did you know my father . . ." Grazina said to no one in particular. "Did you know my father invented fruit salad?"

BJ turned around and bit her lip. "I can see that."

24

The crew picked up the sacks of creamed spinach from the store in Thetford. A pair of laconic workers threw them in, like body bags, and gave BJ a thumbs-up before ambling back to their shifts. There were long stretches of quiet on the way back, punctuated by Sony or Grazina reading aloud whatever words they saw outside: *Chicopee Mutt Rescue, Dr. Klein's prosthetic consultations, Yankee Candle Factory Outlet, Have you seen this girl?, Gavin DeGraw at Mohegan Sun,* and one billboard that read, enigmatically, *God Knows.*

At one point Hai opened the window to let the spring in, and it seemed to lift everyone inside, their heads leaning back to relish the sweet-scented flourish. Only in springtime, it seemed, does gravity work backward here, the dandelion pollen rising in great squalls, the flower buds shooting up, further from the ground, as if pulled by the sky's sudden need for them, all of it under the crisp brilliance of April sunlight. Watching this, Hai felt himself displaced by a wild, untenable gratitude.

After the two-hour straight shot down I-91, they made it to Grazina's house. Maureen and BJ still had to get to HomeMarket for the

afternoon shift after dropping Sony off at the group home. Hai and
Grazina stood waving from the crumbling sidewalk as the van chugged
off. He had to turn away when he saw Sony holding up the headrest to
the back window as if to reassure them it was still there.

"Poor boy," Grazina said. "No diamond, really?" She looked at Hai
like he had an explanation.

"Really."

"We deserve some Stouffer's now, yes?" She kicked at a pebble.

"I think we still have a couple in the freezer."

Hai was about to put the key in the door when he spotted the official notice made out on yellow carbon paper, the ones that have multiple
copies, which meant someone else had a copy—which meant problems.

"What is it, Labas?" Her eyes narrowed at the paper.

"It's a notice from Hartford County Family Services. Says they're
coming back at four p.m. tomorrow to 'escort' you to the Hamilton
Home."

"Of course! All prisoners get escorts."

"You're a special one," he said, not knowing how to joke about it. He
yanked the paper off the door and shoved it in his coat pocket. Grazina's shoulders wilted. She looked genuinely defeated.

They spent the rest of the day watching reruns of *The Office* and
eating Stouffer's and drinking tea like nothing had happened. Then he
gave her a bath and was grateful for the calm of watching her sit in
warm water, hearing the droplets trickle as he sponged her back. "Ah,
that's a nice spot there. Good spot there," she said as the sun dipped
behind the milk-glass window, turning the room deep red.

They were a nightfall away from the end, he thought, and almost
laughed at the absurdity of it. She must have sensed it, because she
turned to him and smiled. "Labas, we did a lot, didn't we? Didn't we do
so much?"

⤎

HOURS LATER, in the middle of the night, a night in which he hadn't slept an inch but lay staring at the peeling wood-panel walls of his room, he heard Grazina scuffing down the hall. She made it to his door and walked in. He pretended to be asleep and through lidded eyes watched her walk to his desk and stand there looking out the window, the bridge light washing her face white. Then she turned to him, as if they were in the middle of a conversation and she was about to say something decisive, substantial. She poked him on the shoulder.

"Labas, you awake? Hey, Labas boy."

He blinked up at her. "Now I am."

"You wanna go to a diner?"

"What? Which one?" They had never been to a diner this whole time. He sat up. "You feeling alright?"

"I'm feeling perfect."

He had given her a double dose of everything before bed, which lately might as well be her new prescription.

"I want to have a cup of coffee at the diner. Please? One coffee."

"Of course, of course. Why not?"

Before long they were riding down the black three a.m. streets on her scooter, wind in their faces, not a soul in East Gladness far as they could see.

THE TOWN LINE DINER was actually one Hai had been to before. He and Noah used to get two-dollar English muffins there after driving all night in Noah's truck with nowhere to go. It was a casual and homely place that served your eggs on paper plates, and nobody ever asked you if you wanted anything else, like your order wasn't big enough.

Hai and Grazina were the only ones there save for the waiter, a scrawny man with raccooned eyes and lips that never moved when he spoke. He took their order and walked away as if they were part of the wall.

"What'd you get?" Grazina asked, even though she had just heard him order.

"Chicken tenders." They were his grandma's favorite, and for some reason he missed her worse than usual. She used to dip hers in straight vinegar, saying the ketchup wasn't "strong enough." Maybe it was the lack of sleep, but for a minute he had this insane urge for Grazina to start speaking to him in Vietnamese, and knowing the impossibility of it crushed him in his seat.

"Why do they call them that?"

"What?"

"Tenders. They're always tough, not tender at all. Especially not *here*." She looked around, her lips curled.

"That's a good point. We should write an email."

"Email my ass. Whose machine will we use?" Grazina said, testing the coffee with her lip.

"How's your coffee?"

She shrugged. "Coffee."

The food came and they ate. He mostly watched her chew.

She reached for one of his tenders and took a bite, then shook her head. "See? Rubber."

"Your meat loaf okay at least?"

"I wanted Salisbury steak."

"It's basically the same thing. You went from a flat meat loaf to a raised one. It's an upgrade."

She was still in her jacket, and underneath was her favorite owl sweater she insisted on wearing, the owl's sad eyes now peering at him over the table's edge.

"So this is the last supper," she chuckled and pushed a dab of mashed potatoes on her lips into her mouth.

The waiter came over and topped off their coffees, which was mixing strangely with the Zoloft he had taken with her hours before, hoping it'd put them to sleep.

Grazina stared off somewhere behind him and he knew she was sliding away too. He tapped her mug with a spoon and she startled awake.

"Did you get the forms from Jerry Bathhouse?" she asked.

"I'll get 'em tomorrow when he's back from Alaska." He knew better than to ask who the hell Jerry Bathhouse was.

"His son was in the Peace Corps in Chile. But couldn't climb the mountains due to asthma, so they gave him a desk job. What a scam."

"I wish I had a desk job."

"You don't want one. Terrible for your bones."

"Okay," Hai said, putting down his last tender.

Just then the door chimed and two men came in. It was the detective from months ago, this time with a stout man with no neck who must've been his partner. They glanced at the pair in the booth, then settled at the bar.

"I don't know if I've been a good mother, Labas," she said out of nowhere, staring morbidly at her meat loaf, which she'd only put a dent in. It looked like someone had shot it with a handgun.

"Hey." He snapped his fingers. "Come on back. We can't be thinking like that, okay? Not tonight."

"But how do I know? He wouldn't tell me, would he? If I sent him a letter?"

"Send who a letter?"

"Pope Benedict." She scrunched her face. "Wait, no . . . my daughter. The apple doesn't fall far from the tree. Marianne from our church told me that once. That bitch." She made her hand into a fist, but could only do it for two seconds.

"Well, fuck Marianne," he said, dipping a tender into malt vinegar.

"You know how many rotten apples that woman's eaten? Thousands." He hadn't known a single Marianne in his whole life. "She even makes apple pie from rotten apples. There's apple cider in her veins, for God's sakes. She should talk. And besides, I heard she wasn't even Catholic. I bet she hates the Pope." Grazina nodded approvingly.

He must've spoken too loud, because the short, older cop looked over his shoulder. He was wearing a fedora like those old-timey detectives, and it made Hai want to laugh and scream at once.

"I wish I knew you when I was a girl." Grazina sighed.

He leaned back, a vague emptiness spreading through him, like his organs were dissolving one by one, and soon Grazina's face, the whole room, started to blur.

"Stop that. Don't cry, boy." She reached out to him, but her arm couldn't reach and she let it lie there by the wounded meat loaf. Then, in a lower voice: "You miss your mother, huh? She good to you? You never say nothing about her. Don't cry. Never cry in a diner. They charge extra if they catch you. Believe me, I've seen it happen."

He nodded and jammed his fists into his eyes and put his head down.

"Listen, I'll call Jerry Bathhouse first thing tomorrow and he'll sort it out, okay?"

"Okay." Hai nodded some more. "Thank you."

She patted the table. "There, there."

Through the window in their booth, the night's curtain was starting to lift, bluing at the edges. Hai put money on the table and they headed out.

"Can I call Lina first?" she said all of a sudden.

He walked her over to the pay phone by the bathroom and pushed in the quarters. She dialed—except it was the number to Grazina's own house, the place where her daughter lived for so many years. It rang and rang, and Hai knew the mint-green rotary phone on the counter in the unlit kitchen was throbbing with no one to pick it up.

She hung up after a long time. "She must be working. She's an ESL teacher, you know, my daughter."

"I know."

"She even won a spelling bee."

"I know."

She gave the phone a few pats, as if to say *good job*, then they headed out.

In the lot, standing beside the chained-up e-scooter, which was beaded all over with condensed mist, Hai took out a cigarette and sucked on it while Grazina let herself down in the seat. Dawn was peeking its red eyes through the tree trunks beyond the lot.

A fine yellowish-white pollen, like the dust you find on the bottom of a Kix cereal box, had gathered around the foot of everything: the cement steps, the stacked cardboard boxes, telephone poles, some of it swirling over little puddles in the potholes. He put out his cigarette against his boots, then removed a butter biscuit from his pocket he had saved from his meal. "Here," he said, bringing it to her face. "You wanna step on it with me?"

She sat in the scooter staring at it, then slowly shook her head and turned away. "No thanks, boy. I'm too kaput."

"Okay." He flung it into the woods.

He was about to get on behind her and speed off into oblivion when he felt something grip his boots and looked down and saw the ground shifting, the yellow dust flowing past his legs like the pavement was melting underneath him. He let out this little yelp, his mouth wanting to say, *Sony, grab my hand. Sony, come grab my hand.* But his cousin was nowhere to be found. Sony was at a group home with no job, inside a fatherless world without diamonds or second chances.

"I'm slipping away," he called to Grazina, who was craning her neck trying to see what was on the ground. "Ma," he said to the old woman out of nowhere, "I'm slipping away, Ma!" He reached out to her but couldn't get any closer. His feet felt crazy. The earth was swallowing him up; it finally had enough of his bullshit, and somehow this made sense.

"Don't be silly," Grazina said, pointing at his feet. "It's just salamanders. Look!"

There they were: a wave of lizards dashing across the parking lot. They were coming from the woods, their backs pollen-doused, like survivors of some nuclear war, some reptilian D-Day, and were now gyrating in slick hordes under his feet. They poured over the concrete, swarmed and wrapped around the scooter's wheels, surging toward the other side of the lot where a slope dipped into a meadow of wild rye.

"This must be Big Night," Grazina said, looking around.

"The fuck is that?"

"Big Night. Every spring, when it starts to get warm, they all run together into a pool of water to make babies. We're standing on highway to sex party."

"How do you know this?" He could see the last of the winter stars reflected off their backs. There were so many he couldn't make out a single individual one. It felt like something you were supposed to witness in a church or from the top of a mountain. It made him want to recite sutras or psalms, but he couldn't remember any. He wanted to tell Maureen about this. That the reptilians, when they weren't eating our bad energy, were fucking in puddles outside of shitty diners by the highway.

He placed his finger on one of their backs, and it stopped and stared up at him, eyes pupilless and curious, as the others pooled around it, before pushing along. "They're so brave," he said, delirious, his voice cracking with awe. "They're so fucking brave."

"Kaip senieji giedojo, taip jaunieji dainuoja," Grazina said, but he didn't hear her.

"Look at them, Grazina! They're crawling across a parking lot in an armpit of a town to make babies. When has anyone ever crawled across a parking lot for anything?" He shuffled over to her, careful not to lift his feet.

"My husband used to be obsessed with Big Night. He would go with Lucas and—"

He kissed her on her forehead, which startled her into a dazed stare. Then they just stood there—the only sound was the radio from the diner inside leaking through the windows, that and the immense swishing of the salamanders as they threw themselves, by the hundreds, toward the beginning of the world.

25

Somehow there was music.

It bloomed from inside him and became something else, something he could touch. So he reached out to it. He opened his eyes and saw Grazina's face hovering above him. He was splayed on the couch and holding her hand as though she was about to pull him up. All around him was the voice of some warped, demented angel, crescendoing into trilling, pitched notes.

"Sergeant Pepper? You're alive. Quick, they have music here. Music. In an abandoned church!"

He sat up and blinked until Grazina's living room clicked into place. There was something spinning on the record player on the sideboard. "Who is this?" he said over the blaring music.

"What?"

"Who the hell is this?"

"You don't know?" She looked at him open-mouthed. "It's Gene Pitney. Hartford's pride and joy."

"Hartford? Aren't you in Europe right now? Aren't I Sergeant Pepper?" The record sounded like a man singing while being flushed down a toilet, the cherubic voice cut with prancing desperation.

"Oh, yes. Why, of course you are!" She sniffed the air, nodding. "Smells like England, Sergeant Pepper."

"Why's that?" He pretended to look around the streets.

"Salt in the air. Seawater."

"Then we're close." He was trying to catch up; it must have been hours since the salamanders flooded over their feet. "Do you remember your orders?"

"To kill anything that moves." She picked up a comb from the coffee table and held it up like a weapon.

"No, to get to America at all costs. Don't you remember your promise to your father, the baker?"

"Of course," she said, finding Hai's eyes. "I'm meeting him in New York."

The digital clock on the VCR read 3:40 p.m. Twenty minutes before social services was to come and end the twilight zone they'd been trapped in.

He walked to the kitchen, trying to think of a plan—but all he found was Maureen's R2-D2 penis statue on the table, somehow larger than before. He tucked the giant penis under his arm, opened the pantry door, and stood staring at the saltine boxes chewed through by mice, and felt sick to his stomach, the house suddenly a tiny cage, nowhere to go, not enough doors.

"They've sent their spies after us. I can tell," she whispered at his back. "They've been following us for days. Two little girls. They use children now, you know. So you won't suspect it."

He was barely listening. He was trying to pretend their pretending was real—when it came to him. "Okay." He turned around so fast she jerked back. "I got it. We can dupe 'em, those little girls. But you have to follow me out of this church. Don't grab anything. Just make a run for it, okay?"

"They're coming, Pepper. I hear them upstairs. Here, put this on;

it's colder than you think." Before he knew what was happening, she was pulling her owl sweater over his head and yanking his arms through.

"You're the best honorary soldier I've ever met," he told her. "Even better than the real ones. Ready?" He took her hand and they rushed for the front door, Gene Pitney's "Only You" blaring on the record player, his voice carrying them through the air, making it feel like they were riding it, floating out on his high, jittery runs. The pride of Hartford County sending them into Hartford County.

Outside, engulfed in a fog so dense it made everything appear underwater, he helped Grazina onto the motor scooter, then sat in front, setting the R2-D2 between his legs, and fired it up. It let out a weak electric moan but managed to pulse forward. He headed to the only place they could go, toward the dead end. Pitney's voice wailed through the opened front door as they whirred down the potholed street, the river to their left roving in bulbous globes like some primordial serpent molting its skin.

"You ready?" he shouted over his shoulder.

"For what?"

"To land in America. We're coming close now." The fog was so thick the houses on both sides had evaporated. The scooter seemed to be floating through nothing.

"How do you mean?"

"That wasn't a church back there," he said. "It was a chapel on an ocean liner. We already docked this morning. Everybody's already gone."

The scooter thumped along and she was quiet for a moment. "We're here, then? We're really here?"

"Almost." He twisted the speed throttle, to no effect.

"Wait. Am I old now? Am I old or am I still in the war?"

"No, no. Don't do this now. You're in the war and your name is Grazina Vitkus and you're seventeen years old. There's war everywhere, alright?" She seemed genuinely scared, and he started to unravel. "Hitler,

Stalin, Germany, the fishhook, Auschwitz, Dresden, Saigon, Iraq, Gettysburg. Remember? Your dead brother, the lake, the bakery. No, don't look back. Look forward. Don't you look back now!" He pulled at her arm until she stared ahead. They were at the end. He tried to do a U-turn, but the wheels caught on a pebble and stalled. He kicked at the ground and wheeled the scooter about, and that's when he saw the patrol car's blue lights cutting through the fog. They were already there— early.

Slowly, he inched the scooter forward. It didn't occur to him that this would be the last time he'd be with her. For reasons he couldn't explain, he nearly lost it when he saw her dove-colored socks rolled down to her ankles.

"I feel like I'm in the middle of something," she said in a worried voice. "There's no floor or roof to me. Where's Lina? Did she ever get to see the salamanders?"

"She's in Texas. And you *are* in the middle. You're in the middle of two countries, but now you're coming to a new one called America, okay? Where you were always headed. You always wanted to be here, remember?" he shouted over the current.

"But I'm losing," she said into his ear. "I'm losing the beginning. Where's the beginning?"

"It's right there, ahead of you." He pointed to the sloping house emerging from the mist, the police lights swirling outside it. "You're gonna go and you're gonna get married in that house up ahead. You're gonna have two beautiful, talented, and kind children who will love you and tend to your every need until your very last breath." His eyes were so wet he thought he was having a seizure as the cloud line on the horizon lifted above the river and a blade of amber light slashed through the valley, diffusing the fog and alighting on the slate streets with a Nordic glaze, gold and grey everywhere. The houses came back into view, their gaping jaws ransacked and mugged. He heard their voices, or imagined them, the people who once roamed the wallpapered rooms, asking for one another, calling out to names lost to every ledger in history. The river sloshed somewhere to the right of him, the swirling lights coming closer.

"Where's the book you wrote, Sergeant Pepper?" she shouted, conflating, at last, all his forgeries into one name.

"I fucked up! I chose the wrong story to live in." He felt something on his cheeks and realized she was wiping tears from his face. Pitney's voice returned as they approached the house.

"Mother Mary bless you, Sergeant," she said as the lights blued his hands. "Bless the demons in your soul. You're a brave soldier. And brave soldiers get broke in the brain when they come home. But what's after America?"

"I don't know what to do. I don't know what happens now! I'm just a kid, okay? I'm not a sergeant of anything. I don't know which crumb of the corn bread becomes corn cake. I don't know when a person becomes somebody else." His voice was breaking in the wind. "I wish I could take you somewhere but I can't, Grazina. I don't have anywhere." He put one hand up to indicate to the officer ahead that he was harmless, then spoke into her ear. "Don't you want to go to the new world?"

"I'm not sure."

"Well, you don't have to stay there. You can go *deeper* into it and see. And maybe you'll go right through it, like a door. America is just a big old door, okay? Look—your son is waiting for you. He's the door. The door you made."

"Lucas? He's not born yet. He's inside me—I feel him kicking."

Agitated voices, spilling out from the cars, were cutting through.

"He's both inside and out of you at once. Like you and me. Golden Triangle."

"Labas?"

Lucas was walking out of the house, trailed by the cop, and cursing. The nurse was digging into a bag, taking out a stethoscope.

"Yes?"

"In the chapel, back on the boat. I've hidden a stack of money in a cookie tin in my room. Take it. My payment to you for getting me across. I can see my father now."

"Don't worry about that. Just go with them, okay? They're gonna take you to get processed, then you can work to be a citizen. Like me."

"Will I see you again? Will you visit?" For a moment her face was stricken. Then everything drained away and she glanced about, confused.

"Of course. And I'll bring—"

Before he could finish, the officer, who was actually a security guard from the Hamilton Home with a tattoo of a diamond under his left eye, grabbed Hai's arm and brought the scooter to a halt by jamming his boot on the wheel. Lucas and the nurse swooped in and took Grazina by the hand. It was all in slow motion. He stepped off the scooter and walked forward in a trance, not caring what they did to him, as Grazina was being ushered into the van, muttering in Lithuanian.

But where was she going? She was going to a place where freedom is promised yet made possible only by a contained egalitarian space fashioned with walls and locks, where measured nourishment is delivered each day through long corridors by staff born from a never-ending elsewhere who forgo watching their own children grow up in order to watch strangers grow old, all this to keep you alive so they can suck up money from your bank account while you're warm, immobilized by tranquilizers, and satiated and numb, a body ripe for harvest even beyond ripening. She *was* heading to America after all. The truest version of it. The one where everyone pays to be here.

"Come on, Mom, we got you. You're safe now." Lucas and the nurse guided Grazina into the van, her white hair disappearing, then reappearing behind the glass. "Look, I get it." In the wind, Lucas's face had purpled to the shade of freshly sawed ham. "You're just a kid. And I don't know what you two were up to. I don't need to nor wanna know. I can tell my mother liked you, okay? And that's fine, but she's not well. And *you* are clearly sick also. I mean, look at this," he said to the guard, and gestured to the sculpture clutched to Hai's chest. The guard shook his head in disgust, saying something he couldn't hear. "Look at him." Lucas's gaze lingered on Hai's scabbed-up lip. "He's mentally ill. I mean, why did you make a penis, dude? It's so *weird*. And you've been taking care of my mom?"

"It's an R2-D2."

"A what?" Lucas opened the passenger door and hopped in. "Just get us out of here, Tonya. I'll come back and deal with the house later."

"She likes Stouffer's," Hai said. "Make sure you get the Salisbury steak from Stouffer's." He stood open-mouthed as the van sped off, the security car following behind, its patrol lights still blazing. "With the brownie in the corner," he said to himself, mist swirling around him. "With rainbow sprinkles." Gene Pitney's voice, still playing on the record inside, was flowing through a cracked window as the car lights faded. He stood for a while listening to it all, letting the air flow over him. Then, clutching the R2-D2 penis to his chest, he walked away from 16 Hubbard Street. And for the first time since the last brick was paved into place over a century ago, the street was truly empty.

HE WALKED IN a dazed aftermath. In the silence the birds called out to the waning day, as if after a flood. He sensed a change and glimpsed, over the highway ridges, new buds forming on shrubs along the river-banks as the valley rolled away beneath him under sprays of broken light. Nestled in a whorl in the current was a burst of pink confetti swirling away from him, the result of cherry blossoms at the 9/11 memorial off I-91, bloomed and shattered by a north wind a mile up-stream.

Crossing King Philip's Bridge, he recalled, from a high school history class, King Philip's ultimate fate. How his uprising was put down by the colonizers and how Philip, also known as Metacomet, was subsequently beheaded, his skull displayed on a stake for twenty-five years as a warning to other Native chiefs against reclaiming their lands. He felt every footstep over the rail ties as he crossed, wood cut from another time, hammered into place to carry the living toward whatever traps them.

It was late afternoon by the time he made it to town. The sun, stronger now in the season, had burned through the fog, bathing houses in a benevolent warmth, lending a butternut glow to the lawns with faded umbrellas left out all winter. In one of the front yards he passed, a cracked kiddie pool was filled with dirt, and April's first tulips were peeking over the lip. Some yards had a mother or father at the edge of them, home from work, just steps from the car and still in retail uniforms, simple slacks and button-ups, floral dresses, name tags glinting, aiming the hose over whatever might grow. One man diffracted the spray with his hand to cover a patch of soil no larger than a greeting mat. Some of them nodded vaguely in Hai's direction as the sound of sprinklers on both sides filled the air and he passed through the place that made him. He took out the orange pill bottle, swallowed the last half handful, then chucked it into a flowerpot and pushed on. He thought he saw early fireflies blink through an alley between two houses and envied them their inner resources.

In a few weeks the roads will be filled with bike spokes you can hear from your room at night, so clearly that you have to put down your book and look out the window to see what propels a person so fast through so much summer, the gasoline sweetness of young skunks and lilac blossoms wafting through the window as a deep urge to make something, anything, mounts in your chest and you decide, once and for all, to plot your escape from whatever tiny name on the map has tried and failed to claim you.

It must have been evening by the time the HomeMarket sign came into view. He passed a telephone pole where, in the coppering filament dusk, a splash of violet snowdrops fanned out from under the base as if tossed from a passing car, remnants from years of memorial bouquets placed to mark where Rachel Miotti was last seen alive, now gone to seed and wildflowered.

He approached the back door, where he sat down on the milk crates and held his head in his hands. It wasn't his shift, but having nowhere to go, he went toward order, consistency, discipline—but mostly toward these people, these little people who make the world turn by making food faster than we have ever prepared it in the history of our species.

It was dinnertime and a car passed him circling the drive-thru as Russia's voice came through the speaker, asking how he could help them. Hai wanted to laugh at the question, absurd in its sincere and brutally reduced proportions.

After a while the door opened.

"Hai? What are you doing here?" It was Sony.

"Here to do my job."

"But you're off today." He tilted his head. "Looks like your lip's healing at least."

"Who knew Asian Ulysses S. Grant would have such a heavy right hook? What about you?" He squinted at the fluorescent lights behind Sony. "Aren't you fired?"

"Maureen's knee is hurting, so BJ asked me to work one shift. She's paying me in cash. Hey, where's your UPS jacket?" Sony pointed to the white owl on Hai's sweater.

"Fuck." Hai looked around helplessly, dismay lodging inside him. He had left Noah's jacket back at the house, still hanging on a hook in his room, along with his unfinished copy of *The Brothers Karamazov*. He thought of running back to fetch them but remembered that, in the commotion, he had also lost his glasses. Maybe that was why the walk over looked so beautiful—numinous and faraway. He looked down at the owl on his chest staring up at him, then took a deep breath and collected himself, his eyes drifting to the abandoned apartments across the lot, their broken windows. "Hey, Sony?"

"Yeah?"

"You gonna be okay? Like, *really* okay?" The knots in his jaw showed.

Sony's sneakers grated the sand as he pushed a pebble to the side, then toed it back. "You know Lee kept fighting after his defeat at Gettysburg, even when he was down to just twenty thousand men—down from one hundred thirty thousand at the start of the war—and it was ten against one?"

"Did he?"

"Yeah, and it was considered immoral by many scholars. All hope was lost, but he was too proud and stubborn to give up. I always felt bad for his horse, Traveller. Imagine being a horse and walking around all summer without knowing you're a loser."

"I wish I was a horse," Hai said.

"Did you know they can gallop up to forty miles per hour for ten full—"

Hai was staring at the scar on Sony's head, the evening light reflecting silver in its valley.

Hai remembered the plaster penis sitting on the ground between his feet. He flipped it upside down and dug into the hole at the base, removing a roll of wax paper.

"Oh, you brought Maureen's monument . . ."

"Here." He handed it to him. The paper crinkled in Sony's hands as Hai stared at the tenements, the spring weeds already creeping along the Reagan-era fencing.

"Oh my goodness." Sony's voice was elsewhere inside him. "No, no, you can't. How?"

"Listen now. That's enough to get Aunt Kim out and then a bit more for a deposit for an apartment for you both." After the diner last night, Hai had stopped by an ATM and emptied his account. That plus what he took from Grazina's tin box that afternoon would be more than enough. He had shoved it into the statue while she was gathering things for their great escape.

Sony tried to ask more questions but started to stutter.

"I'm sorry," Hai managed.

"For what? You didn't——"

"You don't even know . . . And you don't have to."

Sony pressed the bundle to his chest and squirmed, grinning with all his teeth like a child filled to the brim. A car passed them from the drive-thru, the guy giving them an odd look as he rolled up his windows.

"Go on," Hai nodded to the store. "Go tell 'em the good news. They could use some good news."

"Hey, BJ! Hey, Wayne!" Sony shouted with delight as he ran inside. "You gotta look at this. Look at what Hai did! Look what my big cousin did!"

It was Hai's chance—he crossed the lot and stepped over the warped chain-link fence on the other side. The dead grass was high as his waist as he passed the spray of used needles on the pavement, then beyond that, until he was in some sort of courtyard surrounded by boarded-up windows. There were benches with broken seats, wooden planter boxes where a community garden once stood—all of it empty now, the ground littered with glass, a few stuffed animals, fast-food wrappers, spent bottles of single-shot liquor, and cigarette packs. Old furniture and black-rusted shopping carts lay among the detritus.

At the courtyard's far edge, beside a tipped-over washing machine, was a green Waste Management dumpster. He walked over to it, his head feeling boncless, and ran his hand along the lid, then lifted it and peered inside. It was only half empty. Hugging the R2-D2 penis, he pushed the lid open and climbed inside. Dry and warmed by the day's sun, it was mostly filled with black garbage bags and dead leaves. He lay back on the bags and kept very still. Inside the dumpster, the noises from the street arrived altered, their octaves warped, subdued, as if the city that once touched him was now further away.

He thought of all the people who once drank and ate from the cups, the wrappers and boxes now stuffed in black bags that buoyed him toward what he was always becoming: lifted by what this town refused. The trash was no longer just trash—but evidence. Because to discard is to move on. Inside the dumpster, he was pressed on all sides by human forwardness. Everything's a room, he realized, too late. The cars on the interstate nothing but rooms with wheels. The endless prescription bottles. And the body, too, a room, and so is the heart. So is the cell in the blood spilling back to the world, only to be contained by more world, which keeps even the atoms that make up the Styrofoam cups and trays sloughed daily from the back of HomeMarket. The average lifespan of a take-out container is one minute and forty-two seconds. Lying on garbage was the closest to weightlessness he'd ever been, and he wondered if this was what it was like for the astronauts floating in outer space, their soft bodies held by their suits. We always belong somewhere, if only to whatever's holding us, and shouldn't that be a good thing? To have your uselessness become a marker of time, waste being the proof of having lived at all? He had successfully thrown himself into the trash, and the act was so complete, so total, it felt clean. He was a container inside a container filled with containers contained by space—and somehow this made him full.

The bag beneath him started rattling. He looked down and realized his phone was vibrating. He flipped it open and said hello.

It was his mother.

She sounded tired, as if she had just finished returning enormous things to where they belonged. She wanted to know when the semester ended, when he would come home. She wanted to make a big feast, and asked if he could buy the long incense sticks from the Chinese grocer in Boston for Bà ngoại's altar—the small ones burning too quickly. She talked about this new hummingbird feeder she had bought at Home Depot, and as she went on, he heard, in the distance, Russia's soft, gentle voice float up from the drive-thru speaker.

And he was reminded of what they did there. That somewhere, right now, someone is waiting in line asking to be satiated. And those who serve them, who lord over nothing but a stainless-steel counter and its crumb-speckled dominion, stand at the end of the line saying, again and again, *How can I help you?* Because our kind has built a box using four walls and a roof and called it HomeMarket, called it McDonald's, Wendy's, Burger King, Burger Chef, Subway, Panda Express, Pizza Hut. Centuries from now, when the cosmos are no longer mysteries infinitely multiplied by syllables, they will unearth the ancient and mildewed libraries and understand us as the epoch that reheated chemically preserved sustenance we never cooked under red roofs, from which we asked *How can I help you?* endlessly, day and night, through droughts and earthquakes, through wars and floods and assassinated presidents, fallen towers and allegiances, impeachments and suicides, through birthdays, some so insignificant they will be forgotten even by those they crown, knowing so little can be kept—not even the gnomic words that nonetheless birth the histories between two people: *Hello, Hai, Labas.*

"How can I help you?" Sony was saying now as a woman stepped up to the counter, her hair disheveled from the day, single mother to the two girls swaying beside her. They were beaming because this was their treat, for they had waited all day for their mother to come home from her shift at Lefty's Bar and Grille, and had spotted the red roof from all the way down the street, screeching as they hugged and kissed her neck, as the car became a singular kingdom of joy. She looked up now in self-abandonment, finger on her lip, scanning the menu like it was a map for a way out of here. "I don't know what I want," she mumbled to herself. "Oh, what do I want, what do I want?" And Sony's fingers hovered over the screen, ready to manifest her wish. Because whatever it was, they'd have it. For they never run out, not for long.

Hai lit a cigarette, taking a long drag as he peered through the dumpster's opened door. He saw, framed in a perfect square, the twilit sky teeming with the faint trace of stars above him. The same stars that will be shining two years later—when Russia gets his sister, Anna, through rehab, which will finally stick the fifth time. When Wayne moves back to North Carolina to start a smokehouse called The Knighthood. When the growth in Maureen's breast returns, this time with bad cells, and she gets a mastectomy and moves in with her brother in Defiance, Ohio, knitting scarves for the local church in her wheelchair as the sunlight slides each day from her lap to the hardwood. But she'll pull through despite the lizards, living longer still than her little boy. And Aunt Kim will move into an apartment with Sony in Manchester, where they'll both work at Canetti's ravioli factory while Sony studies at night to be a docent for the New England Civil War Museum in Vernon. And BJ will end up managing the HomeMarket in the airport, and also partnering with Miss Magician's daughter, Abra Kadaver, to become the New England Regional Women's Tag Team Champion, her entrance song full of banjos and her new gimmick being a face-painted fast-food manager named Over Time. Tom the mechanic will finally get his "Dominican" ear, the skin an exact match save for the seam, which widens to a hole as he takes it off at night to sleep beside his wife. Seven months after leaving 16 Hubbard Street, Grazina will pass away one afternoon during a nap at the Alzheimer's facility in Rhode Island where she was transferred, her headstone reading, as per her will, *GRAZINA M. VITKUS 1929–2010. Loving wife and mother*—with an American flag etched on each side. A handful of leads will come in for the murder of Rachel Miotti, one of them naming a beige SUV caught on CCTV a few blocks from HomeMarket, cause for her mother to do another round of TV interviews, but the breaks won't come and to this day no arrests have been made.

Within five years, the turnover in the store will be so complete that none of the original crew will be left at the HomeMarket on Route 4. But the HomeMarket will still stand—undefeated—an entire new team, like a new set of organs, implanted and running the same shifts inside its concrete walls. The only sign that they were ever there will be a faded Chewbacca sticker Maureen had placed in the back of the broom closet, next to the industrial tubs of BBQ sauce.

"Are you busy now," Hai's mother said on the phone, "or is the school closed for the day?"

"Colleges don't really close, Ma. They just kinda sit there with the lights on."

"That's right. It's not a nail salon," she chuckled. "You learning anything good? Tell me something new that you learned. About medicine."

"Okay." The bags crinkled under him as he shifted. "Well, it's crazy you called," he clutched the R2-D2 penis to his chest, "cause I'm actually in the lab right now, dissecting a body."

"Really! My goodness, you mean a real person?"

"I'm the last one in here, staying late, just trying to do one more," he said, the dark creeping along the iron walls.

"You mean cutting open a corpse? An actual corpse? You're kidding."

"Wish I was. But it's incredible in here, Ma. A miracle of evolution."

"What's it look like in there? Is it bad of me to ask? Does it look like the meat at the Chinese butcher? Oh, those poor people. You'll have to pray for them."

"It's for science. They've donated their bodies to improve our knowledge. They wanted this."

"What's it look like in there, son? I got goose bumps just thinking about it."

He pushed his invisible glasses up his nose and saw above him a constellation he had failed his whole life to name, one of its stars shuddering between two chemtrails drawn across the dimming sky.

"Space," he breathed, the cold seeping through his sweater. "There's so much space you wouldn't believe it."

"Yeah?" Her voice grew faint. "Even with all the organs and arteries jammed up in there? All that blood?"

"Yes," he gasped into the dark, like a boy seeing his name in ink for the first time, "there's so much room in a person, there should be more of us in here. There shouldn't be just one."

There was a long silence, the sound of his mother thinking.

That's when he realized he'd been falling this whole time—he just couldn't feel it, the trash forming a zero-gravity cushion beneath him. "I'm scared, Ma," he whispered.

"Of what? What are you talking about?"

"Of what's coming. Of the future—it just seems so big."

"That's only because you're young. Eventually, it gets smaller. But don't be afraid of life, son. Life is good when we do good things for each other."

He mumbled something else, the cigarette in his fingers down to the butt.

"What was that?"

"Tu esi mano draugas."

"I can't hear you. Can you—"

"Nothing, Mommy," he whispered in English, an insane beam of love for the world lancing through him. "I was just drifting."

And that's when he heard it—not the river's rush, but the hogs.

Dragged by their hooves into the emperor's butchery, they were screaming from a galaxy far, far away, inside him. And they sounded just like people.

Soft, simple people, who live only once.